About the author

Alan Paisey has published over thirty non-fiction books, variously on educational management, military history, and transfer pricing. His first novel, *A Bond to Serve*, was published by Vanguard Press in 2017.

A RUM AFFAIR

Alan Paisey

A RUM AFFAIR

Vanguard Press

VANGUARD PAPERBACK

© Copyright 2018
Alan Paisey

The right of Author to be identified as author of
this work has been asserted by him in accordance with the
Copyright, Designs and Patents Act 1988.

A CIP catalogue record for this title is
available from the British Library.

ISBN 978 1 784654 40 5

*Vanguard Press is an imprint of
Pegasus Elliot MacKenzie Publishers Ltd.*
www.pegasuspublishers.com

First Published in 2018

**Vanguard Press
Sheraton House Castle Park
Cambridge England**

Printed & Bound in Great Britain

Dedication

To Tim, Pam, Neil, and Claire

Acknowledgements

I thank Ann Blackburn in England, David Duckworth in New Zealand, and John Henry in the United States, for their encouragement and helpful comments. Without the computer dexterity of my wife, Sheila, writing this book, as for others, would have been handicapped.

1

They were seated in the foyer on opposite sides of the same small table, huddled over a cup of make-believe coffee. Their heads were together as if sharing a deep secret. Their animated whispering was interrupted only by glances now and then at the milling concourse of patrons pouring out from the auditorium.

The crowd was thickly studded with men and women dressed in a variety of uniforms, together representing all the many military and support services involved in the war. Some were on leave, staying locally in their homes, but most were posted in the port, air force stations, and army barracks in and around the city.

The minds of those hurrying theatregoers were still reeling from the spellbinding performance they had just witnessed on the stage. But their thoughts, even as they headed for the exits, were being forcibly turned towards the next necessity that faced them outside in the streets, where it was pitch dark under the nights without lights regulations.

How would they get home on a wet night in the blackout, with the continuing possibility of an enemy air raid?

Vanessa Coles and Carol Johnston had no such worries.

'I'm so glad our hotel is just around the corner,' Vanessa said to Carol, as she spotted a few anxious expressions on the faces of some of the people passing across the open foyer.

'A few taxis are still running but most of them will have to catch a bus home,' Carol added to her comment. 'Let's hope the show has put some energy into those who are walking home in the rain.'

They resumed their confidential discussion.

'She forgot her lines twice tonight. I think she had been drinking,' said Carol. 'She cleverly covered it up but upset her partner for a few seconds. But it happens in the best of plays on the best of stages by the best of players.'

Neither Vanessa nor Carol was a principal actor in the musical play, which had been running for a few weeks. It was the second performance that day of a production of the play first staged in 1935 at the Theatre Royal, Drury Lane in the West End of London. They were young and content to have small parts in its revival at the Royal Court Theatre in Liverpool, a premier theatre outside London.

The theatre had remarkably survived the repeated aerial attacks from the Luftwaffe during the Second World War, attracting top people in the stage profession. Vanessa and Carol counted themselves fortunate to have joined them in the cast.

'We ought not to be criticising such a celebrated actress,' said Vanessa. 'We might be in the same boat ourselves one day. Otherwise, it was a good performance tonight.'

'Yes, it's a nice stage, with good acoustics, and the atmosphere in the theatre is very homely,' Carol conceded.

She consulted the brochure on the coffee table.

'It says here that the original building was built a hundred and thirteen years ago by John Cooke, a circus owner. It was redesigned by Henry Sumner as an orthodox theatre and opened as the Royal Court in 1881. Destroyed by fire seven years ago, before the war, it was restored fully by the outbreak of war.'

Vanessa swiftly added, nodding her head in approval, 'Perhaps that's why it survived the bombing. Modern construction methods and materials could have helped it to withstand the bomb blasts in surrounding buildings and anything but a direct hit.'

'It's remarkable that it is still standing when you look at all the destruction and damage nearby and around it,' remarked Carol. 'Did you know that Liverpool is the second most bombed city in Britain?' she asked.

'It must be due to the port,' Vanessa answered. 'Being on the west side of the country, it has always been important for shipping across the Atlantic. Half our food has to be imported and, of course, American supplies and military forces have to be carried this way. They all have bellies to be fed.'

'Quite true.' A voice carried to them from someone nearby, interrupting her comments. It seemed to be directed at them, defying the noise of the rushing people passing. It put paid to their private conversation.

Both girls turned abruptly to face the source of the intruder's voice. It came from a man, who had chosen to listen in momentarily to their conversation, after briefly loitering among the tables.

'Don't look so surprised,' Vanessa said to the man.

In a rather unfriendly tone of voice, Carol thought, as Vanessa continued. 'Girls also know what's what. But please don't try to overhear our private discussion. It's the height of rudeness.'

'Yes, I'm sure they do know what's what,' said the speaker, putting up his hands in mock self-defence. 'Who am I to challenge that assumption?' he asked.

'Yes, who indeed are you to accost us. Be on your way, then.' Vanessa tried to give the man a swift dismissal.

Carol started to feel uncomfortable. She was taken aback by her companion's forthright aggression towards the man. It seemed a bit out of proportion. He was apparently a fan of the theatre, whose patronage guaranteed their actresses' salary.

'May I introduce myself?' he persisted, speaking politely.

Answering his own question, he quickly said, 'I'm Tim Denton. I was standing here, hesitating, wondering how I could get to speak to Vanessa Coles. I saw in the programme brochure that she was born in Swindon. It's also where I was born and raised. Since it is a small town I wondered if our paths had crossed at all. I haven't managed to meet anyone from my home patch before, so I wanted to take the opportunity to speak to another person from the railway town.'

After a moment's hesitation, one of the two women answered. 'Well, it's me, but I don't speak to strangers,' Vanessa said. 'But if you are a Swindonian, I will break the rule in your case.'

'Thank you for such a major concession.' Tim smiled when saying it, trying not to sound sarcastic. 'How strange do strangers have to be to stop you from speaking to them?' he asked, not expecting an answer.

'What is the uniform you are wearing, then?' Vanessa asked curtly, as if seeking his credentials.

She completely ignored his previous baiting remark.

'I have to say how much I enjoyed the performance tonight,' Tim said, in turn ignoring her question.

'That's nice of you to say so,' said Carol.

'But I asked, what is the uniform you are wearing?' Vanessa's hardened voice suddenly sounded as if she was on the warpath.

It crossed Tim's mind that she was a woman to be reckoned with. It stamped an impression on him. She disturbed him, perhaps irritated him a little.

'I don't normally speak to strangers, either, especially in wartime,' said Tim.

'But you are evidently someone special, so I can say I'm in the navy, just put into port after another hazardous Atlantic crossing, escorting your food and war materials.'

His face was a mixture of reprimand and warmth.

'That's marked your card, Vanessa, for tonight,' said Carol, laughingly. 'I am in awe,' said Vanessa, feeling somewhat abashed.

'But not quite,' Vanessa corrected herself, recovering her engagement in the fray, but managing a lovely smile with it. 'What do you do in the navy? Are you a cook or something?' she asked provocatively.

Tim never forgot that smile. It had something very warm inside it as well as a sting of purposefulness, combining into a mixture that made his insides churn. 'Not quite,' he replied. 'Remember, the cook or something, whatever he is, are both vital members of a crew. I happen to be a commissioned engineer officer, who reports direct to the captain.'

'How long have you been in the navy?' asked Carol.

'I joined in the first year of the war,' he replied. 'That's a long time to be in the war,' said Carol.

'So where did you go to school?' Vanessa asked, taking the initiative again, after regaining her breath. She had felt momentarily overtaken by the exchange. 'The College Grammar School,' Tim replied.

'There you are. I knew it!' said Vanessa. 'You never managed to pull one over The Commonweal, did you? But apparently, you have done so on this occasion. So, I am all ears to hear your story.'

She surprisingly conceded the ground to Tim.

Tim acknowledged that The College and The Commonweal were rivals, with the edge on the latter, a purpose-built school in the most salubrious part of town.

But he realised, that from the look in her eyes, the banter had been a front.

There was considerable depth in this woman.

Vanessa was beautiful. Her well-moulded face was crowned with a glorious head of blond hair. Her flashing blue eyes were set in a face disarmingly distant – but capable of breaking into liquid warmth, disclosing a set of perfect lips and teeth.

'My story is not a long one. But let me get you both another cup of coffee,' Tim said, diverting attention. He strode over to the kiosk.

'What a handsome man,' Carol expostulated to Vanessa. 'Do they all come like that in Swindon?' she asked. 'Please save me one if they do.'

Carol must suddenly have been impressed by the atmosphere that had developed out of the blue at the little table. Vanessa's own body language had distinctly changed.

She decided she had become a supernumerary.

'I'll get back to the hotel, Vanessa. See you at rehearsal tomorrow. Don't stay up late.'

'Night, Carol, have a good sleep. Let's hope the sirens don't go in the night.' Carol moved so fast. Tim didn't see her move away.

'Where's your friend?' Tim asked when he returned with the coffee. 'She's gone for an early night. We have rehearsals tomorrow. I can drink her coffee – or we could share it', Vanessa said, with a surprising concession, not lost on Tim Denton. It was a time when nothing could be wasted.

'What about you, then? You will have rehearsals, too,' Tim questioned Vanessa sympathetically.

'Yes, rehearsals are important to maintain the best production, especially for an actress coming new to a part, to iron out the slips. I can spare a few minutes, anyway, now we are talking about the faraway alma mater down south where we were born.' Vanessa made her comment casually.

'So, when did you leave Swindon?' asked Tim.

'At the same time as you said you joined the navy. I was eighteen when I sat the higher general certificate after two years in the sixth form. Results were good enough for university entrance, but I wanted to go on the stage and was accepted on interview at the Royal Academy of Dramatic Art in London. But their theatre had just been destroyed in the blitz. They had to continue at the City Literary Institute. The course was somewhat upset by the war, but as students we had the benefit of extensive touring, giving shows to the troops. It saved me from being directed into war work. Getting on the cast here has been my second success since then. The first was at the theatre in Salisbury. The show has been playing here for about ten weeks but I have only just joined it to replace a young actress who was killed in an air raid.'

'Being on the stage and entertaining the troops is an important job in wartime,' Tim said. 'You shouldn't regard yourself as not contributing to the war effort.'

'Perhaps, that may be. And what happened to you?' she asked. 'You must have been ahead of me.'

'I left The College in the summer, two years before war was declared. I went straight to Cambridge. When I graduated, I was then eligible for call-up and went into the navy, to Dartmouth College for basic officer training, followed by the Royal Naval Engineering College at Manadon, Plymouth. I was first posted from Manadon and have been continuously at sea since then. Mostly on a destroyer for trips across the Atlantic and back.'

'You sound as if crossing the Atlantic is like a pleasure cruise. That's over four years ago,' Vanessa replied. 'Don't you get any leave?'

'From time to time, when duties permit. As a matter of fact, I am just beginning one week's leave before going to sea again,' he replied.

'What do you do as a marine engineer?' asked Vanessa.

'Primarily, I manage the ship's engines and then maintain all the working parts around the ship. It can be a big job, especially if the ship suffers any damage,' Tim explained.

Suddenly the bell rang to clear the entrances of the theatre. It was part of the air raid drill to avoid any unnecessary, persistent crowding.

'Well, it has been nice running into you so unexpectedly. I hope your show goes on. It really helps the war effort. People need an uplift from time to time,' Tim said.

They wandered out to the street, still chatting. 'How far away do you have to walk?' he asked her.

'A couple of streets only, but long enough on a rainy night,' she replied. They continued walking.

'Do you mind if I come to see the play again tomorrow night?' Tim asked.

'Of course not. I shall be looking out for you. I can call you Tim, then,' she said with a certain amount of certainty that was not lost on him.

On reaching her hotel Tim turned to go, with a wave of his hand. But as he moved away, she called out to him.

'Don't go. Come in with me, please. It's not as if we are total strangers any more. Remember, we came from the same town.'

Her change of manner took Tim by surprise. How could she change so radically in so little time? That really disturbed him.

'Was she thinking of him as a passing sailor,' he said to himself. 'If so, too bad.' He was not up to one-night stands.

He fell into a momentary spell of confusion. Until then, she had been so formal and distant.

'Are you sure you can put up with me for another hour? I thought you had to get to sleep early for rehearsals tomorrow morning,' Tim called out.

'I don't want you to go,' she called back. 'But I know you have to.'

It was said in a definitive form, almost as if it were a lasting imperative. For a few seconds he laughed inside himself. He was standing on a Liverpool street in the blackout and pouring rain. He was being invited into a hotel by a woman with whom in other circumstances he could have fallen head over heels in love with, but had known for only a few minutes.

At the same time as that thought happened, he realised that this particular woman would have been the last person he could ever have imagined would be capable of uttering such an invitation.

It was like a request he had never contemplated hearing from any stranger nor had ever been willing to tolerate from an unknown woman.

Her hotel room was warm and comfortable, so different from his stark cabin on the ship and in utter contrast to the inclement weather outside in the street.

Shedding their wet outer garments, they stood looking at each other. For once neither could find anything to say.

Eventually, she spoke.

'I expect you're used to girls asking you in. A sailor has one in every port, I understand. You must have collected quite a few in your time,' she said.

'My trips have been mostly confined to Liverpool and Halifax in Nova Scotia, but occasionally to Russia,' Tim said.

'Well, then you must have three girls already,' Vanessa probed, laughing. 'As a matter of fact, I have none,' Tim said. 'Are you an abstainer?' Vanessa boldly pressed him.

'No, not at all. The war has cautioned me, rather than the reverse.'

'How about having one in Liverpool, then?' she quipped.

'Chance would be a fine thing,' he replied.

'I'm sorry I have no champagne to celebrate our meeting,' Vanessa said, interrupting her own interrogation. 'It's hard to get hold of these days. But how about a hot whisky to warm us up?'

'That will be good,' said Tim. 'I have to drink rum in the navy. Have you ever drunk rum?' he asked Vanessa.

'No. I have never tried it,' she replied.

She brought the two whiskies, fifty-fifty with hot water from the kettle. 'Here's to The College,' she said with her most charming smile, putting her arm holding her whisky through his upheld whisky arm to make the appropriate salute.

'And here's to The Commonweal.' He matched her innuendo, but adding, 'I always thought The Commonweal was a good school, well run, and on a wonderful campus.'

That unexpected closeness to Vanessa enabled him to look deeply into her eyes, where he discovered a quality not noticed before. At least, he thought, it confirmed an unbending determination.

It reminded him of his own predilections. He had always regarded the control over oneself and pursuit of a legitimate objective as the axis of character.

He had been born to devoted and upright parents of humble origins in Swindon, in a residential road, central to the growing town. It was part of many developments that sprang up to fortify the growth of the Great Western Railway in the nineteenth century and first two decades of the twentieth. The houses were all built on flat land below the last line of hills on which historic Old Swindon had been located. He was proud of his parents, who had struggled against the odds to rear him and his twin brothers in stringent economic times.

Tim's thoughts suddenly turned to Vanessa's parents.

'Your surname is Coles. Your father was not one of the three doctors who practised at The Brow in Victoria Road, by chance?' he queried.

She gasped. 'Yes, he was. How did you know that? But Coles is not an uncommon name. How clever to put two and two together,' laughed Vanessa.

'Ah, but you attended The Commonweal, near where you lived in Bath Road,' Tim said.

She felt suddenly stunned.

'How do you know where I lived?' she asked in surprise.

'They were our family doctors as it happens,' Tim replied. 'In fact, your father, when visiting our house one day when I was eleven, asked my mother if I could deliver medicines from The Brow to old and infirm patients unable to collect them for themselves. The College being nearby, I went straight to The Brow after school. They paid me five shillings a week. During the time I worked there I made several visits to your private house with messages for your father.'

'Well, how extraordinary!' Vanessa exclaimed. 'I am astounded.

'Five shillings a week must have seemed a princely sum at the time,' she continued.

'Yes, for a boy it was. It taught me how to value and manage hard-earned money,' said Tim.

'And now here you are with his actress daughter and you in the navy. What are you in the navy?' Vanessa asked.

'I'm a lieutenant,' said Tim

'What does that mean?' she asked. 'I only know about army ranks.'

'It's the equivalent of captain in the army and flight lieutenant in the air force. You start as midshipman, then sublieutenant, then full lieutenant.'

'You are a tall man for a sailor,' Vanessa declared.

'I'm six foot tall – and you are not a short woman,' Tim was pleased to make the comparison.

'I'm five feet seven inches,' was Vanessa's reply.

'And still growing.' Tim provoked her, but then chanced his arm adding, 'But still beautiful with it.'

'Not growing any more. Remember I'm twenty-two and stopped growing four years ago,' she said. 'I had a real fear thinking I might grow to six feet.'

She betrayed no offence in discussing her body.

He thought by then he had a right to question her about her own liaisons. 'You obviously didn't need ports to find boyfriends,' Tim commented.

'But so many in the profession only go for their own sex,' said Vanessa. 'I've had my affairs – all were disappointing. I have spent my time fighting them off,' she said, without any semblance of pride.

'Perhaps one day you will run into the right man,' Tim said sympathetically. 'The waiting may be tedious but the arrival will always be worth it. I must go, Vanessa, but I will book for the show tomorrow night,' he added, preparing to leave the room.

'There is no need for you to do that. I can get you a ticket and will leave it at reception for you. If you can arrive at least an hour before the play starts, come to my dressing room,' was Vanessa's parting word to him.

As Tim made his way out of the hotel, he thought her last-minute invitation might have been the kind of remark many actresses throw away at friends, relatives, and acquaintances. It was just like saying, 'Call in to my house for a drink sometime when you are passing.'

Then he realised he was making defensive excuses for his own fears. She had invited him to her hotel room. Was it the stormy night that had encouraged the invitation? Or was it something else?

He tried to argue with himself. Was he expecting, indeed demanding of himself, that it should be something else?

2

Neither Vanessa nor Tim slept well that night. Vanessa realised that she had fallen in love. It was an experience quite different from anything else she had felt previously. It was as if she wanted to exist inside of him and he in her. He was tall, handsome, slim, well built, and everything a woman could ask for.

But it was much more than that. It was the man, shining through all the appearances that had gripped her. She felt her hesitations about men and her suspicions of their alleged duplicity and negative attitudes being swept away when he was there. On the twinkling of an eye it seemed, her life had been ushered into a new world.

Tim's restlessness was the result of the disturbance to the magnificent hold he customarily had over his emotions. If Swindon had not appeared in Vanessa's brief biography in the play's brochure, it might never have happened. He felt stupefied by the incredibly fine chances by which a life could be turned around. If he had never looked at the brochure – and particularly the track record caption for one of the lesser members of the cast – he would have left the theatre in the same way as he had entered it, oblivious to the chance he had missed.

He realised that his life was never to be the same from that moment. It was a thought that was at the same time disturbing but exciting.

He was in no doubt. She was a treasure, beautiful in figure, face, and personality. He was sure that underneath was the kind of character that could only command his unswerving devotion. He found himself wanting to be one with her. It was a precedent experience. If it was love, then so be it.

For both, as the night wore on, the evening of the next day could not come quickly enough. He had always been able to sleep well, but not that night.

And he must remember the bottle of rum.

He had booked into a hotel for the first night of his leave, expecting to take a train to Swindon to see his family the next day – plans that were about to be upset.

In the morning he returned to his ship, temporarily berthed in Liverpool, to conjure up a bottle of navy rum from the officers' mess. He also collected some more suitable civilian clothes from his cabin, having intended to wear his uniform for travel and self-respecting purposes for his visit to Swindon.

But in the event, he was still wearing his uniform when he turned up at the theatre. He was a sailor and proud of it. Changing into civilian clothes might just be the wrong thing to do so early in the tumultuous relationship that had thrown Vanessa and him together.

During the day Vanessa had briefed Carol about the arrangements. Carol accepted her apology as a matter of fact, that she would be unable to meet her for coffee after the performance that night.

It was almost like being in a play.

'Are you smitten with him, then?' Carol asked her. 'Or is it a one-night Liverpool date, something you will enjoy before you pass on to greater things?'

'You'll see,' Vanessa replied. 'Smitten is the word.'

'It's a bit quick, isn't it?' Carol was serious in her question. 'It's not like you to be bowled over by anyone, least of all by a passing serviceman, even though he came from Swindon.'

'It was you who said to me, "Please save me one if they do",' Vanessa reminded her. 'Or didn't you really mean it?'

'Ah, yes, but that was a figure of speech. Don't forget the old saying, "Take on a man in haste and regret it at leisure",' Carol said quickly.

'But you need to have the wit to judge the exceptional fact that stares you in the face. Sometimes, if a great opportunity comes your way and you are not quick to seize it, you lose it forever,' Vanessa answered her, with a touch of philosophical overtones. 'Life's chances can be very fleeting. And I know my own mind.'

Tim was more than an hour early to find Vanessa's dressing room. She was waiting for him.

When he knocked on her door she felt a sinking feeling in her stomach, thinking it might not be him. He might have had second thoughts. She stepped swiftly to open it.

'Hello, Vanessa. I'm a bit earlier than you suggested. But I've got a present for you.' Tim's greeting was more formal than he would have liked and more than she would have wished.

But decorum still had to prevail. Who could possibly know what might materialise to make anything other than such formalities a premature folly?

He handed her the bottle wrapped in coloured paper. She opened it and exclaimed, 'It's a bottle of rum! What a surprise in wartime. I've never even tasted it. Promise me that we will open it in my hotel, after the show. Will you come back with me?'

'Nothing will get in my way,' he said gallantly, surprised with her forthrightness. It was not an invitation he had any intention of turning down.

'Or was she seizing an opportunity?' he asked himself. 'If this is still the girl in every port syndrome in action, she is pretty good at it.' The question momentarily went through his head. He wanted to dismiss his thoughts, looking for evidence enabling him to do so.

'Now let me into the secret of what an actress does in her dressing room, just before going on stage', he said to Vanessa.

She perceived that he really wanted to know. 'Of course, my clothes have been settled for my part in the play and I have to make sure they are perfect for each performance. What takes a lot of time is the particular make-up I have to apply to my face. It, too, must be exactly the same for every appearance. And then there are my lines to brush up. That's particularly important when taking on a part in the early performances, but as time goes on an actress can recall them with her eyes shut, so to speak. If you make a mistake, it is possible to ad lib over the gap until you can pick up the correct lines again. Usually, other actors can sense when that happens and can be accommodating.'

Since it was Saturday, with Tim in the audience, for Vanessa it had to be a night for a special edition of the show. She wanted to be at her very best.

Tim waited for her at the same little coffee table in the foyer, enjoying the exodus from the theatre after a perfect performance which attracted a rapturous response from the audience.

Tim stood up when he saw her hurrying towards him after she had taken about twenty minutes to change her clothes and remove her make-up.

He thought she was going to stop, but instead, she walked straight at him and into his arms, hugging him for the first time. He realised she was hyped up from her effort on stage but was glad she had overstepped the boundary line of decorum. It implied an invitation to him to relax his own behaviour.

'Let's go,' she said. 'The first few performances, for me as a new girl, are always the most trying. But they are now out of the way. I think I have got my part fixed OK at last.'

'I thought you said one of the principal actresses made mistakes in her lines. You are implying that you have been the same,' Tim commented.

'Oh, there are lapses and lapses, big ones and small ones. Mine were quite trivial,' Vanessa said, laughing it off.

She had remembered to bring the bottle of rum. They hurried out of the theatre. The coffee table had been outclassed. They left it behind, relegated to their past, however short it had been.

Scarcely had the door to her room in the hotel been closed, than they hurriedly embraced, dropping anything they carried, including the bottle.

Did he move to kiss her first or did she kiss him first?

Did it matter? The effect was mutual. It unleashed a torrent of passion that had built up since their first meeting twenty-four hours before, released from the underlying yearnings of solitude, frustration, and sex starvation, which intending lovers had to endure who had never encountered the right person to release them with.

There was nothing to say. Their bodies said everything. Time stood still.

After a few minutes, time was rudely started again. Their reverie was spectacularly broken by the sound of the air raid sirens. Even before the sirens had ceased their dire and mournful warning, bombs were already dropping.

'We ought to go down to the shelter,' Vanessa said, her voice showing apprehension.

Tim, only too fresh from bombs, torpedoes, mines, and explosions in the Atlantic, was resigned to the sound.

'Can I say, no?' he questioned. 'Let's stay here. If I die, I would like it to be with you. Nothing will ever deter me.'

Impressed by those words, which cut to her very core, and without a murmur, Vanessa assented. 'Such a statement of love could be rare,' she thought. 'What else was there to say?'

'I'll fix a tot of rum for us immediately,' she said. 'Where are the glasses?' she urgently asked herself.

'You only need one,' called Tim. 'Make it a loving cup. We have to share it to the bottom. Rum was always circulated to sailors when they were facing a battle.'

She rescued the bottle from the floor and poured a generous amount into a large glass. 'Do you think we are facing a battle?' she asked.

'Well, we are actually on one end of one,' Tim said. 'The Luftwaffe aircrews are on the other end of it. They are facing the Liverpool defences. Their lives, too, are at risk.'

'You sound like a man who sees everything,' she responded. 'You drink first,' he said.

'No, I insist you drink first. I've never had it before.'

She drank after him, making a face from the undiluted rum.

'You soon get used to it. It drove sailors fighting mad in the old days,' said Tim. 'It could do so today if you drink enough of it.'

'Well, there's a thing. I'm feeling fighting mad already,' said Vanessa laughing – and coughing. 'But it does wonders on an empty stomach.'

After a few more sips of rum, their clothes came off. Their passion, which overtook them, could have shattered the strongest resolve. There was nothing left to resist, no impediment to their ardour. All inhibitions were jettisoned.

Vanessa whispered to Tim, 'I told you I didn't want you to leave. Make that a permanent requirement. My resolve is fixed.'

He knew their meeting was once in a lifetime. Tomorrow and all his tomorrows would be transformed by that very day. It was what he had always secretly hoped for, what his whole being said an energetic "Yes" to, the event that would be the catalyst of his life to be. What more evidence could he expect?

They found the comfort of the bed as if it were a shelter and refuge from the air attack on the city. Soon they were transported into a world of their own – far away from the bombing, the theatre at number one Roe Street in Liverpool, and the destroyer in port with a number, but hidden name.

3

Sunday proved to be a continuation of the night. Their hands were never far from each other. It was as if they were condensing their previous years – of yearning and wandering, with no one to satisfy their longing – into a few hours.

As the day wore on they attended to their bodily needs and discussed the way ahead. There was so much to talk about.

Tim knew that the theatre was closed on Monday nights.

'Would you like to come with me on a semi-official visit tomorrow, darling? It would take up most of the day.'

'Where would that be?' she asked.

'I've had an invitation to visit RAF Burtonwood, near Warrington, opened during the first January of the war as a servicing and storage centre, and for modifying British aircraft.'

'But what is so special about it for you to go for a visit?' Vanessa queried.

'It was operated by RAF Number 37 Maintenance Unit for two and a half years. Then it was transferred to the United States to become a servicing centre for the aircraft of their Eighth, Ninth, Twelfth, and Fifteenth Air Forces. It is reputed to be the largest wartime airfield in the whole of Europe. It has a greater number of American personnel and aircraft maintenance facilities than any other base in the United Kingdom.'

'Is that unusual for you to be doing that sort of thing?' she asked.

Tim was getting used to the sudden questions that she asked. They always seemed to be different in purpose, but penetrating. He tried to see a pattern in them, concluding that they were directed at knowing more about him, but mostly for protecting him. He interpreted his own conclusion that her early concern had a long-term meaning for their relationship.

'Not at all. It's common practice to exchange officers between the services for just a day or even for a one-off combat mission,' Tim explained.

'I hope they don't invite you to go on one of those,' she said, feeling slightly alarmed. 'You have more than enough danger on the seas as it is. Surely every crossing you make is a real or at least a potential combat mission. No more is the word,' Vanessa rejoined.

'There's no fear of that at this particular base. It's non-operational, anyway.' Tim quickly set her mind at rest.

'They might not let me in,' Vanessa said.

'Oh, I think they will. I shall tell them who you are and who we are,' he replied. 'I met a number of their senior officers in the officers' club in Halifax before escorting their ships bringing them and their aircraft over here. So, they owe me a small debt.'

'After Monday, what will you do with your time?' she asked. 'I'm back on stage on Tuesday. And I cannot get time off so soon at the start of appearing new in the cast.'

'I shall come and see the show again,' he said with pride. 'And also on Wednesday, my last day. On Thursday I have to report back to the ship. I've cancelled my trip to Swindon. It has been a necessary sacrifice.'

Vanessa was persuaded. 'Actions are better than words,' she said to herself. It was a kind of pledge that was to have far-reaching consequences for her in the future, in circumstances beyond her imagination.

'Oh, don't mention Thursday or Swindon, darling,' Vanessa said sharply. 'I haven't faced up to either yet.'

The visit to Burtonwood went without a hitch, as Tim predicted. It gave Vanessa an insight into his relations with other officers and his standing in the navy. She felt proud to be with him on the visit and introduced as his fiancée. Her designation had to be stated for admission to the base, but she gave no thought to its being premature.

She assumed from that time onwards that he was her fiancé. It seemed so natural to her that it simply reinforced the effects of the tumultuous upheaval in her life in the previous few hours.

His two further attendances at the theatre, however, became an increasing anticlimax. Not that he had tired of watching the production. If anything, he revelled anew in watching Vanessa while she was on stage. He was learning how to enjoy the play, including its appealing songs. He thought he could remember so much of it that he would be able to rehearse it again in his mind in the middle of the Atlantic. It was the approach of Thursday and his departure that troubled him most.

The exuberance of their last night together was inevitably tinged with sadness. They had been conjoined over a period of only a few days. It had seemed so full of meaning and enjoyment, but at the same time had passed in a flash. He began to fear her passion would wane. When he was at the lowest ebb of his thoughts during those few hours, he was suddenly electrified to hear Vanessa whisper to him.

'I'll never forget you, darling,' Vanessa breathed. 'You are in my heart for keeps. You will come back to me someday? May the war spare you till the end. I shall only start to breathe easily when that time comes.'

'I shall find you wherever you are. I shall look in the theatres throughout Britain until I find you, as soon as I can,' Tim promised.

'You look for me. I'll look for you. I can't face the fact you might never come back. The sea is such a dangerous place in wartime,' Vanessa declared.

'And I am not forgetting that enemy aircraft drop bombs on unsuspecting, or at least unknown, civilians,' Tim pointed out. 'The Luftwaffe still has plenty of fight left in it. We shall both be brave as are so many others, but we will have the advantage of being fortified by our love,' he reassured her.

Neither then could have known that the sea could be as lethal in peace as in war. It could produce heartbreaking experiences of equal force as anything imaginable.

'Can you think of two professions that could be so distinctive and removed from each other than the stage and the sea?' Vanessa asked the question, hoping Tim would reveal any doubts he harboured about sealing his own love for her over the time ahead.

'Only that the boards are common to both. We take people on board. The deck of a ship is normally a safe haven. In the acting profession you have to pound the boards of lowly theatres before you can hit the big-time productions,' Tim commented.

'Now that's something I had not thought about,' she said.

'Truly, they are two honourable and vital professions, though contrasting, as far apart as two jobs could be,' Tim commented. 'We live in two different worlds. But doesn't that make it a challenge? Is it not an unending fascination for both of us?' He asked his own searching questions. 'We just have to make it work.'

In prospect, it seemed an impossible combination to cope with, trying to get together again after months apart and not knowing where each other would be living. They just had to find a way to harmonise their movements – two eager people, desperate to renew their love for each other.

That Thursday morning, they walked to the theatre. The show was giving a matinée performance. But few people seemed to be in and around the theatre at such an early time of day.

They paused on the pavement outside the main doors.

'Remember, darling, my heart will go to sleep until you return. It's been awakened as never before and nothing will satisfy it unless you do it,' she said quietly to Tim.

'You cannot say more,' Tim responded. 'I shall live for the day.'

He turned to go.

Suddenly, and without restraint, Vanessa burst into song. As the first notes pierced the morning air, people suddenly appeared from nowhere, standing away at a respectable distance to hear the lilting notes drawing to their brief end, curious to know why such a song should be raised in the street.

'The lark is singing on high
The sun's ashine in the blue
The winter is driven away
And spring is returning anew
Who cares what fortune may bring
What storms may tear us apart
No sadness can kill the wonder and thrill
Of that waltz in my heart.'

While she was singing it, Tim Denton, slightly bewildered at first by the unorthodox event and a little embarrassed, soon quickly filled with pride. Looking over her shoulder, he saw a man about to leave the theatre, obviously intent on walking to a car that had just drawn up outside.

The man momentarily paused on hearing the singing, waiting to hear the end of the cadenza, before stepping out and striding to the car.

Tim heard him call out to Vanessa.

'Good morning, Vanessa,' he said. 'That sounded beautiful. I hope you got all the words right.'

'Who was that?' asked Tim, when the man had gone.

'That was Ivor Novello. He composed and masterminded *Glamorous Night*, the show you have been watching for four nights. It's been around for a few years and revived from time to time in the provinces. He is planning a new production in the West End, called *Perchance to Dream*. It will replace *The Dancing Years,* currently at the Adelphi, which ends this July, but the new show won't open until early next year.'

'I didn't know you could sing,' Tim gently protested.

'That was the chorus of the main hit song "Waltz of My Heart" from *The Dancing Years*,' she informed him. 'Of course, I have never been a member of the cast for that show nor on the stage in London, but one day I hope to get there.'

'I am sure you will make it,' Tim said. 'I should think that spontaneous exercise of your beautiful voice must have registered itself in Ivor Novello's memory.'

'He has heard me sing behind the scenes before today,' Vanessa said. 'Although he has never heard me sing from *The Dancing Years* before.'

'Well, he certainly stopped to listen to it,' Tim pointed out.

'It wasn't meant for him,' Vanessa reminded Tim.

'I am honoured. What other talents do you have?' he asked her.

'One day, I hope to land a principal singing part on stage,' Vanessa said. 'Ivor will be looking for new leading ladies. I hope my time will come.'

'I'm sure it will happen,' was Tim's last word to her, except for one. 'Goodbye, darling,' Tim said. He gave her a last hug and they kissed.

4

With leaden footsteps, Tim returned to his ship that day. Early the following morning, the destroyer left Liverpool port. The captain called his officers together for the briefing soon after leaving.

He had some surprising news for them.

'We have been taken off the Atlantic convoy run, but I don't know for how long. We are going south to strengthen the escort for ships assembling in the Bristol Channel ports, which have to be protected into U-boat alley and Southampton Water. The whole voyage will be dangerous at this time, but especially off the north Cornish coast.'

The destroyer sailed southwards the length of the Irish Sea and patrolled the extremes of the Bristol Channel, until it joined the convoy sailing westwards, circumnavigating Cornwall before turning east and entering the English Channel. The escort vessels were numerous enough to prevent any interference from hostile surface forces, but they had to be vigilant against submerged U-boats.

On entering the approach to Southampton on the east side of the Isle of Wight, Tim, in company with the entire crew of the destroyer, was dumbfounded to see the huge number of ships and activities taking place around them.

'We've heard rumours for a while that an invasion of the continent was about due. So, this is it,' Tim said to a fellow officer.

'It looks like it. What a gigantic scale everything is on. But the weather is not too good at the moment. It's the fourth of June tomorrow and all the meteorology is bad,' his colleague replied. 'It's bound to be delayed.'

The destroyer left the ships at their destination and with other escort vessels put into Portsmouth naval base, nearby to the east. They moored ready to take up their duties, once the signal was given that the weather was at least at the minimum for the invasion to take place. They would join the overwhelming sea forces due to be launched against the French coast early in the morning of the next day. The bad weather continued overnight, however, forcing yet another day's delay in the plan.

It was on the sixth in fact, when the signal was given that the planned invasion of the Normandy beaches should go ahead, in spite of the inclement weather.

The destroyer joined the numerous naval vessels constantly patrolling the waters far and near, guarding against any attempt to prevent the landing itself and threatening the supply ships from reaching the French beaches.

In the following weeks, Tim's destroyer took part in sinking two of the eighteen U-boats sunk, trying vainly to interrupt the invasion and subsequent supply missions, which became a constant feature across the English Channel. The U-boats were totally overwhelmed by the allied warships involved, numbering over one thousand, many reserved only for hunting the undersea enemy.

The constant day and night patrols of navy ships ensured the successful foundation of the allied forces on the continent of Europe. The war still had a long way to run but it was optimistically regarded as the beginning of the end.

Tim was glad when his ship took its turn to be withdrawn for a rest at the end of August, by returning to Portsmouth naval base.

After only two days the destroyer, fully brought up to its full capacity for fuel, ammunition, and food, put to sea once more.

The captain informed the officers and crew that they faced the ocean again. He thought it might be their final stint on the convoy run to and from Halifax, the departure port from Canada for allied ships in the North Atlantic, with Clydeside as their port of arrival.

But first, the ship was withdrawn for a refit in Scotland, before taking up its duties again, staying on station until the cessation of hostilities with Germany at the end of the first week of May 1945.

With the rejoicing over the declaration of the end of hostilities out of the way, the thoughts of a majority of the destroyer's crew soon turned to the possibility of demobilisation. Everyone understood that the men first called up would be first out. Those only recently entering the service would have to serve on after the war had ended.

Tim Denton, being one of the most senior of the destroyer's crew in terms of service time, was demobilised in September on a first in first out basis. He had decided not to pursue a career in the navy, although he was approached to do so. For him, meeting Vanessa was the deciding factor.

Otherwise, he might have continued his career in the peacetime Royal Navy.

At the demobilisation centre at Devonport, representatives from many shipping lines were looking out for men they could persuade to move into the commercial world. Tim was cornered by an agent of the Ennerman Lines, a significant company in the maritime industry, keen to see if he could tempt Tim to enter the merchant navy.

'Are you thinking of going to sea again, sir?' asked the agent who first approached him.

'To be frank, the sea is all I have known since I was called up from university at the beginning of the war,' Tim replied. 'But I am not yet sure what I want to do.'

'I'm from the Ennerman Company, sir. All I can say is that for men with your qualifications there will be great opportunities on the oceans in future. I understand that you are a Cambridge engineer graduate and have been a marine engineer in the Royal Navy for over five years.'

'That is correct,' said Tim.

Tim was keen to know about the kind of company he might consider joining. He asked the agent to describe the status of Ennerman. In reply, the agent delivered the information with a brief rundown on the condition of the company. He was evidently not short of enthusiasm about his job.

'By the outbreak of the Second World War, Ennerman's fleet had been successfully rebuilt and expanded from the First World War. It owned a total of a hundred and five ships with a combined capacity of over nine hundred thousand tons, making it one of the biggest company fleets in the world. Its variety of ships was classed as mixed cargo and passenger, cargo ships with limited passenger accommodation, all-cargo ships, and short sea vessels for service in the Mediterranean.'

'What happened to its ships in the war?' asked Tim.

'For war purposes, many of its ships were requisitioned by the government, serving as troopships and the transport of equipment, others being reserved as cargo vessels taking part in the transport of food and military supplies to the United Kingdom across the Atlantic. They also sailed to Russia for the transport of military aid.'

'Yes, I encountered some of those ships in the convoys,' Tim commented. 'Some of them, I know, were sunk.'

'They suffered heavy losses, particularly from U-boats. Forty-one of the company's ships were sunk by submarines, seven by air attacks, three by mines, and one by a surface raider. Others were lost in accidents or scrapped. In total, the Ennerman Lines lost sixty ships out of its fleet of one hundred and five,' the agent replied.

'Why, that's a huge price to pay,' Tim commented, somewhat in awe. He was only too aware of the cost in shipping that the war had meant to Britain. 'It nearly cost us the entire war. If the Liberty ships had not come along in time, Britain would have had to surrender,' he said to the Ennerman's agent.

'I expect you know that better than anyone else,' said the agent.

'So, what is the present state of affairs in the company?' asked Tim. 'Are they actively trying to build up the company again?'

The agent went on to explain how the company was currently coping. It was a story of systematic and progressive enterprise.

'It will be a repeat of replacing the losses, the same as after the First World War. A new building programme is already under way. We are building fast steam cargo liners that can carry up to about twenty passengers in considerable comfort, sometimes many more. Crew accommodation is also greatly improved in these new ships. For rebuilding our international trade routes with these ships, we have purchased outright twelve cargo ships from the government, which they had been managing directly in the war. Within five years, twenty-five of these new style ships will have entered service, making a total of forty-five new vessels since the war, and a further fourteen for the Portuguese trade routes and Mediterranean services. By then the Ennerman fleet will have been almost completely rebuilt, consisting of a total of ninety-four ships with a carrying capacity of nine hundred thousand tons.'

'That sound like impressive progress,' Tim told him. 'As you said, it looks like a company worth joining. But in my case, what kind of specific jobs are on offer that might interest me?' he asked.

'We have two immediate vacancies in the port of London for third engineer officers. They are both on new cargo liners. Other vacancies are in the offing. But we are most anxious to crew up one of our ships under repair in New Zealand. It's one of the Liberty ships we now use for freight, built in 1944. For the right man, we would appoint him as chief engineer. The ship carries five engineer officers. We have already found four engineers, but two are new, joining the crew after qualifying in New Zealand. We have to get the ship back to London for a ballast loading to the United States. It's a job you might be interested in with your previous experience. If you applied for it, you would also have another advantage in that you have served on one of the American destroyers acquired for convoy work, so you must be very familiar with American marine engines and other working parts on an American-built ship.'

The agent's offer was attractive by any standard. As chief engineer officer, he would virtually be in charge of the entire engineering of the ship, following on from being the chief's deputy, as second engineer, during his final posting in the navy on a British-built destroyer.

The opportunity was especially appealing to him for the delay that would be incurred before he had to sail to New Zealand. He would have time to get his bearings on joining the company and that would give him time to spend with Vanessa before sailing. Against that advantage, there would be some delay in New Zealand for preparing the ship to be ready to sail, assuming the repairs had been completed. Overall, it would eventually entail a long time away from Vanessa.

Tim's first thought on musing with the idea of taking up the New Zealand offer, as put to him by Ennerman's agent, was to discuss it with Vanessa.

'I would like to discuss your offer with my partner,' Tim responded. But where was she? He was left with the possibility of searching and, perhaps, failing to find her.

Even the four months, which had elapsed since he left Liverpool, had been enough to lose sight of her and she of him. He deduced she might have left the theatre in Liverpool by then. The show had been running for some time before

Vanessa had joined it – and when he had seen it – so it was highly probable that she had moved on by then.

The agent was naturally expecting an answer from him more or less immediately, at least on a first refusal basis. Other engineer officers were also being interviewed. Some of them would jump at the chance he had been offered.

He calculated that if he took the offer he could be back in London within another few months for the ship to be adapted to carry ballast. The ship would be in London for a few weeks for that purpose. There would be plenty of time to track her down and make amends for his neglect. He suddenly made up his mind. The balance of probabilities was on his side.

'I'll take the ship in New Zealand,' he told the agent.

'I'm glad you have made up your mind so swiftly,' the agent replied. 'It is an unusual opportunity to be promoted straight to chief engineer officer in the company, but the circumstances are entirely in your favour. You were deputy to the chief in the navy so you are exceptionally well qualified for the job.'

He continued, 'You have to report to the company's offices in London within three days. I will have notified them of your arrival in the meantime.'

Tim immediately set off by train for London but broke his journey at Swindon to see his parents. He had managed during his wartime service to visit them on his all too infrequent leaves.

'So, you are now out of it, Tim,' his father announced.

'Yes, at last, it's all over.' Tim greeted his parents with warm hugs.

'Will you be staying, now?' his mother asked.

'No, unfortunately. My life has been made a bit topsy-turvy lately, Mum,' he replied. 'It's all a matter of competing for the best jobs going.'

He informed them of his lucky break with the Ennerman Company and his liaison with Vanessa. 'I hope to introduce her to you both in the near future. I'm sorry I cannot stay long today, but I'll be back soon.'

On reporting to the Ennerman offices, Tim was given his instructions. He would sail to Wellington on an Ennerman ship in three weeks.

He left the offices with a smile on his face. There was ample time to track Vanessa down. His severance pay from the navy, added to the retaining pay from Ennerman, starting from his engagement date, would enable him to survive comfortably.

But where would he start to find her? There were scores of theatres all over Britain, all potentially open to Vanessa's employment. If she had completed her time at The Royal Court in Liverpool, she could be anywhere, if she had managed to get another casting.

First, he made a telephone call to The Royal Court in Liverpool to confirm that the *Glamorous Night* production had concluded its run there. The show had ceased a month before.

His mind went straight back to her final few words to him as he left her in May. The impression it had made on his mind then came to his aid.

'I wonder if she has already pulled off her expectation to be cast for a prominent part in a new Ivor Novello show,' he said to himself.

It took him no time at all to establish that the latest hit show in the West End was *Perchance to Dream,* showing at the Hippodrome since April, just before the war ended.

He hurried to the theatre.

The booking office was open. A queue of patrons waited to buy tickets.

He looked eagerly on the surrounding advertisements for her name in the cast, but without success.

Following an illogical inspiration that came to him, he joined the queue. 'What ticket would you like, sir?' asked the clerk.

'First, can you tell me if Vanessa Coles is or has been in the cast?' he asked. 'Or is expected to join it?'

'As a matter of fact, she is due to appear for the first time tonight, standing in as a replacement, playing three important parts.'

'Which one is she playing, then?' Tim asked.

'She plays all three. It's a common practice in Ivor's shows,' the clerk replied. 'Now, what about your seat. There are quite a number of people waiting behind you, keen to get their tickets.'

'Have you a seat near the front of the stalls?' Tim asked.

'I think so. One seat only left on the front row.'

Tim was left in a quandary. Should he see the show from the front row in the hope she would never expect to find him there and would not recognise him? Or should he try to gain access to her room before the show and perhaps upset her first night on the stage?

He decided on not distracting her, as a matter of fact completely misjudging Vanessa's professionalism by such a consideration. He had much to learn.

Tim corrected his request to the clerk. 'Please give me a seat in the back of the stalls.' In deferring to Vanessa's dedication to the stage he had made a correct supposition but had wrongly chosen a change in his own behaviour in an acknowledgement of it.

He would beat a retreat to her dressing room immediately the show had ended – but this time without a bottle of rum in his hand.

In his excitement at meeting her, he had assumed the validity of all the talk and promises she had made when they first met. He could not bear to think of her as a person who changed her mind. She could never be a turncoat. She had achieved what she had declared her next objective was to be.

The performance that night was the most stirring experience Tim had ever had in his life. The promise of her wonderful voice, which she demonstrated to him on the pavement in Liverpool, was gloriously fulfilled on the stage of a premier West End theatre. People sitting around Tim gasped at the clarity, lilt, and expression of her singing parts. Her first night on the London stage was amply and rapturously applauded at the end of the performance, when the cast took curtain call after curtain call.

Tim rushed around the theatre to find a way to her dressing room at the end of the show, full of optimism.

He found a small concourse of enthusiasts had gathered in one place that seemed a promising spot for an access to the dressing rooms. But his way through was blocked – by immovable people.

He courteously elbowed through some of those people but found his way barred by theatre staff, trying to protect the cast from being overwhelmed.

'Sorry, sir, we really have to give the cast a chance to recover their wits after such a marvellous performance.'

'I am desperate,' said Tim. 'I must see Vanessa Coles.'

'No chance tonight, sir, I'm afraid,' was the reply from one member of the staff. 'Perhaps tomorrow night you might have better luck.'

'In that case, will you deliver an urgent message to her now, please?'

Tim must have looked so determined but also forlorn, that one of the staff came forward, offering to deliver the message.

'What is your message, sir?'

'Just tell Vanessa Coles that a bottle of rum has just walked in.'

'Say that again,' the man said with an air of disapproval. 'You are not trying to play a prank on me are you, sir?'

'No. I am not. This is serious. Only say that a bottle of rum has just walked in.'

The attendant went on his way. A minute passed. Then another. But suddenly, a loud exclamation could be heard and the crowded corridor was frantically parted to let a woman run through.

'Tim, it's you, it is you,' Vanessa called to him as they threw their arms around each other and were momentarily lost in another world.

The theatregoers standing nearby or milling around trying to contact the cast members were awe-struck. Mostly, they were impressed with the apparent ease with which a man among them had managed to draw out the newly appearing star of the show on her first night when no one else had been able to make any contact. The men among the crowd were excited to be so close to Vanessa, the women among them becoming suddenly aware of the handsome man she had embraced.

She dragged him away from the bystanders back down the corridor and into her room, locking the door behind her, breathless, and brimming over with ecstatic exclamations of delight that he had come back at last.

'I wonder what the papers will report tomorrow about that scuffle and the reasons for it,' said Tim. 'I never expected such a dramatic appendix to the show. I could hardly restrain myself watching you on the stage. It was your voice I recognised first and then your beauty in those different parts.'

'The first thing I have to do is cancel the festivities that the cast have arranged for tonight to mark my joining the cast. I was called on by Ivor to replace my predecessor who had to withdraw. It's been my big opportunity to break into the big-time parts,' said Vanessa.

'Or can I come with you, too?' Tim offered.

'No way,' she replied. 'I'm not sharing you with anyone else tonight. They have to get used to my priorities.'

'What a formidable woman you are becoming,' said Tim. 'But I love you, with all that I am and with all that I can be.'

'You have spoken for me, too, darling,' said Vanessa.

Tim gave Vanessa a rundown on what had happened to him in the interim. The days of wartime secrecy were over.

'I have about twenty days before I get on the ship for New Zealand,' he added.

'Tomorrow is Saturday,' Vanessa replied. 'My parents are coming up from Swindon for that performance. And they have booked a late-night dinner at the Dorchester Hotel afterwards. I will not let them know who you are. I am going to spring a surprise on them.'

They never stopped talking from then until they fell asleep in Vanessa's hotel room. Their demanding day and the excitement of their quick discovery of each other, after losing track of their respective whereabouts, was finally laid to rest where they truly belonged, in each other's arms.

On Saturday, it was Tim's day to meet Vanessa's parents for the first time. And then he remembered. It was the first time only as Vanessa's lover.

The joyous exchanges between Vanessa and her parents on seeing each other after so long a separation quickly gave way to her introduction of Tim, who wondered if she had forgotten his ties with her father from years before.

Dressed in one of the best suits he had bought with his demob allowance of clothing coupons, Tim towered over her parents who were ageing and shorter than he. 'This is Tim Denton,' Vanessa announced to her mother. 'We've known each other since May last year.'

She stretched the truth. 'He is a good friend of mine. I couldn't let you know. He has just turned up from the war. I wondered if you would be able to let him join us at the Dorchester.'

'Of course, of course,' her father said. 'A friend of our daughter is always welcome with us.'

Tim Denton breathed a sigh of relief. The first unintended and risky hurdle had been overcome swiftly and with ease.

But had Vanessa forgotten that her father had engaged this man – when he was a boy – to deliver medicines from his surgery?

Vanessa's mother had not been listening to her daughter's explanations.

She had been captivated by her daughter's friend, using the moments sizing up the upstanding, impressive-looking man before her, leaving her husband to pay attention to her daughter. She offered Tim her hand.

Then Dr Coles smiled and shook hands with Tim. Clearly, he had no recognition of Tim as that young boy he had enlisted for a job some fourteen years previously.

Tim was willing to leave his former contact quiescent, but Vanessa had other ideas.

'Don't you recognise him, Dad?'

'No, I'm sorry I have not met you before, Tim, have I?' he asked.

Tim held up the forefinger of his left hand.

'You put this finger back in the right order when it was knocked out of joint by a cricket ball. I always remember you took me by the left wrist and turned away to shield what you were about to do. Before I could see your intention, you had seized the dislocated finger and put it back into its proper place.'

'Yes, I do recall doing that in the middle of the surgery floor but that was for the boy who delivered medicines to infirm patients in their homes,' Dr Coles replied.

'Of course, it was me,' Tim said with his most charming smile. 'I worked for you as a lad for about four years.'

'Well, forgive me for not recognising you,' Dr Coles responded. 'But who on earth could have recognised you?' he asked. 'I am astounded.'

It took hours of talk – among the general conversation between the four people – to reveal Tim's upbringing and career to date. He well knew that in one way he was on trial for the hand of their daughter, although he guessed that Vanessa, already twenty-three, and a woman of the world, would consider seeking it as a courtesy, rather than a necessity. Perhaps her father and mother would also regard it as an imposition. But he knew that if they disapproved it might make it awkward for his relationships with Vanessa. He told himself that as a couple they had had no contact with either set of parents before that evening. They had made up their own minds as mature people.

The hours passed quickly.

The Saturday night performance, as the climax of the week, was a highlight for Vanessa personally. The audience had clearly identified her as one of the stars of the show.

The four of them joined the late dinner patrons at the Dorchester Hotel, eventually retiring for the night at Vanessa's hotel, where she had booked a room for her father and mother.

Her parents returned to Swindon on Sunday. There being no performance on Monday, Vanessa and Tim joined them on the ninety-minute train journey, staying overnight in their house in Old Swindon.

On Monday it was the turn of Vanessa to meet Henry and Elsie Denton, Tim's parents, at their house in New Swindon.

They were enamoured of Vanessa and intrigued by the connection with their family doctor. His mother remembered the day Dr Coles had asked her if Tim could do the delivery job at the surgery. Family history, invoked so unexpectedly, made their meeting lively and enjoyable.

Returning to London, Vanessa was eager to dedicate herself to her new career in the West End, the premier venue of the British stage.

For the time until he was due to sail, Tim enjoyed supporting her and watching a performance every third night but using the day to attend the company's offices and making preparations for his voyage.

The dreaded day of his departure arrived in late November.

Tim was expecting to be away for several months. But this time there were no enemy perils to face. The voyage to and from New Zealand would occupy three months altogether. He had been told the ship would probably leave Wellington in February or March of the following year for the return voyage to London.

'The war is over,' Vanessa reminded him. 'I cannot say how relieved I am that all I have to cope with is your absence. I don't want you to go. But you will come back to me, won't you?' she pleaded unnecessarily.

'You will be stationary. My travel will involve a long way to come back to where you are,' Tim replied. 'This time I will know where you are and it will be easy to find you on my return.'

Neither could get used to saying goodbye for his long periods away. The separation was part of the arrangements between them, so they accepted it as gracefully as possible, knowing that parting had to be generated to create the expectation and joy of the return.

5

The Ennerman Company had reserved a share in a cabin on one of its ships sailing to New Zealand, leaving at eleven o'clock from Tilbury Docks one morning in the last month of the year that the war ended. Tim Denton was booked to sail in the MV *Southland*. It was a mixed freighter of over eleven thousand gross registered tons, built by the John Brown Company in Glasgow, in the year before the war.

The ship was built for the Federal Steam Navigation Company, a company which later amalgamated with the New Zealand Shipping Company. When they subsequently decided to put it on the market, Ennerman snapped it up.

Completed in the month that war was declared, the *Southland* was immediately requisitioned for war purposes, accordingly painted in wartime grey. At the end of the war, it was released back to its owners and repainted in company colours.

Although many of the company's ships were sunk during the war, the *Southland* came through the conflict relatively unscathed. It usually sailed alone, but once it was incorporated in a convoy as its commodore ship, carrying the man in charge of the entire convoy. Towards the end of the war, it was used as a store ship in the Philippine Islands in the Pacific.

After the war, the *Southland* traded for many years between Australia, New Zealand, and Europe, carrying a combination of general cargo and refrigerated foodstuffs, including meat, rabbits, dairy produce, and fruit. It also had passenger accommodation in two cabins, each for two people.

When Tim arrived at Tilbury to board the *Southland,* he was welcomed as a company colleague by the captain.

'I hear you have been appointed to one of our ships in Wellington,' he said. 'It's one of the Liberty ships, but built late in the war and in good nick, I'm told.'

'Yes,' replied Tim. 'I'm looking forward to it. It will be quite a change for me from the navy. I was in destroyers for over five years across the Atlantic on convoys and was finally made deputy chief engineer.'

'Were you now? Then you must have escorted me a couple of times and I'm still alive to tell the tale,' the captain laughed.

Tim was able to take full advantage of his new appointment as chief engineer to another of the company's ships. He was expecting to have the opportunity to discuss mechanical, operating, and employment matters with the engineers of the *Southland.*

The captain introduced Tim to the *Southland's* chief engineer. Tim saw an older man who had obviously spent his life at sea. He thought he could learn a lot from him. There was always so much not covered in the reference books issued by the company.

'I'm pleased to meet you, Chief. I'm on my way to Wellington to take up my first appointment as chief.' Tim felt deferential to a man who was considerably older than he and who evidently had had a long record as a mariner.

'We can find time to have a chat sometime,' the chief responded. His manner was open and friendly. Tim immediately felt himself warm to the elderly man. He looked forward to having discussions with him about his own pending responsibilities.

He also met the ship's chief steward, who told him about the accommodation. 'You will be joined in your cabin by a young Englishman who is emigrating permanently to New Zealand. I hope you will be comfortable with the arrangement.'

'Yes, of course, I shall. I know there are only four berths for passengers altogether,' Tim acknowledged.

A few minutes later Tim saw a Rolls Royce, driven by a chauffeur, slowly approaching the quayside. It pulled up at the boarding gangway. A smartly dressed young man alighted from the rear door of the car, opened by the chauffeur, who then unearthed an extravagant array of luggage from the spacious boot. The stream of items seemed too large and various for any but a fastidious young man. The final item to appear was a full set of golf clubs.

The chief steward introduced the newly arrived passenger to Tim. 'May I introduce James Ward, who has taken a position in the textile industry in New Zealand with Barry Hales and Company Limited, one of the larger manufacturing and wholesale companies. Mr Ward, this is Tim Denton who has just joined the Ennerman Company. He is a maritime engineer.'

'Hello, Tim, glad to meet you,' James said.

Tim in turn gave James a warm welcome and introduced himself as his fellow passenger, who would be sharing the same cabin. He seemed to be about the same age as Tim.

'Let me give you a hand with the bags,' Tim announced, and immediately helped to carry his luggage to their cabin. They established a good rapport with the customary ease of young men. James Ward told Tim he originated from a wealthy family and had tried to work in his father's construction business in Britain, but had chosen instead to make his own independent way abroad.

The other passengers in the second cabin were two men, Richard Chalmers and Frank Lever, returning to New Zealand from completing business commissions in England. The four passengers generated a friendly relationship together, spending many hours eating, drinking, or playing cards, and exchanging stories. The hours were never dull. All four had been in military service of one kind or another during the war and were quite uninhibited in talking about it.

During dinner one night early in the voyage, the captain asked Tim point blank what his experience had been in the navy. All he had previously told the captain was that he had spent his time crossing the Atlantic.

'I had some ups and downs in destroyers. I left training for my first ship in 1940,' Tim replied.

'Where did you do your navy engineering training, then?' the captain asked.

'At Manadon in Plymouth, but it was a shortened course, as I had spent three years on an engineering degree immediately before joining up,' Tim elaborated. 'So, I was posted to join the crew of HMS *Leamington* based at

Londonderry in Northern Ireland, with the second escort group.'

'That was one of the old ships the Americans managed to give us under lend-lease,' the captain knowledgeably added. 'But it seems that it was neither lend nor lease. I'm told that the United States is billing the UK for everything now the war is over.'

'We were glad to have those ships at the time and they did good work in the North Atlantic, but they were not the best of ships to handle. Heavy weather had a bad effect on them and they were difficult to manoeuvre,' Tim volunteered. 'I was a junior engineer, learning my trade on some very old engines and even older working parts of the ship. Perhaps it did me good.'

'You must have had some nasty scrapes in those years,' the captain commented. 'Practically every convoy at some stage had to face some sort of attack sooner or later.'

'Yes, it was a bad time,' said Tim. 'The *Leamington* shared in the destruction of U-207 near Greenland late in September in my first year, while escorting convoy SC48. On another voyage the next year, while defending convoy WS17 – the ships were carrying troops to the Middle East – we shared in the sinking of U-587 on nearing home in the western approaches. There were no survivors from that U-boat.'

'It was incredible how Germany managed to persuade those men to go to sea in the U-boat fleet,' the captain commented. 'In the early days when they had it all their own way, submariners were the elite led by captains who were the darlings and celebrities of the Reich, but when their famous commanders like Schepke, Prien, Mohr and Endrass eventually failed to return to base, it became a different story. Mind you, it became hard to get crewmen sometimes to man our own merchantmen when the loss rate of ships began to get severe.'

'I think the loss rate was at least seventy thousand U-boat men,' Tim declared. 'Chances became very low that you would return to base, particularly after the middle of the war, when we got the upper hand. It was the heaviest loss rate of any specific arm of any service of both sides of the conflict in the Second World War.'

Tim wanted the captain to be moving on to talk about something else. But the captain was content to continue the topic, which evidently meant so much to him.

'My own worst experience was being part of PQ-17,' the captain told him. 'It was July 1942.'

'Oh, you were in that convoy, too? So was I,' said Tim. 'We were diverted to strengthen the escort screen for it. What happened to you?'

'I was first officer on a former Ennerman ship carrying tanks to the Russians. The ship was one of the twenty-three sunk from the convoy of thirty-five. I was lucky to get into a lifeboat and was quickly rescued. The ship was a destroyer – my God, now I think of it, it was called the *Leamington*. Of course, that was your ship.'

He spoke so loudly, almost shouting his sudden realisation of the good fortune he had just stumbled on, meeting one of the crew who had saved him.

He grinned widely and got up from his seat, holding out his arms to give Tim a hug of thanks, recalling the immensely low temperatures and mountainous seas that they had faced in the lifeboat.

'Do you think it was a wise move to tell the ships to scatter from convoy protection when the news was that the *Tirpitz* was sailing to intercept them?' Tim asked him.

'In retrospect no. But no one knew that the hesitation of the German command would prevent the *Tirpitz* from showing up,' the captain replied.

'But you were fortunate to be one of the first ships sunk,' Tim observed.

'The destroyer escorts were withdrawn from protection of the merchant ships when they were ordered to turn westwards with the cruisers to intercept the expected German navy. The ships were left exposed and picked off by the Luftwaffe and U-boats, when the German surface ships failed to arrive.'

'Did you spend the rest of the war in the *Leamington*?' asked the captain. 'Thank goodness, no,' replied Tim. 'I left it when the ship had a refit at Hartlepool, Durham, between August and early November of that same year, before it was transferred to the Canadians. It resumed convoy escort in the Atlantic. They had some remarkably good fortune soon after that. Later in November, the SS *Buchanan* was torpedoed by U-224. The *Leamington*, directed by aircraft, found the last of the freighter's four lifeboats and rescued its seventeen uninjured crewmen, who had been in the lifeboat for thirteen days since their ship had been torpedoed. The destroyer had only just returned to the sea after its refit. I resumed Atlantic convoys in British-built destroyers.'

It had been a happy and unexpected encounter for Tim and the captain, discovering that their paths had indeed crossed previously. They expected it would possibly do so again as company senior employees.

The voyage from Tilbury to New Zealand lasted six weeks via the English Channel, across the Atlantic in a south-western direction, through the Panama Canal and continuing in a similar direction across the Pacific Ocean to Wellington. Its cargo, being entirely for New Zealand, required no trading stops at interim ports. When the *Southland* crossed the imaginary equatorial line separating the northern and southern hemispheres, the usual ceremony for crossing the equator was held, the "captives" being only two of the passengers, Tim and James, and several new crewmen.

On several evenings, the four passengers were invited to join the captain and senior officers for dinner. Otherwise, they dined separately in groups.

The conversation almost inevitably turned to the conflict which had so recently ended and which had involved them all. One of the two New Zealanders almost apologetically said he had spent most of the war in New Zealand. But his sojourn had been forced on him.

'I was on HMNZS *Achilles* in the first few weeks of the war. You may remember the action the ship was involved in during December of the year when war was declared.'

'Remind us, if you can bother to do so. The first few months of the war seem a long time ago and so much has happened in between.' One of the ship's officers intervened.

'Well, on the thirteenth of December, not long after war was declared, we were with HMS *Ajax* – another light cruiser like *Achilles* – and HMS *Exeter*, a heavy cruiser.

'We detected smoke on the horizon, just after six o'clock in the morning, and confirmed it as a pocket battleship. We thought it was the *Admiral Scheer* but it turned out to be the *Admiral Graf Spee*. A fierce battle immediately opened-up at about eleven nautical miles.

'The German gunnery was remarkably good. They concentrated on the *Exeter,* inflicting serious damage. An early salvo hit the *Achilles,* with some damage. During the exchange of fire, four of our crew were killed. Captain Parry was wounded.

'*Ajax* was hit seven times, suffering five killed and seven wounded. The Germans had greater firepower, but even so, we damaged their ship. Thirty-six of their crew were killed, and many wounded, when the range was reduced to four nautical miles about one hour after the first sighting.

'The *Graf Spee* broke off the engagement half an hour later to head for the neutral harbour of Montevideo where it arrived at ten o'clock that night, having been pursued by *Achilles* and *Ajax* all day. The *Exeter* was forced to fall back, owing to the severe damage inflicted on it. *Graf Spee* was obliged by international law to leave within seventy-two hours. Believing overwhelming odds had been assembled against him in the interim, the captain of *Graf Spee*, Hans Langsdorff, scuttled his ship rather than risk the lives of his crew.'

'What happened to you, then?' someone asked.

'I was a gunnery officer. It was my good fortune to be wounded. Others were killed, but my wounds were bad enough for me to be given a shore job when I eventually recovered.'

Passing through the Panama Canal, the *Southland* began the second leg of its voyage, the long haul across the Pacific Ocean.

One day, at dinner, the captain suddenly asked James if he had escaped being called up in the war.

'By no means, Captain,' he replied. 'In fact, I was in the army by Christmas of 1939 and captured at Dunkirk six months later.'

'You spent all those years as a prisoner of war, then?' the captain asked. It seemed a rhetorical question to ask.

'Yes and no,' James answered.

'Now you have got us all wondering what that means,' the captain rejoined. 'Can't you tell us about it?'

'I was moved with hundreds of other prisoners eastwards by easy stages. I managed to escape twice on the way but was soon recaptured. We were finally incarcerated in a camp in Poland. After a while, I escaped and evaded capture during the winter, early in 1941.'

'Winter in Poland must have been pretty severe,' someone interjected. 'You must have had a tough life trying to rough it at that time of the year.'

'It was bad enough, but I made my way to Warsaw and was fortunate to contact the underground organisation. There was really no option but to join them. They found me useful. I became an active participant. I even fell in love with one of my group and married her. She was an active resistance operative, later killed by the Germans.'

'And did you evade capture all the rest of the war?' one of the ship's officers asked. 'It was a long time to be on the run.'

'Yes. Poland's plight will all be made clear before long,' James continued answering the question. 'But after five years of war, they were anxious to inform Britain of what they were facing in reality. They commissioned me to go to London with a full report on Poland's circumstances and prospects. It was a staggering thought that they could engineer my passage to England at the height of the war, although we should remember they also sent parts of the secret rockets V1 and V2 to Britain around the same time.'

'You must have been welcomed with open arms in London. What with disappearing from prison camp and arriving from Poland in wartime, with highly valuable information – it must have seemed like a miracle to Whitehall,' Tim commented.

'Quite the reverse,' James resumed. 'I was interviewed at length. An important individual in the Foreign Office was guilty of the most deplorable reaction. He treated me as if I was a spy with an elaborate cover. It seems he had strong Russian sympathies. He rejected my written report and all I had to say verbally. One day I hope he will be exposed for the callous and deceitful handling of the Polish interests he perpetrated.'

'What a ghastly experience,' the captain voiced the feelings of all the men present. 'Talk about traitors within. Just to think of it makes my blood boil. We were fighting for our lives on the sea. To think that such people were getting away with it. I hope they will be unmasked before long.'

'It's one of the main reasons why I am now emigrating,' James concluded.

At that moment, Frank Lever, who had been silent throughout, suddenly spoke in a voice so intense that it stirred the attention of everyone.

'In 1942, I completed a tour of operations in Wellingtons in 15 Squadron of Bomber Command at RAF Bourne, narrowly escaping disaster several times. The squadron at one time was down to only five crews. As a gunner, I was grounded to a post as an instructor before being posted to Cairo to join 31 Squadron of the South African Air Force, flying Liberators.'

'They were the long-range aircraft, weren't they?' Tim asked.

'Yes. It was why they were strategically based in the Cairo region, as you will see. We had some sticky assignments. We flew as one of eight aircraft to attack the Ploiesti oilfields in Rumania. Only four of us returned. But I wanted to supplement, and perhaps confirm, what James has been saying. We were involved in the struggle in Warsaw, briefed at Brindisi for two trips.'

Frank embarked on a synopsis of their briefing.

'The Polish Underground forces struggled to survive the German occupation by the most secretive and outlandish means, not the least of which was a clandestine existence in the sewers of Warsaw. They seized on the approach of the Russians from the east as the moment to attempt to take their revenge on the occupying German forces, which had inflicted such oppression, destruction, cruelty, and death on the Polish population, especially that of Warsaw itself. Remember, Russia was supposed to be our ally.

'Unfortunately, they did not factor into their understanding the utterly cynical calculations of Stalin, who ordered his army to pause outside Warsaw. His motive was rooted in the Soviet bid to carry the communist ethic and practice as far westwards as the other allied forces would allow. That ambition was recognised by some but not taken into the reckoning by most – including those who rose up in open defiance of their tormentors in Warsaw itself, naively expecting a collaborative effort by the Soviets to hasten the overthrow of German rule in Poland. In the event, the Soviets were content to invest the eastern bank of the River Vistula, while the Germans unknowingly carried out the work of extermination that indirectly served Soviet interests.

'Stalin was content to see the rebels suffer destruction at the hands of the German occupying forces. Stalin reasoned that men of the calibre of the Warsaw rebels would expect to re-establish a sovereign Poland. He saw the opportunity to destroy their nationalist sentiment and energy, thereby creating a political vacuum, which could be filled by communist people of his own making. In those critical days, before their great effort ended in their own extermination, the Polish rebels were desperate for arms, fresh ammunition, and food.

'We flew very low from the south following the River Vistula, fired on from the Germans on the west bank and from the Russians on the east bank. We used the number of bridges over the river as a sure-fire navigational aid. When we reached the fourth bridge over the river we turned sharply to port and were directly over St Catherine's Square to drop our parachuted supplies.

'I flew to Warsaw twice. Only four of the eight aircraft returned from the first flight. Three returned from the six sent on the second flight. The surviving aircrew were ordered to count those flights as double for service record purposes.'

'It sounds as if we shall hear more about all this in due course. On the face of it, it's unbelievable,' the captain remarked. A comment that evoked murmured agreement from everyone else present.

The days of the voyage passed with easy endurance. It was like a lazy cruise in fine weather, with plentiful food, drinks, and good company.

Christmas was celebrated with the best of food and drinks on board. But it was a quiet affair, perhaps aptly, some men thought.

Tim exhausted the opportunities to tap the knowledge and experience of the engineer officers. He became thoroughly rested but felt growing anticipation as the ship drew nearer to New Zealand.

He had anticipated that keeping in touch with Vanessa would be easy while he was away from London, but it proved to be the opposite. The silence only increased his desire to be with her as soon as possible.

The voyage had a beneficial effect on him. He found plenty of time for contemplation on the voyage as a passenger. It enabled him to put the war behind him. He had found a new determination to work for the peace and his love for Vanessa.

6

The *Southland* approached Wellington harbour, passing Shelly Bay and the international airport on its port side. The ship slowly inched straight to a dockside mooring, aided by a tug.

Once a gangway had been put in place, company agents, customs, and other officials came aboard. Within an hour, three of the four passengers left the ship to pursue their various interests. Tim had nowhere to go. He stayed on the Ennerman ship, where he was met and given a royal welcome by a company representative, accompanied by Derek Rhodes, the captain of the ship he was about to join.

'We've been looking forward to meeting you,' Derek Rhodes told him. 'Welcome to New Zealand. It's a long way from home but it can be a lot like home. You can find features of life here which are more like Britain than it is in Britain, or, as Britain used to be.'

'It is very nice of you to come in person, Captain,' Tim responded to the introduction. At first sight, Tim felt a rapport with his new captain. It boded well for his assumption of his job as chief engineer.

'I didn't have to come too far,' the captain replied. 'That's our ship over there.' He pointed to a freighter at a berth less than a quarter of a mile away by a quayside walk.

Tim noted his reference to the ship as, "our ship". It was customary for a captain to speak possessively of a ship as, "my ship". It was a likeable sign.

Tim refused their offer to carry his sea bag. 'I haven't got much in this bag but I have arranged for someone to deliver my things over to the ship. They are mostly in my sea chest,' he said.

They walked along the quaysides to the vessel that Tim was joining as first engineer officer, or as commonly called, chief engineer.

On the way, the captain put a question or two to him. 'Is this your first visit to New Zealand?'

'Yes, I have never been out of the northern hemisphere before,' Tim replied. 'It seems very quiet here, I must say.'

'Well, it's quieter here now than it was in wartime. Several hundred thousand American troops were drafted in, many thousands at any one time, and the harbour was very busy with naval and merchant shipping. The population of New Zealand in total is still around one and three-quarters of a million people, mostly in the North Island, with probably around half a million of them in the whole of the South Island.'

'New Zealand certainly must have pulled more than its weight in the war,' Tim responded. 'I had no idea the population was so small.'

'As you probably know, Wellington is the home of the New Zealand Shipping Company,' Derek Rhodes continued. 'The company has survived the Second World War but only by suffering the loss of half its ships. Out of a fleet of thirty-six ships, nineteen were sunk in various oceans of the world, mostly by torpedo attacks from U-boats. It's a loss rate that can be put alongside Ennerman's and that of many other companies. As you know, over five thousand ships worldwide went down in the war.'

'It does not bear thinking about,' Tim concluded, trying to end an unpleasant topic of conversation that always evoked mental pictures in him he was trying to forget.

In fact, the company's agent changed the subject for him rather dramatically at that point, with a company briefing. It was news Tim was looking forward to hearing. To their surprise, he also gave the captain and Tim news they were reluctant to hear.

'Two of Ennerman's replacement ships were acquired from the United States, both ex-Liberty vessels. One was the *Samking,* owned by the Federal Steam Navigation Company since May 1945, when it remained unused after the ending of hostilities. It was managed by Ennerman but has just become another modern mystery of the sea. I have to tell you, it has been officially accepted that it disappeared on or about one forty-five Greenwich Mean Time on the eleventh of January when the last signal was received from the *Samking.* Its final voyage began from London three days earlier. It carried a crew of forty-three, its destination Cuba, and was sailing in ballast only, with no cargo.

'The other Liberty ship that the company acquired is the one you are both joining, the *Samqueen.* The loss of the *Samking* is being publicised and might become a notorious incident. Both ships were new, completed in the last month of 1943 in wartime by the Bethlehem Fairfield Shipyard at Baltimore in Maryland in the United States.'

It was a rather sobering piece of information he had imparted, of concern to both the captain and chief engineer of the lost ship's sister ship.

'That's not a welcome piece of news,' said Derek Rhodes. 'The mysterious loss of the *Samking* will cast a shadow over our crew when they know about it and will hang over the integrity of the *Samqueen*. The two ships happen to be similar in type, origin, and lineage. The two ships had so much in common.'

Tim joined in the regrets. It had been the most unexpected news he could possibly have encountered. 'That is not a good omen for us, just starting out. But I think most sailors take it as a symptom of the dangers of sailing the ocean and will put it behind them. After all, we have had years of losing ships by many means and causes in the war, so there is a touch of déjà vu about the loss of another ship.'

The company's agent agreed that in timing it was an unfortunate coincidence. He suggested to the captain that a briefing about the Liberty fleet at large would help to put the minds of the crew at rest, or at least those of the younger crew members, assuming the old hands were far too experienced to bother about it.

Captain Derek Rhodes took Tim to the cabin reserved for the chief engineer and then showed him around the ship, reiterating the key essential facts, which Tim had ascertained previously.

'The ship has a length of four hundred and forty-one feet six inches, a beam of fifty-six feet, and a draft of twenty-seven feet and nine and a quarter inches.'

'This will be the biggest ship I have ever served on,' Tim told Derek Rhodes. 'My last destroyer was three hundred and seventy-seven feet long and considerably narrower at the beam at thirty-six feet six inches. This ship's length exceeds the length of a soccer pitch by just under one hundred feet.'

'It's a good thing we don't have to run up and down our ship, then,' Derek Rhodes said, laughing. He continued giving the vital information, which Tim had already researched, but found it worth hearing again to reinforce his memory.

'Its cargo capacity is ten thousand, six hundred and eighty-five long tons. In wartime it carried one four-inch stern mounted gun for engaging U-boats and a variety of light arms for anti-aircraft use, but the weapons have been removed entirely.'

He concluded his tour by referring to the *Samqueen*'s own crew, soon to be assembled.

'The crews of Liberty ships ranged between thirty-eight and sixty-two. *Samqueen* will sail with a total of forty-five crew members, most of them British in origin. They are now drifting in and will soon be complete, although a small number will not arrive for another two days, including the two new engineer officers.'

The crew were given a time to assemble on the ship for the captain to extend a welcome. When he met them, he included a short reference to policy matters, and then gave a briefing about Liberty ships.

'Altogether, over two thousand, seven hundred Liberty ships were built in the United States. Their suggestive general title was a commentary on the Battle of the Atlantic, which extended for the whole of the Second World War. The U-boats of Germany's Kriegsmarine gradually attempted to strangle the flow of food and war materials across the Atlantic Ocean. The supplies were primarily for the benefit of the British population, but from the end of 1941, when the United States entered the war, it was necessary also to sustain the vast army of American servicemen using Britain like an aircraft carrier.

'Several thousand ships were sunk in the Atlantic alone, the peak losses reaching over one thousand, eight hundred and fifty in 1943 alone, after which date the number slowly declined, but was still left at a menacing, dangerous level until the end of the war. Shipping was Britain's lifeline and means of achieving liberty.

'Although British in conception, Liberty ships were quick and cheap to build in the United States as cargo vessels, becoming the very symbol of wartime industrial output. They were mass-produced in the American shipyards to standard dimensions.

'Orders by Britain to replace ships torpedoed by German U-boats were supplemented by purchases by the United States for its merchant fleet to deliver war material to Britain and to the Soviet Union direct and via deliveries through Iran.

'Eighteen American shipyards were employed in building the Liberty ships over a period of four years. They became easily the largest number of ships produced in the war to a single design. Their production enabled the allies to replace stricken vessels faster than U-boats could sink them, given the introduction of far more effective defensive measures to protect them from U-boat attacks.'

Most of the crew dispersed from their captain's welcome talk to their mess for the meal prepared for their arrival on the ship. Many were old hands but included a few young men with little or no experience of the sea – and had no first-hand or intimate knowledge of the war and certainly not of the part Liberty ships played in it.

Twelve officers were included in the *Samqueen*'s total crew of forty-five, including the captain, the four mates, five engineers, chief steward, and wireless operator. The bosun was in charge of the rest of the crew and had the safety of the hull when docking, loading, and unloading as his special responsibility.

The two new engineer officers were already in Wellington, completing their training at William Boult, the maritime engineering company. International shipping companies, as well as more local companies, had a history of hiring their graduates. Their thorough training of ship's engineers stood the Boult Company in good stead, not only in New Zealand but throughout the ocean-going world.

Their engineer graduates had the benefit of a successful record as apprentices for five years, including considerable experience in working on ships in Wellington harbour. Deemed diligent, punctual, and reliable in their work with the company, and driven by their intention to become engineer officers on ships of the high seas, they were readily snapped up by the shipping companies.

The following day the two men contracted by Ennerman presented their certificates of completion of their apprenticeships and commendations from the William Boult Company when they reported for duty on the *Samqueen*.

Captain Derek Rhodes and Chief Engineer Tim Denton, were pleased to welcome them aboard. Their arrival completed the complement of engineer officers for the ship.

The two young new engineer officers were Ray Williams and Robin Spencer. Ray, the older of the two men, who had been a seaman for a short while before starting his apprenticeship, was appointed as fourth, and Robin as fifth, engineer officers. Tim spent most of that day showing them around the ship, explaining their working schedules, and establishing a relationship with them.

Neither had a formal engineer officer's uniform.

Tim told them that their wardrobe would be completed in London, where the ship was bound. They would be booked in at one of the famous uniform tailoring companies in the West End, which produced made-to-measure uniforms for maritime companies, as appointed by their employers.

Both men would also be subject to a medical examination in London by a doctor appointed by Ennerman.

They had time to learn their way around the ship and meet other members of the crew. For Robin, it was an opportunity to find his sea legs. The gentle undulations of the harbour waters – although they were directly exposed to the Pacific Ocean – provided a painless introduction to the mighty swells of the open sea.

Almost immediately, Tim Denton was introduced to an unsuspected custom in the merchant navy. The first deck officer gave him the information.

'We shall be having a party on board thrown by the officers and attended by women from the city who could be contacted and invited en masse, such as nurses.'

Before it was held, another jaunt was organised into the town to the Majestic Cabaret. The officers went impeccably dressed in their uniforms, including Tim, but the newly arrived fourth and fifth engineer officers were reluctant to attend the Majestic Cabaret since they were bereft of their formal dress.

The resourceful Second Engineer Officer Jack McDonnell, speaking with the third engineer said, 'I think we can fix them up. Let them borrow our second uniforms.'

They were not a bad fit. The extra bars on each shoulder epaulette gave the new young men an inflated feeling of status that inevitably appealed to the women guests at the cabaret.

7

The *Samqueen* was partly loaded over the next few days. 'We are sailing in the first week of February,' Captain Derek Rhodes informed Tim. 'I shall be glad to be on our way earlier than expected. This trip has been a long spell away from home. My family must be wondering what has happened to me. Are you married, Tim?'

'Not yet,' Tim replied. 'I am on a long leash, or, if you prefer, I am holding the loose end of a long leash.'

'Why not both at the same time?' Derek added quickly. Tim looked at him to see if he could detect his attitude behind the comment. He decided he was serious.

'It can't be an easy life for a wife, year in year out, if her husband is at sea,' Tim suggested. 'It is not much of a life for any children, either.'

'Well, I know that's the popular view,' said Derek. 'But in fact, I have a different take on the question. There are huge compensations for a married pair by the irregular absences from home. The intermittent homecoming, remember, is the same for both people. It can be full of renewal, expectations, and making the most of the time. It can be a great antidote to the humdrum daily routine and irritations that constant familiarity can bring. Each return can be like a visit to paradise.'

'Not so good for the children, though, is it?' Tim queried.

'It can be a hazard if they are giving problems. But I am assuming that the wife is resourceful and competent in looking after the home and the children as her job, while the man is doing the same on his ship.' Derek clarified his argument. 'In any case, the man is going home from time to time and has that amount of influence on the children. In fact, the intermittency can be an advantage. Incompetent fathers are no use anyway.'

'It's an angle I hadn't thought about,' Tim admitted. 'I think you have given me something to keep in mind.'

The *Samqueen* left Wellington in the first week of February, as the captain had indicated. It was an early departure that Tim welcomed. The ship first made a very short hop to New Plymouth, where further freight was loaded to complete its total cargo for England.

From New Plymouth the ship sailed across the Pacific Ocean towards the Panama Canal, in summer weather. The sea was calm at the outset but was expected to become rougher as it moved further north.

During that part of the voyage, Tim had the responsibility of inducting the newly formed engineering team into the operational organisation and management of their work. Each took irregular turns sharing the three eight-hour watches each twenty-four hours. In addition, he assigned a regular task to the new men to measure and record the oil reserve in the ship's tanks, employing a specially adapted, flexible instrument.

He also had to deal with an early clash between Murray Scott, the third engineer, and Ray Williams. In the engine room, soon after departure, the more senior officer told his junior to follow a certain painted line on the floor to detect where it ended. As it happened, Ray Williams had noticed the line previously and where it ended. He replied to the order by stating the fact that he had already observed where it ended.

'Just do it,' was the order from Murray Scott.

When Ray Williams reiterated his first statement, he thought Murray Scott was about to lose his temper, to the point that his senior officer was about to strike him.

Murray Scott was about twenty years older than Ray Williams, having been at sea throughout the Second World War. He was a dour Scot from Glasgow, not the most popular member of the crew, but certainly a man with a reputation for being good at his job.

To freshman Ray Williams he appeared to have the disposition of a martinet. Yet strict discipline at sea in the merchant marine could be as necessary as among sailors in the navy, or soldiering – in cargo vessels as well as in fighting ships.

But was he testing out Ray Williams with a nonsensical order to ascertain the man's substance? After that unpropitious start they became good friends.

Tim soon realised that a more relaxed relationship pattern existed on a freighter, even more so than on a ship with only a few passengers like the *Southland*. The discipline he was used to and the formality of relationships had been much greater on a navy ship.

He used his long-standing personal skills to establish a modus vivendi with his team of four engineers. In a short period of time he felt confidently able to rely on each of them.

Although a cargo ship's crew might be isolated from social company, a few compensating factors kept the men in good humour. Cigarettes were plentiful and cheap in an age when everyone smoked. Alcohol similarly was extremely cheap, a bottle of whisky or gin costing shillings, and beer costing pence. Food was nothing if not plentiful, of a wide variety, and well-cooked by the ship's chef.

Meals were in great contrast to domestic cooking. At home, a man might be used to having one large omelette for breakfast on occasion. On ship, he was served with a stack of omelettes laden with butter and maple syrup. True, the sea gave a man an appetite, but he could still be at pains to make headway with the chef's dishes. It was not unusual for the chef to survey the crew halfway through their meal, to see how many were struggling with his latest offerings.

When the sea surface lost its orderly conduct, Tim sent his newest recruits, in turn, to climb to the crow's nest, an observational station on a large ship. It was located at various heights on the main mast in the fore of the ship, anything from twenty to thirty feet or more above the main deck, but varying according to the size of the ship and usually reached by a metal ladder. The ladder might have a security cover for at least its upper length, but then it might have no cover at all.

From its great height, an observer secured distant views, and therefore a long warning of hazards such as icebergs, other ships, or the early sight of land on the horizon, in the days before radar. The crow's nest had served maritime vessels the world over since its invention in the first decade of the nineteenth century.

The *Samqueen* had an open ladder forty-feet up the main mast to its crow's nest, with a double rail around its floor area, six feet long crosswise, in relation to the beam of the ship, and two feet wide.

The first to be ordered to climb to the lookout was Ray Williams.

'Why have you chosen a time when the waves are rather rough?' he asked Tim. 'It could make going up there rather dangerous.'

'To give you the best view you can have of the ocean,' Tim laughed. 'If you can cope with it up there you will never have trouble in future with your sea legs.'

'They didn't tell me this was part of the job,' Ray playfully complained.

'Go on, give it a go,' Tim urged him on. 'I will give you half an hour.'

Ray climbed the steps uncertainly. He expected to be thrown off at any moment. But he made it all the way and could be seen, high up, looking down and out to sea, taking it all in, as if it were a moment in his life that he would never forget. When he descended he looked thoroughly dishevelled but obviously excited. He disappeared to his cabin for a drink and to brush himself up, but not before blurting out, 'It's bound to be the moment of my entire life I shall not forget.'

Robin Spencer was next to go. He looked at the angle of swing the crow's nest was taking in the heaving waters. The extent of the swing seemed to be tempting him to stay on the deck.

'I'm not sure I want to take a dip in the sea,' he told Tim.

'Of course, you can do it,' Tim said firmly. 'You have to stay up there for half an hour. Don't come down before that time unless you are really ill.'

His comment did little to encourage Robin, who was determined to emulate Ray. As a younger man without previous sea experience, he felt he had a greater challenge to face.

'Here I go!' he cried. 'Wish me luck.'

Tim saw him arrive in the crow's nest, clutching the rail. The sea was even more troubled than when Ray had been up there. He saw Robin swing out over the ocean one way and then return for a sortie the other way. He expected him to come down before the time was up. But he stuck it out, before stepping carefully back down the rungs of the ladder, gripping it for his life.

'That was great,' he told Tim. 'It was an unforgettable thing to do, although it was quite frightening when I was hanging out over the water.'

'Well done, man, you have earned your sea legs. You'll make a sailor yet,' Tim said.

The crow's nest was a unique place to be, offering a singular view of the world. The ship looked very different from that vantage point – rather like that from a low-flying aircraft. But it was the view of the sea that gave the biggest thrill. The movement of the waves sometimes rocked the ship like a pendulum, putting the crow's nest from being high on one side to being tossed over the water to the other side. To go to the crow's nest was a real personal risk with safety built into it. Tim was determined to prove his men were as seaworthy as possible.

The *Samqueen* continued its voyage in a generally north-eastern direction for the Panama Canal, leaving summer behind in New Zealand. On the way it crossed the earth's equator, the imaginary line on the earth's surface equidistant from the north and south poles, dividing the earth into the northern and southern hemispheres.

Crossing that imaginary line had long been the occasion for rituals imposed on any crew member or passenger for whom the crossing was a precedent. Tim himself had only recently been ritualised when he travelled to New Zealand on the *Southland.* It was a worldwide practise by the British Merchant Navy and Royal Navy, United States and Russian Navies, and many other national navies and mercantile companies.

The tradition may have originated with ceremonies for passing headlands, or as a folly sanctioned to boost morale, or created as a test by seasoned sailors to ensure their new shipmates were capable of handling long, rough times at sea.

The crossing coincided with the fifth engineer's birthday in February. It happened to be Robin Spencer's twenty-first, so it called for double rituals. He took part in the equator ceremony with several other crew members and then invited all the officers to his cabin for liquid refreshment.

Taking advantage of his temporary celebrity status, he told McDonnell he would like to steer the ship.

The two men went to the bridge at an opportune time of night but the deck officer on watch would hear nothing of the request. He claimed it would be a black mark for him if he allowed an untrained and unlicensed member of the crew to steer the ship. But the ship was quiet in a calm sea. With further pleading he allowed Robin Spencer to take over the wheel from the steersman, for an all too short experience to feel in command of a large ship.

As the days passed, Tim grew accustomed to his regular talks with the captain on conditions and operating problems on the vessel, in addition to overseeing the watches of the engineers and assigning their tasks.

For his job, he had to become familiar with the parts of the ship falling within the purview of engineering responsibilities. They included the maintenance and repair of anything mechanical and complicated, including kitchen appliances, lifeboats, deck apparatus, and the all-important deck cranes.

But the centre of engineering on the ship was the boiler room, and drive shaft to the single screw. The motive power of the vessel had to be maintained to propel the ship by day and night in both calm seas and storms. It was particularly essential to keep the screw turning in rough weather. Failure of the engine would put the ship at the mercy of the waves and place it in danger of foundering.

Tim had briefed the new engineer officers, who were unfamiliar with Liberty ships, with the basic details of their field of responsibility, although exhaustive information was available in the ship's operating texts. He ran through the essentials as if quoting from the handbook.

'The *Samqueen* is driven by a one-hundred-and-forty-ton vertical compound, triple expansion, steam engine, assembled for testing before delivery to the shipyards, and fuelled from two oil-fired boilers, yielding two thousand, five hundred horsepower with a single screw, giving the ship eleven and a half knots or just over thirteen miles per hour over a range of twenty-three thousand nautical miles.

'High-pressure steam enters from the boiler and, passing through the engine, is exhausted as low-pressure steam to the condenser. The engine is of an obsolete design for ships. It was selected to power Liberty ships because it was cheaper and easier to build in the large numbers needed for the volume of Liberty ship production. Many companies were available to manufacture the engine, eighteen shipyards eventually being involved in building the ships. It has the additional advantage of ruggedness and simplicity. Parts manufactured by one company are interchangeable with those made by another, and the openness of its design makes most of its moving parts easy to see, giving ready access, and for oiling.'

During the first few days of sailing from Wellington, the only serious problem arising was the overheating of the crankshaft of the main engine. The engineers anticipated an opportunity to repair it while at Panama.

The ship reached the Gulf of Panama and from it entered the western end of the Panama Canal, a forty-eight-mile ship canal connecting the Pacific Ocean to the Atlantic Ocean, but via the Caribbean Sea. The canal was cut across the Isthmus of Panama, making it a key conduit for international maritime trade.

At Balboa, to the north of Panama City at the western end of the canal, the ship took on board the requisite pilot for the canal passage. The town at the time included the administrative centre for the canal, a port and well-stocked shipyards. Panama City itself was already a large prosperous city with an affluent population.

During the ship's slow movement through the canal, the engineering team was able to close down the offending crankshaft to remove the crankcase bearings. Tim ordered Robin Spencer, the fifth and youngest engineer officer, to climb down into the deep well to remove the bolts for the purpose. The temperature outside the ship was 30°C. Added to it was the perennial differential temperature of the boiler room.

Working in at least 40°C, Robin Spencer removed the bolts but was overcome by the heat. He managed to call out before fainting. Jack McDonnell reached down into the well and using his undoubted strength, hauled him up to the deck and was able to revive him. The engineers succeeded in paring minute quantities from the metal bearings encasing the crankshaft, to reduce the friction responsible for generating the overheating.

With the repair and passage through the canal completed, the *Samqueen* docked in Christobel-Colón at the eastern end of the canal, on the Caribbean Sea. Crew members were permitted to go ashore, for shopping, sightseeing, and savouring the bars, restaurants, and other places frequented by seamen the world over.

Tim felt no attraction for those tempting pastimes. His mind was preoccupied with the thought that he was on his way to London and the woman he loved. He felt sorry for those members of the crew who spent their time ashore looking for a female companion to while away their time. Perhaps they had never met women in their home territory who possessed them enough to deter them from wanting to indulge in the sailors' common practice.

Leaving the Panama Canal, the *Samqueen* sailed across the Caribbean Sea, wending its way through the West Indies and into the Atlantic Ocean, where it set a north-eastern course for the British Isles. Throughout that part of its voyage, it sailed over the graveyards of hundreds of allied ships sunk in the conflict that had only recently ended. The struggle on the ocean had been an epic of risk, courage, disaster, and triumph, carried out by merchant and naval seamen, immortalised as the Battle of the Atlantic.

Through calm and stormy seas, the ship continued under generally wintery conditions and turned to starboard, eastwards, when reaching the English Channel, then the busiest waterway in the world. It sailed the whole length of the southern coast of England, before turning briefly northwards after the ferry port of Dover in the County of Kent, and then to port into the Thames Estuary at the point of North Foreland in the extreme north-east of Kent.

London lay ahead.

'You will soon have brand new uniforms to wear when you go ashore in London,' Tim passed the remark to Ray Williams, once they were in the Thames Estuary. 'I would like you to know that you have earned your spurs so far on this voyage. It will be nice to get out of those working clothes.'

'Thank you, sir. I have enjoyed the trip. It was a special experience to climb up the crow's nest. I shall never forget it. It was something I have never done before. The ships I have been on previously as a crewman were small, so they had no equivalent. In any case, crew members were always expected to do their specific job and not take any liberties. I appreciate the opportunity you gave us to go up there.'

'Well, London is a big place and I'm sure you will enjoy the sightseeing. But of course, it is still in a heavily bombed condition, especially in the city – that's the name given to the site of the original London, about a mile square – and the docklands. Areas were devastated around the old docks in London itself.'

'But shall we able to get into port?' he asked

'Yes, of course,' Tim said. 'We will be going to the modern docks at Tilbury down the river on the outer edge of the greater city area. But I hope you have a nice time here. We shall be staying for several weeks.'

8

'How far is it to London, now?' Robin Spencer asked Tim.

Hearing his question, Tim's mind immediately reflected on the many people over the centuries asking the same question. Dick Whittington and many like him had hoped to find their fortune in London. They were tired and footsore, but Tim's shipmate would never suffer the fatigue and aching feet from the long march to the capital endured by those people.

But was there any kind of fortune that Robin might acquire in London, having arrived comparatively comfortably by ship? It seemed unlikely. Tim himself was far luckier. Coming home to his lover, he rated his chances of finding his own fortune in London as one hundred per cent.

Vanessa would be waiting, only for the finding. He would share his fortune with her.

'Now we have entered the Thames Estuary,' Tim replied to Robin's question. 'The remaining sailing distance is about forty miles to the Port of Tilbury, the principal port for London. It's located on the River Thames at Tilbury in Essex, twenty-five miles below London Bridge.'

'That seems a long way from the city,' Robin commented.

'It had to be, but it is a big city,' Tim stated. 'The original docks consisted of a tidal basin on Gravesend Reach opposite

Northfleet, connected by a lock to a main dock with three side branches – Royal Albert Dock, Royal Victoria Dock, and King George V Dock – constructed over a period of seventy years until completion just twenty-five years ago. Between the tidal basin and main dock are two dry docks. The three docks collectively form the largest enclosed docks in the world, with a water area of about two hundred and fifty acres and an overall estate of over one thousand acres.'

'Those are pretty big figures,' Robin said. 'I can't really take them in.'

'So you see, Tilbury is a big port,' Tim continued. 'It had to be located away from the city itself. It provides berths for large vessels that could not be accommodated further upriver. The docks are a great commercial success. They became London's principal docks, even though unfinished, during the first half of the twentieth century. You will see how many giant granaries, mills, and refrigerated warehouses there are alongside its quays. Their great size and provision of numerous finger quays gave them a collective span of over twelve miles of quaysides. They can serve hundreds of cargo and passenger ships at a time.'

'Hell's bells, that is huge,' Robin said in amazement.

'Well, London has been the largest city in the world,' Tim reminded him. 'Of course, all kinds of cargoes for the country as a whole come in here as well as freight for London, like paper. There are extensive facilities for grain, sugar, meat, and other bulk cargoes. Talk in the industry is that soon goods will be loaded and unloaded in individual containers. If so, they will be the next big thing in the market, together with cars.'

'It's not a passenger port, then?' Robin queried.

'Yes, it is as well. Southampton is the main passenger port in the south of England, but Tilbury handles a lot of passenger traffic for the Far East and South America,' Tim replied.

'I'm looking forward to seeing London,' Robin said. 'It's always been the place I have wanted to visit since we studied it in primary school.'

'You and Ray Williams should report to the company offices as soon as you can, to get appointments for your uniforms,' Tim reminded him.

The *Samqueen* docked on a day in the middle of March at the Royal Victoria Dock, where the New Zealand Shipping Company's warehouse was situated, for the purpose of unloading its cargo from Wellington and New Plymouth.

Most of the crew, being British, were only too glad to hand over unloading to the dockers. With their contracts ended, they were able to escape from the ship, in which they had been confined for so many weeks, to visit their homes.

The purposes for going ashore were different for Ray Williams and Robin Spencer, but they had one thing in common. They were eager to fulfil their contracts by getting appointments under the company's instructions. They had to present themselves for a medical examination to put the final seal on their jobs – and to be fitted out with their coveted merchant navy engineer officers' uniforms.

Tim stayed on board for three days with the second and third engineer officers on arriving at Tilbury. Apart from tying up loose ends from their voyage and overseeing the mechanical unloading equipment, they had to take part in the negotiations about the conversion of the ship's holds for a ballast loading, which needed to be put in hand within a few days.

But on the first day, at the earliest opportunity, he telephoned Vanessa. 'Darling, I'm home but will be tied up for three days before I can have some days off. How have you been?'

To his utter astonishment, without speaking a word, she sang him a song, not for the first time, but for the first time over the telephone. He noted it grossly lacked the quality of her song on the street in Liverpool, but was like a siren call to him, not that he was on the rocks, but that he was home.

'Deep in my heart when the shadows are falling
I hear a voice that is ever recalling
Moments of love with the moonlight above
Magical night, glamorous night.
Each night I make a song for you
Each night my spirit longs for you
Each night when I'm alone
I listen to my heart
And want you for my own.
Deep in my heart like an echo repeating
Sounds a refrain of our first happy meeting
And we will regain with delight
Let us kiss and recapture that rapturous, glamorous night.'

'Darling, I am fine. Those words of a song from *Glamorous Night* have been haunting me every day since you left. I just had to let you hear me sing it. I'm desperate to see you again. Are you well?' she asked.

'I am well and cannot wait to be with you. But I have duties that must be discharged before I can leave the ship. They will last for three days before I have time off,' Tim answered.

'Three days. That seems inordinate. I don't think I can bear knowing you are just down the road. Could I go aboard if I come to the ship?' Vanessa asked him.

'Yes, of course, you can if you can spare the time. You will still have to return for your evening performance, but please come if it is at all possible. It will make my day as well, darling,' Tim answered.

'Give me the directions,' she said, writing them down furiously.

She indulged in a taxi. Two hours later she arrived and swept up the gangway, not knowing where to go for Tim. She accosted a passing member of the crew.

'Can you tell me where to find Chief Engineer Tim Denton?' she asked.

'Tim,' he replied. 'He's my boss. I'm Ray Williams, fourth engineer officer, at your service madam. Come with me. We've had a good voyage and I'm looking forward to seeing London,' he said.

'That's nice of you to say so, Ray,' Vanessa said, as she followed him across the deck to a tannoy location.

'Chief Engineer Tim Denton is wanted on the main deck at once or sooner if possible,' he said on the tannoy, sharing in the general mood of relief after a long voyage completed without any serious difficulties.

It was several minutes before Tim arrived.

Vanessa chatted with Ray Williams while she waited. She recalled that Tim had told her several engineer officers were serving on their first voyage.

'You haven't had a rough trip from New Zealand?' she asked him.

'No, it got a bit rough once or twice but not enough to put me off the sea,' he said. 'This has been my first ship as engineer officer, but I have been to sea before. I was sailing for a few months in New Zealand in ships sailing locally. Here is Tim coming now.'

Vanessa gasped at the sight of Tim, dressed in working dungarees, and with obvious marks of hard work on his face, hands, and clothes.

Without hesitation they melted into each other's arms, clinging until their bodies had realised what was happening and duly generated the requisite bodily responses that made them one again.

Ray Williams was somewhat taken aback. It gave him a different view of the chief, who had been reserved but friendly. He found himself gawking at the sight until his brain told him to move away.

'Can't we go to your cabin?' Vanessa asked. 'Only if you could stand the strain,' Tim quipped.

'What about you?' she queried, evidently bubbling with enthusiasm. 'I've always wondered what a sailor would be like after three months or more at sea,' Vanessa called to Tim as he turned away to take her to his cabin.

'You are very mischievous today, darling,' he replied. 'Let's see if I can find a sailor who has been to sea for three months.'

'No, just this one will do,' she announced. 'Lead on, chief engineer.'

'As a matter of fact, I have always wondered what a beautiful actress would be like after over one hundred and twenty performances,' Tim said, thinking he should give as he had been given. He did a quick calculation – and got the number wrong.

'Which kind did you mean?' Vanessa instantly asked.

Before she could say anything more, he corrected himself. 'I meant of another kind,' he said.

'I'm glad you added that,' Vanessa said, as they both exploded with laughter.

Vanessa remarked on Tim's appearance.

'This will be the first time I have ever made love to a man in the middle of his work. And dirty with it. Do you think it will make a difference?' she asked, not expecting an answer.

'Well, my blood is up,' Tim answered. 'So, look out.'

It was a prophetic thing to say.

'Let's call this a one-night stand,' Vanessa said. 'I am beginning to feel like a lady of the night – or day if you prefer.'

'It will be our version of a girl in every port.' Tim made his contribution to the bizarre commentary. 'All in a good cause.'

'I'm going to see you soon in the normal way,' Vanessa happily announced.

'But not for three days,' Tim reminded her.

There was no inhibition in either. For an hour they gave everything they had to each other. The long absence had cultivated expectations, which nothing else could have satisfied more than exactly what they were doing.

'I shall not be fit to go on stage tonight,' Vanessa exclaimed. 'But what a way to go. I wonder if the cast will notice any difference?' she asked herself aloud.

'I'm quite sure you will give an extra wonderful performance tonight. I ought to come and see it if I can get off just for the evening,' Tim said definitively.

But he was unable to release himself from duty. The pressures were too urgent following the ship's immediate arrival and the preparations for new ballast requirements.

Finally, Tim was able to leave the ship for two days. He had accumulated a quantity of honey and quality scented soap, two commodities still scarce in Britain. Some were for his parents and some for Vanessa. The withdrawal of American aid from Britain, redirected as Marshall Aid to the liberated countries in Europe, left Britain struggling. Consequently, Britain's population continued to be variously rationed or suffering the shortage of supplies for many items of diet, clothing, household furniture, and appliances, for over five years after the war had ended.

The top priority on Tim's personal checklist on reaching London had been to see if *Perchance to Dream* was still running in the West End, and second, if Vanessa was still holding her place in the cast. He had got the answers to both questions after she had finished her song on the telephone. He was delighted that both were in the affirmative.

During the time the *Samqueen* would be in dock, he expected to make several trips into London. He could catch a bus along the never-ending Commercial Road running from the City of London to Poplar, Canning Town, and Plaistow. The route took him into the West End and beyond.

From leaving Vanessa in November until the return in March he had not had any contact with her. It seemed inappropriate time-wise, expensive, and a bit pointless to try to make contact.

It was a time of suspended reconciliation. She was busy on the stage and he was busy on the ship. But it would be worth waiting for the glorious day of reunification. The words of his captain, Derek Rhodes, crossed his mind. If absence makes the heart grow fonder, it makes renewal of contact a regeneration of their first meeting. It could be an unalloyed experience.

But from time to time he had had a few lingering doubts. Would her absorption in a singing career on the stage become his rival? He had heard rumours that great artists focussed all their emotions and normal instincts into their thrust for perfection in their art and performance on stage.

However, his early contact with her had enabled him to sweep away all his reservations and fears, making him content to resume his life with Vanessa at close quarters.

It was late in his first free day when he was able to leave the ship. He made his way to the Hippodrome in Charing Cross Road, Westminster.

He joined the latecomers without tickets at the box office.

'Have you any tickets left for tonight's show?' he asked the clerk.

'Nothing much, apart from a single return in the most expensive seats.' It was a disappointing answer.

'How much is that?' Tim asked.

He was quoted the price, which was normally well outside his pocket. 'It's in a premier box,' the clerk answered.

'That will suit me down to the ground,' he responded suddenly, without hesitation in a wave of wild enthusiasm, to the surprise of the ticket clerk.

There was little time left before the curtain would be raised, but time enough to find his seat and become used to sitting in one of the very best seats in the theatre, with a most advantageous view of the stage, and for that matter, the audience.

He felt rather than saw many people looking at him, as if he were a member of royalty, or another very select body, to occupy such a seat.

'If only I could tell you,' he said to himself, 'that the rising star you are about to see on the stage is my beloved. You would have no doubt that I deserved this seat.'

For a few more seconds he marvelled at the contrast. Only a few days had elapsed since he had been pounding the oceans of the world. And only three days since he and Vanessa had vented their love and passion for each other in his cabin on board the ship, a prohibited indulgence for a crew member on a commercial ship, and unthinkable on a navy ship.

His only comforting option over many previous weeks had been spending many private hours of opportunity conjuring up his own version of perchancing to dream. Within minutes his dream would become a reality when he saw Vanessa on the stage. Within an hour or two it would be fulfilled yet again.

On Vanessa's first entry, it was as much as he could do not to allow his body to sponsor any physical reaction. In his mind, he wanted to wave or call her name. But it was impossible to respond to such childishness. His was the steel-like conduct of a former naval officer and self-controlled public behaviour of a marine officer. Instead, he waited, motionless, enjoying the play, as silent as the entire enraptured audience.

For several minutes into her appearance on stage, Vanessa did not see him. He knew that a good actress played to all parts of the theatre, so it was only a matter of a little time before she found him.

She did so, unmistakably, but without even batting an eyelid, just perhaps a fragmentary interruption of her movement, caused, like a flash of lightning, when a thought momentarily went through her mind.

'If only I could bring him on stage and introduce him as my lover. I want to tell the world how lucky I am.'

Tim knew she had seen him but was intrigued by her utter lack of response.

But he expected nothing less of her. She was an arch-professional.

Was her step after that recognition in a lighter mode? Was her speech suddenly imparted with a supplement of energy? Was her voice in song lifted with greater volume?

He quickly dismissed such thoughts as self-congratulatory, with contempt. 'It is little more than an exercise in egoism,' he told himself. 'He counted for little when she was on stage with a huge audience to woo and delight, to thrill and to court their emotions. On the ship I am important. In the theatre she is important.'

The reputation of the show had evidently been growing, once again amplified by the rapturous acclaim the audience gave it that evening.

As the curtain fell for the last time, Tim made a beeline to Vanessa's dressing room. But she beat him to it. Her face gave away the condition of her heart. They hugged in silence, seemingly forever.

'Do you realise it's been only three days since we last met. How did you get on that same night after coming to the ship?' Tim asked.

'I was as right as rain,' Vanessa replied. 'In fact, I took everything by storm. Two of my close associates asked me what had happened to me. I couldn't enlighten them, could I?'

'You should have said you ran into a sailor down the East End, who was dying to show his credentials,' Tim replied, putting them both into a laughing fit.

'Tonight, when I first saw you from the stage, I thought I was perchance dreaming. It didn't seem real for you to be in a seat normally reserved for royalty. And then I realised it was actually you and how appropriate it was for you to be in that seat. My heart leapt with joy. My drama training didn't really provide for what to do in such a situation. But suddenly my whole being was vivified. A number of the cast told me it was the best performance I had yet given,' Vanessa reflected.

'I thought I would be unable to restrain myself from giving you a signal,' Tim replied. 'Darling I am here – but it all happened inside me.'

'We are together again. Life can be good,' Vanessa spoke her mind. 'Have you got a date for sailing again from London?' she asked.

'At the moment the ship is scheduled to sail on the fourth of April, so for about three weeks we shall be in port. The time will be taken up with fitting out the holds to take ballast,' Tim replied. 'But it could be longer.'

'What does ballast mean?' Vanessa queried.

Suddenly, Tim was hit by the ludicrous contrast between their respective concerns. Her life was consumed by fine clothes, dry conditions, the warmth of the theatre, and the need for mastery of her lines – presented at a premium. Her working associates were top professionals, whose clients were the wealthier part of the population.

His working concerns were considerably different – working with professionals of a different kind but also with unlettered men. He was always exposed to the weather, often in savage conditions, grubby in appearance, and with the lurking dangers of the sea a constant threat.

Tim braced himself to explain the steps that had to be taken in a technology that must have seemed bewilderingly strange to Vanessa.

'Special steel fittings have to be installed in the holds of the ship to store a vast quantity of loose gravel which will be gathered from the riverbed. If it is loosely poured into the holds it would move around in bad weather and might even endanger the ship by piling on one side of it and turning the vessel over,' Tim explained. 'The idea is to make a huge steel frame to contain the gravel. Quite a lot of welding steel fixtures to the floor and roof of the decks is necessary. So, I shall have to be around while the work in going on, but I can be free to get on the bus and head this way most days at some time or other.'

'That's good news,' Vanessa responded. 'We can spend some time together in the West End. Have a leisurely meal and go to interesting places,' she said.

'What about your party time? I thought stage people spent their time going to parties?' Tim asked, revealing his ignorance of the profession.

'Oh, no. I'm not the party type, my darling. A nightly performance is a demanding focus for me. I have to be on top form. In any case, I know that Ivor is working on a further production that we hope will be his greatest work. I am potentially in line to be a candidate for a leading role in it, so I have every incentive to be at my best at all times,' Vanessa declared.

Tim secretly approved of her resolve and determination. It was in line with the character that had won her to him.

'I look forward to the time when you will have the theatre public at your feet, then,' Tim laughed, as Vanessa demurred.

She changed the subject. 'I would like the chance to look round the ship sometime, to see how you live. Apart from that surreptitious call the other day, I've never been on a ship before or met crewmen, except you and the fourth engineer officer who found you for me.'

'That can easily be arranged soon,' Tim said.

He kept his word to meet Vanessa each day, if only for an hour or two. 'This is like calling at a port a day,' he said to Vanessa.

'But it will only cost you a bus fare,' she replied. They both laughed.

'It's not easy to get used to,' Tim added. 'I don't like your being so near and yet so far. It's like a local courtship.'

'All good things come to those who wait. Have patience and you shall have joy. It gives you something to look forward to each day,' Vanessa said.

'Thank you for those words of comfort, madam,' he replied.

They burst into laughter at the pseudo-advice delivered to one another.

9

By waiting only a day or two, Vanessa had a Monday evening free without a show. It was the day Tim called on her to fulfil the visit to the ship she had requested. She was introduced to a few of the crew who were still on duty. In fact, it happened to be a day when an informal event, arranged to mark the ship's arrival, was being held on the ship, attended by a few wives and partners of the officers and non-British staff who had stayed in the port, together with several company men from Ennerman and their wives.

They included the captain, some of the deck officers, and several of the engineer officers, including Tim's recently recruited new engineer officers, Ray Williams and Robin Spencer.

'I am surprised that neither of these two young engineers has been to London before,' Vanessa remarked to Tim. 'Do they know how much they have been missing?'

'They have been into town already, on the second day of our arrival, to be measured for their company uniforms. But they have not been properly blooded,' Tim replied. 'They are both New Zealanders, far from home. It takes six weeks by sea to make the journey, although British Overseas Airways will soon be reducing that time to well under a week. I don't think they will be homesick.'

During the introductions, the news soon spread around that Vanessa could sing and was a member of the cast in a play on the London stage.

'Is there any chance we could hear a number or two?' one of the deck officers asked Vanessa. 'Sorry, we have no piano, but would you need it?'

'Yes, is the answer, and no, I do not need it,' Vanessa promptly replied. 'I can confirm that,' Tim interrupted. 'She sang to me on the pavement outside the theatre in Liverpool in 1944 – no orchestra, no piano. I was riveted to the spot. It was all in tune and sounded just as if she was on the stage.'

Vanessa sang for them "We'll Gather Lilacs" from the current show *Perchance to Dream*, "Glamorous Night" from *Glamorous Night*, and "Waltz of My Heart" from *The Dancing Years*.

Not a man stirred.

But they all erupted in applause when she had finished.

The captain thanked her. 'We shall have to see your current show now,' he conceded. 'That's one of the best advertising ploys I've heard and seen for years.'

Afterwards, Vanessa suggested to Tim that as it was her night off the stage, they should introduce Ray Williams and Robin Spencer to the famed nightlife of London.

They asked the two men if they were free for the evening.

'We would like to take you for a *Dine and Dance* evening at the Piccadilly Hotel. It ranks as one of the most famous hotels in London. It's in Piccadilly Circus, central to the West End theatres, cinemas, food outlets and fashionable shops. It is close to main destinations like Leicester Square, Shaftesbury Avenue, Regent Street, and Trafalgar Square.'

They were glad to assent.

The four of them caught a number 15 bus to the West End.

The evening promised to be a great success. Each of the three officers was dressed in his best, Ray and Robin wearing their brand new uniforms for the first time. They displayed the confidence that went with their splendid outfit.

The West End was crowded. Everyone walked to, and around, the West End, especially enjoying the exercise. A bus ride or underground train brought them from the suburbs. Car ownership had been beyond the financial reach of most people. In any case, the sluggish reconstruction of the car industry from war production to making civilian cars had so far yielded figures of only miniscule proportions, relative to demand from a population starved of new cars throughout the war.

They had every opportunity to savour the delights of the West End while visiting the Piccadilly Hotel. The lights of London had been restored from their wartime blackout. Tens of thousands of working people from the hundreds of offices in the area returned to their homes after their day's work. They were replaced by the masses of evening pleasure seekers, drawn from far and near, who crowded into the West End. They turned themselves into theatre devotees and cinemagoers, mingling with those aiming for dining delights, but also included those attracted for a variety of very different reasons.

While dining in the Piccadilly Hotel's spacious restaurant, the two new men, Ray and Robin, were eager to join the dancing with the couples already enjoying the bon vivant of the evening on the adjacent dance floor. By chance, their dining table was quite close to a family party, one of whose members caught the eye of the ever-vigilant Robin Spencer. Boldly and impeccably correct, he strode over to their table and addressed the apparent head of the family.

'Excuse me, sir, but may I have the pleasure of inviting your daughter to dance?' Without hesitation, the face of the addressee lit up. He was tickled pink to find himself involved in quaint British customs, even if they reflected a hierarchical attribution of sovereignty to the man of the family.

'Of course, you may, and after it please come back and join us,' the man said. His pronounced American accent caught Robin momentarily off-guard. But the daughter was nothing if not captivating. One dance led to another until it seemed appropriate to return to the family table.

The rest of the evening was spent in the company of Judge A. Cantor and his family of Philadelphia, ensconced in London on holiday. He had brought them over from the States to show them where he had spent several years in the services in Britain. The young maritime officer evidently made an impression on the family. He was enamoured of the judge's daughter, Janet.

It may have been the trials and tribulations that were soon to afflict him in the days ahead, but after that evening Robin allowed that promising liaison to be neutralised or at least pushed to the back of his mind.

For Janet, her heart had been stirred. She sent him a Christmas card in time to arrive before the day. But it arrived in January, a month late, having been sent speculatively to the New Zealand Shipping Company's offices at the Royal

Victoria Docks at Tilbury, where the *Samqueen* had unloaded its New Zealand freight. It had then found its way to the Ennerman offices and finally to the intended recipient.

Robin got in touch with her immediately. It was a delayed realisation of the original promise of their relationship, but still the fulfilment of a romance that sprang from that brief contact at the Piccadilly Hotel.

Meanwhile, Ray Williams had severed himself from the others in the arms of a young English woman, who was celebrating her twenty-first birthday with her parents. She had taken his breath away when she agreed to dance. Her parents were evidently well-heeled and prominent in the building industry.

Something must have happened between them.

He danced with her time and time again. Finally, he came over to Tim and Vanessa to apologise, disclosing that he had been invited home with the family.

'I thought we could be introducing them to the West End, but never that thoroughly and not that quickly,' Vanessa whispered to Tim. 'We might never see him again. Come on, let's go and dance.'

'I hope you are wrong with that assumption darling,' Tim replied. 'It's his turn on watch tomorrow night. I hope he remembers.'

Tim felt his new recruits had been shepherded enough. They had acquired their company officers' uniforms, subjected themselves to medical examination to meet company standards, and had been launched on the delights of London. But he had not expected them to be enraptured with members of the opposite sex so immediately and, it seemed, absolutely.

During the voyage from New Zealand, Robin Spencer had been troubled with skin irritations that turned to rashes, a result of the heat and oily atmosphere of the engine room. When he arrived at his medical appointment, the doctor considered that the extent of the complaints was serious enough to raise the question as to whether it was only a temporary setback or a recurring liability. In any case, the medical certificate was issued subject to a further review, which took place three months later and which he passed with a clear sheet.

Both Robin and Ray had inadvertently found their fortunes in London.

10

The *Samqueen* spent fifty-two days altogether in London moorings. Having arrived on the thirteenth of March it was scheduled to leave on the fourth of May. It was a month later than previously envisaged, the delays being caused by dockers' strikes and unexpected difficulties over the ballast loading.

All five engineer officers were committed to share the watches while the ship was in port. Off duty, they were free to go ashore, sightseeing, or visiting family members or friends.

Additionally, the fleshpots of London, historically entrenched in the capital for centuries, were routine destinations for seamen in port.

For the more discerning and wealthy few, the West End attractions, which Ray Williams and Robin Spencer had savoured with their chief and Vanessa, could be an occasional indulgence.

After his visit to the Piccadilly Hotel, Ray Williams had his own destination in mind. He had a ready access to the home of the newly found daughter of a wealthy building tycoon.

For those without friends or relatives in the area, as well as the numerous less discerning and impecunious, the sometimes rowdy and salacious venues in the East End were to hand.

One night, Robin Spencer savoured the latter with his shipmate, Second Engineer Officer Jack McDonnell. While the *Samqueen* was still in the Royal Victoria Dock, Robin and Jack returned very late that night from a local public house, noted for its high jinks among seamen in nearby Canning Town.

They were the worse for wear.

The port was still alive. Some ships were being unloaded and loaded by nightshift military gangs, standing in for dockers on strike. Other ships were silent and inactive, like ghosts in the darkness of the night.

Making their way on foot back to the ship, they found some of their rights of way had been reduced to only a degree above the hazardous, particularly on such a rainy but black night.

To reach their ship they had to cross a lock gate, protecting the water level in the three Royal Docks from the rises and falls of the River Thames. On that particular night, the eastward exodus of river water for the North Sea was swift and strong.

The lock gate was a substantial structure like a giant door, whose two halves came together at an angle facing into the docks, enabling the water pressure inside the docks to guarantee their closure. The gate opened when the river water level was commensurate with that in the docks, allowing ships to enter and leave. The distance from the top of the gate to the water on the side of the river was around fifteen feet. Pedestrians had access over it, walking on top of the gate along its substantial four feet width, with a safety handrail on the River Thames side.

Somehow Robin managed to fall over, through, or off the safety rail on the lock gate into the River Thames. The swirling current immediately sucked him under, carrying him to one side. It was a sobering plunge into cold water. It would have been worse in January, but cold enough in March.

The only ameliorating factor for him was that in falling he missed crashing onto the defensive boom – a huge timber log, at least two feet thick, floating in the river but chained to the gate, protecting it from ships not quite under control. He landed in the narrow strip of water, three feet wide, between the boom and bottom of the gate.

He instinctively resisted the pull of the tide to stay under the gate, struggling until his strength began to ebb, groping as he did so for any support he could find. A chain hanging down from the gate fell into his hands. The chain was oily and greasy, as was the water, full of the swirling debris of the river being swept on its way out to sea on the racing tide.

McDonnell, thoroughly roused from his evening's reverie but physically severely handicapped by it, reached over the rail to try to pull Robin out of the water by the chain he was grasping.

But even for him the odds were impossible. The distance was too great to sustain his effort. Neither man was able to grasp the chain with sufficient firmness to hold and sustain it for long enough with the necessary strength. The boom moved in the tide, chopping from one side to another and threatening to injure or even drown the man in the water.

The prolonged and desperate efforts to save Robin were fortuitously terminated about five minutes later when another member of the ship's crew happened to return by the same route.

It was Chief Engineer Tim Denton, fresh from a day spent with Vanessa, including a leisurely lunch and visiting the best shops in Regent Street.

His arrival permitted McDonnell to look around for an alternative method. He found a rope neatly arranged in a flat spiral but mercifully not sodden with rain.

The two men eventually hauled their nearly drowned crewmate out of the water. He was very cold and exhausted.

A return to the ship for a hot bath and a good night's rest prepared Robin for his duties the following morning, although his newly bought sports coat and other clothes were completely ruined by oil. His hands were cut and bruised from his ordeal.

Captain Rhodes had the habit of walking the entire ship first thing every morning. While Robin was sounding the oil levels in the ship's reserves the captain sauntered by. Without stopping, he muttered to the embarrassed fifth engineer officer, 'I hear you went swimming last night. Don't make a habit of it.' And he went on his way.

As soon as the *Samqueen's* cargo from New Zealand had been unloaded when the ship first arrived, shipwrights and carpenters had been on board installing a series of vertical steel stanchions along the ship's midline on the 'tween-deck, the lower as opposed to the main – sometimes called the weather – upper deck.

The tops of the stanchions were welded to the underside of the weather deck. Between each set of stanchions horizontal planks of fir, three inches thick were fitted. The design and workmanship were considered of substantial enough quality and durability to guarantee that ballast loaded into the holds in the artificial space created would be held in place, preventing it from shifting to one side or the other and destabilising the ship.

When the construction work had been finished and inspected, the ship left the Royal Victoria Dock for an anchorage in the River Thames nearby in Gravesend, on the opposite bank of the river. Unless a ship is loading or unloading, it pays to vacate a dock, since fees paid on an empty vessel are an unnecessary expense on its owners.

The movement of the ship to its new anchorage was primarily necessary for it to undergo preparations to take on board ballast in place of cargo. The ballast equalled a portion of the ship's cargo tonnage, to give it the stability and safety to cope with the vicissitudes of ocean swells and stormy conditions, en route to a distant port to fetch a normal cargo.

In the case of the *Samqueen,* the ballast consisted of sand and gravel sludge dredged from the bed of the River Thames. Two scows, flat-bottomed boats with blunt bows, used on the Thames to haul bulk freight to and from larger ships, were located one to each side of the ship. Cargo booms from the ship hung out at right angles carrying scoops or clam buckets for removing the sludge from the scows to the holds of the ship. The operations could be a busy time for the ship's engineers, the steam driven winches working overtime to complete the ballast loading.

Vanessa made another visit to the ship when the loading was completed. She wanted to know some more about ballast loading, which was so evidently in a different world from the one she inhabited.

Tim told her the basic facts that he was then able to disclose.

'Altogether, a total of one thousand, four hundred and ninety-eight tons of Thames shingle have been finally winched aboard. The whole of the solid temporary ballast is stowed in the 'tween-decks of four of the five holds, with one hundred and ninety-one tons in each of the bilges numbered between two and five.'

'But what about all the water in with it, surely that will slosh around quite a bit?' she asked.

'Most of it drains away during loading and the rest of the wetness serves to form a solid mass, levelling the surface out and well below the level of the boards to hold it from shifting,' Tim explained.

'Why is it necessary to carry ballast anyway?' Vanessa asked.

'The economics of merchant ships allow it; indeed, they require it,' Tim answered. 'It would be nice to take a full load of freight one way and pick up a full load to return. But that is not always possible. You have to get your business wherever you can. If you can fetch a full load from afar, the cost of the outward trip in ballast is covered by the income from the freight carried on return.'

He took her into the depths of the ship to show her what had been done. 'It seems too small a portion of the total freight tonnage the *Samqueen* could carry to do the job,' she observed.

'Yes, it does,' said Tim. 'But it is equal to deadweight cargo and the amount is calculated to reduce the buoyancy of the ship by enough to enable it to overcome the buffeting of the wind and waves in mid-ocean. When the ship leaves Tilbury it will have a draught of water forward of ten feet eleven inches, but nineteen feet three inches aft.'

'But why such a big difference between the bows and the stern?' asked Vanessa, immediately fastening onto his figures.

'You don't miss much darling, do you?' Tim said. 'Let's say, we would not want the bows of the ship to be in danger of nosing into the ocean, and we must have the stern in the water to keep the engines going at all times for the propeller to drive us forward to overcome the waves.'

'Even I know the propeller is at the stern end of the ship. But if it failed, what would happen then?' she queried.

'It could be disaster,' Tim replied. 'It would depend on the state of the sea. In a calm sea all could be well, but in a storm, the ship could capsize.'

Vanessa had seen all she wanted to see. Her time was limited.

Tim accompanied Vanessa back to the theatre after that visit on the day before the ship was due to sail.

'We should be back in London in one month, darling. Good luck with the production. May it continue to be a great success. It has certainly achieved a notable slot on the London stage,' Tim said, as he took his leave at the theatre entrance, with a long hug and kiss, as if it were to be his last.

The *Samqueen* pulled up its anchors precisely at two o'clock in the afternoon of the fourth of May, a month later than originally scheduled, sailing from its temporary mooring on the Gravesend side of the river. The timing of its departure depended on the tidal flow of the River Thames.

The voyage facing the ship was nearly three thousand miles to New York, still under the command of Captain Derek Rhodes, a man still in his mid-thirties. The departure must have evoked unwelcome memories for him. Tim had by then learned the true facts of the significance of the loss of the *Samking* for the captain.

It had been in January, only four months previously, when the Liberty ship *Samking* had set out in ballast from the same port. Derek Rhodes should have been in command of that ship but his indisposition with pneumonia had denied him his assumption of that duty in favour of another captain. Illness had saved his life when the *Samking* was lost with all hands. All investigations into the loss of the ship had proved negative.

The weather in the early days of May, as the *Samqueen* left London, was fine. Prospects for their voyage were good. Eight of the ship's twelve officers, including the captain, had seen war service. Their familiarity with the Atlantic Ocean had been established in far less promising circumstances. In wartime, in addition to the normal ravages of stormy seas, the ever-present threat of torpedo attacks from U-boat fleets had to be faced. German naval attacks by surface warships and U-boats on mercantile shipping caused the loss of over thirty-five thousand British seamen, over fifty thousand allied seamen in total.

For the voyage, Tim appointed the third, fourth, and fifth engineer officers to resume their duty to be in charge of the main engines and boilers, each for watches of eight hours continuously, out of every twenty-four hours of clock time.

The total complement of crew members numbered forty-five, most men still retained from the voyage from New Zealand, but nine replaced in London by new crew members.

The ship made good headway eastwards along the Thames Estuary on the ebbing tide. It turned to starboard southwards at North Foreland and to starboard again westwards at Dover, entering the busiest waters in the world. It sailed the length of the English Channel until it reached a position south of the Isles of Scilly, thirty miles or so off Land's End, when the open Atlantic Ocean to the United States lay before it.

The North Atlantic rollers had begun.

11

The weather for the first five days of the voyage was dictated by high pressure over the Azores, spreading premature calm across the central Atlantic Ocean. Having passed the Lizard at noon on the fifth of May, the *Samqueen* set course on Track C for Ambrose Light and New York harbour, one of the recognised headings for ships across the Atlantic.

The voyage across the Atlantic Ocean was nothing more than the endurance and seaworthiness for which the *Samqueen* had been built. It was made for the oceans of the world.

In slack moments Tim, who had access to the ship's log, supplemented his knowledge of the ship's sailing record from it, as well as from conversations with Captain Rhodes.

'The first captain was with the ship for nearly three years,' Captain Rhodes informed him. 'He was Captain Prindle, who first took command at the Baltimore shipyard at the end of 1943 when the construction of the ship was completed. He made several ballast voyages like ours and had no qualms about sailing the ship anywhere.'

'Where did he get to, then?' asked Tim.

'He really went everywhere in that time,' he continued. 'For his first voyage, he sailed from New York to Alexandria, Egypt, after which the ship was formally handed over to be managed by the New Zealand Shipping Company under the control of the British Ministry of War Transport.

'Returning in ballast to New York, the ship made a second voyage to the Mediterranean where it was engaged for six months shuttling troops and supplies from the Middle East to the war zone in Italy. But then, in contrast, it carried a cargo from India to England.

'It was put under secret orders and commanded to sail to Okinawa, but Japan surrendered during the voyage, so the ship was diverted to Singapore to be one of the first merchant ships to reach the port after its liberation. Several voyages with military supplies from India to Malaya were followed by the repatriation of one thousand, four hundred Japanese prisoners of war, from Hong Kong to Japan. After finally returning to Hong Kong, it sailed to Australia to load a cargo for Britain.'

'When did you first come into contact with the ship?' Tim asked.

'Captain Halward took over command for a short time before handing over to me in Wellington. He made the voyage from Vancouver to Britain and then to New Zealand via Singapore. The ship took cargo to Britain and voyaged to Montreal, for a load to Australia, before he relinquished command,' Derek replied.

The *Samqueen's* previously unblemished record was not expected to be put at risk on the present Atlantic crossing. It was fully anticipated that the voyage would be routine in a sturdy ship with an experienced and competent crew.

The engineer officers maintained their daily round of eight-hour watches in the engine room. The constant, simultaneous monitoring of the triple expansion steam engine, boilers, and drive shaft to the propeller ensured the smooth running of the ship day after day.

After each engineer's watch was completed, he repaired to the mess for a meal and then to his cabin for a well-earned sleep. The cabins of the engineer officers were nearly amidships on the starboard side under a companionway to the upper deck.

The rest of the twenty-four day they spent sometimes with colleagues, playing cards, reading, engaging in discussions, drinking, and leisurely meals. The younger engineer officers still indulged in visits to the crow's nest after their first initiation by Tim had whetted their appetite for it. They also spent idle time in the bows of the ship, watching the flying fish.

Familiarity with the ship and its new members of crew was soon well established by everyone. But throughout the twenty-four hours the prime duty of the engineer officers demanded that they were formally available at all times, for any unexpected job that required immediate attention. Dealing with the failure of pumps or any other malfunction of machines and equipment – on which the current performance of the ship depended – was their constant responsibility.

The weather provided a propitious start for the voyage in ballast to the United States. But there was no room for complacency. The following day Captain Rhodes personally checked the ballast arrangements, accompanied by Chief Engineer Tim Denton and Bosun Charles Skipton.

The captain noted that the material had solidified so well that his shoes scarcely made marks on it. He checked every hold for the trim of the ballast itself, the security of the supporting timbers, and their steel stanchions.

It was a comforting sign to see that the solutions for ballasting the ship had been so successful.

'Everything seems to be satisfactory and in order, Tim,' the captain remarked.

'Yes, it seems to be a solid job,' Tim replied. 'We ought not to be too worried about it.'

'Well, we should be especially wary of the construction of the ballast caging. We are repeating the voyage of the *Samking* in ballast, although we do not yet know whether it was the shifting of the ballast that caused the ship to founder,' Captain Rhodes said, expressing his concern.

Tim forthrightly added the comment. 'It's always been a moot point about the installation of ballast constructions. The company must depend on the integrity of the contractors, the ship's crew on the checks of their own engineers, and on God for moderating the storms sufficiently to preserve the ballast arrangements. Of course, freight loading itself can also be a ship's undoing, if the storms are bad enough.'

'True enough, but let's hope the weather on this trip will not be too savage,' the captain agreed.

'We should be all right,' said Tim. 'May is normally a sublime month for storms, although I have met them in every month, apart from the peak period June to November. Occasionally they start early in May or stay late in December.'

The ship's owners had voluntarily offered *Samqueen* as a weather-reporting ship in cooperation with the International Meteorological Organisation. Under the terms of the contract, the ship's wireless operator was obligated to report the state of the weather in the ship's area twice each day throughout a voyage. In return, the ship received a general synopsis of weather conditions and the forecast for the next few hours.

The *Samqueen* reached the midway point between Ireland and Newfoundland, making steady progress at eleven knots, its near full speed, at a rate of around two hundred and fifty sea miles each day.

The latest forecast indicated deteriorating weather.

In response to the latest weather information, the captain ordered the bosun to rearrange the distribution of water ballast in the double-bottom tanks to improve the ship's trim.

Adverse weather materialised on the evening of the ninth of May when a force six wind blew up from the west. Stormy conditions developed during the night.

The ship rolled more than the captain expected, but it always recovered its posture, although sometimes slowly, it seemed to him.

Nevertheless, Derek Rhodes took the precaution of ringing the engine room to order a reduction of speed to six knots. It was a welcome order to the engineers since the ship had been maintaining a high speed for over five days.

He also ordered the bosun to make three inspections of the ballast over the time of the bad weather. Charles Skipton's successive reports to the captain confirmed that it had not shifted, even when the rolling of the ship was at its heaviest.

By the afternoon of the tenth, the light improved and the waters abated as the storm eased. The captain, who had not left the bridge for its duration, retired thankfully to his cabin, desperate for sleep, but satisfied that the voyage had been in good order so far.

Far away, disturbed weather in the area of the Verde Islands had not diminished. It moved slowly, at first undetected, its anti-clockwise winds around a centre of decreasing pressure, but gradually gathering momentum. When no reports of it had been delivered, the United States Weather Bureau eventually dispatched a long-range aircraft eastwards over the ocean from its base in Guantanamo in Cuba.

After five hours of flying, the sky darkened, the sea became indistinct, and then faded into invisibility. The pilot rashly opted to fly into the storm. The aircraft bucked and threatened to disintegrate for twenty minutes until it suddenly emerged into sunshine and a windless sky, but its altitude had plunged, leaving it flying at only a thousand feet above the sea. It had reached the eye of the hurricane, where the waters of the ocean were stirred into white foam as far as the aircrew could see, throwing huge mountains of turbulent waves into the air.

The aircraft climbed out of the eye of the storm at sixteen thousand feet and climbed still further until, at twenty-five thousand feet, the aircrew had a bird's eye view of the whole hurricane.

The cost to the aircraft could have been fatal. It suffered quite badly from superficial damage. The pilot was surprised at the runs of rivets he could see missing in the aircraft's wings as he turned for home.

Further flights to monitor the storm were frustrated, owing to the unavailability of aircraft, or mechanical failures of those that were available.

Those omissions allowed two vital days to pass for monitoring the storm. On the eleventh an updated report was obtained. The hurricane had taken a change of direction to the northwest.

Meanwhile, the *Samqueen* had maintained a speed of nine knots during the night of the tenth of May. The ship was by then only one hundred miles southeast of the Flemish Cap, an area of shallow waters, centred about three hundred and fifty miles east of St. John's in Newfoundland. The ship was approaching the edge of the Grand Banks, to the east of Newfoundland. About two hundred fishing vessels from many nations had been fishing on the Grand Banks but had sailed to calmer waters on receiving the meteorological warnings.

The *Samqueen* crossed the southern part of the Grand Banks, sailing into fog during the afternoon of the eleventh.

'This fog has upset transmissions of the ship's wireless in and out,' the wireless officer reported to the captain. 'I shall have to repair the system immediately, but in the meantime, we are unable to report weather conditions for the rest of today and probably for tomorrow as well.'

'That's not good news,' Captain Rhodes replied to him. 'But do your best. We cannot afford to be incommunicado with weather like this around.'

Captain Rhodes had been anxious to notify his company's agents in New York of their expected arrival there on the seventeenth.

At midnight of the thirteenth, the ship was two hundred miles south-east of Cape Race, a point of land located at the south-eastern tip of the Avalon Peninsula on the island of Newfoundland in Canada.

Tim was well aware that the ship would soon pass his frequent, former wartime destination of Halifax in Nova Scotia on the starboard side, as the *Samqueen* followed its south-western course towards New York.

12

Captain Rhodes awoke suddenly at seven o'clock on the morning of the fourteenth to sense that the ship was rolling with a long, slow, ponderous motion.

He went straight to the bridge.

'How long has this current swell been running?' he asked Cadet Officer John Thorne, the duty officer.

'For about an hour, sir,' said the young officer on the watch. 'The barometer has been falling since midnight.'

The captain noted that the swell appeared to move at thirty knots, enough to put it well in advance of the storm that caused it.

'Keep your eyes skinned on the southern sky and inform me at once if it hazes over,' the captain instructed him. He gently upbraided the cadet officer for not reporting the long decline of the barometer but made allowance for his lack of experience.

The captain then visited the small wireless room to find the operator, James Desmond, still wrestling with his re-assembly of the deficient apparatus. 'How is it going, James?' he asked.

'I shall need another two hours' work to set it up and get it running,' James answered. 'Unfortunately, it's proving more of a problem than I expected.'

'That is bad news. Of all the times to go wrong, this is the worst possible one. Do your best to get it going. We need it urgently now,' the captain called out as he left the wireless room.

James redoubled his efforts immediately, spurred on by the captain's injunction to secure an immediate weather report.

At just after eleven o'clock he rushed to the bridge with a message he had managed to receive. 'Sir, there is a report of a hurricane. At eight o'clock this morning it was five hundred miles away from the ship.'

After delivering it, he beat a hasty retreat to his wireless room to complete the repairs to his apparatus.

'Let me look at the data again,' the captain said to the first officer. On recalculating the progress of the hurricane, the captain came to his own conclusion.

'I make it that the ship is now only four hundred miles away from it. If the hurricane and the ship continue on their respective courses their paths will cross.'

He asked First Officer Gerald Berkeley to tell the wireless operator to contact any ships to the south-west of the *Samqueen* to send them their local weather reports.

Gerald Berkeley left quickly to discharge the order but was met with a dismayed wireless operator, who explained his equipment had once again broken down.

He reported back to the captain, who sent for Tim Denton.

'Come up to the bridge. I want to get to grips with the storm. You have had a lot of experience of these waters, Tim, so your experience will be useful.'

The three of them discussed the information to hand and the prospects, finally deciding that three alternatives were open to them.

'It will not be easy to pick the right choice, but let me reiterate them,' the captain said.

'One, we could change course to the south, or two, stop where we are now, or three, return on our course eastwards.'

They dismissed the second and third in favour of the first, in an attempt to pass behind the storm. The captain ordered the ship to alter course accordingly at noon to due south.

The sky and ocean became less than inviting as the *Samqueen* on its new course encountered increasingly heavy swells, while still making uneasy progress.

The meteorology authority monitoring the track of the hurricane decided to issue a further warning to all shipping, after receiving a weather report from the German vessel *Badenhaver*. From a position sailing on an inbound course, one hundred and fifty miles east of the hurricane's predicted track, the German ship reported that the hurricane was still registering winds of one hundred miles an hour. The message read:

14 September 1300 AST Broadcast on 500 KCY from all eastern seaboard wireless stations handling marine traffic All ships western approaches general hurricane warning Atlantic hurricane now believed centred approximately 3800 north 6300 west predicted track now shifted to the eastward centre

Expected pass 200 miles south-east Cape Race by 1200 AST on 15 All ships proceed accordingly.

The *Samqueen* did not receive that message. Unfortunately, it must have been sent at a time when its wireless reception equipment had been out of action or malfunctioning.

Reducing speed a little, the ship sailed on against an ocean of wide swells. The day was hazy and windless but with a darkening sky in the far distance, to which they were heading.

By late afternoon, black and threatening clouds appeared on the horizon. The captain decided to alter course by three points to the east in the same direction as the storm seemed to have moved.

The chief engineer, Tim Denton, noting the change of direction, reminded the engineer officers and engine-room crew that maintaining their engines would be crucial if they had to face the worst.

The signs had been enough to send everyone to check every lashing on the ship. Another inspection of the ballast showed it to be intact.

The chef hurriedly prepared an evening meal, which the crew consumed without delay, anxious only to return to their tasks to make the ship as ready as possible for a stormy passage.

By seven-thirty in the early evening, the barometer was falling more sharply as the wind increased its velocity to force four. The surface of the ocean had become turbulent.

The captain then ordered the helmsman to alter the ship's course by 94 degrees, virtually eastwards and away from New York, away from their destination.

Only fifteen minutes later the light was obliterated, as the wind rose with terrifying suddenness to force seven from the east, while the sea rose and fell with intensifying motions. First Officer Berkeley entered the following in the ship's log around nine o'clock.

Weather deteriorating rapidly Barometer 30.1 and still falling steeply Wind ESE Force 9 to 10 Steep head sea and heavy southerly swells Heavy rain reducing visibility to three hundred yards Vessel rolling and pitching heavily and taking some solid water across the foredeck Speed reduced to 40 revolutions making good about 5 knots on a course of 44 degrees Ship steering badly.

Twenty minutes after nine o'clock, the wireless operator reported on the bridge telephone that he could now transmit messages but was still unable to receive them. First Officer Berkeley took note of the message and informed the captain, but the latter was too fixated to rejoice over the information, while staring at the compass at the side of the helmsman, who struggled with the wheel.

At that very moment, the ship fell away from the wind by three points while the helmsman fought to hold its swing and restore the ship to its course.

After a few more minutes the awful thought swept over the captain that soon it might be impossible to steer the ship. He rang the engine room, ordering the chief engineer to reduce the ship's speed by ten revolutions.

An hour later, the noise from the storm completely overwhelmed speech on the bridge, an isolated construction to the fore of the ship, where the captain commanded the ship and from which the ship was steered.

Captain Rhodes decided to assess the state of the ship, in relation to the sea by a general view from outside on the platform extension to the bridge. The wind speed meter was reading at least ninety miles per hour. The wind almost snatched the door to the port wing platform of the bridge from his hands. Sky and sea seemed to be one. Drops of water carried by the wind had the properties of ice as they hit his face. He returned quickly to the bridge to find the barometer still slowly falling.

Although the helmsman fought to keep the wind in the starboard quarter, the wind changes and the sea in response to them were following contrary directions. Consequently, the ship was stressed and torn first one way then another, often broadside to the main attack of the sea, then to the wind, then to both simultaneously.

On board, no one could pursue any movement. Crewmen just clung to whatever secure structure was nearest to them. The ship shuddered, rolled, and creaked in a wild dance of madness. Every crewman was inside the ship. It was impossible to access any deck, as mountainous waves successively swept the superstructure, tearing at any item protruding in their way.

The fourth and fifth engineer officers viewed the monstrous waves from their cabins with ultimate apprehension. They looked up in the direction of the sky to see the crests of the waves up to a hundred feet above their heads. Their only thought at that instant was that they would crash like a torrent on the ship and engulf them.

The *Samqueen* dutifully buried itself in the trough of one wave before rising swiftly aloft with the next crest of the wave.

The thoughts of many crewmen were on the fate of the *Samking* loaded with ballast that disappeared in the same area without any trace.

By eleven o'clock that night the ship was patently out of control. Even having two men on the wheel had failed to hold the vessel to its chosen course.

When the wireless officer reported that he had restored some power of transmission, Captain Rhodes ordered him to send the following message describing the *Samqueen's* plight.

Steamer Samqueen position 4220 north 5800 west in full hurricane Having difficulty steering All ships keep clear.

Collisions in the open ocean were not unknown, but the chances of two ships colliding in those conditions were virtually impossible. All ships had scattered for safer seas, once the broadcast warning from the meteorological office had been issued. If another ship similarly out of control crossed the path of the *Samqueen* and then collided with it, no one could have taken any steps to prevent it.

Since the ship's wireless reception apparatus was still out of action, the virtue of the outgoing message was to alert the maritime world of the whereabouts of the ship, which in the interim had been lost.

It was the last known signal to be sent from the *Samqueen*.

The *Samqueen* had unwittingly become exposed to one of the greatest storms known in modern times. Charles Baker, the second officer, wrote in the ship's log.

We got a warning of the approaching hurricane just before noon on Tuesday and altered course. By seven o'clock that evening there were hot gusts of wind hitting us and the ship started rolling very badly in the mounting seas. The barometer dropped to the bottom and on Wednesday morning, just after midnight, the ship took a list of 65° after several huge waves hit us broadside. I've never seen waves like it before. They were straight over the ship, one going down the funnel.

13

The silence of the *Samqueen* had been long enough to alert the meteorological centre in America, which had been the destination of the ship's weather reports twice daily. The sudden cessation of reports evoked their concern.

The centre alerted Ennerman, the ship's owners, in London.

When the latest and last transmission arrived after an enforced silence, it only confirmed the ship's plight. All attempts to make contact after that had completely failed.

The difficulties of the *Samqueen* were made doubly significant, both to the owners and the authorities, in the light of the recent loss of the *Samking*.

In no time the expected disaster about to overtake the *Samqueen* was leaked to the media. The possible loss of a major ship was newsworthy in any case. The connection between the two Liberty ships became grist for both the broadcast and printed media.

The thousands of ships lost during the recently ended war had had no publicity at the time of their loss. The strict censorship of wartime shielded the public from the horrifying number of ships and their precious cargoes destroyed, their passengers and crews frequently perishing.

The *Samqueen* was at the mercy of the ocean. Its motive power and carefully balanced engineering to give it buoyancy had been overcome by the very medium for which it was built to exploit.

The listening and reading public waited with bated breath for the outcome.

Newscasts and newspapers variously reported the catastrophe as an almost accomplished fact, matched against the loss of the *Samking* without trace.

Vanessa had been on stage in the evening. She had an undisturbed night's sleep, during which the news broke. She normally turned on the radio to hear the BBC newscast on waking.

The brief mention of the unfolding disaster was an unmitigated shock. She listened to the news item with devastating anguish, clutching desperately for ameliorating facts that would lead to hope that the ship would survive.

None was given.

She cried out in despair. 'My darling, my darling, you promised to come back to me. How cruel can the ocean be? How can I sleep until I know that you are safe?'

Although it was early morning, before business hours, she decided to telephone the Ennerman Company. She was able to contact someone. They, too, were unable to sleep.

'My partner is the chief engineer. I suppose lots of other relatives of crew members must be worrying you at this time, but I would certainly like some kind of assurance, if you can give it,' she told the official on the other end of the line.

He replied without hesitation.

'We had a signal from the ship to say the storm was severe, but we have had nothing since then. It may be that their transmissions have been interrupted or that their wireless equipment is damaged. So, it is far too early to be clear what has happened,' her informant explained. 'Give me your telephone number and I will let you know whenever we have further positive information.'

His parried interchange was enough comfort to carry her through that day and give everything to her performance in the evening at the Hippodrome. She fell asleep that night with the same assurance. But she knew that the next day or two would be exacting to the last degree.

In the engine room of the *Samqueen* the collective skills of the engineer officers and their combined long experience at sea were producing a story of wonderful seamanship, self-control, and courage. In the bowels of the ship they had a slight advantage over those on the bridge who faced the maximum movements of the ship at the mercy of wind and waves.

The difference between the two locations, like the crow's nest, was parallel to, and illustrative of, the swing of a pendulum. Those in the depths of the ship were nearer the fulcrum as opposed to those on the bridge at the end of the pendulum, experiencing the full rigour of the ship's swing.

Every member of the entire crew was hanging on firmly to unmovable machinery and fittings. In the engine room, every time the ship plunged into a deep valley of the ocean, the ship's stern rose well out of the water.

Something had to be done to prevent a catastrophe.

Chief Engineer Tim Denton and Third Engineer George Scott worked in unison. Tim explained his orders to George.

'When I raise my free hand, I shall hold it up until the ship's bows have sunk well beyond the horizontal. Then I will drop it.'

Using the fixed inclinometer, which measured the ship's tilt or forward slope, Tim hung on for safety to something immovable with one hand but raised his other hand when the ship was plunging bows first into the ocean. On the signal, the third engineer spun the control wheel cutting off steam to the pistons. The single huge shaft turning the propeller to drive the ship slowly reduced its revolutions.

When Tim dropped his hand in an authoritative manner, George reversed his orders, opening up the steam valves to the pistons. It was a vital operation. The propeller was being carried out of the sea by the obscene dive of the ship's bows into the deep. The reversal of the routine as the bows recovered their dominance, gave the ship back its driving power and the chance of steering it safely against the waves.

The engineers knew what the fatal end to their voyage would be if the ship's engines failed. To prevent that outcome, they adopted this process to curtail the excess speed of the engine and use it at its most economical level. The endless revolutions of the propeller, if unchecked, could soon cause irreparable damage to the shaft and driving mechanisms, unless modified as far as, and when, possible. It was a solution they adopted to keep the engines and transmission machinery under control.

The propeller's revolutions were being increased intolerably, when, at a designed minimum speed for driving the ship, they were successively subjected to excessive freewheeling when the propeller was out of the water, followed by the sudden cessation of the revolutions when it plunged into the sea again. The entire mechanism was being strained beyond its endurance.

Correcting that imbalance was the object of their concern.

The ship was heeling over as much as 32 degrees but so far recovering from it, but slowly. Its ballast in the 'tween-decks – unfortunately above the level of the turbulent sea – had a detrimental effect on the speed of recovery compared with ballast that could have been alternatively placed in the bottom of the ship.

On the fourteenth of May, First Officer Gerald Berkeley wrote an entry in the ship's log:

2400 hours Full Hurricane Wind WSW gusting to 110 mph Barometer 29.8 Zero visibility Mountainous broken sea Ship taking heavy solid water fore and aft Rolling to 30 degrees Barely maintaining steerageway at 30 revolutions Vessel answering helm only with extreme difficulty.

The ship's position was probably abeam the hurricane centre and very close to it. The wind dropped suddenly to forty miles per hour, only fifteen minutes after Gerald Berkeley had written that report.

Any relief that overcame the captain and crew, however, was muted by the state of the ocean, which seemed to increase its turbulence more than ever.

Their hopes were very soon completely obliterated by the astounding sight of a huge, towering column of water appearing from nowhere. It descended on the bridge wheelhouse with a noise characteristic of an explosion, shaking the entire ship, as if to destroy it.

Within seconds, before the men on the bridge could regain their feet and senses, a second avalanche of water of even greater proportions struck the ship on its starboard side.

Those pillars of water were the stuff of ultimate fatality to a ship in a storm.

The *Samqueen* heeled over through 30 degrees to 40 degrees and beyond, throwing men around, tearing their hands from their chosen supports.

The ship stayed on the 40 degree mark for a life-threatening minute. From his place on the bridge, Captain Rhodes felt a low rumbling sound beneath his feet, extending throughout the ship.

It seemed to continue interminably. But at last, it ceased.

As if waiting for it to do so, the ship slowly righted itself from the extreme listing but only as far as 30 degrees to port.

The captain rang the engine room but could make no connection. He managed to move himself near enough to signal to one of the two helmsmen to leave the wheel and come to his side.

Struggling against the noise, he charged the crewman to go below decks and tell the chief engineer to transfer the oil from the port to the starboard tanks. It was a limited remedy to reduce the risk that the ship would roll over completely.

The *Samqueen* was still slowly underway but lying almost on its side in the cockpit of a hurricane.

Twenty minutes later the captain decided to assess the effects of the oil transfer. He had difficulty in opening the door out to the port platform of the bridge – so violent was the wind – but succeeded in clawing his way out clutching the rail as if his life depended on it, which in fact was obviously the case.

Almost immediately a colossal torrent of ocean assailed the *Samqueen* from astern, engulfing the entire vessel in its turbulent waters.

Captain Rhodes was swept like a cork out to sea, half-drowned and deafened by the turmoil of the collision between steel and water. He fought to the surface just in time to be caught on a second mighty surge of sea lifting him as before but miraculously throwing him back on the ship, against the railing of the boat deck, thirty feet aft of the bridge, which he had just left.

Remarkable escapes in the hands of nature could never have been more exceptional. His life was lost in one second and saved in another, but only by the intervening existence of the wrecked ship. He could so easily have been the first casualty that day.

Those two mighty cascades of water had pummelled and destroyed all resistance to the vicissitudes of wind and wave left in the ship. No one could walk on the deck, its list always increasing to danger point.

Just as Tim, as chief engineer, had activated the pumps to transfer the oil from number three port to number three starboard deep-tanks, to comply with the captain's order to try to lessen the ship's list, the first of those two cascades of sea water had struck.

No one knew that it had carried the captain into the ocean and near-death before gratuitously returning him to the ship.

With incredulity, Tim Denton watched the inclinometer, measuring the ship's list, reaching the end of its range, indicating a virtually horizontal position on the ocean, before watching as the ship gradually recovered to a 30 degree list to port.

Everyone in the engine room heard and felt the huge ominous rumble of the ballast breaking its anchoring structure and moving to the port side of the vessel.

At the time of the shifting ballast, the maximum roll of the ship was almost enough to put its funnel parallel to the ocean. The lee rail ended in water which poured into the ship, successive waves entering open doors and portholes and running down into the ship's holds and engine room.

The ship listed from 30 degrees to 80 degrees, its port gunwales plunging up to twelve feet into the sea. At the extreme listing everyone expected the ship to capsize.

First Officer Berkeley was still in the wheelhouse, having seen the captain go out on the port wing only to disappear in the torrent of water.

A few minutes later the half-drowned captain reached the bridge again, covering the thirty feet of severely sloping deck on its starboard side with enormous difficulty. His re-appearance astounded the beleaguered Berkeley, who realised either that he had just seen a miracle, or was grossly wrong in his perceptions of what he thought he had seen, or perhaps that he was suffering from hallucinations.

But he had no time to wonder about the reality. The captain was already yelling to him, 'Sound the emergency signal.'

Ironically, the propeller was still driving the ship slowly forward at three or four knots but completely out of control and moving broadside to the waves. The helm had been lashed down, since human hands could no longer control it.

The pumps transferring oil and water from port to starboard tanks had stopped working. When the emergency bells rang everyone assumed the end was imminent. The crew made a desperate exodus from the engine room and other below-deck locations towards the main deck, where many congregated amidships.

Cabins, favourite seats in their mess deck, working stations, and sleeping quarters for the crew members, which had become home for long voyages and where life on board had been lived, suddenly lost their comforting appeal. The inclement weather, from which the inside of the ship had always shielded them, now clutched at them for death at worst and in the darkness of the night.

Several of the crew had by that time allowed their fears to overcome them. It was indeed an extreme strain on the self-control of every man.

Signs of utter resignation could be seen, as if nothing could prevent the inevitable loss of the ship with all hands. Those given to resignation included several officers and various crew members.

Previously, Fourth Engineer Ray Williams had gone to the wireless room, trying to assist the wireless officer. But the latter's recent struggle with the underperforming apparatus and threatening repercussions of its failure had not prepared him well for the intense and overwhelming environment of destruction and death that had descended on the ship.

Ray Williams tore him away from his wireless room, the two men dragging each other to Ray's cabin. Ray desperately tried to calm him down but the wireless officer was bordering on panic. He tried to read to the man from his mother's small pocket Bible, but all his efforts were unsuccessful. It was while they were in Ray's cabin that the ominous and cataclysmic roar of the shifting ballast was felt rather than heard around the ship.

Hearing anything was a past luxury. The endless crashing of waves and the unremitting oceans of water sweeping over the vessel had driven the frail human voice into insignificance. They deafened the most seasoned of sailors and tore at their minds, ultimately threatening madness.

With the captain's signal, thoughts of using the lifeboats were in the minds of some crew members. But the impossibility of using them restrained most men.

14

The successful launching of a lifeboat at sea from its parent ship required a considerable number of steps performed in logical order.

But in conditions of extreme weather and the impending foundering of a ship it is unlikely that a lifeboat could be launched in an orderly fashion, unless the process was in the hands of a well-trained crew.

Unfortunately, in the case of the *Samqueen* the prolonged fight against the elements had eroded the confidence and self-control of many of the crew.

The expectation of a textbook launch was out of the question.

When the emergency bells rang, some crew members assumed that the order to abandon ship had been given or at least had used it to prepare to escape.

The wireless officer, the fourth engineer officer, and several other members of the crew managed to reach the number four lifeboat, one of two lifeboats on the port side of the ship, matching two on the starboard side, but found difficulty in boarding it. Each lifeboat had a length of twenty-four feet with a capacity for twenty-five passengers.

Between them they tore off the canvas covering.

Two of them climbed on board. Meanwhile, another crew member removed the gripes, which lock the lifeboat onto its chocks and fix it to the ship, leaving the boat secured only by its falls and ropes, which allowed the lifeboat to be lowered to the sea.

The captain, assuming no one had mistaken the alarm calls, ordered First Officer Berkeley to cut the falls and loosen the gripes of the two lifeboats attached to the port side of the ship.

The falls were adjusted to allow the lifeboat to drop to the water level at an even keel – but decidedly not when a ship was lying on its side. Having been cut, the ropes would normally fall into the water when the lifeboat was launched.

Gerald Berkeley crawled aft at his peril against the repeated attacks of the storm-driven waves. When he reached the number four lifeboat in the blackest of nights he could see no more than a few inches and could hear nothing in the constant noise of crashing water. Speech, man to man, and communications by mouth in the ship were temporarily impossible.

He hacked at the falls with a knife, assuming that they should be cut before the gripes were removed. But as he fought to sever them, a savage wave struck him and covered the boat deck, taking both port lifeboats with it spinning and disintegrating into the ocean. The force of the ocean overcame the remaining ties by which the lifeboats had been fixed to the ship.

The two crewmen who had managed to board number four lifeboat, the wireless officer and an able seaman, were swept away in the raging seas beyond the help of humankind. They were the first casualties.

Berkeley's own struggles obliterated every other consideration, as he tried to empty the water from his lungs.

As a sudden flash of lightning illuminated the ship, he was horrified to see a crewman crashing down the sloping deck of the *Samqueen* in free fall, colliding with the bulwark and washed away at once into the dark night and ocean.

He was the third man to be lost.

Berkeley's task had been wrenched from him. Realising how useless it would be to attempt to cut the falls on the two starboard lifeboats, he crawled painfully back to join the captain in the bridge.

When the ship was restored to its more modest, but still dangerous, listing position, Chief Engineer Tim Denton knew he had a final duty on behalf of all the crew. In deciding that all was then lost, he had to discount his engines as being instrumental any more in saving the ship.

He called on Second Engineer Jack McDonnell to join him. If one failed to reach the engine room the other might still be able to achieve their joint objective.

They undertook the hazardous journey back to the bowels of the ship. Clawing and swinging their way down the companionways to the boiler room, their mission was to prevent the ultimate catastrophe to a ship at sea.

They had to avert the build-up of steam pressure in the boilers that would cause an explosion when it was not used to drive the propeller at full speed.

It was a risky expedition. Whatever it cost, it was a mission that had to be accomplished. With the ship on its side, it was the work of acrobats to climb boiler room ladders, walk on floors at crazy angles, and to reach and turn off valves and pumps with no sure foot or handholds.

The chief and second engineers themselves ran high personal risks. One paid the price.

After accomplishing their task, Jack McDonnell slipped on an oily ladder, falling several feet to the deck but gashing a long wound in his head, as he fell unconscious. His body rolled between the machinery with the constant buffeting of the ship.

When the two men failed to return after fifteen minutes, the Third Engineer George Scott, the Fifth Engineer Robin Spencer, and a fireman made the intrepid journey to the engine room to find Jack seriously injured and Tim Denton trying to care for him.

The four men carried out their nightmare rescue mission at great cost to their strength, and with personal risk, carrying Jack McDonnell along, but sometimes up the companionways and ladders, permanently distorted by the sloping posture of the ship, to reach the main deck.

Each man took it in turn to bear the main weight of Jack's body. They carried him laboriously with no sure footholds, taking an age, each man exhausted by his efforts.

Alongside the gathering of the crew on the main deck, they joined everyone waiting amid the noise, cascading waves, and confusion. They wedged Jack's body securely between a hatch and a stowed cargo boom.

The cold air and flying sea soon restored their second engineer's consciousness, but not sufficiently for his own good. In a dazed state, he struggled to his knees, only to be pitched down the full width of the main deck into the port side scuppers, just as the ship took another lurch which dipped them for another ten feet deep plunge into the turbulent sea, sweeping Jack away to his death. He became the fourth man to die.

As if it had been a signal to abandon ship, most crew members struggled to congregate under the starboard bridge wing, joined by the captain and two other officers. The shouting of men and orders given could scarcely be heard over the chaotic scene that developed and which seemed to be nearing its ultimate finale.

The ship's carpenter from Edinburgh became the fifth fatal casualty while trying to make his way to the rendezvous. He was caught on the open deck by a merciless wave over the bows which swept him the width of the main deck to the port side bulwarks, smashing his body to pulp. It remained for a few minutes as a reminder of the perilous risk to move anywhere on the ship, before it disappeared, claimed by the unforgiving ocean.

Near Fifth Engineer Robin Spencer's cabin, where the remaining crewmen were congregated, was a sealed locker housing various emergency rescue aids. The bosun had already shown himself as an unflappable seaman, conducting himself with steady, rocklike behaviour. He and Robin secured an axe to break down the locker and recover whatever implements were available to facilitate their rescue.

The bosun handed the axe to Robin, who reflected on the times he had wielded an axe in his early farming life for so many purposes in New Zealand. They found two Very pistols. The captain grabbed one and Robin the other.

It was still in the early night hours of the fifteenth of May.

They each fired off one shot. The captain turned to Robin with a modicum of humour, despite their extreme predicament, to say, 'You nearly blew my head off.'

With the engine room shut down and steam pressure falling, the generators finally ceased. Nothing remained to save the ship, nothing to correct its fatal list.

Five of the crew had already been lost.

A number were injured.

The majority congregated in the saloon or starboard companionways. Several deck officers crowded on the bridge. Third Officer Norman Gale and another crew member tried to revive the transmitter but they found that the ship's aerials had been swept overboard or were damaged beyond repair.

Evidently, the buoyancy in the *Samqueen* was just marginal enough to prevent its sinking. The ship was sluggish in the water, which at times reached up to the centre of the hatches, remaining at the mercy of the crests of the waves and floundering into their troughs, but all so slowly, refusing to succumb to their tireless incitements to surrender to the deep.

By four o'clock the next morning the wind and seas abated noticeably, the centre of the hurricane having moved away from them at a distance of perhaps ninety miles to the north.

Optimism raised itself.

The captain discussed with Tim, the chief engineer, if steam could be raised again and steps taken to reduce the ship's list in a calm sea.

Tim volunteered to explore the possibility but returned in half an hour declaring that four feet of water covered the gratings of the engine room. The fire boxes had been flooded. Without fire there could be no steam to operate the pumps.

Dawn came on the day when Armageddon had overtaken the ship. During the night the long hours of perdition had merely seemed to be a prolongation of their agony, a tortuous way to die.

Second Officer Charles Baker wrote in the ship's log:

The waves caused the ballast to move and with a terrific roar the ship turned on its side and stayed there. By morning the list was up to 80° and gradually increasing. We were bang in the middle of the hurricane by then. The crew were at boat stations and we lost five men that day.

Vestiges of cloud, wind, and sea visible in the daylight were the only evidence of that terrible night, while the *Samqueen* sluggishly wallowed in a waterlogged and damaged condition, as testimony to the overwhelming power of the sea.

15

Waiting was the only option open to the crew. But waiting for what? There could be no incoming signal by wireless. No message could be sent for help.

In that vast expanse of ocean, only the sight of another ship would be their ultimate relief. The sea remained too stormy for comfort to be clinging to a waterlogged ship, which had played such a prolonged and perilous gamble with the graveyard that lay beneath it.

With two lifeboats already lost from the port side and the launching of the two starboard lifeboats apparently only a parlous prospect, the captain decided he would encourage the crew to construct some rafts. If the ship sank they would provide a lifeline for at least some of the crew, particularly if the sea had resumed a calmer disposition by the time it became necessary to use them.

At least it would give the crew something to occupy their minds and exercise their energy, rather than lounging for endless futile hours. Unfortunately, only an inadequate supply of suitable materials was available and nothing like propitious for the task. A few spare hatch boards and some empty barrels were the sum total they could gather.

Ropes were cut randomly from the rigging. Raft-making had not been part of the experience of many – perhaps none – of the crew members. By the early afternoon, the first product of their labours was launched on the end of a long rope to test the raft's lashings. The bindings lasted only for a few minutes. The restless waves, still storm-driven, tore them apart, scattering the timber in all directions.

Even late in the day, the stricken *Samqueen* was still pounded by occasional heavy waves. At half past six in the early evening, a particularly heavy wave struck the starboard side of the ship, sending it rolling to port and remaining in an undignified and perilous semi-capsized position for long enough to cause crew members to believe that their time had finally arrived.

The captain and First Officer Berkeley concluded that a final attempt to launch the two starboard lifeboats should be made, whatever the outcome. It was still daylight. In spite of the heavy waves, the sea had lost its ferocious element.

Their only chance of deliverance lay in those two starboard lifeboats. They had just enough capacity to save the entire crew between them – provided they could be launched with impunity.

Both were still intact but perilously perched sixty or more feet high up from sea level on the sloping starboard side. With both port side lifeboats destroyed and all attempts at wireless transmissions failed, nothing else remained. They had no knowledge if any of their emergency transmissions had ever succeeded in reaching intended destinations. The crew had almost exhausted all their options.

The construction of rafts had lacked appropriate materials. The first accomplished products of raft-making had been dashed to pieces as soon as launched. Investigations in the engine room to revive power in the ship had been undertaken, but all possibilities had been thoroughly discounted. After the first night there had been no power in the ship. The pitch darkness of the night could be relieved only now and again by a flare fired into the air, more to alert a would-be rescue ship than to supply illumination for the dying *Samqueen*.

The bosun had remained an inspiration to crew members, active and optimistic to the end. He masterminded the preparation of the two lifeboats concerned with several other crew members. The falls were not initially released, but the gripes, that held the lifeboat to its structure, were removed to allow the first lifeboat to be moved onto the slanting deck.

The falls were then eased, a line being attached to both ends of the lifeboat, before its final descent down the side of the ship into the sea. On contemplating the removal of the gripes, the boson realised the lifeboat would need to be steadied all the way down the precipitous, sloping distance of the starboard hull of the ship.

As the falls were finally released, the lifeboat swung out and began its slow descent, but almost immediately, when the *Samqueen* made another watery lunge into the deep, it smashed back on the hull of the ship, its gunwales turning into firewood. After the accident, the damaged boat would not budge at first, but with an hour's manoeuvring it was lowered towards the water, too unseaworthy to carry any passengers.

The heavy seas had one more ploy to play. When the lifeboat reached the projecting edge of the bilge keel it tipped over, spilling all its contents into the sea before being carried away to its own destruction.

It was proving to be an almost impossible task to save themselves in their own lifeboats. Only one was left. Despair was rife. The onset of night did nothing but cast utter gloom over the crew. The mid-May night was expected to be their nadir.

By that time several members of the crew had gone to pieces, distraught and resigned. Some comforted themselves with alcohol. Third Engineer George Scott himself repaired to Robin's cabin and spent the time helping himself to a drinking spree.

The crew all thought the ship would sink imminently.

Dramatically, any hope of survival depended on the one remaining lifeboat.

The evening brought fading light, the clouds gathering with the fresh north-west wind heralding more, not less, unruly weather.

At nine o'clock one of the seamen penetrated the galley, foraging for easily carried food for the crew. Emerging from the starboard alleyway, he swung himself to climb the ladder to the boat deck when he happened to look out to sea.

His was an experience at sea that would prompt any man to rub his eyes, or realise he was hallucinating, since the crewman's vision encompassed a view long dreamed of, yet never materialising, that had lain beyond hope and expectation.

'Lights. There's lights out there!' he shouted at the top of his voice, the quieter weather conditions allowing his voice to be heard.

Following his pointing arm, every head of the gathered crew turned. In the pitch darkness of the early night the lights were clearly identified as those on the mast of an oncoming ship.

They fired their flares and rockets from the ship's store previously broken open. Daylight suddenly descended on their vicinity of the Atlantic Ocean. The hopes of the stricken crew rose miraculously from the edge of perdition.

The ship – not in sight, but with mast lights that could be viewed at sea level, long before the ship itself was visible – that brought salvation to the *Samqueen*'s crew was the *Cuthbert Browne*, another Liberty ship, laid down in the first month of 1944 and launched early in March. It was number two thousand, four hundred and fifty-seven of the Liberty ships to be built. It took part in the convoys to Russia during the rest of the Second World War, under the ownership of the American Liberty Steamship Company, New York.

The *Cuthbert Browne* had also sailed from Britain on Track C, heading for New Orleans, but had changed course on that same mid-May day when the hurricane moved away and the *Samqueen*'s crew lost the last but one lifeboat remaining on the ship. According to later information from the *Cuthbert Browne*'s wireless operator, the captain was persuaded to avoid the relative ocean congestion when he found that thirty-seven other ships within a radius of fifty miles were crowding the western end of Track C.

The crew members of the approaching ship were overwhelmed by the voluminous spectacle of fire exploding suddenly at night in the middle of the Atlantic. In return, they let loose their own rockets in recognition.

Within an hour their ship was lying to at the dangerous distance of a quarter of a mile from the *Samqueen*. Before long it was compelled to manoeuvre to a different position at a safe distance from the stricken wreck, a move dictated by the rough sea and wind which were developing again towards storm conditions. It was also to a location where the ship would be of most assistance to enable the survivors of the *Samqueen* to transfer ships, by using the flow of water and wind to their greatest advantage.

The plan to launch two lifeboats windward of the *Samqueen* from the *Cuthbert Browne*, while the rescue ship was manoeuvred to leeward to take them back aboard, was easy to plan, but nearly impossible to execute.

Launching the lifeboats in stormy seas proved hazardous. The first was successfully sent on its way towards the *Samqueen*. The second was so badly damaged by colliding with the hull of the parent ship, that it had to be hauled back aboard.

The first lifeboat fought a perilous passage between the two ships, aided by a searchlight on the *Cuthbert Browne*. While the coxswain tried to manoeuvre the lifeboat to the *Samqueen*'s lee side, a vicious wave removed its rudder from the pintles and swept it away.

Fortunately, it was close enough for the coxswain to yell out their dilemma.

The lifeboat was rudderless. As he was unable to steer it, he faced the danger that the lifeboat would crash into the wrecked ship and founder.

A lamp trimmer on the *Samqueen* removed a spare lifeboat rudder from the deck storage. Tying a lifeline around his waist and the rudder to his back, he bravely plunged into the sea, swimming to the lifeboat to restore its mercy mission.

It was too much to expect the lifeboat to try to tie itself to the *Samqueen*, the ship continually heaving and falling as it was in the troubled sea. Anything attached to the wreck – whose only prospect was to sink suddenly – would be dragged down to its own destruction.

The port side bulwarks were still being immersed with the swing of the ship in the waves. The lifeboat and heavily listing ship were like corks on the ocean, thrown around at will and never in the same place at the right time. In any case, if ropes had been attached between the lifeboat and the *Samqueen* they would have been quickly snapped by the differential rises and falls between the two – but a much more likely result would have been that ropes would have committed the lifeboat to contrary plunges into the sea and its own ultimate fate.

It was a chaotic, terrible scene.

The list of the *Samqueen* was getting worse, reaching 80 degrees for longer periods. Men were jumping overboard and clinging to wreckage and anything else they could find with enough buoyancy to guarantee a man's survival.

Jim Moleman, one of the youngest of the crew, an able seaman, jumped into the sea with his friend, Charles Jameson, the donkey greaser. Both men were sucked under the sinking ship. Jameson disappeared, becoming the sixth man lost. Moleman was sucked straight under the ship and out the other side, from where he swam to the *Cuthbert Browne*, involving a swim of nearly two miles. It took him two hours to make the agonising trip in such a forbidding sea.

Captain Rhodes personally helped men down the sloping deck of the ship into the water. At the midnight hour, eleven crewmen were successful in swimming to the lifeboat and laboriously boarding it in the relentlessly stormy sea. The lifeboat's coxswain was anxious about overloading it in the conditions, ordering the lifeboat to pull away to avoid being shipwrecked.

Although the lifeboat was built to carry twenty-five passengers – on the assumption of sailing in a reasonably stable sea – the coxswain decided that eleven soaking men plus its crew were all that the lifeboat could take to navigate the dangerous return trip to the *Cuthbert Browne* in safety and, if necessary, to be reloaded onto the parent ship.

Nevertheless, he fully expected to make a return journey for the remainder of the crew. The lifeboat with its eleven saved men, however, took four hours to reach the parent ship, a distance of less than two miles.

The prolonged difficulty of the lifeboat's voyage back to the *Cuthbert Browne* left it in such a damaged state, that the decision was made it could not make a return journey. The rescue ship had only two intact lifeboats still on board. The services of the third had already been lost when rendered unseaworthy by smashing against the side of the *Cuthbert Browne,* on being launched to the aid of the *Samqueen*. With its fourth lifeboat damaged while carrying out the rescue, it was time to be prudent, time to preserve the safety of the *Cuthbert Browne's* own crew.

Fortunately, the compulsorily aborted rescue operation by the *Cuthbert Browne* was completely sidelined when another ship appeared from the night.

The pyrotechnic display, frantically mounted to light up the ocean by the *Samqueen*, had been more than enough to carry a long way over the ocean. It was also seen at a great distance by the *Proveedor*, which made haste to the scene, joining the *Cuthbert Browne*.

The Argentinian Steamship Company's freighter *Proveedor*, of the Cia Argentina de Nav Dodero, Buenos Aires in South America, was a modern ship. It was northbound from Buenos Aires to Montreal with a full cargo of frozen meat, when it too had to alter course because of the shifting path of the hurricane, diverting through seas which were more unfrequented by shipping. The *Samqueen's* surviving crew were being rescued by those compulsory changes of course by its two rescue ships.

The *Proveedor* arrived in the night on the same day with stormy conditions still raging. On approaching the *Samqueen*, the *Proveedor* launched two lifeboats but it proved far too dangerous for them to move anywhere near the *Samqueen*, which created all the hazards of an island of rocks.

The remaining crew members still aboard the stricken vessel could see the lights of the *Proveedor*'s lifeboats lying off, but unable to risk any further advance towards the wrecked ship.

Many of the castaways then plunged into the sea. Some successfully reached a *Proveedor* lifeboat, others miss-located it and turned to the *Cuthbert Browne* itself, still lying off at up to two miles and easily seen with every light on it lit up.

Four more men were lost.

Meanwhile, the strenuous efforts to release the last lifeboat on the *Samqueen* had been intermittently continuing.

Having failed previously with three lifeboats the crew were determined to succeed with what they believed had been their only hope, until the *Cuthbert Browne* had miraculously appeared on the troubled waters.

Painfully they had inched the lifeboat down the steep starboard side of the ship and at an opportune moment negotiated the bilge keel – which had previously wrecked the other starboard side lifeboat – and dropped it into the sea.

They were then benumbed to see the lifeboat fill rapidly with water. They expected it to sink.

But it resembled its parent ship. It failed to sink, suspended in the sea by its buoyancy tanks. The rope controlling it from the deck enabled the remaining crew members to pull the lifeboat, as gently as the cascading waves would allow, alongside the starboard side of the ship to the stern of the *Samqueen*, where the movement of the waves would imperil it less than on its broadside. The lifeboat was clearly only half a rescue conveyance for a limited number of the crew remaining on the ship.

The captain urged several of the remaining men to jump. Robin Spencer, the fifth engineer officer, was one of those who availed himself of the last opportunity. The lifeboat was wallowing uncertainly and moving around in the dark. With the stern of the ship in the air, a jump of over seventy feet was involved – not a mean feat to accomplish in the night – necessity proving to be the arbiter between several evils.

Five men succeeded in boarding the damaged lifeboat.

In the lifeboat they sat in waterlogged seats with water up to their shoulders. The unserviceability of the lifeboat, with its sluggish and unstable movement, was dominating their minds, always accompanied with the expectation that the latest heavy wave would send it to the bottom.

It took them over four hours to drift towards the *Cuthbert Browne*. They fired flares to indicate their whereabouts and the track they were trying to take to the ship.

A scrambling ladder was strung over the gunwales of the *Cuthbert Browne*. Soaking wet, frozen, and exhausted, the five survivors needed the ship's crewmen to help them on board.

Being on the ship felt as liberating as stepping on to land. They were taken below, given hot showers, clothed, and fed. The young fifth engineer officer later wended his way to the engine room, only to find that the American way of conducting engineering conflicted with his own.

At half past four the following morning, the remaining officers, including Tim Denton, the chief engineer, and a few other members of the crew who had stayed on board, were ordered by the captain to jump overboard. With approaching daylight, they had the best chance to be seen by their rescuers.

They clung to boxes and anything afloat while swimming towards the *Cuthbert Browne*. It seemed to take hours. The rescue ship had been using its searchlight to sweep the ocean constantly. The crew directing it were timelessly patient, giving unstinting toil over the long hours of the rescue attempt. The last crew members to leave the ship were picked out by the light.

The *Cuthbert Browne* moved to meet them.

It looked terrifying to see a huge ship towering into the sky and bearing down on the men in the water. It brought back vivid memories of wartime incidents to Tim.

But its crew were all committed to the rescue. They threw lifebelts down to the swimmers, who by that time had exhausted their strength. It was all they could do to hang on to the lifebelts while they were hauled one by one up the side of the ship to safety.

Captain Derek Rhodes was last to leave the *Samqueen*. He had done all in his power to retrieve his first command. He was then about to sustain the best traditions of the British maritime profession. When he was satisfied that the last member of his crew had escaped from the ship, he tied the essential ship's documents in a waterproof container to his waist with a lanyard.

With very mixed feelings he jumped overboard.

After half an hour in the sea he reached a *Proveedor* lifeboat and was hauled safely onto it. Of all those who had plunged into the sea, or been washed away by the waves that assaulted their ship, ten were lost: two men in the first lifeboat to be swept away; two falling down the sloping main deck into the sea; the fifth dying when swept under the ship; the chief steward as the sixth man to perish; and four men attempting to swim to the *Cuthbert Browne*.

The swimming ability of some of the crew may not have been equal to the demands for their survival, but in those waters, sharks could also be a menace. Crew members remembered seeing sharks during daylight on that crucial day.

At a quarter to six in the morning of the rescue, the *Cuthbert Browne's* searchlight was switched off. Suddenly the seascape was reduced to near darkness.

Undoubtedly, the captain and crew of the *Cuthbert Browne* had displayed seamanship and bravery in the best of maritime tradition. Its captain, Edward Stephens, was making his first voyage as master. His control of and persistence with the rescue were absolutely magnificent. On arriving at the scene of the disaster he had tried to sail his ship as close to the wreck as possible but realised his position was contrary to the wind and waves. He then used his expertise to sail his ship several miles for another approach that in the end was appropriate for the rescue operations.

The two rescue ships set a course for land, the *Cuthbert Browne* towards Bermuda, the *Proveedor* to Montreal, leaving the *Samqueen* abandoned and harried by turbulent seas. The waters were expected eventually to penetrate the ship's apertures, tipping the balance against its buoyancy, and confining it to a lonely and unsung grave.

16

Still at sea, Tim Denton had escaped from a horrific ship disaster. As one of the eighteen men rescued by the *Cuthbert Browne,* he was still chief engineer, but no longer exercising his engineering duties. The hurricane had reduced him to a shipwrecked survivor, content to be a passive passenger, dressed in makeshift clothes supplied by the crew, who collectively had become host to his guarantee that he would be able to step on to dry land once again.

The other rescue ship, the *Proveedor,* sailed on to Montreal with the other seventeen of the surviving crew. They would soon be repatriated on the regular liner voyages from Montreal to Britain.

During its passage to Bermuda that day, every effort was made by the *Cuthbert Browne* to wireless information about the survivors to the authorities, shipping company, and next of kin.

The ship made good progress during the hours into darkness. A United States Air Force air-sea rescue boat from the Kindley air force base was ordered to meet the ship at sea, to avoid the necessity of its putting into harbour at Bermuda.

Under the command of Warrant Officer John Cameron, the boat kept the ocean rendezvous in the storm-tossed sea at about half past two in the early hours of the next morning, seven and a half miles east of St George's Harbour, Hamilton.

The rescue boat circled the *Cuthbert Browne*, closing onto its leeward side, but the heavy swell crashed the boat against the side of the freighter.

The two captains talked by wireless.

It would have been inviting a disaster to transfer the survivors in such conditions. The captains were anxious to play it safe.

The captain of the *Cuthbert Browne* decided to steam three miles closer to the shore and to calmer waters for a second attempt. At that new rendezvous the rescue boat managed to secure a line to the ship. A Jacob's ladder was thrown down from the freighter's deck onto the boat, watched intently by the eighteen survivors.

Once the formalities had been completed, Second Officer Charles Baker called out to his fellow crewmen first to throw down any personal belongings they carried and then scramble down the rope ladder. All survivors were safely transferred by four o'clock.

As the rescue boat detached its line to the freighter, the eighteen men in an assortment of clothing, standing together, raised three resounding cheers to the captain and crew of the Liberty ship, who had saved them. The *Cuthbert Browne* then turned away southwards for New Orleans.

In a short while the rescue boat reached shore at Hamilton, where the survivors stepped on to land at Kindley air force base, freed at last from their great ordeal.

Three officials of the Ennerman Company – Captain W. Holland, marine superintendent; P. Baldwin, naval architect;

and F. Stravan, engineer superintendent – had flown from England to welcome the survivors ashore. They gave each survivor sufficient money to kit himself out with new clothes and to cover his day to day expenses. Hamilton, the capital of Bermuda, was an ideal place to spend some money in shops used to catering for wealthy Americans.

Accumulated mail and telegraph messages for the crew were distributed, followed by a message from the Ennerman Company read out to the survivors by Chief Engineer Tim Denton, before they were all taken away for breakfast.

To the chagrin of the four officers among the group – Chief Engineer Tim Denton, Second Officer Charles Baker, Fourth Engineer Ray Williams, and Fifth Engineer Robin Spencer – the officers and the rest of the crew at first were separated. After a strong representation by the officers, all the crew were fetched back from the seamen's home to be reunited with their officers at their accommodation in the New Windsor Hotel.

Tim Denton had a surprise in the hotel when the receptionist handed him a message from London. Opening it feverishly, he just read the briefest of notes, *Contact the Bermuda Rotary Club.*

'It couldn't have said much less,' he said to himself, 'but it could have said a bit more – perhaps the club will have the full message.'

He made his way at the first opportunity to the club's address as fast as his tired legs would let him.

He was addressed by the receptionist. 'Good morning, sir, what can we do for you?'

'I came ashore in the night from my ship, which was wrecked in the storm. I have been told you have a message for me from London,' Tim explained.

'Oh, you are off the *Samqueen* then?' she queried. 'How wonderful to see you. The whole place has been on its tiptoes about it since we got messages from the rescue ship during the night.'

She was more interested in enjoying his salvation than in giving him the message. But what more could a shipwrecked man want, than to be welcomed?

'What is your name, sir?' she asked.

'Tim Denton,' Tim replied, presenting her with the official identity document issued to each survivor on the *Cuthbert Browne,* and his identity disc. 'I was chief engineer on the *Samqueen.* Now I have no ship.'

'All that matters is that you are safe,' she replied.

'We had a message from a source without a name from London. We were reimbursed to give you this bottle of rum and this money. Please sign for it here.'

The receptionist must have seen the transformation that came over his face as she spoke. He was nearly moved to tears.

'Are you happy with it, sir?' she asked.

'It's from my beloved darling. She must know about the shipwreck and now my survival. The bottle of rum has become a symbol between us.'

'You sound like a lucky man, although I could say she must be a lucky woman,' she replied. It brought a tired smile to Tim's face.

She made it her parting remark as Tim turned to leave the club. But he had second thoughts, reversing his movement. He spoke to her again, wanting to show his appreciation.

'You are being kind. I need a bit of a morale boost at the moment. By the way, can you direct me to a men's clothing store?'

'Yes, of course.' She directed him to two shops. 'They can supply everything you need between them, including underwear, socks, shoes, suits, and outer garments.'

Just then the manager of the club arrived and spoke to the receptionist. 'Tell the man who collects the bottle of rum that I would like to speak with him when he arrives. I hope I haven't missed him.'

'He is standing over there,' she told him.

The manager walked over to Tim. 'Good day, sir, I am pleased to meet you. I congratulate you on your survival. It was a nasty one. I have since had a second message from London. It was from a Vanessa Coles. She said she was acting on the stage of the Hippodrome, asking if you had arrived yet. She hoped you would be able to telephone her when it's convenient, perhaps after you have had a sleep, she insisted.'

'Thanks for the message,' Tim said.

'I have a favour to ask of you,' he went on. 'Would you be good enough to talk to the members at lunch today about the rescue? The club would be pleased to pay the cost of your telephone call to London in return.'

Tim thought for a moment, deciding that it was too good an offer to resist. It would be an expensive call to Vanessa in London. 'All right, I will go and get some clothes and see you at twelve o'clock.'

Tim had money to spend. The amount was sufficient to exploit the best shops in one of the most salubrious retreats and holiday spots for celebrities in the world, particularly for the purchase of clothing and footwear, which included the latest, fashionable, double-breasted grey suits.

Elegantly dressed, he attended the Rotary luncheon and addressed the members, before being taken on a privileged personal tour of Hamilton.

He returned to the club to make his phone call to Vanessa in time to talk with her before she went to bed. He was overcome with excitement as he made the contact.

'Vanessa, darling, this bottle of rum is safe and well,' were his first words to her. He was lost in his emotions. How could he say all the things that were in his heart about her that had kept him going, when all seemed lost?

'Thank God for that,' Vanessa replied. 'You gave me a very anxious time before the good news came through. I thought you were lost for all time but now you have been found. I cannot wait to hug you.'

She poured out her heart with such relief, bringing tears to Tim's eyes as it did to hers, in mutual rejoicing.

'I shall need to stay here for a while before returning to England,' he told her. 'There will be a delay before passages on a ship can be arranged. My time will be taken up for two days with various duties I have to perform and also to get my sleep back.'

'How long will it take to get a ship back?' she asked.

'At least a week, perhaps two,' he replied. 'Bermuda is not a major port of call for the shipping lines.'

The following morning the survivors visited St Paul's Church to honour the ten members of their crew who had been lost from the *Samqueen:* Wireless Officer J. Desmond, Able Seaman C. Latino, Able Seaman H. Southwark, Second Engineer J. McDonnell, Carpenter W. Walker, Greaser C. Jameson, Able Seaman S. McCall, Chief Steward P. Richmond, Able Seaman G. Thomas and Fireman F. Parker.

In the afternoon, the survivors met local dignitaries representing the seamen's home and customs service. Later, they attended the churchyard where Chief Engineer Tim Denton, on behalf of all the surviving crew, including those taken to Montreal, laid a wreath on the merchant marine seamen's vault. By the grave, the Reverend Frank Keats led a short memorial service in memory of their lost crew members and in gratitude for their own survival.

The following day, Tim relaxed with several others of the crew members. They were approached by a number of newspaper and radio reporters. He also had some time for sightseeing. The Ennerman Company representatives confirmed to the survivors that they would be picked up by a ship bound direct for Britain. It was due to leave Kingston, Jamaica, but it would be about a fortnight before it could call at Hamilton for them.

The next morning Tim was awakened by the ringing of his house phone.

'This is reception, sir. I'm sorry if I woke you up, but someone has just walked in who wants to see you, as soon as you can.'

'Is it another reporter?' he asked her.

'I do not know, sir,' she replied. 'They do work early hours these days. You just have to get used to being newsworthy at the moment.'

He reminded himself that he was chief engineer and a senior officer on the ship that he had left to founder in the ocean. He had to put a brave face on the disturbance. Reporters, too, had their job to do.

He spruced himself up and shaved in quick time.

Reporting to the hotel reception desk, he asked the receptionist where the caller who wished to see him had gone.

'Having a coffee. It was my suggestion, since I thought you were still in bed,' she replied. 'It gave you time to show you had fully recovered,' she quipped.

'Smart thinking, just the right thing to do, thanks,' he said to her. He walked from the foyer to the restaurant.

As he turned a corner he could not believe his eyes. Vanessa was striding out, coming back to the reception area.

In a second his eyes took in how beautiful she looked, if tired from her travel. She must have lost a lot of sleep, he thought, but she looked driven by hidden energy that could only mean one thing.

The mutual sighting let out a shriek from Vanessa and a 'My darling,' from Tim at the top of his voice, as they both broke into a run towards each other.

The minutes passed with such a grateful clinging, as if they were one body, in their favourite posture, dating from time immemorial.

'How on earth have you managed to get here, darling?' Tim asked, after getting his breath back. 'Don't say you have had to abandon the stage? What trouble you must have taken to get here so quickly.'

'No, of course not. Time for my understudy to shine,' Vanessa replied. 'I just had to see that you are safe, whatever the cost.'

'I can think of nothing more I could have wished for,' Tim exclaimed. 'In those terrible days having you in my head kept me going and hoping against hope that we would meet again. The lines of your song to me on the pavement in Liverpool kept going around and around in my head. "What storms may tear us apart. No sadness can kill the wonder and thrill of that waltz in my heart".'

'How long will you be able to stay?' he asked.

'I've got five days leave from the stage after today,' she said. 'But you have never flown before,' Tim said. 'Were you nervous?'

'Not nervous, but excited. It all went quite smoothly,' she replied. 'The main problem was getting a visa. Did you know the Americans introduced the visa after the war? The official at Ennerman's warned me I would have to get a visa if I contemplated going to see you. Fortunately, our flat is near their embassy in the West End. I had to go around there and wait until I laid my hands on it.'

'I shall be leaving by ship but in about two weeks,' Tim told her. 'We can enjoy the time together. Which way did you come?'

'Tortuous, three flights,' she told him. 'Did you know that commercial flights for civilians have only just resumed from Britain to the United States? The pre-war Imperial Airways and flying boat system has only this month been overtaken by

Pan Am, operating out of Herne Airport in Bournemouth, to La Guardia airport in New York. It went via Gander in Canada for refuelling and a stopover lasting several hours. The whole flight took eighteen hours altogether, flying in a Douglas DC4.'

'No wonder you are exhausted,' Tim expressed his concern. 'I've never heard of that aircraft before. Was it comfortable?'

'Apparently, it's a development from the DC3 from the wartime, designed and constructed for long flights. It had four engines and manufactured with proper seats for civilian use,' she replied.

'How did you get out here? It's over eight hundred miles out into the Atlantic,' Tim reminded her. 'You had to take another flight to get you here in time.'

'Yes, from New York I had to fly in a DC3. It took about four hours. But here I am, but I'm not sure yet whether my spirit has caught up with my body yet.' They moved on into the reception area.

On the way past the receptionist, Tim threw her an accolade. 'You did a very good job concealing my visitor's identity. You had me guessing. I fully expected to see another reporter looking for my story.'

'I can see you are a lucky pair,' she called back. 'Good luck to you both.'

Over breakfast in his room, they exchanged their news and comments. A lot had accumulated since they had last been together.

Her career in the interim had been firmly consolidated, while Tim's had come to an untimely end.

They didn't linger long over breakfast.

'You must have some sleep, darling,' he said to her. 'I will stand watch,' he assured her. 'And promise not to fall asleep.'

'I don't need a watchdog,' she replied. 'I expect you can do with more sleep yourself. You couldn't have slept on the shipwreck, could you? Anyway, who said you go to bed to sleep?'

They didn't need a second bidding to place the Do Not Disturb sign outside their door and embrace between the sheets.

Sometime later, sleep claimed them. For nearly nine hours they made up for their dire previous lack of rest, compounded as it was by the expenditure of their stored-up energy, that just had to be dissipated in their love for each other.

When she awoke, Vanessa's first word was a recognition of her lover's caring. 'How can a shipwreck be so empowering?' she declared. 'Your prowess is as undiminished as ever.'

'And your allure is as alive as it always will be for me,' Tim breathed, as he squeezed her to him. 'And where do you get the energy from after your long trip?' he asked.

'Same as you. Saved and safeguarded,' she said, poking him in the ribs.

The rest of the day was spent lazily. But they decided the next day they should take advantage of being in an out of the way place. 'It is unlikely we shall ever be here again,' Vanessa said. 'We must go somewhere special to mark the occasion.'

17

When Tim went back to the reception desk to enquire about sightseeing they could do together, the receptionist greeted him with another message. It was from a former undergraduate friend of his from Cambridge days. It invited Tim to the Turks Islands. His friendly note was quite persuasive.

'Tim, I have heard about the disaster. It may seem a long way between Bermuda and the Turks Islands but you are in this part of the world and unlikely to be here again. Please come if only for two or three days. It will be a refreshing experience for you after your terrible ordeal and nice for us to have visitors.'

He showed it to Vanessa.

'I've just been handed this note from an old friend, who wants us to visit him on the Turks Islands. Do you know where they are?' Tim asked her.

'Never heard of them. But I think Bermuda is isolated. So, they would have to be a good way from here,' Vanessa replied.

They consulted the receptionist again. She fetched a map.

'You would have to go back to New York, then to Miami, then from there to Nassau in the Bahamas, and finally a shorter flight to Grand Turk. I can explore the possibilities for you if you want to do it,' she said.

'What do you think, darling?' Tim asked Vanessa.

They looked for the location of the Turks Islands. The receptionist told them it would take four flights to get them there – New York, Miami, Nassau, and Grand Turk.

'Well, it would use up my return flight to New York, which I have to do anyway. It's one of the longest legs of the total journey the receptionist is indicating,' Vanessa ventured. 'Why don't we look into it. It does seem a chance not to be missed.'

In perusing the map, Tim noticed that Kingston in Jamaica, was closer to the Turks Islands than Bermuda. 'I wonder if I could get on the ship in Kingston,' he said to Vanessa. 'I shall have to explore the possibility. It has only just occurred to me.'

She enthused about the idea. 'Give it a try', she said.

He contacted the Ennerman Company representatives, asking permission to board the ship, scheduled to take him back to Britain, at Kingston, rather than Bermuda. The unusual request was explained by the arrival of Vanessa and the invitation from his friend, who was in the diplomatic service. Accordingly, he wanted to take advantage of the opportunity, which would be at his own expense up to boarding the ship at Kingston.

Their answer was in the positive, although they quibbled over the additional fare from Kingston to Bermuda, but eventually conceded that the company would pay.

Vanessa and Tim found themselves facing the expedition with a little apprehension. Tim was making his first ever flight, Vanessa her fourth – with the stopover at Gander counting as two. They would both be amassing more flights in as many days on their planned trip, including their first flight together.

Consequently, they set off at their earliest possible time for their intrepid journey, fraught not so much by the distance but by the novelty, infrequency, and slowness of the flights involved.

The novelty of flight for them was extended when they reached Nassau. Having booked their flight in an aircraft carrying twelve passengers to the Turks Islands from Nassau, they found that smaller aircraft had less stability in the air. It could be a more upsetting way to fly than in the larger airliners. Nevertheless, they were having a taste of the unfolding post-war life that would take flying for granted, opening up distant destinations to masses of people and making those faraway places as familiar as their own hometowns.

The Turks Islands, with the larger Caicos Group, formed one of the British territories in the general area of the West Indies and Caribbean Sea. Full of anticipation for their local expedition, they flew to Grand Turk Island, the largest of the Turks Islands. Grand Turk – and the much smaller Salt Cay – were the only inhabited islands in the group.

At that time, Grand Turk's inhabitants were numbered by a total of only a few more than one thousand people and Salt Cay by less than one hundred. They were exceptionally small islands, Grand Turk being a long, north-to-south island of six plus, and Salt Cay two plus, square miles.

It was exceptional for the islands to have visitors.

The British administrator on Grand Turk welcomed them in the tiny inhabited area, later to be called Cockburn Town, on the south-west coast. His official house, of wooden construction, was in little better condition than any of the other local properties. But the weather was warm enough for outdoor living and the preferred place to be.

He explained that the islands were currently a constitutional dependency of Jamaica. He was responsible for the governance of the Turks Islands to the governor of Jamaica.

Tim took the opportunity at that point to discover how he would be able to travel to Kingston at the conclusion of his visit. Vanessa would simply reverse her journey by the same flights back to New York by which they had both arrived.

The administrator surprised Tim. 'That is no problem. I go to Kingston once a month. You are welcome to travel with me and it won't cost you anything.'

'Thank you, sir, that is a wonderful bonus for me. I am grateful.'

Tim's former friend, who had sent the invitation, was the deputy administrator. He took them first to the north of the island to visit the only hospital, which was in the hands of Matron Molly Layton, a British qualified nurse. Then they visited the little school between the hospital and the capital being run by a male British teacher, its sole member of staff.

They were driven around the island for those and further trips in a pre-war, ancient Morris 8 by the assistant administrator. There were no paved roads. Scattered over the tracks were conch shells and other debris, constantly disturbed by the wind that dislodged the flat, desert-like surface of the island.

Lunch with the administrator and his assistant was fully occupied with their respective life stories. It was one of the most entertaining meetings over lunch Tim and Vanessa had ever experienced. They were all able to talk freely about their background and careers.

The administrator told them about his time in Japanese captivity, following his capture as a minor member of the diplomatic staff in Singapore. His assistant had graduated from Cambridge University, taking his appointment in Grand Turk as his first substantial posting in the foreign service, after discharging several previous, proving, elementary jobs in several countries.

The administrator assumed that they would be staying for a night or two. 'You ought to have a swim in the delightful waters nearby. Later in the day I will fix up a seat on the plane to take you back to Nassau on the day you prefer, Vanessa. Tomorrow morning it would be great fun to go over to Salt Cay.'

'Is there a hotel here where we can get a room?' Vanessa asked.

'Oh, don't worry about that,' he replied. 'You are welcome to stay here in Government House. As my deputy invited you to come, we both assumed you would stay with us. As a matter of fact, there are no hotels as such. The United States has a small base on the south tip of the island. A few places provide accommodation for their visitors and family, but they are far from the hotels that you are thinking of.'

With their arrangements satisfactorily made, Vanessa and Tim walked a few steps towards the nearby seashore.

With no one in sight, they stripped off and swam in the sea from a narrow, gently sloping sandy beach. The water was proverbially crystal clear and unbelievably placid.

They were standing in the sea, up to their waists only ten feet from the shoreline, when Tim suddenly alerted Vanessa. 'Stand still. But turn around. Look to the shore.'

She did so and exclaimed with surprise. 'What is that – a shark?'

'Don't move,' Tim reminded her. 'It's a stingray. They seem to be fond of following the shoreline. It's a big one, isn't it?'

'And the water is so clear you can see it so well,' Vanessa said.

They watched it slowly pass them, foraging as it went by, and gradually moving out of sight.

The next morning, they boarded a very small plane, with two passenger seats, to fly for fifteen minutes over the ocean waters of the Turks Island Passage to Salt Cay. It was a low altitude flight. They saw nothing on the water, nor in the air. It was as if they had the Caribbean to themselves.

The plane landed on a simple beach airstrip, close to the settlement which would later sport the title of Balfour Town. As they went into land they were momentarily disturbed to see a plane, similar to the one in which they were flying, crashed on the beach.

Tim and Vanessa walked over to the makeshift, tumbledown building, where fishing vessels brought in their catch. On the simple quayside they saw the biggest fish they had ever seen in their lives.

The administrator had arranged for a local man to show them around. He explained that the fish was a shark. It was about eight feet in length. It had somehow become caught in fishing nets. The fishermen had dragged it back into the harbour.

The local children, assisted by the fishermen had then killed the shark by throwing lumps of coral rock at it.

'What will happen to it?' Vanessa asked their guide.

'Some people eat it. You have to clean shark meat very thoroughly. They urinate through their skin, so it is easy to eat tainted meat if it has not been cleaned properly,' he replied. 'But people get used to eating it and have no difficulty in preparing it for a meal.'

Vanessa spied a crude notice declaring one word: Lavatories.

'Where are they?' she asked Tim. 'I need one.'

'I'm sorry,' he replied. 'I have never been here before.'

They both laughed at his humour but more at the reality, which they quickly grasped. Lavatories were evidently notorious by their absence.

The lavatory consisted of one wide plank with four holes cut at equal intervals along it, suspended at each end but hanging directly over the water of the harbour.

'That's the most economical and efficient lavatory I have ever seen,' declared Vanessa. 'It's a good job the weather is warm throughout most of the year.'

'You certainly have to come prepared,' Tim added. They both laughed at the innuendo in his remark.

The guide then took them on a tour of the tiny island in a small, decrepit car – one of only two vehicles on the island.

It was boiling hot. The temperatures seemed to be amplified when they came to the salt pans which were the reason for the island's inhabitance.

The pans were extensive, once occupying the entire island.

Tim and Vanessa were intrigued by an area where harvested salt had been piled up like mountains. It resembled the snows and ice of the Arctic, with which Tim had been acquainted during his war service. To Vanessa, it was a novel and impressive sight.

It was a white wonderland, frightfully reflecting the powerful rays of the sun. The interaction of the sunlight and the salt mountains, some standing ten or fifteen feet high, was too overpowering for their eyes, compelling the use of their sunglasses.

They saw the second vehicle on Salt Cay – an even more decrepit, small truck. It was used to move the salt on the site itself and to the nearby harbour only two hundred yards away.

It never had to travel far. There were no paved roads. But the truck was completely covered in rust from the single freight it had always carried.

They were astounded to see an old man, who had evidently been born and bred on the island, whose entire life had been shaped and cultured by salt, walking on the white substance, dressed only in a tattered pair of short trousers and a straw hat. His body was burnt black by the sunlight over the years. The skin on his feet was so thick it provided him with ready-made boots.

It was his home, his job, and his purpose for living.

Soon the visitors took their leave of the guide. Vanessa and Tim returned to Grand Turk in the light plane for Vanessa's last night. Her time of parting was fast approaching.

Next day Vanessa began her long journey back home, travelling alone. She took the four-hundred-mile flight in the small aircraft back to Nassau on New Providence Island, as the first of her four-sector flight back to Britain.

18

The *Samqueen* continued to confound the expectations of the surviving members of its crew, the crews of the rescue ships, and the maritime authorities. The day after its remaining hulk was left to sink, the *Berndon,* bound for Baltimore from Marseilles, fortuitously came across the ship, still wallowing in its severely listed trim and with no signs of life on it.

The *Berndon*'s mystified crew reported the wreck's position. Several salvage tugs also picked up the message. Sensing a spectacular salvage possibility, three tugs were soon on their way towards the reported position. The Dutch tug *Wadden Zee,* which had just arrived at New York harbour, soon found that two rivals from a Canadian port had also abandoned their current activities to join in the search. They were the *Patsy,* a smaller, coastal tug, and the *Christine,* an ocean-going tug.

The *Patsy* won the race to reach the *Samqueen* first. Its crew were astounded to see the posture of the ship, high in the water, but almost on its port side – with about ten feet of the starboard hull below the bilge keel actually clear of the waves. The *Patsy*'s crew eventually boarded the abandoned Liberty ship, attaching the Canadian red duster – the civil ensign of the merchant service – and their firm's flag to the wreck.

They noted the sea around the stricken ship was alive with sharks.

Captain Vernon Cranwell, master of the *Christine,* reported that his tug had sailed to a point eight hundred and twenty miles east of Bermuda. After searching the area for the wreck, they sighted the *Patsy* and the *Samqueen* in the early hours of Monday morning. His crewmen boarded the ship with burning gear for welding the towing chains.

It was a difficult operation. The *Samqueen* was rolling about in the very high seas. Finally, everything was accomplished. The tow began using only one line, eventually reaching six knots. The prize money for the *Samqueen* was fixed at one hundred and sixty-five thousand pounds sterling, a major rating for its time.

The *Christine* had taken the *Samqueen* in tow just before midday on the third day from the end of May, accompanied by the *Patsy,* choosing to head for Bermuda, eight hundred miles away. The choice of Bermuda was in preference to Newfoundland, also at eight hundred, or Halifax at nine hundred, or New York at eleven hundred miles distance, each of which alternatives posed more insuperable problems of navigation and weather conditions than towing to Bermuda.

In the early afternoon on a day a week later in early June, the *Samqueen* was manoeuvred by the *Christine,* assisted by the *Patsy* and a local tug, into the two-mile-long Murray's Anchorage at Hamilton, Bermuda, where its unwieldy size and buoyancy in the sea made very difficult handling problems for the tugs. Eventually, the ship was attached to a battleship mooring.

Its arrival was the signal for animated and protracted disputes between the authorities, the owners, and the salvage company, lasting for several days.

The three officials from the Ennerman Company found it impossible to walk on the deck of the *Samqueen*. The main deck was washed clean. Scattered personal debris from the crew was lodged in nooks and crannies, flung or wedged there by crew members as they emptied their pockets to maximise their buoyancy in the sea, before jumping overboard.

The gunwales of the ship were freely littered with hurriedly cast-off clothes and shoes, including jackets with their owners' effects still in their pockets. In the cabins, all the personal belongings of the crew had been ripped into complete disarray. Cascading out of open doors was a mass of clothes, plates, knives and forks, and half packed kit-bags and holdalls. Pictures looked crooked but were still straight, in relation to their walls, while furniture lay everywhere, overturned, or piled up, damaged, smashed to pieces, or in distorted shapes. Jettisoned bars of chocolate, tins of sweets, books, diaries, razors, rubber boots, and photographs littered the cabins and companionways everywhere. Everything was wringing wet. The smell of fish assailed the entire environment. The macabre inside of the ship, where order and the lively activities of a large crew had once dominated the scene, was as still as death.

They found four feet of water swilling around the machinery in the engine room. Ropes and Jacob's ladders hung without purpose on the exposed starboard hull of the ship; the means by which many crewmen had escaped into the sea.

Within days, a new hurricane threatened Bermuda. The moorings of the *Samqueen* on the battleship fixture and those of the remaining tug *Christine* were doubled in anticipation of the storm. Winds reached one hundred and forty miles per hour, mercilessly battering the two vessels until both were wrenched apart from their moorings and driven onto coral reefs. The *Samqueen*'s rudder was torn off and new holes punctured in its hull, admitting a flood of more water into the ship.

When the hurricane blew itself out, urgent engineering steps were taken to prepare the *Samqueen* to be seaworthy enough for towing to a major shipyard for comprehensive repairs. In preparation for that voyage, the rest of its ballast was unloaded, the sea water in the ship was pumped out, and the holes in its hull were filled in with concrete. This effective emergency treatment enabled the tugs to slide the ship slowly clear of the coral and towed to a dock in St George's Harbour, Hamilton.

Five days later at noon, the ship left Bermuda in tow for New York. The weather northwards, however, was stormy enough to flood the *Samqueen* again, the sea eventually penetrating through the temporary concrete patching. It was serious enough for the tow to be diverted to Newport News, Virginia, arriving in the afternoon of the last day of June. Later, it was moved the short distance to Baltimore, Maryland, where complete repairs were to be carried out.

The *Samqueen* was a ship that just would not die. Its salvage, repairs, and the thorough investigation of its hazardous voyage marked a milestone in maritime history, particularly in terms of the conditions and dimensions of loading ballast. The inquiry into the event suggested that the provision of lifebelts, whistles, lights, and other aids for the crew would have facilitated their rescue and probably saved the lives of those lost.

Ironically, the *Samqueen,* in finally moving to Baltimore for repairs during the later months of 1946, had returned to its place of birth, the original shipyards where it had been completed in December 1943. It had led an eventful life of three years.

19

Without further delay, the *Samqueen*'s owners arranged passages for the seventeen survivors, who had been brought ashore in Bermuda, to begin their return journey to the United Kingdom. They would embark on the SS *Orbita*, due to leave Kingston, Jamaica, nearly two weeks later.

Tim Denton, as the eighteenth survivor, embarked on the ship before it left Kingston, and was able to welcome the rest of the survivors on board when it arrived in Bermuda. The ship was a somewhat ageing ocean liner of just under fifteen thousand, five hundred tons, launched before the first year of the First World War, for the Pacific Steam Navigation Company, by Harland & Wolff in Belfast.

During the Second World War the *Orbita* was engaged as a troopship. After the war, the *Orbita* began transporting emigrants to Australia and New Zealand, before playing an important part in the immigration policy of the United Kingdom. The *Orbita* was therefore in familiar waters when picking up the survivors.

Consequently, Tim Denton found himself in a ship already full of immigrants when he went on board in Kingston. It arrived in Bermuda to pick up the main group of the survivors, who joined the first large group of West Indian immigrants to arrive in Britain.

The disbursement of money to the surviving crew members had been enough to ensure their clothing and footwear were adequate for the journey. Everybody involved was brought up to date with developments. The *Samqueen*'s owners had promptly informed each survivor's next of kin of the arrangements for the return of his or her family member or friend to Britain.

The survivors, who joined the immigrant passengers, felt, like them, that they were sailing into a new life, if not a new land. Arriving at Liverpool, the survivors virtually had no luggage to present to the customs. Their ad hoc landing cards told nothing of their ordeal.

Despite being shipwrecked, they were subject to the formalities of landing in the United Kingdom without documentation, other than the survival certificates given to each man on the *Cuthbert Browne* and the Immigration Regulations Landing Card issued on the *Orbita*.

On disembarkation, Tim made for Lime Street railway station where he found he had about six hours to wait for the next train to London. He went to a pub to fill in some of the time.

When he later left the pub, he saw a large open space opposite the station. It had been created by clearing a large bomb-damaged building from the wartime blitz on the city. He learned that on the site there had once been a Lyons Corner House, a two-storey Mecca for teas, with a spacious restaurant and dancing floor. The Lyons Corner Houses were popular in

London and the great cities in the interwar period, lasting for a decade after the war.

The cleared site had been adopted as a form of Speakers' Corner, the internationally famous locus of free speech adjacent to Marble Arch on the edge of Hyde Park in London. Several entertainers and speakers were using the site at the time. Some were demonstrating their skills in acrobatics or juggling to entertain the crowd.

Tim used part of the waiting time to visit the Royal Court Theatre. He simply stood outside on the spot where Vanessa had sung to him. Then he wandered into the foyer to remind himself of the very first time he had set eyes on her at the little coffee table.

He was a little surprised at himself taking such a sentimental journey. The thoughts that raced through his mind as he did so gave him an emotional boost that brought a tear to his eyes. He truly loved Vanessa.

It was time for his train. The company had booked Tim into a hotel in London, but he eschewed the booking and made his way to Vanessa's flat, which she had purchased by that time in expectation of a more extended professional connection with the West End theatre world.

He awaited her return from the Hippodrome.

They were deeply moved to be together again. Their relief and underlying fatigue were finally assuaged by the most relaxing sleep either had had since the beginning of the shipwreck.

They were home in more senses than one.

As a survivor of the epic *Samqueen* disaster, Tim was temporarily a newsworthy item. Several newspapers approached him for his account of the shipwreck.

Once they found out that Vanessa Coles was his partner, their interest doubled. Photographs of them together appeared in two magazines with joint interviews, incidentally providing free publicity for *Perchance to Dream* and a further boost to Vanessa's career.

20

Britain was still in recovery mode from the dislocation of the Second World War. Service men and women were streaming home from foreign parts. Together with those in domestic postings, everyone was desperate to be demobilised, fortified by hopes of a better life, employment opportunities, and a prosperous future.

There were many job vacancies to be filled.

The industrial unrest, which had surprisingly plagued the war effort in some occupations, was fed by a widespread mood among the demobbed service men and women that the pre-war social and economic structure must be left behind.

Attempts to jettison many former practices and attitudes – in an effort to break their continuity – even led to militant action, steered by anti-establishment attitudes and foreign sympathies.

Notably, ports were disrupted by the strike action of dockers, particularly in London and Southampton.

Tim and Vanessa enjoyed their life together for about ten days, during which time they took the train from Paddington to Swindon to see both sets of parents. Between them they had a whole host of memories to share in both homes.

'Telling my story time and time again certainly rivets it on my mind for ever,' Tim remarked to Vanessa one day.

'You had better watch that it doesn't become embellished with telling it so often then,' she warned.

'I don't think there is any danger of exaggerating anything,' he told her. 'It will always be impossible to convey the feelings of being in the pitch darkness of the night and battered by the untamed waves. It was so long, drawn out and terrifying that every conceivable embellishment that could be imagined had already become embodied in reality.'

'I can understand that,' said Vanessa. 'When I look at you, my heart jumps with anguish when I think of what you went through. I only hope it was a once in a lifetime experience. That must be enough for any mariner. I don't think I could stand the strain of something like that again,' Vanessa said tenderly.

Vanessa had only limited time off from her endless round of appearing in nightly performances on stage, rehearsals, and business engagements. Tim was busy making visits to the Ennerman Lines offices for discussions on the loading and usage of ballast, as well as negotiating for the next seagoing appointment. They savoured their free time together.

The remaining months of the year allowed Vanessa and Tim to share her flat, while he took a succession of limited voyages from Tilbury to North Sea and Mediterranean ports, usually as chief engineer, but sometimes standing in to fill a vacancy in the engineer ranks.

It was in January of the following year that he heard that the *Samqueen* had been refitted to seaworthy standards and would soon be ready for sea again.

'Do you think the company will invite you to join another crew for it?' Vanessa asked Tim when he relayed the news.

'I just do not know,' he replied. 'But I think something is in the offing.'

The company called him to an interview. A senior official, Colin Smithson, explained the situation.

'You probably know already that the *Samqueen* is ready to leave the shipyards. It will be given short sea trials when we have crewed it up, before it returns to London,' he began.

'Yes, I have heard. It's the sort of news that everybody wants to hear, yet no one wants to welcome,' Tim said.

'Yes, I know what you mean,' he told Tim. 'It's a wonderful thing to recover a badly damaged ship but crewmen might regard it as an unlucky ship.'

'At the moment, we don't know how easy it will be to get a full crew for the ship, but we are going to man it from London,' he continued.

'Some seamen think it bad luck to take a twice floated ship, but others don't care a cuss about that sort of thing,' Tim commented.

'What about you, then, Mr Denton? Would you be happy to be offered a position on it again?'

'Yes, of course, but I shall soon be looking for some kind of advancement. I would be happy to join the new crew on the ship again, at least in the interim,' Tim declared.

'The ship will be renamed, of course… ' Colin Smithson continued.

'It should be called "unsinkable",' Tim interrupted him.

'… yes,' he said, and they both laughed.

'The new name will be *Stormguard*,' he informed Tim.

'That sounds very appropriate,' Tim commented.

'We have hoped you would be willing to join the crew,' Colin Smithson said. 'We don't expect to recruit many, if any, of the former crew. Most have got other jobs now, anyway.'

'Depends on whether I can keep my current job in the company as chief engineer,' Tim said cautiously.

'There is no doubt about that, but something unusual has cropped up,' came the unexpected reply. 'We have had a communication from the Admiralty. It was one of those requests – "if you are interested, please do it". Underlying the request was an implication rather like a covert order for us to take action, but with deference to the wishes of the individuals involved. We have been asked to give any ex-navy officers an experience in another branch of ship management other than the one they are qualified for. We were left with the option to select men we thought suitable for it. You are one of the men on our books we wanted to consult.'

'Why do you think they have taken this step?' asked Tim.

'You can speculate as well as we can,' the official replied. 'There is always a reason. The navy has discharged so many men who have then left the sea. But even as we are unwinding from the war, there appears to be disquieting news from various parts of the world that might impact on the navy's ability to respond as fully as they might wish to do. It's a bit like the years before 1939 when Britain was not as well prepared as they might have been to take on the implications of declaring war on Germany.'

'What did you have in mind for me, then, on the *Stormguard*?' asked Tim.

'You are an experienced engineer and former senior officer of the ship, so we would second you to the crew as second mate. The chief mate would be your mentor. There will be two third mates who will be informed of the arrangement,' the official explained. 'You do not have to make up your mind right here and now, but we would like to know your answer within, say, forty-eight hours.'

'When would this be put into effect, from the shipyards or later? By the way, who will the captain be?' Tim questioned.

'Derek Rhodes is taking the captaincy again,' Tim was informed. 'You would be chief engineer from the shipyards to Tilbury. The captain would not hear of any other arrangement. It is expected that you would take the new job as second mate for the ship's first long voyage to New Zealand from Tilbury. We hope to appoint an alternative chief engineer to replace you and an experienced chief mate to be your mentor.'

'This is all rather sudden. But I will let you know by the deadline you have given me.' Tim stood up to leave the office, while the official took on an informal demeanour.

'By the way, I saw *Perchance to Dream* last weekend. Someone told me that your partner was Vanessa Coles. I have to say what a wonderful voice she has, and her acting was superb. Please give her my thanks and best wishes.'

'I will, and thanks for the compliments,' Tim responded and went on his way, proud in his heart and exalted by the company man's remarks.

When Tim welcomed Vanessa home after the show, they kissed and cuddled for a while. They were usually silent during those nuptials, but Tim was itching to tell her his news.

'How did it go tonight, darling?' Tim asked. 'You must be getting used to it from habit by now. I often wonder how moved the actors are on stage when the night's audience makes such an original and sincere response to the performance.'

'Professionalism for me means treating each and every performance as if it were the first. There is always some small nuance of improvement I can make. I always remember the audience is new. I sing and act to them as new people. They are there to be entertained and charmed. Nothing but the best will do,' Vanessa replied.

'You have spoken like a hardened professional, but I know you mean it. It happens to be in tune with a very nice compliment from one of the top officials of the Ennerman Company today,' Tim reported.

'But did they give you a job?' Vanessa intervened.

'Not about me, about you,' was Tim's swift rejoinder.

'Yes, there will be something for us to discuss,' Tim continued. 'He had recently been to see the show. Someone had told him about us. He waxed eloquent about your singing and acting. You are one of the very best according to him. He actually congratulated me. I am not sure whether that was for your performance or for our liaison. I began to think he thought you were in some way part of his company.'

Vanessa said laughingly, 'I think that might have to be another day. I've heard of ageing prima donnas getting lucrative jobs on liners and trying to perpetuate their fame, long after it has passed them by.'

'As long as they can still sing in tune,' Tim said, making them both laugh. He saw the funny side of the proposition. 'Just imagine,' he suggested, 'a tuned-up piano but a singer slightly off pitch. Nothing could be more excruciating than such a discordant duet.'

'It's a hopeless dream for a young career woman to have,' Vanessa told him. 'It might be useful one day when you run out of income, or when the stage won't have me back.'

'When we are old and grey. But you will still have a voice then, my darling,' Tim added. 'I shall only be able to make a noise like a duck's quacking.'

'But you said there was something to discuss. What is it?' she asked.

'Apparently,' Tim said, 'the navy has been privately nudging the major companies to widen the experience of selected former naval officers. No reasons have been given. The circumstances are that we have all been trying to get out of the Second World War.

'Demobilisation and withdrawal of some ships from front line service have preoccupied the navy. But, of course, life with all its upheavals goes on. New ships are being built. Someone must have watched developments of policy around the world and come to the conclusion that we have to be vigilant again.'

'So soon?' Vanessa expostulated. 'Surely everyone is glad that the war has ended and is looking only for peace.'

'You would think so,' Tim agreed. 'But it seems that whispers about the potential difficulties lying ahead seem to be radiating behind the scenes in the intelligent services and power centres of the military.'

'But how can that have any bearing on what the company has asked you to do?' queried Vanessa. 'I don't see any point or purpose between the two.'

'It takes long training and seagoing experience to provide senior officers for ships. That goes for merchant ships as well as navy vessels. That is why after initial training and shore studies, you join a ship as a fifth engineer or cadet deck officer, to work your way up the ladder of experience in command at sea,' Tim explained. 'The idea behind the navy's request is to broaden the command experience of ex-navy men still at sea but in the merchant navy.'

'But how can that be of interest to the navy. Surely, they have demobbed hundreds of senior people?' she asked, beginning to suspect the worst.

'Demobbed men have been out of service now for various lengths of time. Most have chosen not to sail the seas, some will be sick or have died,' Tim answered.

'I'm getting there,' said Vanessa. 'They would recall you to the navy. Is that what you are going to say?'

'It's a question of having reserves. If there is a conflict and the navy runs short of officers I might be called on,' Tim confirmed.

'So, what will you be doing that's different?' Vanessa wanted to know.

'I shall be chief engineer until the ship arrives in Tilbury,' Tim replied. 'But I will take over my new job as second officer, known as second mate in the profession, for a voyage to Wellington, New Zealand. The chief or first officer will supervise me. I already have an understanding of the scope of responsibilities involved, but it's a question of actually discharging them satisfactorily. I have to become familiar with and prove my competence in coping with the varying ups and downs of reality that a ship goes through on any voyage. Two third officers will also be appointed.'

'What is the job?' she asked him.

'Any functions that are not mechanical or electrical. They are responsibilities lying with the engineers. It's really the rest of running the ship – cargo loading, storage, unloading, supplies and stores for the ship, handling of anchors, derricks, management of the crew, disputes, and importantly taking turns all round the clock to maintain watches on the bridge,' Tim said, listing the main categories of the job. 'If the captain became ill, the chief deck officer – or first mate as he is generally known – would take over.'

'What are the watches?' Vanessa questioned from his list. 'I've never been clear what it means.'

Tim continued his explanation.

'It means being on duty on the bridge, keeping an eye on everything on behalf of the captain. A captain cannot be awake twenty-four hours a day, every day for a long voyage. Besides, he has other things to attend to on the ship and needs time off in his cabin and for meals. If a ship has only one third officer, the chief officer will be on watch from four o'clock in the early morning, until eight in the evening, as well as doing his executive duties. The second and third officers would cover the rest of the twenty-four hours between them, from eight in the evening until midnight, and from midnight to four in the morning.

'If two third officers are carried, the chief becomes a dayworker, carrying out his work in general from eight in the morning until five o'clock in the afternoon.

'In that case, the second officer will do the watch duty from four o'clock early in the morning until eight in the evening. It is a tradition arising from the second officer's duties to fix the ship's position from the stars for sunrise and sunset. He is also responsible for the ship's charts, publications, all navigational equipment, gyrocompass, and the ship's log, recording the type of cargo and tonnage, time in port, time at sea, pilotage of the ship, and any unusual factor, such as a hurricane or other event involving the ship. The senior third officer does the midnight to four watch, the junior third officer completes the twenty-four-hour watch duty by doing the eight in the evening to midnight watch. The third officers are responsible for handling the ship, regularly fixing its position, and piloting the ship in coastal waters. The senior third officer must also prepare the position data of the ship at noon daily for the captain and chief engineer.'

'You have overwhelmed me. Sailing a ship sounds so complicated. I never dreamed there was so much to it. Why does the chief engineer need to know those data?' Vanessa shrewdly asked.

'Mostly for checking fuel consumption and because he is the ship's senior officer next to the captain and first deck officer,' Tim replied. 'He needs to know the critical facts all the time.'

'I can see that you are caught in a web, not of your own making,' Vanessa concluded. 'But we really have to face each difficulty as it comes up. You will be away on the New Zealand voyage for at least three months. It will make me feel like a singleton again, although I always tell myself that every day you are away is one day nearer your return. The navy part might never happen, so let's not worry about that.'

21

Tim was given a date to report to the crew assembly office at the shipyards in Baltimore, Maryland in the United States, together with a ticket for a free passage to the port of Baltimore on one of Ennerman's passenger freighters, the newly launched *City of Pretoria*. He looked forward to a relaxing week of travel, with time to study various documents on the responsibilities of deck officers in merchant ships, supplied by the company, as opposed to the duties of engineer officers.

On the second day after leaving Tilbury, he met on board one of his former colleagues, another survivor from the *Samqueen,* who had been taken to Canada by his rescue ship. Tim had gone to the main dining room for dinner, early enough to have a chat with a few other passengers and a cocktail.

The passengers began to be seated for the meal when they were joined by the ship's representative for the evening. He was Norman Gale, who had been the third deck officer on the fated *Samqueen.*

At first, Norman failed to recognise Tim, dressed like any other male passenger, but Tim saw that he had been promoted to second officer, and assumed that he had just finished his long watch.

A round of formal introductions followed.

They didn't get very far when Norman's and Tim's eyes met, instantly with joyous recognition. But it was not the place to demonstrate other than normal conduct for a dinner gathering of people who were strangers to each other. And, of course, there could be no reference to their former experience in a shipwreck.

Passengers want to be entertained with glib talk, humorous banter, and exploits at sea, but not from the fear and suffering that disasters can bring.

Tim was always a good listener. For his own contribution to the bonhomie of the occasion, he recounted his boyhood record of delivering medicines to aged or infirm people for Vanessa's father in Swindon during wartime.

'That sounds like a straightforward little job for any young man to do,' an attractive woman opposite him on the wide table levelled at him. 'Don't say you got up to any fancy antics with it.'

'My worst moments were causing the neatly wrapped bottles of physic to cascade across the street,' Tim told her. 'It happened on several occasions.'

'How did you manage to do that?' another woman asked.

'I had to put the bottles in a small saddlebag, attached to the seat of my bike, fixed at the back of the saddle behind me. The bottles were heavy and my saddlebag was pretty old. A few times, when I took the bend from one street to another at a reckless speed, the bottles chose to slip out of the bag and keep going in the same direction. It was very embarrassing for me to return to the doctor's little pharmacy with my tail between my legs and confess my sins.'

'The old folks must have been grateful to have their medicines delivered to their door,' the first woman continued.

'Yes, they were, and sometimes too grateful,' Tim said laughing.

'What do you mean?' she queried.

'Sometimes the patients were not that old. They had been ill but recovered enough to be mischievous. One day when I knocked on the door of a house, a woman's voice from inside called out, "Come in, please". I went in to find a younger woman standing naked. I actually dropped her medicine on the floor in fright but the carpet prevented the bottle from breaking.'

'You must have thought your day had come,' she said.

'It was the first time I had ever seen a naked woman. It scared the life out of me. It was not part of the job.'

She laughed heartily and then said, 'I bet you wouldn't drop the bottle now. Or would you put it into her hand carefully.'

'I was only fourteen at the time,' Tim said, ignoring her provocative suggestion.

After dinner, the passengers dispersed. Tim and Norman Gale couldn't wait to get away to have their secret talk together.

'Norman, it's great to see you again. Where did you get to?' Tim spoke first. 'Was it plain sailing to Montreal? You certainly had plenty of ships to choose from to go back to Britain.'

'Yes, it was fairly straightforward. We reached Canada, had a wash and brush up in a nice hotel at the company's expense and then took a ship back home,' Norman said, but didn't elaborate. He was a man of few words at the best of times.

'But how about you?' he asked. 'We heard stories of further cyclones that you were trapped in.'

Tim filled him in briefly but hurried on to ask him about his promotion to second officer. 'When did it happen?'

'I did several short voyages quite quickly on returning. But after that the company informed me that the navy was interested in giving suitable former naval officers exposure to wider experience. But I turned it down. I think the Ennerman Company calculated that if, in the near future, the navy takes away any senior crewmen from company employment, they might end up becoming short of seasoned officers themselves. So, they promoted me, anyway, and here I am.'

'It's a good promotion to be second mate on a large ship like this,' Tim observed. 'I am still destined to rejoin our old ship in the Baltimore shipyards. I shall be first engineer again back to London, but I have agreed to take the same offer from the navy and have been promised secondment to the second mate's slot out of Tilbury.'

'Perhaps we can get together to talk about it during this trip. I can't stop now but will be pleased to help in any ways I can later,' Norman replied, taking his leave.

Tim managed to discuss the job of the second officer with Norman during the third day. He was invited to the bridge as a servant of the company during Norman's long daily stint on duty there.

At dinner that night the senior third officer represented the company. After introducing himself, he announced that there would be a cabaret at ten o'clock after dinner.

Tim found himself sitting opposite the same woman, with whom he had previously exchanged pleasantries. She was sitting in the same seat as the night before, her companion alongside her.

Most passengers were busy talking to their immediate neighbours to their left and right. It was later that the woman opposite happened to glance across the table and asked him, 'Are you enjoying the voyage?'

'I am enjoying being relaxed. But being on a busman's holiday is never quite as refreshing as being on a genuine holiday, is it?' he said, returning her question.

'What on earth is a busman's holiday?' she asked. 'It sounds like a saying the English use. Forgive my ignorance. I'm an American. I'm Angela, by the way.'

'And I'm Livonia, Livvy for short,' said her companion. 'Angela and I met on the ship but found we both came from the Baltimore region.'

'A busman's holiday just means that when you take a day or week off from work for a holiday, you still end up doing something closely resembling the work you always do. Like the driver of a bus who goes on a long coach ride as a passenger.' Tim did his best to elucidate the meaning of the saying.

'Oh, I see, it's a bit like taking coals to Newcastle,' she commented. Tim was surprised that she knew that well-known conclusive comment, originating from the north-east of England, but responded with encouragement.

'Yes, in the sense that you are presented with an experience that you have an abundance of already.'

'So, I take it that you are used to the sea as a job, then. What do you do?' she asked him.

Tim told her something about his war experience and life in the merchant navy since the end of it, but avoiding any mention of the shipwreck of the *Samqueen.*

At the end of it, almost apologetically, she said, 'And here was I thinking you were a regular landlubber.'

Tim put a more philosophical question to her. 'Do you think it's possible to guess a person's profession and standing from his appearance? I could tell you are American by your speech, but would be hard pressed to identify your employment, that is, if you are not a housewife.'

'I'm not married,' she replied. 'But my partner is always away for long periods from home. No, I am not a housewife. Far from it. I own a chain of hairdressing and cosmetics shops, so my life is normally hard work from dawn to dusk. Sometimes, I have to take a break and get away from it all or the constant claim on my time and perennial responsibilities would drive me round the bend.'

'Well, I would never have guessed that, but I suppose I could have translated your beauty into such a profession, but it never crossed my mind – I mean giving employment to your beauty, not that you are not beautiful,' Tim said candidly.

She laughed.

'That's why you confused me, too. How could such a handsome man be a sailor? If I had asked myself what does this man do, I would have opted for the stage or films – you are not on your way to Hollywood, are you?'

They both laughed. 'No,' Tim reminded her. 'This is the wrong way to Hollywood.'

The third night Tim was late getting to the dinner table. He felt a little unsure about his growing familiarity with the American woman. She was impressive. With a lot of jet black hair and dark glasses to match, he could see by the frown and worry lines on her forehead, and by the laughter and grimace lines on her cheeks and around her mouth, that she must have been around fifty, but her figure belonged to a twenty-year-old. Her brown eyes didn't quite match her hair.

'What kept you so late?' she asked.

'I have been in discussion with members of the crew,' Tim answered. He didn't elaborate on a subject of no concern to company passengers.

The meal was eaten in a pleasant atmosphere. The weather and how to spend lazy days on board were always good for conversation on a ship.

When the dinner party broke up, she called out to Tim, 'I hope you will deliver my medicine bottle to my cabin later.'

'I have no bicycle,' was the first thing Tim said as his immediate reaction, taken aback by her invitation. 'But how exciting that you ask me, as long as you have all your clothes on.'

Her smile was intriguing, if a little forced, faintly reminiscent of someone he knew. He suddenly felt out of his depth. He had never been propositioned by a woman before.

Later proved to be an hour later. He knocked on her cabin door with a half bottle of whisky in his hand.

She opened the door, exclaiming that she thought he would never come.

'Here is your medicine ma'am.'

'Is that a bottle of rum?' she asked him. 'Since we are at sea,' she said teasingly.'

'Rum, no, it's whisky. Please follow the instructions for taking it.' He thought it strange she should make such a remark.

They laughed. He turned to go.

'Oh, won't you come in?' The disappointment in her voice was so deceptive it was almost real, he thought.

'You are a fine-looking woman,' he said. 'But I have the woman in my life waiting for me in London. She is my universe. I can't wait to make the return journey to be with her.'

'But I'm not asking you to marry me,' she said, with laughter. 'Just a sweet evening. I wonder what she does while you are away? A one-night stand with someone you like and of your choice is all right these days, isn't it?'

'You would have to ask her that yourself. It's not for me to comment. Partial fidelity may be acceptable to some people but it is not my preference. Shall we say that if I had no attachment, I would love to spend a night with you. I am not quite sure what it is that makes you appeal so strongly to me.'

He asked her if she was going to the passengers' cabaret at ten o'clock.

'Of course,' she replied. 'I'll see you there.'

Most of the passengers and about fifteen crew members had assembled in the dining room, which had been adapted into a cabaret setting, with a small bar nearby. Some subdued lighting had been added to the scene, creating a suitable atmosphere.

Tim looked around but could not see Angela. She was late, but perhaps she had decided not to come after her disappointment. Or, perhaps, she had imbibed the half bottle of whisky too freely.

The senior third officer himself appeared. He warmly welcomed the audience, explaining that it was usual to provide any diversions for passengers on an ad hoc basis which happened to become available. 'We are lucky to have one of our stewards, Jim Hollaway, on the piano. The limited facilities need to be adapted, but, as you see, it is quite easy to arrange something or other. But we depend on someone to give the sparkle to the venue. I'm glad to tell you that' tonight we have a special guest to entertain us. Drinks are available as usual at the bar for the duration of the show.'

With that said, Tim looked towards the entrance. Angela was walking in. She had an air of triumph about her. She was evidently not embarrassed by being late.

The officer at a well-timed moment then said, 'Let me introduce you to one of our own passengers – Miss Angela. Give her a round of applause.'

Tim was astounded, as were many others, to see Angela come to the focal point of the cabaret at the microphone, with an air of complete stage confidence and dignity, which transformed the audience into an attentive posture.

In her familiar American twang, she said, 'How happy I am to be able to stand in for another person. Let's hope the sea will remain calm, as my sea legs are not as competent as they used to be.

'It would be a shame to spoil the evening,' she continued, embarking on a few more pleasantries.

It was then that Tim knew why she invited him to her cabin that night. She never intended him to take advantage of it.

In a provocative voice, Angela proclaimed loudly. 'It's so hot in here, I shall have to undress.'

A puzzled murmur rolled among the audience – with a few passengers suddenly feeling uncomfortable, sensing something untoward was about to happen.

But her declaration completely misled the audience.

What actually happened, did so all at once, as if it were a well-rehearsed integral part of an act on stage for the entertainment of the audience.

Her friend Livvy went to her with a jar of cold cream, quickly sponging her face and neck, wiping away her forehead grooves, the lines on her face, and other intricate make-up that revealed a different woman underneath. Angela took off her dark glasses and removed the large wig from her head and the pads from inside her mouth, before stripping off her mature lady's dress to reveal a more fetching attire for a twenty-plus year-old. She straightened up her stature and threw her arms in the air.

In short, in a twinkling of the eye, and very smoothly executed, she transformed herself from being a fifty-year-old to being a mid-twenties woman, calling out in a modulated English woman's voice as she did so.

'Welcome to the show,' she cried.

At that precise moment of timing, the senior third officer bounced back to call out above the applause.

'I have pleasure in introducing Vanessa Coles, star of the smash hit London's West End musical *Perchance to Dream.*'

Tim thought he was in the middle of a dream. As soon as he realised who she was he involuntarily stood up, partly out of utter disbelief, partly out of a sudden awareness as to why he had been drawn to Angela.

His action triggered the rest of the audience voluntarily to emulate him. Everyone stood up and gave Vanessa another round of applause.

'For my first number I need one of the passengers to join me,' she said. 'You, sir, will do nicely,' she called out, pointing at Tim.

Tim was embarrassed. He had never been on stage before, not even on as humble a stage as the makeshift cabaret venue of the ship.

Vanessa took him in her arms, gently, and sang the chorus of "Waltz in My Heart" before releasing him to render the entire song. Jim Hollaway seductively and softly picked up a skilful accompaniment.

'The lark is singing on high
The sun's ashine in the blue
The winter is driven away
And spring is returning anew
Who cares what fortune may bring
What storms may tear us apart
No sadness can kill the wonder and thrill
Of that waltz in my heart.'

The clarity and pulsations of her voice immediately reduced the audience to silence and respect. Even the barman stopped in his tracks to listen.

Tim hugged her before returning to his seat. No comment nor explanations were made evident, nothing communicated to the audience. It was all part of the act as far as they were concerned.

For the first time in his life Tim felt sick with excitement. He had had no previous idea of her accomplishments, other than what he had witnessed in his many visits to the theatre to see her discharge her set parts in the productions.

For an hour, Vanessa then treated the smallest audience she had ever acted in front of to an endless medley of Ivor Novello songs, the well-known songs of the Second World War, and traditional sea shanties.

There was no sleep that night for Vanessa and Tim.

'How on earth did you manage to pull off that coup?' asked Tim. 'It was superb. It completely fooled me, although something about you drew me to you.'

'It must have been what is inside me for you. I could have no hand in meddling with that. I was afraid my eyes would give me away. But I was lucky. The theatre had obtained some of the new plastic corneal contact lenses. So, I had to borrow two that matched my dark wig,' she explained. 'The mouth pads are very misleading. The best make-up artist at the theatre showed me what I had to do. It was a challenge for me.'

'But how did you manage to come on the ship?'

Vanessa answered his question succinctly.

'It all depended on Colin Smithson, the senior official at Ennerman, who interviewed you. I contacted him at the last minute to find out if a cabin was available, to give you a surprise, without any mention of my plan, but promising some entertainment for the passengers and crew on the voyage. He duly informed the captain, who appointed the senior third officer to get it organised for the third evening. They were sworn to secrecy about my plans, which they accepted when informed it would all be part of my act. In fact, Colin gave me the cabin free on the promise of providing entertainment on the ship, combined with entertaining the new crew of the *Stormguard*, while the ship is waiting to sail in the shipyards at Baltimore, before I fly back to London at my own expense.'

Tim was genuinely impressed.

'So, you have become a singer on a ship after all,' he declared.

'Well, it just happened to suggest itself,' she said.

'Vanessa, darling, you take my breath away. Who would have thought you had such dash, imagination, and persuasive powers?'

'Just remember, I am a trained actress as well as a singer. The make-up, clothes, and disguise were all done by my assistants at the Hippodrome. Acting the part was child's play and anyone can imitate American speech,' she said modestly.

As might have been expected, the several dozen passengers enjoyed the cabaret so much they plagued Vanessa to sing to them again. She reserved her privacy for the next night but eventually was persuaded to perform again on the last night before the ship's arrival at Baltimore. She limited herself to all genuine cabaret items, her voice croon-like for the purpose, while many passengers who felt active enough danced around the polished floor.

22

Tim stood on the quayside in the early morning, looking at the newly named *Stormguard* moving slowly under the command of port tugs across the water from the shipyards. Vanessa remained in her hotel, preparing the entertainment she had planned to give the new crew later in the day.

As he watched, Tim's thoughts were electric. The whole gamut of shipwreck scenes cascaded through his mind. They had brought considerable damage to the ship, its severe listing, death to ten members of its crew, and peril to the rest.

Yet the sight of the ship was beautiful. It had once nearly secured his death. Now it looked as serene as ever. But he shrugged off his sentimental feelings. Life at sea, he told himself, was all a matter of the interaction of the forces of wind, sea, the structural integrity and adequate motive power of the vessel itself, its cargo and accommodation loading distribution and fixtures, and seamanship of the crew.

Competently repaired and painted, the approaching vessel had all the appearances of a new ship preparing to battle the oceans of the world. For the moment it was still only a little way from the slipway, which had been its home for some months and on which the repairs had been delivered to bring the ship back to life again.

With mixed feelings, Tim wondered if any of the newly appointed crew included those who had already sailed in the ship on its previous voyage and were known to him. Then he remembered he had been more or less notified by the official of the company in London that there would be none.

There was no cause for qualms. The ship approached the quayside where he stood, slowly and gingerly occupying its berth, assisted by a port tug. It was neatly tied up, behaving impeccably in every way as a proper adornment of the seas, a ship which had never known anything but triumphant conquests over the oceans of the world.

His spirits soared when he heard a shout from the ship, 'Tim, Tim!' He looked to the main deck and then the bridge, surprised but greatly elated to see Captain Derek Rhodes calling from the walkway, extending from both sides of the wheelhouse to the side of the ship for enabling observations and docking supervision by the captain.

Tim read the ship's new name, *Stormguard,* boldly emblazoned across its stern. 'Truly appropriate,' he thought.

When the gangway was secured from wharf to ship, Captain Rhodes was the first person to disembark expressly to greet Tim, his former chief engineer. He was soon followed by the skeleton docking crew from the shipyard.

The two men went back on board, Tim assuming a privileged rite of passage as the first crew member to board the ship after the captain. They repaired to the captain's cabin for a drink and chat. He soon discovered that apart from the captain, and himself, the stalwart bosun was the only other previous crew member expected to return as a crew member in the newly overhauled ship.

'Tim, I have something to give you. Please come with me. It's rather large as a present, but I have been as surprised about it as I think you will be.'

The captain led the way to Tim's former cabin, opened the door, and entered, followed by Tim, who was astounded at what he saw.

'I have great pleasure in handing back to its owner, your old sea chest. I know it went through the Second World War unscathed. Apparently, it must be unsinkable. It remained secured to the floor in your cabin, surviving the disaster to the *Samqueen*, the long tow to the Bahamas, the hurricane you went through in the Bahamas, and then the repairs in the shipyards at Baltimore.'

His speech sounded like introducing the best man at a wedding.

'I'm astounded!' Tim expostulated, as he moved to unfasten the lid. The contents were more or less in Spartan condition, especially his former chief engineer officer's uniforms. 'What a pity they are in such good condition – now that I shall soon have no need to wear them.'

'Ah, yes, it will be prudent to wear a second officer's insignia when we leave London. It will be good for you and will give normal confidence to the crew,' the captain said. 'It looks as if the navy is needing to make some adjustments in a hurry.'

'Yes, it does. Our new crew members are turning up today, aren't they?' Tim asked. 'It will seem like a new ship to them.'

'Between one and two o'clock, the chef and cook will be coming in, or at the end of the morning. And the company is installing a new domestic music centre during the day. Your partner, I understand, has agreed to take part in the celebrations this evening.'

'That's right. The company offices thought a refitted and modernised ship with a new name is a bit special. It would get us off to a good start and asked her to do it before she flies back to London,' Tim elaborated.

Vanessa had spent some time at a stage dress and supplies dealer's shop in Baltimore City. She had planned to repeat her first performance on the *City of Pretoria,* but with changes of dress to match the kind of songs she sang.

Early that evening, the captain called the new crew together in the dining room after their first meal on the ship. It was his opportunity to set the tone of the working relationships he preferred, and the kind of authority he wanted to establish. They had to see the kind of working climate he would strive for.

After the business of running the ship had been initially introduced, it was time for the entertainment. Captain Rhodes introduced Vanessa as a star from the London stage. She was accompanied by one of the ship's stewards, who had been appointed partly because of his prowess on the new music centre.

She sang songs from the musical stage, then sea shanties, and finally, popular songs of the moment, intermixed with those from the Second World War. In the intermissions she changed her attire accordingly.

With her charm, beautiful voice, and repartee, she wooed and won the audience. The evening produced a sense of solidarity among the crew, exactly as those responsible for commissioning her act had anticipated. Perhaps the sing-along she initiated helped considerably towards that end.

On the following day Vanessa flew back to London. Tim and she promised each other to meet as soon as the ship arrived in Tilbury.

The crew had several days' work to make the *Stormguard* ready for its Atlantic crossing. But first, a day's testing of the ship along the coast exercised the various performance levels of the engines and other mechanical equipment. Everything was in good order.

The weather forecasts were good as the ship left for London five days later. It took on a small load of freight in Baltimore itself, before sailing to Halifax in Canada where it docked, loading up commercial cargoes to equal its maximum tonnage, all for delivery in the United Kingdom.

Tim had the opportunity to renew his old acquaintance with Halifax from the war years. He did the rounds of his old haunts, meeting a few former friends and people still in their same jobs.

It proved to be an uneventful passage to Tilbury.

Although it was expected to be an efficient turnaround in dock for the ship, enabling it to proceed at the earliest possible time on the long voyage to New Zealand, the *Stormguard* was still in port after the two scheduled weeks allowed for the transformation had passed. It should have been enough time to unload its freight from America and Canada and to load a full cargo for Bombay and Wellington, and to make any crew adjustments.

In the event, the *Stormguard* was caught in one of the numerous ongoing dockers' strikes in Britain. Both unloading and reloading, in turn, were disrupted. The strikes lasted so long, if intermittent, that the government was still regularly using the army, ostensibly to unload vital perishable cargoes, but also to unload ships that had to keep a tight schedule, the integrity of which was important for either export or import commitments.

The delay caused by the strike and the initial amateurish handling of unloading and loading ships by army personnel moved the date of departure for the *Stormguard* on for another two weeks.

'Bad luck on one hand can be good luck on the other,' Tim told Vanessa.

'We can use the time. What a bonus. I never thought I would welcome any strike, which always seems to me to be the ultimate folly,' Vanessa replied, revelling in the extended time they enjoyed with each other.

23

It was well into 1947 when the *Stormguard* sailed from Tilbury for New Zealand, on its round the world voyage in an eastward direction.

It sailed the familiar and quickest route to India via Gibraltar, the Mediterranean Sea, Suez Canal, and the Arabian Sea to its destination in Bombay. When the *Stormguard* sailed there, it was the very year in which Indian territory was ceded from being part of the British empire, to become two independent states as India and Pakistan.

The city was still the Bombay of old, the gateway to India. It retained its same name for years after India became independent, until it was renamed Mumbai, only five years from the end of the century.

Since leaving London, Tim had been acting as second deck officer, to which rank and job he had been seconded by Ennerman on the prompting of the Admiralty, and supervised by the First or Chief Deck Officer, Roy Salter.

The *Stormguard* was in port at Bombay for a week – long enough for the crew members to have time to go ashore. Tim had not been to India before, but for Roy Salter the place was as familiar as his hometown.

It was, in retrospect, an experience that Tim did not regret. Their visit for him opened-up a vision of life on a scale with such complexity that he had never previously imagined was possible.

On leaving the dock gates, they were beset by masses of people on foot. 'It looks as if most of them are walking with great determination about their business. The crowds are interspersed with policemen, military men, and others in uniform. Bombay has come out to greet us,' Tim said, with a laugh.

A few were idling on street corners or staring at some unusual event.

Cyclists wended their way in and out of the crowds. Men strained to pull carts loaded with vegetables, or bedding, or construction materials. The road vehicles included old, dated cars, laborious ancient lorries, and ancient double-decker buses.

'I can see the policemen have a constant struggle coping with the chaotic scenes in the streets. Apart from the few people in uniform, everyone seems to be wearing white,' Tim remarked to Roy.

'It's the coolest colour to wear. India has always been a good market for Manchester,' Roy commented. 'We've arrived at a crucial time for India. Tensions are rising. In some parts it is feared there will be a lot of rioting and genocide among Hindus, Muslims, and Sikhs.'

"Everything looks normal here,' Tim observed. 'I believe Bombay is one of the largest cities in the entire world. I wonder how many can speak English after the British rule of so many years.'

'Yes, it's about two centuries altogether,' said Roy. 'So I expect English is pretty common, at least among the professional classes. But I wonder how many English people in India can speak Hindi? I think they kept themselves too much in their own community to bother to learn it. The British officers in Indian regiments were a notable exception. I've met some of them in my travels.'

Despite the heat they walked through to the glorious bay area, with its long curving coastline. The beach and gently lapping sea were thronging with people. They arrived in the middle of the horse racing season, the races taking place on a well-developed course running parallel with the sea.

During their return in the cooler evening they had the chance to absorb the contrasts of Indian life. The ramshackle homes of the shanty areas of Bombay were in such stark contrast with the outstanding buildings of British rule, including the homes of the former overlords, long since occupied by commercial companies and local private owners.

Tim was stunned to see the central station.

'What an amazing building it is,' said Tim. 'It's a glorious eye-opener. I shall not be surprised if one day it is designated as one of the wonders of the world. I think there is a movement world-wide to preserve the gems from the past. Strange to think that after the destructive ravaging of the recent war that has destroyed so much of our heritage, we are now talking about saving the best we have left. The damage throughout Europe in particular is horrific.'

'The guide book says it is called the Victoria Terminus, built sixty years ago,' Roy read aloud. 'It's the headquarters of the central railway. Among classical older buildings in the city from before British rule, they saw the exquisite Mumba Devi Mandir temple, built in the seventeenth century, in honour of the local Hindu goddess, patron of the fisherfolk and salt collectors.

'Tim, the proposed new name for Bombay is derived from the name of this goddess. Apparently, she was supreme to the original inhabitants of the seven islands which form Bombay,' Roy said. He was so knowledgeable that he had little need to consult the guide book for his comments.

On their perambulations they saw scenes which riveted themselves on their memories. 'No wonder the Indians are so good at cricket. Just look at those kids,' Tim pointed out.

They were passing a piece of desolate ground, dusty, uneven, and pot-holed. The length of the bowling pitch had been marked out, with old sticks for wickets hammered into the dry ground. 'They learn to hit the ball at an early age.'

Tim sized up the benefit from that desolate spot to the national game. 'They have a passion that seems to be waning in England.'

'Making do in life with the barest of elements seems to go with maximum motivation,' commented Roy. 'Our playing fields in Britain are strangely silent too often.'

The lack of capital in cricket was reflected in the absence of capital from so much commercial activity. They saw two vivid examples on their walk back. 'Their building industry reminds me of the way it is thought the Egyptians built the pyramids. That stream of men passing the earth in small baskets from excavation to transport is a case in point. Have you met the wanton use of labour for coaling ships in your travels in the Mediterranean at all?' Tim asked Roy.

'Yes, I have. Of course, that is by far the most efficient method when the use of mechanical means is inappropriate. But imagine trying to do that in the same way in a choppy sea from coal tenders to merchant ships,' Roy replied.

'It's a good job we are getting rid of coal for driving ships. Mechanisation is truly the servant of oil,' Tim added.

'Perhaps there is no incentive around here to use mechanical aids. Just look at the number of men involved in the brickwork on that building. Many are involved like a chain gang moving about eight bricks from the stack to where they are needed,' Roy pointed out.

'In the east the weather makes such a difference to life. You don't need a barber's shop to shave a man or cut his hair. You just do it on the sidewalk. How many have we passed like that?' Tim asked a rhetorical question.

It was evening when they finally reached the port area again. Selected street pavements and sidewalks were being favoured as choices for a night's sleeping. It was rumoured that millions were already on the move or contemplating migrating from one area of India to another, seeking a new home, based on their suspicions of where the boundary lines would be drawn when the vast continent was divided up. With the children of their large families, they were greatly swelling the flood of people from country to town, as they were drawn to seek work and a more amenable life in the city.

On the *Stormguard*, more freight had been offloaded than new cargo had been taken on board. Some delay was incurred with a labour dispute, but eventually the ship moved out from its mooring to sail without a further stop to Wellington in New Zealand.

One of the responsibilities of the second deck officer was the safe loading of cargo and attending to its security in the holds of the ship. After two days had passed since leaving Bombay, Tim decided it was time to take a look in the holds to make sure all was well.

Going down into the depths of the vessel was always a slightly macabre experience. He remembered his wartime days when working in the engine room. A torpedo hit was usually fatal for those in the bowels of a ship. Then his mind turned to the *Samqueen,* recalling when its ballast broke free from its restraining structures and brought disaster to the ship.

He mused about the kinds of cargo those holds had formerly held. Their maximum of nearly ten thousand tons of freight had once consisted of nearly three thousand Jeeps, or two hundred and fifty-two medium tanks, or nearly four hundred light tanks, or over two hundred million rounds of ammunition, with aircraft, more tanks, and locomotives lashed to the ship's deck areas.

Tim checked holds one to four. He was looking forward to climbing back up into the daylight and fresh air. But he still had the fifth hold to do. He entered it and moved around. The rats scampered.

Stopping suddenly, he was arrested in his tracks by a cough. He switched off his lamp, not wanting to give his own position away.

'Did I dream it?' he muttered to himself. He waited, still, and silent.

A moment later he heard another cough, clearly muffled. 'There should be nobody else in this hold,' he told himself.

He crept towards the area where he thought the cough had come from, picking up a slight rustling sound. When he calculated he had arrived at the source of the coughing, he switched on his light.

There, lying prone on the deck between two crates on a makeshift bed was a young Indian woman, dressed in a colourful sari wrapped tightly around her.

His powerful lamp temporarily blinded her. Tim was at a loss to know what to say. It was useless to mention that she had no right to be there. But he did so anyway.

'Do you speak English?' he asked her.

'A leetle,' she said.

'You have no right to be here,' he said to her. 'You cannot stay here. So, get up and come with me. I notice you have a supply of water and some food. Where did you get it?'

She offered no answer, but stood up and gathered her bits and pieces together, as if to comply with his command.

They made their way to the ship's office. Tim sent for the captain. 'Can you come to the office? We have a stowaway, a woman who evidently came on board at Bombay.'

The captain was as surprised as Tim at the discovery.

'It looks as if she was helped on board,' the captain said. 'The supply of water and food points to a member of the crew. I shall have to root him out. The trouble would be that if I appeal openly to the crew for the man to step forward, he might be reluctant to do so for fear of the consequences. I doubt if the woman would agree to identify him.'

'There is another way, sir,' Tim said. 'We have to take her into custody anyway. If she were locked in a cabin, I could lie in wait in the same spot in number five hold. I think the culprit would take her food late at night.'

It was agreed. After completing his watch, Tim secreted himself in the same spot where he had found her and sure enough around midnight he heard someone groping his way towards him.

At the last minute, Tim switched on his lamp, surprising one of the deck hands. 'You have committed an offence,' he told the man. 'The captain will want to see you.'

The young sailor was patently shocked at being discovered. He tried to explain the reasons for what he did, but Tim told him to save it until the morning. 'I met the girl in Bombay,' he told the captain. 'She told me she wanted to leave India. We got on well together. As it happened, I planned to jump ship in Wellington. So, it seemed everything fell into place for me.'

'Did you not know that the New Zealand authorities will put you in prison for six months if you jump ship, before you can stay as an immigrant?' the captain asked him.

'No, sir, I didn't, but if I had known it I would have been willing to put up with that. The girl was also prepared to suffer with some punishment to become an immigrant, too,' he replied.

'Well, I shall have to hand you both over to the authorities when we arrive in Wellington. You have miscalculated your chances. It is an offence to aid and abet a stowaway. You have been a good crew member. I am sorry you have brought this on yourself. You will lose your ticket in the merchant marine.'

When the ship arrived at Wellington the captain duly handed over the member of his crew and the stowaway. It was the last he heard of them. But it was not the end of his troubles.

The customs routinely checked the *Stormguard's* cargo.

The captain was alerted that something was amiss when a senior customs officer came on board and asked to see him.

'Good morning, Captain,' he said, affably enough.

'What can I do for you?' the captain asked him.

'I bring some unpleasant news, Captain,' he replied. 'We have discovered a cache of hard drugs from hold three, worth about half a million New Zealand dollars. They were hidden as goods from India. Which port did you call at?'

'Bombay. We were in port for a few days. Is there any evidence of complicity from any members of my crew?' he asked.

'No,' he assured the captain. 'They were craftily built into legitimate goods. We shall need details of when they were stowed on board and by whom if possible. Unfortunately, since the war ended the traffic in illegal drugs has been growing. We are doubling our vigilance to prevent New Zealand falling into a niche market. But if you can supply whatever possible details, your ship will not be delayed.'

'We are scheduled to be here for several weeks, anyway, so I hope to see your arrest of the contact people at this end of the chain,' the captain said. 'How will you go about it?'

'We shall not disclose our discovery but carefully monitor the people who collect the goods and keep a close surveillance on where they are taken and by whom. I think we shall be in for a good scoop over this consignment.'

Saying that the customs officer left the ship, leaving the captain disturbed by his report and the possible repercussions for the Ennerman Company. He realised that once they were committed to transit he could not be held accountable for drugs hidden so expertly. In future, there would have to be a closer examination of export goods before being loaded. It was just too easy to hide drugs in well-packed packages for export.

24

The freight loaded on the *Stormguard* at Tilbury had mostly consisted of British goods destined for New Zealand, supplemented by additions at Bombay. After being unloaded in Wellington, the ship was fully reloaded with a cargo of New Zealand goods for the consumer markets in Britain. The return sailing tracked the direct route across the Pacific, via the Panama Canal, and then the long stretch of the Atlantic to the United Kingdom.

For Tim Denton, the return voyage of the *Stormguard* to Tilbury represented a strange twist of fate. He had joined the ship in the same port, when it had a different name and before it succumbed to shifting ballast, taking its entire crew to the brink of disaster. The captain and bosun shared the irony of the voyage with him. They talked about it, but only in matter of fact terms. As hardy mariners, they had already put it behind them, as part of their decision to choose the sea as their profession.

Tim's dominant thought was reuniting with Vanessa. His experience at sea and as chief engineer had prepared him to learn the job of the deck officer quickly. It had been with confidence that he had assumed this position for the voyage to New Zealand and back.

But he wondered if the voyage to New Zealand and return, although about the longest any ship could make in the world, would be acceptable as the further training the Admiralty had requested. He would soon see.

London, like most of Britain, had suffered from the worst winter weather for over a hundred years. Rationing of some goods was still in force. Britain was somewhat struggling.

But Tim's spirits were buoyed up by meeting Vanessa again after such a long absence, lasting many weeks, for that return trip to New Zealand. When the ship docked in Tilbury once more, after completing his watch schedule he lost no time in catching the bus into central London to see her.

He opened her front door and called out, 'Vanessa.' She responded out of sight from the back of the flat.

'My darling,' she cried. 'You have come back to me.' Both hurried to close the gap between them, throwing themselves in each other's arms. Embracing him with sighs of relief, she murmured, 'I am always afraid you may change your mind during a long absence.'

They kissed passionately for a minute or two.

'Vanessa, you are the centre of my life, no less,' Tim whispered to her. 'If this is love, I have surrendered to it. The saying "absence makes the heart grow fonder" is certainly true in my case. I can't guarantee to come back from the dead but I will come back to you from the four corners of the earth.'

'Oh, for goodness sake don't mention death, but I can put up with the four corners of the earth. We've all got our living to do. You make me nervous again,' Vanessa said. 'There is a letter for you.'

'I'll look at it later,' Tim said casually. 'Only one letter? I thought there would have been more after so many weeks.'

'You have other letters, too. But I should have said it seems a special one this time.' Vanessa had a concerned look on her face, which persuaded Tim to be inquisitive.

'Where is it, then?' he asked. 'Perhaps I had better look at it if it's that special.'

'I'll get it, darling,' she declared, walking to the kitchen.

When she handed the letter to Tim, his heart immediately missed a beat. It was evident that Vanessa had interpreted the contents of the letter from the imprint on the envelope. It bore the letters *OHMS*.

'I wonder what His Majesty wants to tell me?' Tim asked as he opened the letter. 'Maybe it's only about my tax affairs.'

He was soon disillusioned. It was typed on good quality paper from a Whitehall address, with the imprint *Admiralty* boldly across its heading.

Vanessa grabbed a squint at the letter as Tim began reading it.

'Whatever do they want?' she asked. 'This looks ominous.'

'It depends on how you look at it, darling,' Tim immediately replied.

'I was in the navy during the war long enough and with the seniority, for my rank as lieutenant to be made substantive. That means a permanent rank as opposed to an acting or temporary commission. On that basis the navy can always call on such officers to resume their service, without the force of compulsory call-up, as operated in the case of being at war. The navy is short of having absolute power to command me but they are relying on my previous pledges, current goodwill, and physical ability to comply with its interests.'

'But what does it mean for you in practice?' Vanessa was eager to know. 'Are they short of men or is something sinister afoot for this to happen?'

'In wartime, with a constant flow of new recruits being called up, the navy could afford to keep each cohort of intake waiting to fill vacancies at their choosing. In peacetime, sometimes they run short of manpower and can't quite find a particular man for a particular job,' Tim replied.

'I think you are putting me off a bit. I have been reading in the press of disquieting news from China and Korea, to say nothing of the pressures Russia is putting on Europe,' Vanessa said, surprising Tim with her current grasp of worldwide geopolitical knowledge.

'The good news is that I will be down the road at the Royal Naval College at Greenwich,' Tim announced, triumphantly.

'Oh, that's a surprise. What on earth will you be doing there?' she asked.

'Yes, it is something I never expected, and never thought about,' said Tim.

'This is good news. That's a very classy place,' Vanessa commented. 'I went on a tour there once with a group of stage people. It really is a magnificent set of buildings inside and out. What do they do there?' she asked.

'You are right,' Tim reinforced her comment. 'It is the staff college of the navy. Officers attend for training to take command. The course includes law, politics, history, strategic, and management studies.'

'Does that imply that you will be a captain?' Vanessa queried.

'I don't know about that. It might, to a small ship, but not necessarily. I might not pass the course. Or I might be posted to a large ship as third or second in command, or even to a desk job in Whitehall, perhaps even as an attaché to one of the less important overseas countries to which Britain sends military representatives.'

'You will have to let me know about all those possibilities again, to let me take them in. I shall have to weigh up my chances, where I would fit in, for each of those options. Could this affect us much?' she asked.

'Whatever happens, darling, rest assured,' Tim spoke firmly. 'I shall always come back to you. I shall have four months of being on your doorstep at Greenwich. After that, I may have a choice. I do not know what process is involved. But in any case, that is a problem for tomorrow. Today is the most important day. Let's make the most of it.'

Tim tossed the letter down and threw his arms around Vanessa. 'Please stay in my sight – at least until you have to go to the theatre tonight,' he said.

'You are coming with me,' Vanessa reminded him.

They celebrated his homecoming from New Zealand before they left home together. It was the intimate part of their relationship. He went with her to the theatre for her appearance in *Perchance to Dream*. After their return from it, they continued their celebrations – until they were exhausted.

The next morning came, with a renewal of their energy. Tim had to return to the *Stormguard* for a port watch. Only a skeleton crew remained on the ship.

Of course, he was going to reply to the Admiralty with thanks for his recall. It was within his keen sense of duty to do so.

The Admiralty had already written to Ennerman with the requisite information. Tim followed it up by writing to the company informing them that he would respond to the navy as a duty. He included a special note of thanks for the opportunity the company had given him. It was a sad moment for him to say farewell to his captain and finally step off the *Stormguard*, a ship which had meant so much to him since he came out of the navy.

'How long will the navy give you before you have to report?' Vanessa wanted to know.

'It will depend on when the next course starts. They will pay me from the date that I cease to be employed by Ennerman. But I will probably have to wait for a month or six weeks before a course vacancy is available. I shall need time to kit myself up with uniforms and other requirements, which I am sure they will be advising me about.

'By the way,' Tim continued. 'Have you heard any more about the successor show to *Perchance to Dream* that you thought could be in sight soon?'

'We think *Perchance* will run on for the time being, but it's common knowledge among the inner circle that Ivan is well advanced with the other production. So, it looks as if *Perchance* will end sometime next year, leaving six to twelve months for finishing and preparing the other play. Ivor is not enjoying the best of health, so it might be his last stage production. It's too early for casting yet, but I am still hoping to get some promotion.'

Tim received instructions to report to the Royal Naval College at Greenwich in the middle of February. He and Vanessa relished the intervening weeks. Constant cohabiting over those weeks developed their mutual tolerance of their individual whims and ways, bonding them closer together and sealing their devotion to each other.

One day during their conversations, they had a sudden flight from their normal topics of discussion, doubtless triggered by thoughts about their longer-term future and Tim's being away from home. It turned into a brainstorming session.

Tim had realised that the navy might not approve of an extended liaison with Vanessa. Was it a courtship? Was it a partnership? If so, it would be expected that it would end in marriage, sooner rather than later. She would be regarded as his fiancée, as she had been for a long time already, and with the implied consequences.

As it happened, while they were talking about her part in the stage productions, Vanessa suddenly asked Tim what he thought love really meant.

She expanded her question. 'Look how freely we use the word, in all kinds of contexts. Parents love their children – but that can vary between several children. People love a bunch of roses or going to a football match. Even London female bus conductors frequently use it with their passengers.'

'Yes, that's true. But have you ever asked yourself that same question, darling?' Tim surprised Vanessa with his riposte.

'I have some definite views. But have you?' she asked him.

'Of course, I have, but I can't really get a handle on anything other than a passion in me for you,' Tim lamely replied.

'That's an accolade I didn't expect when I asked the question, darling, but thanks for such a gratuitous assurance,' she said, laughing. 'If you think of your passion, do you agree it carries three assumptions.' Vanessa picked up his own remark to carry her argument.

'You sound impressive. You sound like a professor. Remember, I am not starting at the college until February,' Tim interrupted her.

'Never you mind,' she commanded him. 'I bet that's exactly the sort of introduction one of your own professors on your undergraduate course used time and time again.'

'But that was appropriate for engineering,' Tim countered.

'And so, it is in any field of thought.' Vanessa shot her reply forcefully. 'Remember, my own background is in acting and drama. Apart from physical behaviour and practical studies, so much psychology permeates the profession – both the study for it and the practice of it. There is also a lot of organisation involved, with objectives, research, and motivation taking their part.'

'Well, it's a closed book to me, but I love the outcomes from it. There you are, I have used the word love again without thinking about it,' Tim announced, making both laugh at his candour.

'Let me continue,' Vanessa asserted. 'If you analyse that passion, I think you will agree, it has three elements. Ask yourself this. If I am on one side of the world and you are on the other from me, what comes first?' she asked rhetorically.

She answered her own question. 'It's being physically with the other person. So always wanting to be with the other person becomes dominant. Going places and doing things together. Even long absences don't kill it.'

'You are going to tell me what number two factor is. I'm guessing about the order,' said Tim. 'But let me know what you think and I will tell you what I think.'

Vanessa said, 'I think it's sex. I may be out of order with past culture but we are starting to go through a revolution in relationships between the different and the same sexes. We shall see it in our lifetime. The primary purpose of copulation has always been for procreation. The emphasis today on the primary purpose is the enjoyment of sexual relations. Large families were the result of lack of restraint and the absence or neglect of preventatives. Populations are growing anyway, somewhere in the world, and people are moving around more than ever before. Perhaps, one day, science will produce an absolute safeguard.'

'You have surprised me, darling, with that view. I would have put it after compatibility,' Tim commented.

'For me, compatibility is the third factor,' Vanessa immediately replied. 'When you consider it thoroughly, sexual relationships, apart from one-night stands, eventually become part of the compatibility world. Respect for your partner is born of a recognition of the qualities and feelings of complementing each other. And here I end my short lecture,' Vanessa concluded with a smile.

'For me, compatibility of temperaments is essential, but not necessarily beliefs. Think how views change over time,' Tim said. He acknowledged how tersely she had presented her views. 'Your three elements are not necessarily sequential. They interact and develop simultaneously. I've noticed there must be a strong balance of mutually related elements to have a lasting love. An introvert may or may not balance an extrovert. It's the total balance that counts.'

'That's true,' said Vanessa. 'The total array of compatible elements must be balanced. One pair of people might be incompatible in the case of one element but that could be counterbalanced by other factors. Two extroverts might not be a good idea in one case but works in another because of other counteracting elements. If being a good talker is a factor in extroversion each partner could be a good talker on different things.

'I hope talking about love won't dampen your ardour,' Vanessa said in a seductive voice. 'I am finding it the opposite. Talking about it turns me on. I say, always let the passion roll when it rolls.'

'That's the most instructive thing you have said,' Tim replied. 'I can still hear you singing to me on the pavement outside the Royal Court Theatre in Liverpool. I shall always love you, whatever it means.'

'The thought of another woman touching you drives me insane,' Vanessa responded.

'I am destined to work with men and I will always come back to you,' Tim said with a touch of gallantry. 'But I can imagine the temptations of stage and theatre life. They worry me quite a bit.'

'Have no fear,' Vanessa declared. 'As I have said before, so many of both sexes I meet are of different persuasions.'

And with that, the space between them disappeared as they came together with the sudden firmness and power of two magnets being brought into contact. Time stood still while they expressed the passion that overcame them. It was all they could do to break for Vanessa to make her way to the theatre, where her singing that evening was just a touch more vibrant than ever.

25

When Vanessa had the opportunity, they continued their exploration of London. Tim gave a lot of his time to the studies he would be undertaking at the college. It absorbed his mind during Vanessa's time at the theatre. During those weeks, they took a trip to the college in a group of tourists, travelling by boat from Westminster Pier.

'The buildings of the college are particularly beautiful,' Vanessa remarked to Tim. 'The architect had a wonderful knack for pleasing the eye of the beholder.'

'Yes, I find the proportions are breathtaking,' Tim replied. 'The college was designed by a master architect, Sir Christopher Wren, who also designed St Paul's Cathedral and many of the churches in the City of London. The college was actually built in the first decade of the eighteenth century as a hospital, but has been used regularly for the training of navy officers since the end of the First World War.'

Tim later continued his brief explanation of the function of the college. 'Many thousands of navy officers were trained here during the Second World War. As well as for the initial training of officers, it is now also used for the advanced training of navy officers, parallel with the staff college of the army at Camberley and the staff college of the air force being developed at Bracknell.'

The visit whetted his appetite for the day that he would enter those portals as a trainee and student. The date was getting close. When it arrived, he was pleased to receive first of all an invitation to attend a reception held on the evening before the course began for the new intake of sixteen young officers, selected for potential promotion. Each course member could bring his wife or fiancée. The in-house residential staff members running the course would also be in attendance with their wives.

Tim knew that if he invited Vanessa to go with him to the reception, it would almost certainly be in keeping with what everyone else would do. If she came it would be her first official involvement with the navy. Tim shared the common knowledge with his fellow course members that higher promotion in the navy as in the other services went with marriage or bachelorship, rather than partnership.

Any aspiring officer in the higher rank orders of the services who married and was subsequently promoted to a rank that normally carried knighthood status, knew that he would be deprived of that award if he had been involved in divorce proceedings.

He had kept putting off formalising his relationship with Vanessa. He wondered if the recent discussion over love had been a way for Vanessa to question his thoughts about it. He thought marriage seemed in some ways antithetic to people on the stage. But he had to admit that perhaps he was only covering up his own apprehensions about tying himself in marriage. Was his fear simply a matter of ignoring the married state as a closed book rather than seeing it as a new life opening out to be made, to be lived, through thick and thin?

He realised how he had been shielding behind the dangers and separation of the sea as a reason for not marrying. But how many men were living dangerous lives and facing occupational hazards? Coalminers, men on the new oil rigs, air force aircrew, deep sea divers, commercial airline pilots, men handling explosives, and thousands in the building and agricultural trades were all facing dangers at some time or all the time in their jobs.

It was time he faced up to the issue – no more dodging it, nor shelving it for some other time. He decided he would raise the matter with Vanessa. But was it a subject for discussion or should he present her with a ring in the good old-fashioned way and ask her to marry him? Perhaps, she might ask him to marry her? Had she too been putting off formalising their relationship? She might have been happy with it as it had always been, while she was making her way on the stage.

'Darling,' he addressed her at a suitable moment. 'I have received an invitation to attend an official reception at the college sent to all course members and their spouses. Would you like to come?'

'Try keeping me away,' Vanessa replied. 'Let's hope it's not on a stage performance day but I could get my understudy to stand in for me if it is. She is always glad of the opportunity.'

'As a matter of fact, it is on a Monday night, with the course starting the following day,' Tim replied.

'In that case, with no performance, of course I will come. I would never go anywhere where we can't be together, if at all possible. You can't be with me on the stage and I can't be with you on your ship,' Vanessa responded immediately. 'I take it that partners are as welcome as wives,' she added.

'It will be the first official function in the navy that you will have attended. So, I shall have to introduce you as my fiancée. The concept of partner is not current in the navy – nor the other armed services for that matter,' Tim informed her. 'Remember we had to use the term when we went to RAF Burtonwood.'

'Oh, why's that, then?' she laughed at Tim. 'Are they short of vocabulary?' she asked.

'You have to be either married or officially engaged,' Tim explained, realising he was being dragged onto a slippery slope that might make him overcome with embarrassment.

'I thought we were already married,' Vanessa blurted out. 'What could be nicer than our lives for the last several years?' she pleaded, but in such a very delicate way that averted any uncomfortable feelings for Tim.

'I appreciate what you are saying, darling,' Tim replied. 'And you are right. We have found and established the strongest bonds of all. From that point of view, we are married in the natural sense. I am pledged to you and you to me.'

'So, you are talking about civil marriage.' Vanessa interrupted him.

'Marriage with documentation and ceremony has been the institution favoured by the church and now seems increasingly becoming the creature of the state.'

Tim was surprised at the forthright manner of her last remark and realised she was talking from a different sub-culture of thinking from his. He had become very traditional in the naval context, she had tasted the freedom of libertarianism in her growing career on the stage.

'Have no fear, darling. I am happy with the bonds we have made. Anything else is supplementary, if not superfluous.' Vanessa smiled. She looked at him as she said it with such love on her face that he made the obvious remark with confidence in his reply.

'So, if the navy expected us to be married in the civil sense, would you do it?' he asked.

'Darling, is that a proposal? I thought you would never ask me.' She was nearly helpless with laughter. 'That is the standard thing to say, isn't it? I always thought you were happy with the status quo. Sometimes, I nearly decided to ask you to marry me. Now what would you have said to that?' Vanessa responded. She asked the questions but expected no answers, or at least none that she could not have thought of herself.

'I was anxious not to get you involved legally with a man who has a habit of being away a lot and not in a safe job.' Tim feebly tried to make an excuse for his lack of action. He then explained about the navy's expectations of their senior officers, mentioning the practice of denying a knighthood to an officer who was divorced but promoted to a rank that normally justified that award.

'I like a man who lives dangerously and you have done that so far. But don't worry about the navy. If it ever came to the point, you can always say you married a woman for a knighthood. Fortunately, in the acting profession we don't have constrictions like that to worry about. I might have had some doubts if you had ever asked me to marry you at the beginning, but I am so in love with you and am convinced you love me. The history of our relationship reminds me of the wonders of it.'

'But you already have admirers all over the country who would come to your aid if you needed it,' Tim quipped, with a piece of irrelevant nonsense that made them both laugh, as they put the subject behind them. 'I dare not put a foot wrong,' he added.

'That makes two of us,' Vanessa concluded. 'You can do no wrong in my eyes,' she said.

'You are just beautiful,' he called, as they went their separate ways.

26

She looked stunning. He looked immaculate. It was time for both of them to rise to the occasion as never before.

Vanessa and Tim attended the anticipated opening reception party at the college. It had come soon enough. They both turned out in their finest attire. Tim had to wear his formal naval officer's dress suit. Vanessa took the trouble to visit her favourite West End costumiers, who supplied her own stage costumes, to order a unique dress for the occasion.

The design made the very most of her remarkable figure. Low-cut around the shoulders and breast, the simple material in navy blue was decorated at the hem and around the lower line of her breasts with wavy patterns resembling the rolling sea.

The most beautiful historic room at the Royal Naval College was used for the reception. It was a formal event, in keeping with the practice of all three armed services. A chief petty officer announced their names on entering, and a naval rating at hand offered them a glass of champagne. Not being the first to arrive, they had plenty of opportunity to mingle with those who had come before them, while those who came after them soon completed the entire complement of course members, together with at least half a dozen course tutors who would be contributing to the course at some stage or other.

The head of the college, Captain Bruce Fowler, had just assumed command on the first day of February for a two-year posting. His wife Madelene immediately took a liking to Vanessa and engaged her in conversation, while her husband welcomed other members of the course.

'I guess you are not in the navy,' she said to Vanessa.

'You are right. I am very much a devotee of dry land, but I understand women in the navy don't actually go to sea. But now we have to get used to being in the air. I recently crossed the Atlantic by ship and returned by air, which enabled me to judge the benefits of sea and air travel rather well.'

'Life gets speeded up by air, doesn't it?' Madelene said. She had made her own conclusion about travel developments.

'Yes, but I wonder if the more leisurely time spent on the sea is not more beneficial to busy people,' Vanessa commented.

'But it looks as if the airlines will be taking over from passenger services by ship in the near future,' Madelene suggested.

'Yes, I am sure you are right about that. Life will be different then for us all. Rushing between engagements with little time for reflection. It will seem like being on a mass production machine,' Vanessa said.

'You sound as if you live a busy life?' Madelene queried.

'Some people might call it busy, but I'm afraid many would call it by some disparaging word or other. But I know how busy it can be and very demanding,' Vanessa said.

'Now you have got me intrigued. What do you do?' Madelene asked.

'I'm an actress. So, you see, some people might see me as a layabout not doing any useful work for the community,' Vanessa said, rather pensively.

'Well, I don't think any of that,' Madelene said. 'Are you in a job at the moment, then?'

'Yes, I'm very fortunate to play opposite Ivor Novello in *Perchance to Dream* on the London stage at the Royal Hippodrome,' Vanessa said.

'Well, I never recognised you. I have never met a great actress face to face before. What with the stage clothes and make-up in the theatre you now look so different from how I remember. I have seen the show more than once with my husband. We love it. It's a great hit and has had a wonderful run, hasn't it? I am sorry I did not latch onto your name when you were introduced as Vanessa but you must be Vanessa Coles. You've become famous for your performance in the show.'

'You are more than generous in your comments, Madelene. I don't think I deserve all of them,' Vanessa smilingly said to her.

'It's your wonderful voice. How on earth did you fall in with a sailor? Or is that asking an impertinent question?' Madelene asked the questions, hoping for replies.

'No, not all. Tim and I met in the foyer of the Royal Court Theatre in Liverpool in wartime. He had been on convoy work all through the war on destroyers. One week he was in Liverpool docks and took a night off to see the show. I was playing a small part in an Ivor Novello production, *The*

Dancing Years. Another girl in the cast and I were head to head over a cup of coffee when he walked by and complimented us on the performance. Just in talking for a few minutes we found we had some background in common. I fell head over heels for him. I love to think that he fell for me. We've been together ever since,' Vanessa explained briefly.

'That's a remarkable story, Vanessa. I'd love to hear more of it but I've got to rush to catch up with my husband. It's been great talking with you. See you later.' She moved away, looking for the captain.

Vanessa momentarily thought she had been too forward. 'It is not characteristic of me,' she said to herself. 'to reveal so much about my personal life to strangers. But this time it is the right thing to do.' She consoled herself with the reason she had been so giving. 'I know I have lodged a positive note in Tim's favour,' was the thought that lingered in her head.

The rest of the evening allowed the new course members to meet each other and their tutors. The event was intended as an ice-breaker. After about two hours an air of bonhomie had been established. It was a good first step to a course, which was to last four months, starting the following morning.

At his opening address the next day, the officer leading the course, Commander Thomas Southwell, made several trenchant remarks, which stirred the perceptions of the course members rather more than they had expected.

'We are in the aftermath of the greatest war ever fought. It has cost this country the loss of control of its empire and thrown it into enormous debt. The world is dominated by the United States. Europe is partitioned between them and the Union of Soviet Socialist Republics. On the strategic military side, nuclear fission as a weapon of war now hangs over the world. On the tactical front, air power has taken over from the sea. The capital ship in future will become the submarine.

'Against this background, the course will endeavour to equip you with knowledge and patterns of thinking to help the Royal Navy to play as great a part as possible in serving our country. It will be in a world where huge powers and dangerous policies sometimes cast their shadows on our country and threaten the way of life we have developed as our culture, the freedom we have come to enjoy.'

For day after day, the course demanded a heavy work output from the course members. It stretched their mental capacity and concentration on a scale they had never expected. Many lectures and discussions over the weeks were delivered or conducted by prominent politicians, military men, and commercial captains of industry.

They undertook visits to many key institutions governing their interests, notably the Houses of Parliament, the Royal Air Force College at Cranwell, the Royal Military College at Sandhurst, the Royal Naval College at Dartmouth, and the Admiralty in Whitehall.

One day when Vanessa was asking Tim how the course was going, she probed him to find out what differences it would make to his knowledge from the ordinary military training she assumed went on in the three services.

'What sort of lectures are you getting and how do you spend your time for most of the day when you are not out and about seeing inside the sacred institutions that control our lives,' she provocatively challenged him. 'Now don't tell me it's secret.'

'Oh, it's not secret in that sense,' he replied. 'Navy officers normally do not deal with "TOP SECRET" papers or information in the course of their duty in peacetime, although it might apply to higher positions of command.'

'If I happened to drop in on you at the college one morning, what would I find you doing?' she asked. 'Would you just be chatting away or listening to a speaker?'

'Now you are trying to pull my leg,' he protested. 'I think most of the time in the college is spent either listening to a guest speaker – which is usually accompanied with questions to the speaker and discussions about it afterwards – or in workshops.'

'What kind of workshops do they have there, then?' she asked.

'No, it's not workshops in the physical sense, although you could compare it with being in the chemistry lab or art room at school. It's the contemporary buzz-word for actually doing things for as near virtual reality, as you can possibly get,' Tim explained. 'Instead of physical objects we deal with facts, information, and ideas, often presented from previous naval experience.'

'What sort of things do you do in it?' she wanted to know.

'The main activities are problem solving,' Tim said. 'A problem is not a problem if you already know an answer for it – or have a series of options for your choice. You have a problem if, at the time you consider it, you are without an answer. You have to find one. In other words, you are in new territory. It's a daunting but exciting exercise.'

'That means we use the word rather loosely every day, doesn't it?' Vanessa perceptively said. 'You were saying it was a main activity?' she egged him on with the question.

'Other workshop activities incur case studies of historic or recent navy experiences in manpower, logistics, communications, law, and, of course, actual combat. They all involve learning the facts and then offering critiques of the decisions made,' Tim continued.

'That makes sense to me', replied Vanessa. 'It's a bit like the reviews of a new stage performance. Sometimes, it means that many heads are better judges than one.'

'That's a good way of putting it,' said Tim.

'So, what else are you doing?' Vanessa pressed Tim relentlessly.

'A main feature is the talks by experts on developing subjects. We ask questions and follow it up in a workshop context afterwards,' Tim replied.

'Can you name some?' asked Vanessa.

'Yes, of course, but I would prefer not to divulge what was said by the speaker in discussion nor in the group. Not, that it's so secret, but it would not be fair to share it with someone external to the course. The really big topic is the beginnings of what will ultimately be a permanent joint headquarters for all Britain's military services, headed in rotation by the navy, army, and air force.' Tim surprised Vanessa by the thought.

She was quick to comment. 'That would sweep their independent pasts into the history books and create a new way of thinking in the old rivals, would it not?'

'Germany showed the way during the recent war when they combined their disparately organised forces into what we know as the blitzkrieg, which the allies had to emulate later in the war. It is a fundamental move in place that is overshadowing all we do at the college.

'One of the concrete developments we deal with is considering the strategic implications of a communist takeover of China in Asia Pacific, involving the Far Eastern fleet. The loss of the *Repulse* and *Prince of Wales* not only heralded the supremacy of air power over surface ships, but invited the development of an undersea fleet driven by nuclear power,' Tim explained.

'My word, that is pretty big stuff,' Vanessa replied.

'It involves the terms of what lies ahead that have to be taken into account,' Tim concluded.

The intensive course of four months prepared its members for higher command and other responsible jobs in the navy at home and abroad. It had reintroduced Tim into the navy culture and renewed his outlook and familiarity with the service in which he had spent his war years. It had been an invigorating and enjoyable experience. His intellect had been reawakened and challenged on a different level.

Hopeful of having met all the requirements of the course, he awaited the outcome. His posting would be nothing if not a testimony to his determination to excel in everything demanded of him on the course.

Vanessa and he had something to celebrate. They did so privately. Tim had come home again from a nearby destination. He expected to receive his appointment and posting orders within one month of completing the course.

Tim was out for the day when a large envelope was delivered by post one morning. Vanessa had to sign for its receipt. She could see it was from the Admiralty. Tempted as she was to open it, she refrained from such a presumption.

As soon as Tim came through the door later that morning, she called out to him. 'Darling, you have got your marching orders.'

'What are they?' he called, obviously assuming their mutual right to open their letters. It came under the heading of having no secrets from each other.

'This is a special occasion for you, darling. I want to see you open it,' Vanessa called.

They met in the sitting room.

'It's a big enough package,' Tim immediately observed. 'I wonder what it will be?'

He slit the envelope and rescued a single sheet of paper, which formally stated that he had been appointed as the assistant naval attaché to China. He would join the embassy, located in Nanking, and was promoted to the rank of lieutenant commander to take the post.

'Well, that is a change of life for you, darling, isn't it? You are coming off the sea for the first time for a landlubber's job. But you have had the past months to get used to it,' she said. 'I can only say that it gives me some relief to know that although you will be away from home, at least you will not be facing the dangers of the sea any more. It must be important if they have promoted you for the job.'

'It's a well-trodden path to higher command appointments,' Tim replied.

'What are all the other documents?' Vanessa asked.

'Mostly briefing papers, information about the staff already there, and some historical stuff about the embassy and history of China,' he answered.

'We ought to let our parents know about it as soon as possible,' Vanessa said.

'Yes, it would be nice to share it with them,' agreed Tim.

They found the first opportunity to catch the train to Swindon on the following Sunday.

27

Vanessa's parents, Dr and Mrs Coles, met their daughter and Tim at the Swindon railway station. After warm greetings between daughter and parents, Tim expressed his pleasure at seeing them again. Vanessa and her mother immediately went into an intense conversation about members of the family.

Tim had her father to himself for a few moments.

'It has been quite a while since I saw you last, Dr Coles. I have been to New Zealand since then and have run into more complications with my job and future employment in the interim.'

'Oh, don't call me that,' Dr Coles said. 'I think it's about time you called me John and my wife Margaret. Please tell me about your trips. I would be interested to know what has happened to you since we last met. It's a long voyage to New Zealand I imagine.'

'About six weeks. It will soon only be for freight. People will all be travelling by air,' Tim said. 'It's not easy for me not to think of you as Dr Coles. When I come back to Swindon I still think I am a boy,' Tim laughed. 'Seeing you makes me think I am still running around with medicines for elderly people who are unable to fetch their own prescription from the surgery.'

'Well, time has passed, Tim,' John Coles said kindly. 'Our relationship – shall we say – has undergone a fundamental change. I have to remind myself that you could be my son-in-law one day, but of course, I am not suggesting anything more than a potential fact. What I can say now to you is that Margaret and I cannot thank you enough.

'You have evidently brought great joy into the life of our daughter. I could tell from her behaviour while you were away. She's pretty serious about you, you know. I have never known her to be so determined and passionate about her life as she showed after you came along. I can honestly say we have seen a great change in her since you came into her life. Before then we always thought she enjoyed her job but that she had put herself into a sort of state of isolation, you know – a self-imposition of denial, almost like a nun. But don't tell her I used that word. She would hate me for it.'

'What you are saying goes for me too, John. I hope I am as serious about her as she is of me, as you say. She is the person who has given me life with a purpose. I love her as intensely as I know how. I cannot say I was like a monk before meeting her, but I had little time for liaisons or relationships. But when I met her I knew that my own forced abstentions were well worth it.'

'Well, that's good to know, Tim. She is precious to us and we would only wish for the very best for her. And I think she has found it. I hear you are going to sea again. Is it a secret where you are going?' John asked.

'Not really. And not to sea. We are not at war. But some countries are.' Tim wanted to put him in the picture but knew it would be imprudent to do so. Perhaps the general picture was potentially public knowledge but he would not disclose his precise orders.

'I heard that,' said Margaret Coles, suddenly joining the conversation.

'I have been posted as assistant naval attaché to the Far East,' Tim elaborated. 'To China, in fact.'

'Did you get promotion with the appointment?' asked John.

'Yes, one step up to lieutenant commander,' Tim replied.

'But what exactly are you going to do, and where will you be going?' Margaret asked. 'Will you be away long?'

'I am being posted to the British embassy in Nanking. The Yangtze River is like a huge estuary from Shanghai westwards into China. Then it turns south-westwards as a great river at the point where Nanking was founded,' Tim replied. 'It differs from London, where the estuary runs up to the city.'

'Shanghai is on the coast but how far inland is Nanking?' asked Vanessa. 'The distances in China are very large compared with here.'

'About two hundred miles,' Tim told her. 'China has been in turmoil since the civil war began twenty years ago. I have to thank the course at the naval college for most of what I can tell you,' he explained.

Vanessa intervened. 'But why on earth could a civil war last so long? I thought everything had been settled when Japan was defeated in 1945 and had to withdraw from China.'

'It's amazing how ignorant we all have been of what has transpired in China,' Tim declared. 'Apparently, the confrontation started when a communist movement was formed and challenged the nationalist government. It survived spasmodically until the Japanese invaded China and seized huge areas, causing vast suffering and millions of casualties. Both government forces and the communists buried the axe to fight the Japanese when the country was overtaken by the Second World War. Remember that Russia was our ally then as well. Since the war the communists have been gaining strength and look like eventually winning the prolonged struggle.'

'Will you not feel surrounded and threatened with civil war going on around you?' Margaret asked. 'Where will you be, then, in relation to the civil war?'

'The communists now control the northern bank of the Yangtze, the nationalists the southern bank,' Tim elaborated. 'The navy has a ship stationed regularly nearby on the Yangtze River, as a protection for the embassy staff and if necessary as a refuge and possible means of escape. The ship is changed about every three months. At the moment a destroyer, HMS *Convort*, has been on duty guarding the British embassy during the civil war.'

'The presence of the ship sounds like tokenism,' said John.

'Of course,' replied Tim. 'Embassies are sacrosanct, provided governments and anti-government forces keep to the rules. The presence of the navy is to reinforce traditional rights, in case elements arise which want to ignore them.'

'But why is the British embassy in Nanking?' Margaret wanted to know. 'Has it always been there?'

'Well, Mother,' Vanessa interrupted. 'Simply because Nanking has been the capital of China on and off for centuries. It was the capital for the republican government during the

Second World War and post-war fighting. It was one of the great cities of the world until Japan tore it apart during their invasion of China in the thirties.' Vanessa remembered enough from her university days to make the point, finding herself warming to the conversation.

'Yes, you are right,' said John. 'The Japs made a mess of that city. I seem to remember the horrific stories that leaked out not long before the Second World War began.'

Tim responded, 'They certainly wrote themselves into the pages of terror, rape, and unwarranted killing. My father used to save pictures from our national newspapers. There were two Chinese laundries in Commercial Road at the time. Do you remember them?'

'Yes, I do. One at the top of the road near the Town Hall, the other at the bottom near the covered market,' John agreed.

'Dad used to take the pictures into the one near the market,' Tim continued. 'He must have assumed the proprietors didn't read the national newspapers. But his action was kind in intent. I went with him on several occasions. He used to commiserate with them about the warfare the Japanese were deluging on their country. Of course, he never realised the vast extent of China and the fact that perhaps those Chinese expatriates came from parts not touched by the Japanese.'

Tim and Vanessa could only stay in Swindon for a short time because of Vanessa's continuing appearance nightly at the Hippodrome from Tuesday to Saturday. But they spent the rest of Sunday with John and Margaret, staying overnight, before visiting Tim's parents, Henry and Elsie, in their Commercial Road house on Monday.

Tim's father was much more knowledgeable about the situation in China. Tim gave his father more detail about his posting, including a hint of the risks he might be taking. But China seemed a long way away. The thought of his going there did not cause a great deal of joy to his mother, but she knew it was in the pursuit of her son's chosen career.

'Ah, Nanking, what infamy that city can tell,' said his father. 'From a total population of a million and a third, around about a sixth of them survived the Japanese attack and wreckage of the main area of the city.'

'That must be an all-time massacre of a city's population,' Vanessa declared.

'You are probably right. Have you heard the story of John Rabe?' Henry asked.

'No, sounds like a German,' Tim replied.

'Hundreds of those who were saved were through the direct asylum given by John Rabe, a German official working for Siemens. He opened his house and compound, under the protection of the German flag flying over the property and the Nazi swastika armband, which he wore. They deterred the repeated attempts by Japanese troops to intrude into it to gain access to the refugees. He was also instrumental in creating a safety zone to save thousands of other citizens of the city, who found themselves without shelter and exposed to every conceivable act of brutality and deprivation meted out to the civilian population.'

'It was a brave stand to take,' said Tim.

'Especially so,' said his father. 'In the evening of one day in the middle of December, two years before the Second World War began, the entire horizon to the south was a sea of flames.

Women and children pleaded to be let into John Rabe's compound. They sat on the grass, pressed close together to give each other warmth and to give each other courage. The wailing of the stricken children in his garden echoed in John Rabe's head for hours afterwards. Over three hundred women and children were packed into his garden of around only five thousand square feet. But that number of refugees eventually more than doubled.

'Children were unable to avoid the arson – still being perpetrated one month after the Japanese had occupied Nanking – the pointless mass murders, and the bestial rape that punctuated the daily life of what was left of the city. John Rabe saw the body of a little boy, around seven years old with four bayonet wounds in it, one in the belly about as long as your finger. He died two days after being admitted to the hospital, without ever once uttering a sound of pain.

'Young girls were being raped – about a hundred alone one night in the same month at the Ginling Girls' College. Many abused girls still in their childhood were admitted to the American Mission Hospital, one of whom had been violated twenty times in succession. Two girls were found, aged eight and four, whose entire family had been gruesomely murdered. The two girls had remained in a room with the body of their mother. They were rescued by a neighbour fourteen days later. The older girl had fed herself and her sister from a small store of rice that had been overlooked by successive marauding Japanese troops.'

'Can human conduct ever be worse than that?' Vanessa broke the brief silence that followed Henry's account.

'Look no further than the horrendous crimes committed by Russian forces moving westwards in Silesia towards the end of the Second World War,' Tim commented, without elaborating.

28

On their return to London, they settled down to their remaining time together, relaxing as far as was possible under the circumstances. Tim was reading in preparation for his posting to China.

Vanessa dreaded the day of his departure. She was mystified when she found out that he was not going on a ship. 'If you are not going by sea, how are you going to travel that far? Do they want you to swim?' she quipped.

'I am going by air, of course,' Tim tried to end the conversation, which Vanessa had every intention of pursuing.

'Stop pulling my leg,' she protested. 'And will I be able to see you off?'

'Yes, of course,' he assured her. 'We will go to RAF Northolt in West London. I shall have a flight to RAF Portreath.'

'Where's that?' she asked.

'It's a station that became operational about eighteen months after the start of the Second World War, near the coast, southwest of Porthtowan in Cornwall, north of Redruth. It was first used as a fighter base, but later on it fulfilled the vital job of being the stopover for aircraft transiting to or from North Africa and the Middle East,' Tim answered tersely.

'Are the military still flying in those places, then?' Vanessa queried.

'There are many RAF stations abroad left over from the war and still operating. And apparently, with the partition of India, British Overseas Airways is transporting many thousands of migrants between the new India and the new eastern part of Pakistan and vice versa, using existing or former RAF airfields. So, I shall be flying by courtesy of the Royal Air Force.'

'It's a long way to India. Where do you think you will be stopping?' Vanessa asked.

'Probably Malta, Cairo, Bahrain or Sharjah in the Persian Gulf, and finally Karachi, now in western Pakistan – at the RAF base at Mauripur, four miles to the north west of the centre of the city, which the air force is still using.'

'But you are still a long way from China. How will you get beyond there?' Vanessa pressed him further, full of doubt.

'I shall fly from RAF Mauripur northwards to RAF Delhi, then from there south to RAF Agra, then south-east to RAF Allahabad, and finally south-eastwards again to an air force station at either Dum Dum, Agartala, or Comilla in the Calcutta area of East Bengal,' Tim said.

'That's still not China. My geography is sorely lacking but it seems to me that you are far from getting there,' Vanessa chided Tim.

'Not so far really,' Tim defended himself. 'During the war, the American air force and the Royal Air Force flew from those bases over the mountain ranges straight into China. They flew in supplies and people to the nationalist forces. They have been retaining some links with nationalist

271

China. Time enough for me to be delivered, at least. Of course, we don't know what the outcome of the civil war will bring in China, so we are in an interim and uncertain position.'

'You are beginning to talk like a naval attaché,' Vanessa ribbed him.

To say that some of the details she had squeezed out of him enlightened her might have been true, but at the same time she was alarmed at the picture he implied of the chaotic effects of the partition agreement of India and the bitter civil war in China. It suddenly opened-up in her an unprecedented fear for him.

'You are taking me out of my cosy life once again, darling. This is back to the worries of the war. First, the war, then the shipwreck. I hope all goes well, as long as you don't get involved in anything that seems like peril number three.'

'But you have your career on the stage to absorb your worries. It looks like *Perchance to Dream* will finally come to an end in the London theatre fairly soon. I hope and believe you will rise to new heights with the next show Ivor is planning. I'll survive, you'll see. I will come back to you. That's a promise,' he said to Vanessa, looking her straight in the eye.

Vanessa felt a glow of comfort at his assertion but at the same time she doubted if he had fully taken into account the random, unaccountable, and warlike actions of people he had never met to be so certain of himself.

'I have implicit faith that you will keep it,' she said.

Only days before Tim was due to leave for his overseas appointment, Vanessa was surprised to have a call from Madelene Fowler.

'How are things going?' she asked. 'It must be near the time Lieutenant Commander Denton has to leave?'

'Yes, very soon,' Vanessa replied. 'It is very good of you to remember.'

'That's all right. We regard Tim as one of our graduates now. We are interested in his progress,' she said. 'But Bruce and I wondered if you and Tim would come to dinner on Sunday evening in a week's time. It would be just the four of us.'

Vanessa was uncertain about the protocol of the invitation but she warmly responded.

'Of course, we would love to come. What time did you have in mind?' Vanessa asked.

'Say seven o'clock,' Madelene suggested. 'Wear mufti, of course.'

'That would be fine. Thank you both. We will see you then,' Vanessa replied.

When Tim came home she told him about the invitation, wondering if she had made the right decision, without knowing if he wanted to respond to it.

'Madelene and I got on well together at the reception. She always made plain that she would like to meet us again some time,' Vanessa said.

'Your instinct was right, darling,' he said to Vanessa. 'It can't be too common for a senior captain to entertain a more junior officer at his private quarters. Perhaps he has something up his sleeve that he wants to tell us.'

'She told us to wear mufti. I had a job to remember what the word meant. I just assented at the time. Where does the word come from?' Vanessa asked.

'Particularly from Indian army days. But it comes from Arabic, meaning an Islamic scholar. It became commonly used in the nineteenth century for the private clothes of off-duty officers – and has spread around a bit,' Tim answered.

Both were warmly welcomed at the private home of the Fowlers in the Greenwich College grounds. Madelene had obviously become fascinated by the career of Vanessa. They talked endlessly about it.

Tim was soon deeply engrossed in conversation with Bruce Fowler, once the latter revealed that his previous appointment but one – before commanding the college – had been as chief naval attaché to Chiang Kai-shek. Tim was able to glean a wealth of information from the captain about life in China and in particular the work of the British naval officers in liaison there.

'If Mao Tse Tung wins the contest it will mean a sharp decline in British influence,' Bruce said at one point. 'In fact, it will disappear. Hong Kong is still under our control but we are treaty bound to return it to China at the end of the century. You will have to look out for moves that will spell hidden hostility.'

Vanessa and Tim came away from their visit with the feeling that a friendship had been established and would one day come to full fruition.

And so, on the appointed day of his departure, Tim and Vanessa arrived at RAF Northolt, near Uxbridge, early in the morning. It was surprisingly busy with British European

Airways flights, temporarily using the airfield while awaiting the completion of London Airport.

Tim had been directed to report to an air force department, where he found that his flight was in an Avro Anson. It was evidently a personal flight laid on for him. During the preparations for leaving, Vanessa asked the RAF commander if there was any chance she could fly with Tim to Cornwall.

'Yes, I think that would be in order, provided you come back with the aircraft later today,' he said.

'It would have to be a condition that I did so,' Vanessa smiled at him. 'I am on stage this evening. What time will it return to Northolt?'

'Weather permitting, the Anson is due back here at 3.30pm. The weather is always a risk. It will only stop at Portreath for refuelling and a short break,' he replied. 'By the way, what sort of show are you in?' he asked.

'I'm at the Hippodrome in *Perchance to Dream*,' Vanessa informed him.

'Well, I'm surprised. I saw the show several months ago. But I would never recognise you. You must be Vanessa Coles?' he queried.

'Right in one, sir,' Vanessa laughed.

'It will be a pleasure for us to fly you with Lieutenant Commander Denton. I gather he is bound for a difficult assignment,' he continued.

'Yes, he is, but please don't remind me of it. I am apprehensive for him,' said Vanessa.

Both Vanessa and Tim were suitably dressed for the flight with additional flying gear. The Anson was used mainly for training navigators but had been used operationally in the early stages of the war in RAF Coastal Command.

The flight plan followed the Great Western Railway line westwards. The pilot pointed out Reading and then Swindon.

'Our parents would be amazed if they knew we were flying over their heads at this moment. It's a pity we can't drop a note to them on our way,' said Vanessa.

Then they flew over Bath, followed by Bristol and along the southern coastline of the Bristol Channel, landing at RAF Portreath.

'That was a very smooth flight,' Tim said to the pilot when they left the aircraft. 'It makes flying an attractive proposition.'

'Yes, the aircraft has always had the nickname, Faithful Annie, reflecting its gentle handling qualities. It's been around now for over ten years and still going strong. It's a joy to fly,' the pilot responded.

They went to the officers' mess. 'We take off again in half an hour,' the pilot told Vanessa.

'I have to check in at the passengers' desk,' Tim said. 'Then I shall be able to see you off.'

After a cup of coffee in the mess, Tim went with Vanessa to the Anson. On the way they stopped at a distance from the aircraft, to say their private goodbyes.

They looked at each other in a strange way. It was as if they both wanted to rivet the face of their lover in their minds. Dark thoughts remained unspoken at the moment of their separation.

Suddenly, and softly, Vanessa sang.

'I'd like to get you on a slow boat to China
All to myself alone

Get you and keep you in my arms evermore ... '

She finished the lines.

'It's me who is going,' Tim said. 'I should be singing that to you.'

'Oh, it's only a bit of nonsense,' Vanessa replied. 'I wanted to give you something cheerful to take you on your way. I know your heart is not made of stone and never will be, my darling. Just remember the song and come back to me when you can.'

They hugged and then she took her seat. The pilot and navigator, already in their seats, were waiting for her, with the Anson's engines running. The aircraft taxied out, waiting for the signal to take off. When it received the all clear, the engines roared into full power. It headed down the runway, gently lifting into the sky and turning its nose in the direction of London.

Tim found the seat for his own flight to be among the twenty-one passengers carried by an Avro York of RAF Transport Command, serving the critical route to India. He had travelled far in his life but he looked forward to the new destinations the aircraft would enable him to visit.

The York's first stop was Malta where it landed at RAF Luqa, the continuing main air force base from the Second World War. He reflected on the terrible suffering visited on the island during the war from bombing, starvation, and shortage of supplies. Thousands of sorties of German and Italian aircraft had assailed it. By valorous acts, the air force defenders of the island, together with the merchant and navy seamen, who sailed their ships to succour the population, had withstood that aerial assault. The island had richly merited its award of the George Cross.

From Malta the aircraft flew on eastwards to RAF Muharraq in Bahrain for a second overnight stop, the following day flying direct to RAF Mauripur at Karachi. His orders at Karachi were to fly to RAF Delhi and report to the embassy there.

He flew in a DC3 Dakota on a regular RAF flight from Mauripur to Delhi of around seven hundred miles. His two days at the embassy were enjoyed in a beautiful room, staying in a building originally constructed by the British as a hotel for visiting family members of senior army officers serving in the Indian army.

Tim reported to Captain Charles Jenkins, the chief naval attaché to the government of India.

'I hope your trip was to your liking, Lieutenant Commander. My instructions have been to fix you up with flights with the RAF to Agra, then to Allahabad, and the final stop will in fact be Comilla. You will have a companion from Delhi. Lieutenant June Wetheram RN has been posted from here, where she has been deputy administrative officer, to Nanking as head of the administration. Things are pretty difficult up there at the moment. You will both go into a messy situation, I fear, but I wish you all the best of luck.'

'Thank you, sir, and for your impeccable hospitality while I have been here.' Tim saluted the captain and left his office.

Delhi to Agra was a flight of about 120 miles. They flew in another Avro Anson, just the two navy officers, with its pilot and navigator. Tim realised how ubiquitously the Anson was still serving the RAF around the world.

The aircraft from Agra to Allahabad was due to leave the next day. They were billeted in RAF quarters for the night and had most of the afternoon and evening to see the city. Top on Tim's list was the Taj Mahal in Agra.

June agreed to go with him. She had long since promised herself a visit to the temple but had never previously found the opportunity. She read from her guide book, that it was commissioned and completed in its entirety during the first half of the seventeenth century by twenty thousand artisans – at a cost at the time of approaching a billion United States dollars.

Tim and June were lucky. The site had not yet attracted the six million visitors who later came to see it annually from abroad and from India itself, all made possible by the airways, which people increasingly afforded.

Consequently, they were able to go around the complex unhindered, without marshalling and free from the irritating task of dodging round hordes of other people.

From Agra to Allahabad, a flight of about 250 miles, they flew in a Liberator ex-bomber from the war, adapted as a supply aircraft. With only a short break in Allahabad, a city with a vast and variegated history, recognised by the British for its strategic position, they took off again in the same aircraft for the RAF base at Comilla, right on the frontier with Burma, a flight of about 600 miles. They had had a taste of the huge distances that characterised India.

Tim knew something about Comilla, which he communicated to June. 'This place is one of the most important military bases and the oldest in East Bengal. It was widely used by the British Indian army and was its

279

headquarters during the Second World War. Many RAF squadrons were based here during the war. It's the area where the Japanese army tried to invade India. By definition, it was the area where the British army finally defeated the Japs and drove them back into Burma.'

'That must have been an epic event of the war and yet so little seems to be known about it,' June commented. 'It will be the jumping off point for our last leg. I am looking forward to it.'

After another overnight stay, they expected to leave for Nanking the following morning.

In the officers' mess that night they heard a lot of discussion about the geopolitical situation developing in China. They were drawn into much of the conversation.

'It's become very unstable up there since the end of the war,' one officer said. 'At least they had a common enemy in Japan. But now the Japs have gone, the local knives are out. There's a great amount of bloodshed. The communists are making their own rules and they don't agree with ours.'

A colleague added to his comment. 'We used to make runs to Chinese armies at the peril from Japanese guns. Now we are faced with communist guns. We don't always know the latest territory they have captured. Chiang Kai-shek seems to be losing ground all the time now.'

Turning to Tim and June he added, 'It will be a difficult posting for you at the moment. You will be inevitably involved in the war zone, possibly a retreat.'

'What is their present advantage, then?' asked June.

'They hold the north down to the Yangtze River. Chiang sits on the southern bank but for how long who knows. It's a big river to cross but they will find a way by outflanking Chiang or a direct assault across it,' an army officer spoke up.

The pilot, Squadron Leader Jeffrey Purbeck, and crew members who were flying Tim and June to Nanking were also present in the mess. 'We are scheduled to take off at seven o'clock tomorrow morning for the flight,' the pilot informed them.

'How far is it?' asked June.

'Around sixteen hundred miles. It should take us about eight hours at the most,' their navigator replied. 'We shall be flying light so it should not be more than that.'

Tim remembered Vanessa's comment that he would still be a long way from China when he reached that present point.

Neither Tim nor June slept well that night. The full reality of their respective commissions was forcing itself in on them and coming very close. But they dutifully arose and after a splendid breakfast in the mess they reported to the aircraft at the due time.

The flight gave them wonderful views of the hump, the nickname for the mountainous ranges, the highest in the world, which they had to fly over before the vast land of China gave way eventually to low lands in the Yangtze basin.

On the way, they caught up on their sleep and talked about their future jobs in China, which they were on their way to fulfilling.

'How many staff will you be responsible for in your new job?' Tim asked.

'There have been five navy personnel apart from the chief attaché and, of course, local employees for maintenance, cooking, and cleaning,' she replied. 'Add in the air force and army attaché staff. The main part of my job will be coordinating the activities of the embassy as a whole. The ambassador's personal staff of advisors and assistants are more numerous. I have to be a sort of house manager.'

They were escorted from the airfield to the embassy. After introductions they were accorded one day's rest.

Tim had a briefing from Commander James Stafford, the chief attaché. 'Welcome to China, Lieutenant Commander,' he said with a sense of warmth that evoked Tim's trust immediately. 'Between us, please call me James. If you wish, I would like to call you by your first name.'

'It's Tim, sir, and that's fine by me.'

'As it's your first appointment, I will try to give you a variety of jobs to get you conversant with being an attaché. But at the moment we have a pressing responsibility on us.'

'What will that be?' Tim asked.

'As you know the *Convort* is currently guard ship nearby for the embassy. But her time is up. It is due to be replaced by the *Amartyst* which is already waiting at Shanghai and poised for the signal to proceed up the Yangtze River.

We received the ship's readiness signal this morning at six o'clock. I wanted to mention it to you first. If we give the signal to sail it could be here during the night. But unfortunately, I have to go with the ambassador to see Chiang Kai-shek about an important issue, later today,' James explained.

'Do you usually have any trouble over replacing the ships?' Tim asked.

'No, but the circumstances are different this time. Since the last changeover the communists have occupied long stretches of the northern bank. We don't know whether they will retain a benign attitude to us or object to the transfer,' James replied.

'Well, it seems we have no option but to try them out by giving the ship orders to move immediately, do you not agree?' Tim ventured.

'Yes, agreed, or we shall be forced into a stalemate. I'll send the signal off right away,' James said, as he left the office. Neither he, nor Tim, nor Lieutenant Commander Donald Swinscombe, the commander of HMS *Amartyst*, had any inkling of the terrible events that signal would unfold.

29

At Shanghai, on the bridge of the *Amartyst,* the captain of the ship, Lieutenant Commander Donald Swinscombe, picked up the ship's telephone. It was a call from the radio cabin with the order to sail to the embassy headquarters at Nanking. 'The call has just been delivered at half past seven, sir,' the radio officer reported.

'Thank you, Jenson,' the captain called into the phone.

Turning to his first officer, Lieutenant Henry Dawson, the captain said, 'Let's hope we don't have any trouble. The trip should take us between twelve and fifteen hours, provided we don't run into any problems. We can take it steady at about fifteen knots.'

The *Amartyst* got underway almost immediately, edging between the numerous sampans and vessels of all shapes and sizes that swarmed around the waters of Shanghai. For the next hour it approached the mouth of the Yangtze, which had the dimensions of an estuary stretching for a hundred miles westwards.

The captain ordered action stations for the ship's crew. He then spoke over the tannoy system to the ship's company, once they had taken their precautionary stations to defend their ship.

'We are now underway to our station at Nanking. As you know, the nationalists and communists are at loggerheads for control of China. The nationalists still control the country on our port side. The communists have captured most of the land on the starboard side. They seem to have had the better of the struggle so far. Soon this estuary gives way to a very wide river. It is from that point onwards that we might encounter any interference with our passage. Any opposition offered will come from the communists who are potentially likely to object to our short voyage to Nanking. They may see it as some kind of support for the nationalists, so any protests will come from our starboard side. Keep vigilant. Report anything suspicious. And let's hope for the best.'

Unknown to the captain, Colonel Jian Li, the People's Liberation Army commander of the relevant part of the northern bank of the Yangtze, had radioed his orders to each of the divisional commanders on each section of his command along the river.

'The British destroyer *Amartyst* has left Shanghai and is on its way to Nanking. My orders are to stop the ship, by one means or another. We should try to deter the British as far as possible and only use force if all else fails. So, the command has decided on a three-point plan. The ship will be coming along the estuary during the morning. When it clears the estuary and enters the river, I want the 52nd Infantry Company to let go a fusillade of small arms fire while the ship passes them. They will know we cannot harm the ship by that means, but they will surely get the message that we object to their passage and will turn back. If that fails, the 4th Artillery Company will fire a salvo of up to twenty rounds at the ship but falling short. That should make it plain that we mean business. If the ship continues on course and shows no sign of submission, the 15th Artillery Company will attack the ship to achieve its destruction when it reaches Kiangyin. That is all. Do not fail in your duty.'

All went well for the *Amartyst* until about nine o'clock. Soon after the ship reached the end of the Yangtze estuary and entered the river, the firing of small arms could be heard on the starboard-side bank. It was as if individual soldiers were firing their rifles – and occasionally sub-machine guns – aimlessly across the enormously wide river, the longest in Asia and third longest in the world.

'They just seem to be registering a protest, or do you think they are so cocky they could turn us around and send us back to Shanghai,' Henry Dawson said to his captain. 'Is it just a first warning to an intruder?'

'Perhaps, perhaps,' the captain replied. 'Tell Jenson to send off a signal to Nanking: "Under small arms fire from the starboard shore around nine o'clock".'

The destroyer kept on its course, undeterred by the show of infantry weapons aimed in their direction. No sooner had the commanders in the destroyer concluded that they had escaped with only a feeble protest, than its entire crew were alerted to the possibility that worse than small arms fire might soon confront them.

The ship's lookout reported to the bridge. 'I can see flashes from artillery fire inland. There are so many, it must be a whole battery of guns involved.'

His words were overtaken within seconds, when the first of a salvo of shells shattered the crew's confidence by exploding between the Yangtze's north bank and the *Amartyst,* but uncomfortably close to the ship. In fact, the first and subsequent salvos churned up the calm river to resemble ocean waters. A few pieces of shrapnel hit the ship.

The captain noted that the range of the guns was nicely judged to intimidate them but not to hit the ship. The shots were clearly meant as a serious threat, calculated to deter the ship from proceeding any further up river. But he assumed from his own navy culture that the British embassy rights would be respected.

The captain picked up the internal telephone to the radio cabin. 'Jenson,' he said. 'Send another signal. We are under severe intimidation by shore-based guns. Between ten and fifteen shells have been fired. But so far clearly as a warning.'

At the embassy, James Stafford was disturbed by the signals from the *Amartyst.* He sent for Tim Denton, his new assistant attaché, to report the news. 'Do you think those shots could be part of the regular softening-up of the nationalist forces on the south bank, by this demonstration of strength against the British?' he asked Tim.

'It's possible, but I don't think so. The signal definitely says that the captain interpreted the range of the salvo must have been specifically calculated to be a warning to the ship itself,' Tim replied. 'As an indirect message to the nationalists, it's too subtle in this context. They must know it's a British ship and entitled to relieve the embassy as a guard ship. I wonder how high the seniority of the command is on that sector. It may be a junior commander trying his luck, but it's more likely a concerted scheme to prevent the ship getting through.'

'Surely, they can identify the flags the *Amartyst* is flying. If they know the ship is British they are probably trying it on, capitalising on their newly won victories. But you can never tell how much understanding the lower orders of rebel troops have in a particular location. They obviously don't think the ship is on the side of the nationalists or they would have fired to hit it. But they must think it gives comfort to the enemy they are fighting, if not military help,' James observed.

'The ship should display British insignia as boldly as possible,' said Tim. 'And see what happens. Shall I tell the radio room to send such a signal to the ship immediately?' Tim asked the commander.

'Yes, immediately,' James replied. 'And tell him to cancel my appointment with Chiang Kai-shek. Something tells me this situation is not likely to get better.'

On receipt of the signal, Donald Swinscombe ordered two ratings to hang union jacks over the rails along the ship, each man working down one side of the destroyer.

He also rang the engine room to tell the chief engineer to increase speed. The firing stopped with the combined manoeuvre. He thought the cessation of shelling was due to his actions, not knowing that it was in keeping with the plan agreed by the communist commander with his subordinates. The increased speed had merely confirmed the need to implement part three of their plan to stop the ship.

After another hour or so the *Amartyst* reached Kiangyin, about half the distance from Shanghai to Nanking. On the way, the captain sent a modified situation report to the embassy, reporting that the crew was still at action stations.

Commander Stafford replied that artillery duels were commonplace across the river and perhaps they had unwittingly become involved in them.

'Well, that was much about nothing,' Henry Dawson remarked to the captain. 'The shelling we faced was definitely not part of an exchange between the two sides.'

'Perhaps it helps if you show them a determined face,' the captain replied. 'It has stopped and we are on the way again.'

No sooner had that brief conversation taken place, than the lookout suddenly rang the bridge, reporting artillery flashes on the north shore.

'What will it be this time?' the captain said, breathing a sigh of relief that he had kept the crew at action stations.

Was this the routine exchanges of fire between north and south banks of the Yangtze that the embassy had mentioned?

The first shell passed over the ship before exploding, lending credence to that view. But he suddenly put the worst interpretation on the facts.

The captain called to Henry Dawson.

'That's no accident. It was a warning shot if ever I have seen one, or if not, it was a ranging shot. Sound the alarm that we are being attacked. Prepare for action. Open fire at will.'

The captain's reaction came too late. The first three high-explosive shells inflicted immediate, wanton damage, landing on the bridge, wheelhouse, and the ship's low power room, which controlled the destroyer's guns.

The shock of the attack momentarily stunned the entire crew. But the medical staff immediately went to the assistance of the captain, Donald Swinscombe, his first officer, Lieutenant Henry Dawson, and Petty Officer Frank Jameson, the three men on the bridge. They found the captain mortally wounded. He was to die the next day.

Henry Dawson, assisted by Frank Jameson, both badly wounded, tried to take control of the ship. Unfortunately, the coxswain, Leading Seaman James McDermott, who was at the wheel when the second shell struck the wheelhouse, was unconscious from his injuries. Steerless, the *Amartyst* turned its bows to the south and ploughed into the mud of a small, island-like promontory, part of the south bank shore.

Stationary, the destroyer was then an easy target for the enemy gunners. More shells landed on the destroyer, hitting the sick bay, the port engine room, and ship's generators. The destruction of the low power installation by the first salvo of shells to hit the ship, robbed the gun turrets of electrical power for their operation. Emergency local power was finally generated but neither of the two forward gun turrets was able to bring its guns to bear on the enemy guns. Only the stern gun turret managed to fire a few shells in reply before it was hit again and silenced. The artillery batteries continued to fire at the *Amartyst*, causing more damage and casualties.

The sudden, ferocity, and accuracy of the artillery fusillade had taken the *Amartyst* by surprise, although the crew had been at action stations and were expecting some kind of protest from the communists.

The casualty rate rose instantly and continued to increase. The officers on the wrecked bridge immediately grasped the intention of the attack was to wipe out the crew and destroy the ship.

With the destroyer grounded, the only sensible response to the shelling was to evacuate the wounded in the hope that their lives could be saved.

The *Amartyst* became a defenceless, badly damaged, and grounded ship. Henry Dawson ordered a boat to be launched, which managed to take a large number of serious casualties to the southern shore. More crew members swam to the refuge of the south bank, some of them wounded. Jacob's ladders were thrown over the side of the destroyer for the more able wounded to escape.

A good start was made to the evacuation, focussed as it was on the quarter of the ship least exposed to the vision of the enemy. It was a fortunate factor that minimised the communists' opportunity to turn the attack into a complete disaster.

The evacuation was soon assisted from the south shore by nationalist personnel, but the unexpected and sudden emergence of the crisis in their midst revealed only their unpreparedness for such an emergency. Their efforts were spasmodic and ineffective at first, but gave way to more organised and decisive help within an hour.

The wounded senior officers trying to maintain command on the destroyer then read the intentions of the enemy utterly to destroy the ship and its crew. Their inference was soon justified. As the evacuation of the many wounded continued and believing the whole crew was escaping, the communists ordered their guns from the north shore to switch their fire to the sampans, swimmers, and their rescuers involved in saving the wounded. It was a merciless attempt at the massacre of the entire complement of the destroyer.

The guns fired continuously, their fire being directed primarily at those struggling in the water, lying on the sampans, or helplessly wounded in the destroyer's boats. Some shells hit the ship causing more damage and casualties.

Lieutenant Henry Dawson, though fighting his own wounds, retained consciousness long enough to order the radio officer to inform the embassy of the unfolding events. Fortunately, the radio cabin had remained undamaged, the equipment functioning to the last.

A crewman informed Henry Dawson that the accurate shellfire, landing on the evacuation area, had become so severe that the point had been reached of imposing suicidal certainty for any further crewmen to survive in it. Dawson ordered that a message should be sent immediately to the embassy.

'I have ordered the evacuation to be terminated. Any further attempts for crewmen to abandon the ship will certainly cost them their lives.'

A few minutes afterwards, Dawson finally ordered the radio officer to send the following transmission, which included the vital data for their salvation, should it be possible, both for the ship and its crew, before allowing himself to be given whatever help the medical staff could offer him.

'Under heavy fire. Am aground in approx. position 31.10' North 119.50' East. Large number of casualties.'

The guns for the moment suspended their attack, their gunners assuming complete success. The wounded endured the next hour in the excruciating heat, awaiting the outcome. The medical staff worked without ceasing to tend the casualties. Some died from their wounds. The lives of many crew members were saved by the medical staff, operating in the most primitive conditions. They removed shrapnel from shellfire – or bullets from infantry weapons, fired from the north shore – from the wounded, and applied bandaging or tourniquets to arrest the blood flowing from their open wounds.

Unfortunately, they had no antidotes for blast injuries.

Later in the day, the assistance of the nationalist forces on the south bank in the area was soon organised at a higher level. The embassy had immediately contacted the local commander, explaining the situation and requesting help.

The wounded men already assembled on the shore were joined by the more seriously wounded, the evacuation of whom had been surreptitiously restarted by carrying them to shore clandestinely by sampan.

Several more crewmen had been drowned while swimming to the shore. The count by then was over thirty dead and over fifty wounded, evacuated from the *Amartyst's* total complement of a hundred and eighty men.

Remaining on board were over ninety crewmen, who were mostly uninjured, but including a few more lightly wounded who were treated on board. The shelling had stopped, but no one could move on the open deck without drawing the attention of communist snipers, who obviously had the ship under view in their long-distance rifle sights.

As the day wore on, the emasculated crew on board breathlessly awaited the next salvo of shells. Under those officers who had escaped injury, crew members were moved around the ship as adroitly as possible, replacing those killed or wounded and evacuated.

The chef and his assistant cook performed noble work in difficult conditions, supplying crew members around the ship, still in their action stations, with sustenance to keep them fit for the fight and to maintain their morale.

The coming of night enabled the destroyer to land the last of its wounded.

The following day, both groups of wounded already on shore in the custody of the local nationalist forces were taken to a missionary hospital in nearby Kiangyin. A party from the British embassy in Nanking, in the charge of Tim Denton, met them and arranged for their transportation by train to Shanghai, where more advanced hospital services were available. From there the wounded could be distributed later to Hong Kong and Britain, as soon as they were able to travel.

The chief attaché at the embassy had contacted Rear Admiral Charles Mason, second in command of the navy in the Far East. He immediately ordered the *Convort*, under its captain, Lieutenant Commander Robert Sinclair, still the incumbent guard ship at Nanking, to sail to the assistance of the *Amartyst*.

With the destroyer stranded, Colonel Jian Li regarded his order to prevent the ship from arriving at Nanking as accomplished. If any further developments were to take place in dealing with the stricken destroyer, decisions about it would be in the hands of his superiors. He would await their future orders in that case.

So, for the time being, the guns remained silent. But lookouts kept a tight eye on the gun sites on the north bank. Meanwhile, as soon as the ceasefire looked as if it would continue, the rest of the able-bodied crew on the stranded ship slaved to assess and repair as much damage as they could handle, under the skilful guidance of the ship's engineers.

A certain amount of welding took place. Otherwise, bedding, concrete, and materials of all kinds, were resourcefully collected and applied to the over forty damage sites below the ship's waterline. The superstructure was cleaned up and repaired as far as possible, with the main emphasis on securing the facilities to make the ship seaworthy again – albeit on calm river water, rather than the open, forbidding ocean.

It was fortunate that the destroyer had been attacked and disabled by field guns of a limited calibre, rather than by naval guns firing armour piercing shells, as would have occurred in a battle at sea.

30

It took the *Convort* just over an hour to be ready to leave its berth, to go to the aid of the stranded ship. It had to wait for some crew members who were ashore. The ship had come under orders from the Flag Officer Far East, Rear Admiral Charles Mason, to prepare for action stations. Fortunately, the *Convort* had already been refuelled and revictualled in preparation to sail at the completion of its stint of service. Rumours pervaded the ship, as news of the plight of the *Amartyst* filtered in. Out of the blue, at the end of their peaceful service, they were threatened with combat.

After months of their passive, leisurely life, it was a sudden shock for the crew to be faced with peril from a self-appointed enemy. The adrenalin levels of crew members, long exposed to low levels for a relaxed duty, began to rise to fighting pitch. Immediate and severe danger was at hand.

The captain, Lieutenant Commander Robert Sinclair, spoke to the entire crew over the tannoy, when they had all reported on board.

'The *Amartyst* has been attacked on its way to relieve us at Nanking. The damage has been done by artillery from the communist-held bank of the river. The barrage was sufficient to drive the ship out of control, fortunately to the south bank and friendly forces, where it ran aground. There have been many casualties. Our plan is to try to tow the *Amartyst* off the mud and to safety. We must expect the communists will resist our efforts. I am therefore declaring actions stations for the entire crew from the end of these orders. We plan to arrive at full speed to spoil the aims of the artillery batteries. Gun crews must be ready to fire at will to silence any opposition from the north bank. Light arms must also be ready to deal with any boats they may employ and any firing from the shore itself, including snipers. Towing apparatus must be prepared immediately. I have to say; the British navy's reputation is at stake. Two other ships from Shanghai are also on the move to Kiangyin as backup, forty miles down-river from the *Amartyst*. We have our duty to do. Good luck everyone.'

The *Convort* cast off and moved into the middle of the Yangtze. Along its deck rails, as a message to both sides of the civil war, the crew had fixed an assortment of union jacks and British navy ensigns.

The coming of the *Convort* during the afternoon gave the remaining crew of the *Amartyst* a huge boost of confidence, as they waited in a helpless condition for the navy to take steps to extricate them from their exposed and powerless plight.

The *Convort* arrived in the reach of the river where the *Amartyst* lay grounded, awash with the waves it made as it disturbed the calm river water.

It presented a difficult target for communist guns, lying away from the shore, to range on such a fast-moving ship, cutting the river water at well over twenty knots and giving itself part of a screen from the spray created by its bow wave.

Nevertheless, the enemy shore guns fired salvo after salvo into the area surrounding the *Amartyst* to deter the *Convort* from going to its aid. In that, they succeeded. The rescue ship found the barrage too lethal to stop for its purpose.

'Look at that,' Chief Petty Officer Richard Palmer said to Lieutenant James McGreggor, the chief engineer, on the *Amartyst*. 'They know how to play military tactics well enough. The *Convort* has had to keep going or it would have been blown out of the water if it diverted to help us – and risking the obliteration of our ship.'

'We have to wait to see what the navy now has up its sleeve,' McGreggor replied. 'It's a pretty tricky situation. If it can't be solved militarily, the navy might face a humiliating climb down and have to be rescued by politics.'

Unknown to both men and the rest of the *Amartyst*'s crew, Lieutenant Commander Robert Sinclair was made of sterner stuff. He arrested the high speed of the *Convort* two miles further downstream, when the gun crews had concluded they had driven him off.

He rang the engine room. 'Reduce to five knots.'

Then to the helmsman. 'Reverse course.'

Then to the crew at large. 'Prepare for action. It's us or them.'

The *Convort* moved at low knots close to the cliffs of the south shore for camouflage for as long as possible, before disclosing its presence by closing with the stricken *Amartyst* to take the destroyer in tow, away from its unwelcome, imposed, and fatal mooring in mud.

Unfortunately, communist spotters finally saw the *Convort*, returning to the fray. The enemy guns quickly opened fire again, but this time the *Convort*, though more or less stationary, was ready for the fray.

Its gun crews, working with demonic and energetic skills, finally released from their frustration and fear, gave everything to their task, determined to discharge their orders to a man. Every heavy and lighter gun on the ship opened-up a broadside of shot, creating a precedent the communist soldiers had never before experienced.

Following their prearranged plan, the *Convort's* armaments carpeted the inland areas where the communist guns were located. Medium weapons made the opposite shore completely inhospitable to enemy marksmen, supported by lighter weapons, which made continuous sweeps, as had been agreed beforehand, preventing any movement of enemy gun crews or reinforcements.

Robert Sinclair kept the embassy informed of his destroyer's progress or lack of it. With the *Convort's* barrage he had virtually destroyed the enemy's firepower that had continued to endanger the grounded ship.

At least temporarily.

He imagined that his sudden attack would have stunned the communist troops. But he knew that he had only a short time before the enemy would bring up fresh forces and reserve weapons to renew their onslaught.

Prepared as his crew had been for towing the *Amartyst*, his attempt to take the damaged destroyer in tow, however, failed. The stranded destroyer just would not budge from its mud anchorage. Having turned downstream again, the *Convort* made a second attempt to take the *Amartyst* in tow from a new angle.

The second attempt was suddenly frustrated when further artillery shelling began again, just as the *Convort* was committed to attaching a further tow to the beached destroyer. Some shells hit the rescue ship, impairing its steering, and causing casualties. Once again, the *Convort* had to discontinue its rescue operation and withdraw downstream out of the combat area. It had lost nine men killed and over twenty wounded.

On the report of the explicable failure of the *Convort* to salvage the *Amartyst* by towing it off its grounding and away to safety down the river, Commander James Stafford, the senior attaché at the embassy at Nanking, consulted the Flag Officer Far East, Rear Admiral Charles Mason once again.

'I have recently been joined as my assistant by Lieutenant Commander Tim Denton. He came to me from the staff college course. Previously, he had several appointments with the Ennerman Lines, including second deck officer, following his over five years' experience as engineer in destroyers throughout the war. He was chief for two. Would you consider appointing him to take charge of the *Amartyst*? He is a very resourceful officer. It will take some imagination and some radical ideas to salvage this situation. The navy's reputation is at stake. He could be given twenty-four hours to see what he could do with it. Otherwise, we shall have to go cap in hand to the communists with all the unwelcome implications that might entail.'

'That is sound reasoning,' the admiral replied. 'It's a good idea. Give it a try. I think it should be exactly as you have outlined. Brief him accordingly and keep me posted.'

James Stafford lost no time. Tim was away from the embassy, dealing with the transfer of the wounded to Shanghai. He was ordered to return immediately to the embassy, arriving late in the same evening.

'Tim, Admiral Mason and I have been discussing a possible solution to the plight of the *Amartyst*. The attempts to tow the ship away from the mud have failed. We want you to go down there. You will be formally appointed as captain. As you know, the ship's own captain and first officer have been wounded and are off the ship. There are about ninety to a hundred crew members still on board uninjured, but including a few with minor wounds. Time is running out. We think you should be given carte blanche to do whatever you think fit to get that ship off the mud and out of the firing area. Let's say twenty-four hours. If there is no hope of recovery we are going to have to make embarrassing approaches to the communists, with all the difficult political implications that would bring. As you will appreciate, this is an order from the highest level, now ratified by the Admiralty in London, so all I can say is the very best of luck.'

'I'll get to the ship right away,' Tim replied. 'I may have to get them out of bed.' It was a flippant remark in a serious situation. It was his way of concealing the severity of the commission he had just been given.

'I don't think so, Tim, they aren't having much sleep on board,' his chief replied. 'They are waiting for the navy to do its stuff.'

Tim was driven by embassy car as near to the site of the stranded destroyer as it was possible to reach. His thoughts were churned up.

It was the most unexpected order he could ever have as a captain. But he disciplined his mind to consider what steps might have to be taken to discharge it. Some thoughts were already crowding into his head.

And then he thought of the crew and hoped they would not object to being captained by a man from the office. But as he glanced at his jacket hanging in the car, he noticed his many ribbons from the Second World War. After all, he mused, he had had an outstanding war record. But then as now, in the end, it is performance that counts and his immediate task was going to be tough.

The stranded ship had been informed of the decision by the embassy. Two sailors were waiting for him with a sampan. They saluted. 'Welcome aboard, sir,' one of them said. 'We really need you.' They rowed him the few feet to the side of the ship shielded from communist eyes, where he climbed a rope ladder.

It was not the usual way for a new captain to board his first command, or any other for that matter. It was the most inglorious assumption of a captain's duty that could be imagined, but he realised that he had been offered a win-or-win challenge. If he failed, the circumstances that prevailed would be blamed for the failure. They would simply be attributed to being beyond the capacity of anyone to bring about their transformation. If he succeeded, he would have made his mark for ever in the navy.

Climbing on board, Tim was welcomed by the surviving senior officers. They included Lieutenant James McGreggor, chief engineer on the *Amartyst*, who had taken temporary charge of the ship, Sub-Lieutenant Walter Twyford – the deputy to Lieutenant Henry Dawson, the first officer, who had been evacuated badly wounded – and Chief Petty Officer Richard Palmer, who headed the ratings. Tim noted Palmer's wartime ribbons on his uniform. They matched his own and gave him quiet reassurance.

Darkness had fallen. It would give his plans the best chance of fulfilment. He was hoping for the darkest of nights.

'We have twenty-four hours to see if we can do it by ourselves,' Tim told the three men. 'It has to be pretty prompt, or there will be hell to play with the communists. Are many men asleep already do you think?' he asked.

'No one is sleeping,' Richard Palmer said. 'We are all waiting to see what the navy would do next.'

'I would like to recommend a five-point plan. If you agree with it, Richard can assemble all the men on board. I will explain it to them so that we can all pull together to get us out of this mess.'

He then itemised the five points.

'First things first,' said Tim. 'We have to lighten the ship. Anything that can be moved must be thrown overboard, including ammunition and removable weapons. Walter, that can be done immediately after I have spoken to the crew. Richard, I want to be absolutely certain that all the damage sites under water have been made as watertight as possible. Perhaps you would give thorough checks with the best crewmen to guarantee the repairs and temporary solutions. We face river water but everything will fail if any leaks decide to open-up again.

'The engines will play an important part in the extrication of this ship. James, after all the battle damage, you will have already monitored the state of the engines. Can you check all systems so that on my signal, the engines can run very briefly at full power? This will only be for a few seconds. I shall then ask for minimum revolutions of the screws. We shall need the initial reverse power but then utter silence to avoid awakening the opposition. Also, make sure the engineers are ready with as much black smoke as possible to confuse the gunners. We shall need it once daylight returns.'

'Chief,' Tim spoke again to Richard Palmer. 'Does this crew, or what remains of it, include a diver with equipment, or at least crew members who are experienced in diving?'

'Yes, sir,' Richard replied. 'A trained diver was added to the crew specifically for this posting, which was meant to include a long period on the river at Nanking, in case of any interference with the ship. I know that he was involved in underwater mines and explosives, during his training.'

'I'm glad to hear your last remark. You may already have guessed my mind,' Tim said. 'Would you give him precise orders and stress that so much will depend on him.

'Brief him to follow the line of the bows and assess the depth of burial of it in the mud. Ask him to check that it is confined to mud and does not involve rocks. We can't afford to get onto the river only to sink bows first. I want him to lay not less than four low-charge dynamite capsules each side of the bows, buried as much as possible around the bow keel. But the final number could depend on what he finds. They will have to be on a timer. Once they blow, the engines will drag us off, hopefully nearly simultaneously.

'Finally, from now on everyone must only use shielded lamps. When the ship moves, all lights must be extinguished except those in the bowels of the ship. Action to be timed for two o'clock, when I hope the communists are asleep or at least drowsy. For the moment that will be all. I will now relay the plan to the crew as soon as possible.'

The three officers suddenly felt a surge of confidence. They judged their new captain was a man of decision and determination. They went away eagerly to discharge his orders.

The surviving crew members gathered together below deck in dim light to listen to an appraisal of their situation by their new captain, Lieutenant Commander Tim Denton. They were in good heart but somewhat quiescent. Tim thought they were weighing him up. He outlined the overall situation and told them that a cruiser and another destroyer were leaving Shanghai to escort the *Amartyst* downstream out of harm's way. But he stressed that the situation was entirely in their hands. He had been given twenty-four hours to see if the destroyer could be recovered. If not, they would have to yield to the communist rebels.

He then said that the five-point plan he had described to them was immediately to be put in place as they dispersed from the meeting. Everything depended on each element of it working to plan. They were reminded that everything relied on every man directly involved in being able to discharge his task with the greatest accuracy and determination.

Within the hour, Tim received confirmation from the chief engineer that the ship's engines were checked and ready for the task he had outlined. Within a second hour, the chief petty officer reported that the diver was optimistic about their chances. The bows had been snared by about nine feet depthwise of mud, and a horizontal length of the keel of fifteen feet. The mud varied in its density but there were no rocks. He would plant four charges accordingly, buried on each side of the bow line, and three more on each side, back from the bow line and low down on the keel, with a timer fixed to fire them simultaneously.

The chief reported that many more adjustments and improved fixtures had been made to the damage sites under the waterline, including more welding. He was confident they would withstand the river water pressure, as long as the speed of the ship was not excessive.

With all preparations completed, tension mounted. If the retrieval failed, the communist gunners on the north bank, roused by the sounds of their attempt, would have a stationary target despite the darkness.

Exactly at two o'clock, the captain rang the chief engineer to start the engines. Within seconds, after the revs built up, they were put to full power. At that point, the captain ordered the fuses to be blown on the underwater charges. For a moment, nothing happened. Then came the muffled explosions of the underwater mines.

Suddenly, the ship, as if shrugging off its impediment, moved backwards sharply. The captain immediately ordered the engines to be run at minimum speed. It seemed a lifetime to the crew members scattered around the ship at action stations, yet, it was in fact only a minute or two. Everyone gritted his teeth, awaiting the arrival of the first enemy shells.

The coxswain on duty allowed the ship to reverse the course it had taken onto the mud. The captain ordered him to arrest the reversal of the ship at the earliest opportunity and to move ahead at low knots, steering the ship close in, keeping as near as possible to the nationalist shore. Although it was moving against the flow of the river, the destroyer, having reversed its crash course into the southern bank, had thereby begun heading in the direction of Nanking, as if it were still trying to fulfil its commission.

Such a fulfilment, however, was not to be achieved. Firing blindly into the night on the sights already set from their daylight attacks, the communist guns went into action a few minutes after the destroyer had broken free from its torment, but without further hits.

The destroyer made a mile or two and lost the attention of the guns. It was a manoeuvre the *Amartyst* used for the next two days, playing hide and seek with the communists, who were still striving to prevent the ship's advance to Nanking. Each time local batteries opened fire, the destroyer moved on. Keeping close to the southern shore it successfully evaded further damage, moving several times up river.

However, the struggle weighed progressively against the ship. Apart from the increasing capacity of the communists to track the ship, they had time to assemble more guns ahead of its course, and the river was slowly getting narrower. The *Amartyst* was forced to anchor finally a mere ten miles towards Nanking. It was still afloat but impossibly trapped.

At that point, Tim received the bad news that the cruiser and destroyer dispatched from Shanghai to assist the *Amartyst* were heavily shelled as they moved along the first miles of the Yangtze River. Damage to both ships and the numbers of killed and wounded inflicted on them by artillery hits had forced them to turn back.

During the next few days the *Amartyst*'s crew stood down from action stations, but still living on the alert. Tim realised the hopelessness of trying to struggle on as the further preparations of the communists made a noose around his neck.

After two weeks had passed they became resigned to an interminable wait. It seemed only too probable that some kind of negotiation with the communist enemy would have to be conceded. It looked as if the British navy had fallen foul of a cunning and persistent, self-appointed enemy.

It was plain that the communists recognised they had made a coup and were determined to exploit it to the full. In the campaign with the nationalists, they had frustrated a routine, long-standing, arrangement between their enemy and the British.

They calculated that their successful apprehension of the ship could be interpreted as a symbol that they were getting the upper hand in the civil war.

31

The *Amartyst* was virtually helpless in the hands of the communist forces – an imprisonment betokened by the armed guards on small boats nearby on the river, and the gun emplacement that had appeared on the shore of the north bank, with its gun barrel aimed at the stationary destroyer. The next week or two lengthened to more than a month, during which time the delivery of any supplies was formally prevented by the communist blockade. Visitors to the ship were forbidden.

Fortunately, the enemy was unable to cut off the ship's communications by radio. It enabled crucial supplies to be secreted in during the darkest of nights from the nationalist shore.

One day a Chinese delegation approached the destroyer. They came unarmed. Tim Denton knew it was fruitless to resist their request to board the ship.

They brought a linguist whose mastery of English was good enough for their purpose. Through a loud hailer he called to speak to the captain from about twenty yards away.

'As you can now see, Captain, your ship is damaged and cornered. We have waited several weeks to let you see that a rescue attempt is now impossible. Soon your food and water will be exhausted. Perhaps some members of your crew are sick or injured and are in need of treatment. In other words, you are now in a parlous position. We would like to come on board in the hope that you will accord us the courtesy of meeting to discuss the situation in a friendly atmosphere.'

Tim could see the obvious. Their number was too small to be a threat. And unarmed. Their guns would not fire while they were on the ship or in the vicinity.

He really had no option. At their mercy, he ordered a table to be placed on the deck, only feet away from where they would first embark from mounting the ladders.

He then ordered crewmen to drop Jacob's ladders over the side. The four members of the delegation, including the interpreter, climbed aboard, secretly confident their mission would be fulfilled.

The leader of the group, infantry Captain Jin Hong, saluted Tim, but the latter did not return it. Jin Hong wasted no time in getting to the real objective in the mind of the delegation, speaking through his interpreter.

'Captain, we do not wish to destroy your ship nor cause further casualties among your crew. My commanders have been in touch with the highest levels of the leadership of the People's Liberation Army. We had to take action when your ship first violated Chinese waters without permission, before opening fire on our positions on the way from Shanghai. You will understand that it was our military duty to defend our men and installations when we were attacked. Our leadership will be happy to release the ship if you can confirm that you were responsible for instigating the exchange of fire between your ship and the coastal guns of the People's Liberation Army.'

Tim was somewhat taken aback by the effrontery of those charges. He later reflected on what a good example it was of the human predilection to turn an initial action by an offending party to the perpetrator's own advantage. In such a case, he ignores the time sequence of subsequent events but quotes them as offences, enabling him to pose as the injured party. It was a question of overwhelming the original offence, by focusing on the defensive steps then taken by the injured party as if they were of offensive intent.

Tim replied with a full version of events, which he had taken the trouble to amass from his discussions with the wounded crewmen he had sent on their way to Shanghai, from his personal embassy orders, and from subsequent communications, as well as from the reports of the members of the remaining crew on board.

'The British government have customarily stationed a ship guarding its embassy at Nanking. No Chinese government has declared the Yangtze a prohibited waterway. The ship was always used only as a guard ship for the British embassy. The strategic changes your army has made were not previously announced and ratified. At the moment, your army and that of the nationalists share the entire Yangtze River system. Since the embassy is still in the hands of the nationalists we had a right to continue our relationship with it.

'As a matter of fact, I was not in command of this ship from Shanghai but have gathered reports from all sources. I can see that you decided to forestall the progress of this ship on its lawful mission. Small arms fire was first used to deter the ship's progress, then artillery fire on an intimidatory scale, and finally on an attack basis. It was only when the last phase of your attempts to deter the ship was committed that this ship opened fire in self-defence. This is my decided position and I have no intention of changing it. It's the true story of this sorry affair and I ask you to persuade your commanders that enough is enough. Damage to the ship is severe. There have been heavy casualties. We would accept an apology if you let the ship go free.'

Captain Jin Hong saluted Tim, who returned the salute. The delegation departed. Tim half expected that a salvo of shells would soon be delivered on the *Amaryst*. But their guard boat was still in position on the river. Nothing came.

A further week passed. It felt like being in a prisoner of war camp. But there were many compensations.

He knew there was no hope of continuing to Nanking. In any case, the ship was in no condition to fulfil its duty there. Having had to renounce his determination to reach Nanking, Tim Denton was forced to switch his objective to the reverse options.

He soon accumulated his mental energies and set his mind, with a never relenting determination to reach Shanghai.

He alerted his remaining senior officers to the possibility of escape. 'The arrival of that delegation has made my mind up. They have no intention of alleviating our misfortune. They will exploit it to the full. There is no doubt that our incarceration and suffering mean nothing to them in the interim. The only hope we will have is to take advantage of the status quo. They are used to our imprisonment. Day after day they are becoming accustomed to the situation. It is something we can turn to our own use. Keep a close eye on their habits and routines. They may come in useful to us.'

The time in forced captivity allowed for the more systematic repairs and checks on the battle damage that could permit water penetration. He encouraged the crew to make the ship as seaworthy as possible to sail at high speed if necessary. The engines were regularly run and maintained in operating condition. Their fuel stock was still more than adequate for a getaway. They were only about one hundred miles from Shanghai.

The day of opportunity came on the last day but one of July. Tim noticed that the numerous craft surrounding the destroyer when first cornered had given way to several small craft, eventually only one. He also noticed that the soldiers acting as guards had become slack in their duty. At night they failed to retain their vigilance of the day.

The guns had long since ceased firing. Tim hoped the gunners, too, were sleeping at night. He saw that commercial traffic on the river had resumed after the battle. It included boats carrying passengers as well as goods.

He put his mind to work on an escape, using the new circumstances and opportunities. He knew that the battle had transferred to political wrangling internationally. Perhaps the communists thought they had the upper hand with the semi-possession of the vessel.

How unjust the communist attitude had been. He planned to turn the tables on them. He would take his chance.

During those intervening weeks, he advised the whole crew that one day they should to be ready for instant action stations. He told them that the ship's officers were working on a plan that would be implemented at night, when the right opportunity arose.

His policy had the benefit of maintaining morale. There was also plenty of work to do for an escape to succeed. Tim had initiated a two-fold programme. On the one hand, he was anxious to repair as much damage as possible, on the other, he wanted to disguise the appearance of the *Amartyst*, to reduce the ability of enemy watchers to recognise the ship and if possible to deceive people on shore that it was a warship.

Many men were involved in restoring the damage to the superstructure as far as was within their skills and available materials. More importantly, they secretly busied themselves making simple, easily erected structures, to change the silhouette of the *Amartyst*. Crew members went ashore in the middle of the darkest nights, collecting materials and equipment for their purpose supplied by the local nationalists, as clandestinely as possible, to avoid communist spies infesting the onshore regions.

The ammunition and all moveable weapons had been jettisoned, so the gun turrets could be completely obscured. The crew practised fitting the fixtures at night that would give the ship a different look.

An escape would be a daring dash under disguise and without arms.

The officers briefed duty crew members, who were acting as sentries guarding the destroyer, and the lookouts on duty every day and each night. They kept a close eye on the comings and goings on the river, reporting anything unusual.

Once Tim had satisfied himself that the work on the ship had reached a level of suitability for their purpose, he issued a general order to the officers for briefing the crew. He himself then opted to remain on duty early each night to be able to deal with any possibility to escape if the correct conditions arose.

'Once it's quite dark, lookouts should sound the alarm if they see a larger ship sailing down-river. All the better if it is a passenger ship and lit up. They will have to keep their eyes focussed as far up river as they are able to see with their binoculars.'

Nothing happened for ten nights after the plan had been finally agreed and preparations for it completed. But about half-past midnight on the eleventh night, the lookout on duty rang the bridge, which had been repaired to a temporary state for the captain to direct his command.

'Sir.' Able Seaman King, on lookout, spoke to his captain. 'There's a pretty large ship for river traffic in sight well up river from here. It's lit up, suggesting some passengers are aboard, although they will probably be asleep by now. It's not going very fast so I reckon it will be at least fifteen minutes before it draws level with us.'

'Good work, King,' Tim replied, turning immediately to sound the signal throughout the ship to go into action. The crew had rehearsed the drill so many times they moved their materials into place with the speed and expertise of a crack team of scene changers on the London stage.

Tim waited until the ship sailed slowly towards them. When it reached a position mid-stream between the *Amartyst* and the north shore of the river, he ordered the chief engineer to start the engines at slow revs. It was an order to keep the noise to a minimum and muffled by the passing ship's engines.

The *Amartyst,* with every light extinguished, slowly slipped its anchorage by dropping the chain attaching to the anchor. It moved out into the darkness well behind the passenger ship, avoiding being illuminated by its reflected light. The solitary guard boat lying several hundred yards away showed no signs of movement. The men on board were probably in a drunken sleep.

The crew of the *Amartyst* knew they had a distance of just over a hundred miles to cover for their freedom, without lights or usable armaments. They would have to sail between hostile guns from the port, north bank, and, perhaps, mistaken guns from the starboard, south bank.

The passing passenger ship had doused most of its lights and increased its speed, to pass as soon as possible through the danger zone of the river where the fatal combat had taken place. The facts of the contest between shore and ship had become well known during the intervening weeks and noted by the many users of river shipping.

The passing ship was followed gratefully by the *Amartyst* at a respectable distance, completely blacked out, the crew hoping that if the enemy gunners attacked the passenger ship, they would completely fail to see the destroyer following incognito in its wake.

Tim Denton assumed from the conduct of the ship ahead of him that it was from the nationalist ranks and therefore hostile to the communists. He waited with bated breath for signs of a response from the north bank military cohorts – alert to see if they had seen the ship and planned to attack it. Obviously, the vessel had planned to get through the fighting zone during darkness.

Soon enough he saw flashes from artillery fire on the north side of the river. As soon as he did so, the guns of the nationalists on the south side replied to protect their ship. The duel to destroy or defend the passenger ship was fierce and prolonged.

Tim Denton had to discipline himself. It was difficult to concentrate on his mission. He found himself being constantly torn away from it by the cacophony and interminable succession of instant transformations of night into day that the cascading shells bestowed on the river.

He ordered the chief engineer to reduce speed to ease the distance from the ship he was shadowing. It was proving hard to remain concealed from the flashes of the shells fired by the communists on and around the passenger ship. It took nerves of steel to give that order, impetuous as he was to go for freedom at the fastest possible rate.

Presumably, either the captain of the passenger ship had had no idea of the extent of the communist advances and strength of their armaments, or he had assumed that his innocent ship carrying the citizens common to both combatants would be respected.

It was to be an assumption with an outcome of terrifying dimensions, as the communist guns eventually ranged their fire accurately on the passenger ship.

The hostile gunfire tore the ship apart, killing or drowning most of the passengers and crew. The salvos from the south bank were clearly ineffective in deterring the savage assault of the guns on the north bank.

Fortunately, the wreck of the passenger ship did not catch fire. Tim was afraid he would never get through without being seen if it burned before sinking. The wreck drifted towards the north bank, leaving scores of people swimming, or clinging to wreckage, or drowning in the middle of the river.

He ordered the steersman to veer to starboard as near the south bank as safety would permit, after arresting his speed yet again, in judging the course of the battle.

At last, as the shellfire ceased and total darkness returned, he ordered an increase of speed. He relied on the combatants to be either licking their wounds or dancing with rejoicing. The destroyer's two diesel engines slowly increased the ship's speed, with crew members stationed at the most vulnerable damage spots under the waterline to check that the repairs were holding. Unlike the modest rate of knots at which the *Amartyst* had originally sailed up river from Shanghai, it now approached the maximum revolution of its screws to carry the ship forward at near maximum knots eastwards along the widening river and into the estuary.

At an opportune moment Tim ordered the radio officer to send a message to the embassy at Nanking. 'We have escaped from the communist trap and are now at full speed down-river for Shanghai.'

He had an immediate reply from Commander James Stafford. 'Unexpected but most welcome. Brilliant accomplishment. All news later. Well done. The navy's thanks. God save the King.'

The *Amartyst* headed for the final hazard, the communist-held forts at Baoshan and Wusong in the mouth of the Yangtze. By a prearranged signal it met the destroyer *Convort*, still lingering after its relief of duty at Nanking and failure to tow the stranded ship off the mud. In the intervening weeks, it had offloaded the dead and wounded from its unlucky encounter with the communist artillery and received emergency repairs from shell damage.

Since *Amartyst* was without usable armaments, it was intended that the *Convort* should provide covering fire to enable the unarmed *Amartyst* to get through. In the event, the ships in the closing hours of darkness on the last day of July escaped without detection at Baoshan but by the time of reaching Wusong, the searchlights sweeping the entrance to the estuary mouth were no longer effective in daylight.

Tim Denton and the skeleton crew of the *Amartyst* were exultant. Tim ordered the radio operator to send a message to naval headquarters, Far East: 'Have rejoined the fleet south of Wusong. No further damage. No further casualties. God save the King.'

They had indeed achieved a remarkable escape from the clutches of a hostile and not yet legitimate power in a heavily damaged destroyer whose guns had been rendered useless by the need to jettison everything movable into the river waters. They had used stealth and delusion to conceal their identity and movements from a point over a hundred miles up the Yangtze River to reach its mouth and liberty.

The two ships reached the Saddle Islands at midday, where they were topped up with oil, supplies of food, medical supplies, and ammunition. The skeleton crew of the *Amartyst* was supplemented by crew members from the *Convort,* enabling both ships to sail to Hong Kong, joined on the way by another cruiser and destroyer as escort.

The Admiralty in London had been continually informed of the successive events. When the *Amartyst* reached Hong Kong the ship received a signal from King George VI:

Please convey to the commanding officer and ship's company of HMS Amartyst my hearty congratulations on their daring exploit to rejoin the fleet. The courage, skill, and determination shown by all on board have my highest commendation. Splice the main brace.

The signal from the king contained an injunction dear to the hearts of navy sailors at any time. On that particular occasion, Tim thought his tot of rum was the best he had ever tasted – and the most dearly earned. If only Vanessa could have been there to share it with him.

32

The *Amartyst* was admitted to the shipyards at Hong Kong for sufficient repairs to enable the ship to sail back to its British base. The work was scheduled to take several months. A fresh crew would have to be assembled.

Soon after his arrival at Hong Kong, a telephone call to Tim Denton came from Commander James Stafford in Nanking. 'Your ship will be made seaworthy for you to sail back to Britain. You are to retain the captaincy, taking over the *Amartyst,* when repaired, and when you are available to do so. The remaining crew will be posted to other ships. They are needed. The Far Eastern fleet has lost over a hundred crewmen killed and badly injured, including those from the *Amartyst*, so they will make up the losses in the three other ships that suffered casualties. Eventually, new crewmen, as needed, will be drafted from Britain for your return trip.'

'What is happening in Nanking, then?' Tim asked him.

'The situation in the civil war is changing dramatically. We will have to evacuate the embassy from Nanking. The communists have got the upper hand in the civil war. They are currently attacking the city, but are meeting fierce resistance and have made little progress after crossing the Yangtze. But we cannot underestimate their military ability. We hear they have erected a monument on the south bank to commemorate their feat. They have outflanked the nationalists and obviously intend to drive them towards the south coast and annihilation,' James replied.

'So, the stalemate on the Yangtze is now over,' said Tim. 'It would have been impossible for the *Amartyst* to survive, if we had still been grounded, only to be overrun by the rebels within a few days.'

'Yes, it was just as well that you escaped at the time you did,' James replied. 'It will remain as an example of resourcefulness and opportunism in the annals of the navy.'

'So, what is going to happen in the meantime?' Tim asked.

'We want you back here to help in the evacuation. We have received orders to travel to Canton, over five hundred miles to the south. It seems a drastic step to take but if things go the way that seems likely, it will only give us a few weeks' respite before we shall have to find another solution,' James told him. 'How soon will you be able to travel?'

'Immediately,' Tim replied.

'It will only be for the interim. I would expect that you will return after a few weeks to your ship to oversee the repairs and tidy up all that has to be done,' James assured him.

'Ring up the RAF at Kai Tak. They will be expecting you. I have arranged for an aircraft to fly you to the south of Nanking at your earliest possible time. It may have to fly the round trip without refuelling but it will be the best bet to get you here safely. But that possibility means there is a snag.'

'And what would that be?' Tim asked, fearing the worst.

'It would require a parachute drop. I understand you did some preliminary ground training with the Fleet Air Arm in the navy during the war,' James cheerfully stated.

'That's true, but I never had cause to put it into action for real,' Tim replied.

'Now's the time to do just that,' James asserted.

'In that case, I am on my way, sir. I hope you will still be there when I can make it,' Tim said, breaking the call.

He called the RAF and was driven in a navy car to the base at Kai Tak, Hong Kong's airport, opened twenty-five years before. It later became the territory's international airport, famous for its close proximity to city buildings, and notorious for the technical skills required by the pilots who had to land there in its city surroundings.

Squadron Leader Dennis Johnson, as pilot, had been allotted to take him on the flight, with his crew, consisting of a co-pilot, navigator, radio operator, and jump-master. Tim was briefed by the jump-master, step by step from exiting the aircraft to landing. Tim's personal belongings were encased in a special container normally used for dropping arms. It would be dropped separately on a self-opening parachute.

'I hadn't expected to be leaping into the unknown when I came into the navy,' Tim mentioned to the jump-master, as if he could expect the man to excuse him from the flight.

'You know what to do,' the jump-master replied. 'It will be a daylight drop onto level soil. All you have to do is remember the drill and follow it exactly. How much flying have you done in your service, sir?' he asked.

'Not much, but I was flown out to China not so many weeks ago by the RAF, so I think I have had some recent preparation for this flight,' Tim replied.

He then went to the officers' mess for a meal and to meet Dennis Johnson, who greeted him with a warm handshake and a light-hearted comment about his mission, which had an underlying indication of the danger he faced.

'You made a remarkable escape from the communists. We have all been impressed with the way you rescued that ship. And now, so soon after escaping, you are going back into the lion's den,' Dennis said to him.

'You know how it is. It's the call of duty,' Tim replied. 'There is one question I have for you, Dennis. Does your flight path keep strictly over nationalist-held territory?'

'Fortunately, at the moment, yes,' he replied. 'Both sides have some aircraft, mostly dated types. But we can keep to the nationalist-held territory all the way, so there is no risk of being intercepted by communist aircraft.'

'How long will the flight take?' Tim asked.

'Well, the flight will cover about eight hundred miles. The Dakota is not the fastest of aircraft, but we should have you in the drop zone between four and five hours.'

'That sounds about right, thanks,' Tim commented.

'What will you have to do this time?' Dennis asked. 'I understand it will be the second visit you have made to Nanking in only a few weeks. I hope there isn't a second ship to be rescued.'

Being of the same rank as Tim, he felt he could learn something about the purpose of Tim's mission. It was a matter of being brought up to date in the civil war, whose mysterious twists and turns were not understood by, nor reported closely by media people.

'The communists have crossed the Yangtze. They will overrun Nanking. The British Embassy, as you know, has been located there for a long time but it will have to be closed down and moved immediately. As assistant naval attaché, I have to get back there to retrieve our assets and move them somewhere else. We must hold on to our interests as long as possible. It is not clear yet what the outcome will be in the civil war, although many are now expecting the nationalists will be beaten,' Tim explained.

'The RAF has staff up there as well, so they will be caught up in the turmoil,' Dennis added. 'It's always a risky business being at the whims of another country as a representative of your own. I have orders to drop you at a nationalist airfield just south of Nanking. A car should be waiting there to take you to your destination. We take off in half an hour.'

The reliable Dakota took off and headed northwards. Tim was interested to see the panorama of China laid out below him, both highlands and lowlands. He slept for part of the flight but was awakened by the jump-master when approaching the drop zone. The aircraft, flying at the optimum height for the drop, circled the airfield, which Tim was pleased to recognise as the terminal he arrived at when he first flew to the embassy in China with June Wetheram, some weeks before.

His personal kit was tumbled out first. The aircraft still circled to watch it land safely. Then the jump-master alerted Tim to be ready to go. He did everything by the book, landing safely on the turf, and unclipping his parachute.

The car took him into the embassy building a few miles into the outskirts of the city. He could see the dust rising from artillery shellfire, wondering if he might be too late to help in the rescue of the embassy from the advancing communists.

The embassy building was still standing but had the appearance of a hive of activity. Several ancient trucks were lined up near the front door, being loaded with office furniture and records. He saw army, air force, and navy men and women working frantically and with a will.

Tim quickly found Commander James Stafford.

'James, you have started without me,' Tim called out with a laugh. 'I've come as soon as I could.'

'Tim. Welcome home. We have our own truck. All our records and office furniture need to be loaded and the staff will have to squeeze into it at the last minute.

'We are driving all the way to Canton in the south. The nationalists have loaned us the trucks, but the way things are going it looks as if we can regard them as a gift,' James said.

'It's that bad, is it?' Tim queried.

'Reports coming in are not good,' James replied. 'It looks as if the communists are determined about their objectives and are united behind them, but the nationalists do not have the ideological drive of their opponents and are probably divided on how to combat their enemy. They have also been guilty of mismanagement. Consequently, they are on the run now. I don't know whether they will ever be able to stop the communists, but we shall see. By the way, June Wetheram has been great. Find out where she is and see if you can help. We should be ready to move off in another hour.'

The navy part of the beleaguered embassy set off on their long journey, vainly trying to join up with the elusive headquarters of the nationalist government. An overnight stop they were forced to take was uncomfortable and makeshift. They had sufficient water but were short of food.

No sooner had the nationalists moved their headquarters to Canton than they moved again north-west to Chungking and from there north-west again to Chengtu. When Sichang to the south-west fell, it caused Chiang Kai-shek and two million supporters to flee to the island of Taiwan, off the south-east coast of China.

Since the British government had not been able to assist the nationalists in the civil war, when that decisive turn of events took place – and facing the inevitable – Britain declared its recognition of the People's Republic of China only three months later, once it had declared itself as the legitimate government of China, with its capital in Beijing.

By the end of the year it was time for Tim to close the book on his experience in China. He had arrived full of expectation that he would spend perhaps two years, gathering knowledge of the job of attaché and hopefully travelling the immense length and breadth of the country, which had had such a long history and had made such an impact on the rest of the world.

At the time he received his marching orders he was still travelling with the embassy naval staff, thrown into itinerant disarray by the sudden invasion of the communist forces over the Yangtze and attack on the city of Nanking.

The Admiralty, through the Far Eastern fleet command, formally reversed his posting to China, confirming that his temporary and emergency assumption of the captaincy of the *Amartyst* had been converted by appointing him as its substantive captain.

'It's a well-deserved appointment, Tim, congratulations.' James Stafford made an immediate response. 'I shall be sorry to lose you. We have worked well together through some very difficult times.'

'My stay was short and sharp,' Tim replied. 'It has not given me a lot of time to learn much about the job in the embassy.'

'There is another way of looking at it,' James suggested. 'You have had to face events and deal with problems in your short posting that you would have had to wait for over many years in the normal way of the life of an attaché.'

'What will happen to you?' Tim queried.

'I've been here quite a while. My normal posting was up at the end of the year, anyway,' he replied. 'Although the British government has recognised the new regime, we don't know if they will continue the practice of embassies or not. But I will be out of it in a few weeks.'

'I hope our paths will cross again someday, James,' Tim remarked, as he took his leave, to keep an appointment at the Far East fleet headquarters with the officers responsible for crew postings.

33

Tim Denton had several weeks to take over the *Amartyst* as its captain and to organise the ship for sailing back to Britain.

The news was good. A number of the wounded crewmen had recovered in the interim and were ready to return to service. Some new men were sent from Britain. Another ship, which had returned to Britain for scrapping with a skeleton crew, had shed some of its crew, who were transferred to the *Amartyst*. Those additions, when supplementing the few original remaining crew, who had been given shore jobs and loaned to other ships in the interim, together yielded a total crew complement, bringing it back to a normal level for the ship, a hundred and eighty-four men.

The shipyards duly completed their repairs. The *Amartyst* was declared free from its troubles and ready for the high seas once again.

The destroyer's uneventful voyage back to Britain reflected the skilful restoration of the vessel itself, the integration of the newly formed crew, and the overall management of the captain, Lieutenant Commander Tim Denton. Tim ruminated on the large difference in travel time between his flight to China and the destroyer's return via the South China Sea to Singapore, the Indian Ocean, Arabian Sea,

Red Sea, Suez Canal, Mediterranean Sea, Gibraltar, and the Atlantic Ocean, which took around four weeks.

On a fine day the *Amartyst* arrived at Portsmouth naval base. It followed directions to its allocated berth. It was just another ship coming home. The British media had made the most of the ship's exploits, but they had been reported many weeks earlier. In deference to Britain's recognition of the new regime in China, celebrations on the dockside were notable by their absence. But several moored navy vessels sounded their sirens as a welcome and acknowledgement of the *Amartyst*'s accomplishments, as the ship slowly moved towards its berth.

But the nearly two hundred crewmen on board had eyes only for the people standing on the quayside where their ship would tie up. Many had been in the Far East for an extended absence from their families. All were mariners who had been on their naval postings abroad, missing their wives, children, partners, and home comforts.

Not least among them was the captain of the destroyer himself.

Tim Denton had descended from the heights of excitement and his novel preoccupation with his appointment as assistant attaché, to an unexpected job that had escalated into exposing him to personal danger and precarious work.

The fiasco over the attempt of the communists to deter, and then destroy, the *Amartyst* was probably a unique event in the annals of British naval history. He had endured a task that had claimed all his accumulated knowledge and experience. It had generated and evoked still further skills of character and action that he did not know he possessed.

Away from Britain for over a year, he felt as if he had been out of the country for a lifetime. His customary thoughts about life in Britain had been pushed into the background by those of life in another country, where ways and means, and the landscape itself, were so radically different. He had to make an effort to revive the familiar sounds and sights of Britain in his mind. He wanted to be sympathetic towards them. Being comfortable with them would once again seal his homecoming.

Tim's consuming thought overtook his attention even as he entered the naval base. He had to make his way to London at the first opportunity. Vanessa was on the stage that evening. Would she be different in his eyes? Would he be different in her eyes?

It was the longest time they had been separated since they first met. Was it too long to keep the flame of passion alive?

Suddenly, the preoccupations of the preceding months paled beside the hope of seeing her and finding that overpowering emotion of love in her presence again.

Many wives and whole families were awaiting the return of fathers, husbands, and friends. The concourse on the quay was not huge but very animated.

When his duty as captain was done by handing over the vessel to port naval custody, Tim finally took his leave from the *Amartyst*. It was not the done thing to become sentimental about a ship. But before stepping off the vessel his mind raced over the sequence of events involving the ship. The communists had dictated the destroyer's attempt to discharge its commission to replace the *Convort* as guard ship for the British embassy in Nanking.

His indulgence of reminiscences continued as he stepped ashore, but was rudely arrested as he approached a door to the quayside building. A person was standing there, still, and patient in waiting.

It was Vanessa.

The sight of her stopped him in his tracks.

She looked tired, but her face lit up when she spotted him.

It was undignified under the circumstances for Tim to run to her. But she ran to him.

He dropped his case and held out his arms, engaging in an unashamed and heartfelt hug, followed by a mutual searching in eye contact and an end of the world kiss.

Several crew members saw the encounter.

'Crikey, the skipper's onto a winner there,' one rating called to another.

'By God, he deserves it,' was the rejoinder.

Vanessa knew she had to return quickly to London for her performance that evening. She had cut her trip finely. There was no time to lose.

'The navy changed the date and time of your arrival. I had to keep to my stage commitments but it was possible to fit in a quick trip late morning,' she explained.

'I never expected to see you in Portsmouth. I was hoping to give you a big surprise at home when you came back from work later tonight. But how could you do more?' Tim asked.

'You have come back to me, darling. This time you have returned as it were from the dead. I followed all the news about the terrible loss of life from the crews of several ships and knew you would be in real danger. But here you are, at last. Darling, I love you. This long spell has been agony. I feel I can get on with my life again in full. Thank you for coming back to me.' Vanessa poured out her heart on the quayside, oblivious to the many navy men and their families, coming and going around them.

'My love for you gave me the inspiration I needed,' Tim told her. 'It then brought me back to you. And now it binds me together with you for a lifetime'.

There was a brief silence. She looked at him with a quizzical look in her eyes, mixed with a touch of mischief.

'Was your last remark a proposal?' she asked. He was momentarily thrown.

Seeing his temporary confusion and before he had time to think of anything to say, she interrupted his thoughts.

'I have a proposal for you,' she said. 'Will you marry me?'

'Yes, and Yes,' he said with utter conviction but no more words.

The kiss that followed was ever to be the quayside seal of their lifetime for a lifetime.

'Are you free to come home with me now, or do you have things to do?' Vanessa asked.

'Not immediately. I shall come back and report tomorrow. So, yes, we have the rest of the day together,' Tim replied.

'In that case we should hurry to the station. I have to get back to London. I was expecting that you would not be free to walk away from your ship today,' Vanessa said.

The fast train service to Waterloo took them conveniently to their familiar surroundings in the West End and their apartment.

All the way Vanessa pressed Tim to relate the story of his time in China. Every time he dodged an issue or evaded an explanation for an action, Vanessa rigorously prodded him into a reconsideration of what he had said or indeed compelled him to consider what he had not said.

Vanessa asked Tim, 'Why did the navy chief attaché, Commander James Stafford, order you to be the captain to get the destroyer off the beach? You were doing a valiant job on shore caring for the wounded and facilitating their transport to Shanghai. Why didn't he step in himself? He was senior to you and a more experienced officer.'

'It's always the responsibility of a commanding officer to remain in command, to keep the overall view of all the aspects of a situation. The adjustment of any element in a problem, must be handled as far as possible by a subordinate. Only in an extreme case, where no one is suitable for a given task, should a commander take it on as a personal responsibility,' Tim replied.

'But he could have left you with running the navy's contribution to the work of the embassy,' she added.

'I was new to the job and had little experience by the time the crisis occurred,' Tim reminded her. 'As commander, James had the necessary contacts with the various higher command levels with problems that involved British national priorities.'

'Why did he order you to assume command so soon after the grounding?' Vanessa asked. 'Why was it not possible to leave the destroyer where it was? The attacks on it had ceased. Proper talks with the communists could have solved the impasse and further disaster avoided'.

'There was the question of original liability. The navy's reputation was at stake. We had done nothing wrong unwittingly. Severe damage had been done to one of its ships and a large portion of its crew killed or wounded. The fact that the communists had decided to change the rules out of the blue was unknown to us. Furthermore, it was important to try to re-float the ship as soon as possible. It could have settled deeper in the mud and become a hopeless wreck.'

'It must have been an unbelievable relief and release when you finally shadowed that river passenger ship away from your confinement under the communists' guard.' Vanessa clearly had empathised with Tim for those agonising weeks. 'It must have seemed like being in a prison.'

'I guess prison is worse,' Tim reflected. 'But then, I haven't been in prison. I had fresh air, sunlight, close comradeship, something to hope for, and a Spartan diet, instead of the good meals usually served up by navy chefs. So, the shortage of food was a disguised benefit for people who could not be working hard every day and might have become very fat.'

'Were you tempted to stop and rescue any passengers and crew from the passenger boat that the communists shot to bits ahead of you?' Vanessa was draining every possible understanding of what Tim had been through. 'I wondered if the communists might have relented their attitude if you could have saved Chinese citizens.'

'Not at all, because we in turn would have been a sitting target and shot to bits. In a civil war there is no room for clemency. They were glad to sink the vessel and kill all the people on it. When I saw what was happening, of course, I realised a tragedy was unfolding before my eyes, but I had to put it in the back of my mind. Memories of wartime flashed through my mind as it all developed. The terrible decision one has to make from time to time not to pick up struggling and drowning people in the water near one's own ship is not an act to be taken lightly. It leaves scars on those who suffer the experience forever. It happened to me several times in the Atlantic. I never expected to have to go through it again.'

'It was a remarkable feat, darling. I am so proud of you. Just to think, when we said goodbye in Cornwall, who could have imagined what lay ahead of you. You have ended up being the last assistant attaché to China – at least for the time being, perhaps for a very long time,' Vanessa declared.

'So that must be a distinction worth having.' Tim laughed.

Vanessa had sorted out some of the salient thoughts worrying her. She reluctantly turned to the matters of the day.

Tim thought she was hiding something. She seemed excited underneath her normal extrovert behaviour and tiredness. It never occurred to him that her ecstasy could be entirely due to his homecoming.

Vanessa did have more to say. She reserved it until they were safely at home and had finished their meal. It was nearly time for her to leave for the theatre.

'Darling, there is something I have to tell you.'

Tim could see by her countenance that it could not be unpleasant news. But he had been ushered into another world since he last saw her and had lost track of her interests.

'I am waiting with bated breath to hear it,' Tim said. 'All the talk has been about me and I will be glad to dispense with it.'

'You know I always said Ivor Novello was working on what might be his swansong, since he is not in the best of health. While you have been away he finished it and it was put on stage at the Palace Theatre on the fifteenth of September as *King's Rhapsody*. He chose me to be the leading lady. I have to sing seven songs.'

'I knew you would do it, darling. That is absolutely wonderful news. I am thrilled to be in your company. Presumably you are performing tonight. So, I would like to accompany you to the theatre.'

He got up and hugged her until she was breathless.

'Of course, you may,' she said, when she could speak. 'I have taken the liberty of reserving a seat in the grandest place in the house.'

They set off together for the theatre. Tim had no idea what he was about to see. But he relied completely on the fact that Vanessa had said she presented seven songs during the show. He knew that he would be more than recompensed for spending his evening at a theatre, even if it failed to raise a modicum of enthusiasm as an overall production, provided Vanessa could have him riveted to his seat with her glorious voice and charm.

It was a long time since he had been to a theatre production. So, in principle he was excited to be going with her to see whatever Ivor Novello had delivered to the London stage.

Vanessa disappeared to her dressing room, leaving Tim to while away the time until the curtain went up. He had never been to the Palace Theatre before, although he had many times noted its dominating, red-brick, independent position on the west side of Cambridge Circus. It was suitable as a venue for the *King's Rhapsody,* since it had been built with a view to house the *English Grand Opera* sixty years before, commissioned by the producer of the Gilbert and Sullivan operas, Richard D'Oyly Carte.

In the foyer of the theatre, Tim ran into a former shipmate from his war years, Jack Clements, with his wife, Hilda. Being very early for the performance, he suggested they went to the bar. Going over old times and talking about their respective fortunes or lack of them, absorbed them for the entire time until the bell went to signal the stage curtain was being raised.

'It's nice to meet you Hilda,' Tim said, 'Jack and I go back a long way.'

'You're still single then?' Jack observed.

'No, I have had a partner now for six years,' Tim told them.

'But perhaps she doesn't like the theatre?' Hilda ventured.

'Oh, quite the contrary,' Tim responded. 'You will soon see her on the stage.'

'You mean she is in the cast!' Hilda exclaimed. 'How exciting for you.'

'Yes, she has been in several previous Ivor Novello's plays with smaller parts, but this time she is the leading lady,' Tim elaborated.

'She must be Vanessa Coles, then. I hope you are not too parsimonious as her critic,' Hilda remarked. 'Does she ever sing to you in private?'

'That would be telling,' Tim said. 'But as a matter of fact, she does from time to time. I have to leave home for my job, sometimes for as long as a year or more. She seems to derive comfort from my pending absence by singing to me.'

'That is the most impressive thing I've heard for a long time,' said Hilda.

'What are you doing now, Jack?' asked Tim.

'When I came out of the navy I joined an engineering company and have ended up as its director. What about you, Tim?'

'I went into the merchant navy, the Ennerman Lines. Later, the Royal Navy offered me an opportunity I fancied and I am still in it. As a matter of fact, I put into Portsmouth only this morning from a long stint in the Far East.'

'Good God, Tim, I have just put two and two together. It was you who rescued a damaged destroyer and then managed to escape from the Chinese communists. It was all the news here some time back. What a bloody good show you put up. I hope the navy appreciates it.'

The bell rang.

'We'd better go, or we will be blackballed,' said Jack.

'Vanessa has reserved me a seat in a box as a welcome home again sign. I may see you during the interval, Jack, but good to meet you again,' Tim replied, as they parted.

He had a grandstand view of the stage from his seat reserved for very special guests.

The musical turned out to have a vintage Novello mixture. Its diet of royal houses, personages with high-sounding titles, expensive tastes, grand residences, and the tangled web of relationships between people, who had no need to worry about the workaday life as lived by most people, all contrived to take audiences away from the recent war, food rationing, and a Spartan struggle in a difficult world.

It was the last escapist show on the London stage offered by the past master of the genre. Already, *High Button Shoes* from Broadway had invaded the West End, full of dancing and high-spirited dialogue.

Yet a generation or two had loved the Novello pattern and remained loyal to the end. It would run for eight hundred and forty-one performances, with Vanessa staying the distance.

Some of her songs – among others from the show – notably "Someday My Heart Will Awake", "Fly Home Little Heart", and "The Gates of Paradise", were top-scoring contributions to the song stock of British singers.

Tim only had eyes for Vanessa. After all, it was his first day back in Britain. He had been deprived of seeing the only woman in his life for many months. She knew where he was sitting and seemed to be addressing him with the many songs that had carried her to even greater fame after *Perchance to Dream*.

After the final curtain, Tim raced round to her dressing room. He recalled the difficulty he had encountered when he tried to do the same on the first night of her previous show. But there was no concourse clamouring to see the stars on this occasion. The show had been ongoing for about four months.

Nevertheless, the audience had awarded the cast call after call. They loved Ivor Novello, the cast, the music, and the theme of the story.

34

Although Britain had recognised the ascendancy of Chiang Kai-shek during the Second World War, it had been forced to acknowledge the inevitable only five years after that war had ended, when, with the remnants of his army, Chiang absconded to the island of Taiwan to retain his independence in defeat.

In London, Tim Denton was busy for the next few days being debriefed at the Admiralty and intelligence services. Among the representations he faced were approaches from various newspapers for articles about his escape from the Chinese – plus an invitation from a publisher. But he turned them all down categorically.

The one he was glad to accept, however, was a suggestion from the Royal Navy Greenwich College that he should spend a day in its glorious walls, contributing a talk to the current course of officers, followed by a workshop session.

He was excited to be invited to attend as a speaker on the course in which he had been previously a member.

'I think you may have to thank Bruce Fowler for the invitation, darling,' Vanessa commented to Tim, when he had read the letter of invitation from the college.

'Do you think I will have enough to say to make the visit worthwhile?' Tim asked her, revealing his own inhibitions and showing some reluctance.

'Of course, you must respond. It fell to your lot to be the man on the spot at the critical time and you made a success of the commission given to you. You don't have to be that reticent,' she urged him.

'It's just that they will be used to dealing with big-time events and it may not be that captivating to focus on the fortunes of one little ship,' Tim said, guarding his retreat.

'Don't believe a word of that, darling. You were up against overwhelming odds. It will do the members of the course good to hear about it from the man himself and get the chance to discuss the ins and outs of the struggle, which you eventually pulled off with a great deal of skill and aplomb,' Vanessa concluded.

She added something from his own training that was meant to persuade him. 'Remember, success counts, or in the language of the course, you set objectives which were successively reached. You can't present a better example before the course than that.'

On the day appointed for his visit, Tim surprised himself by feeling cool and collected. The nervousness and doubts he had about his ability to fulfil a task in the college from the opposite end of course membership – indeed, in the job of an instructor – had subsided. Fears afflict everybody, but he had learned that truly courageous people were able to put them aside when the moment for action arrived.

Bruce Fowler introduced him to the assembled members of the current course. Tim had been sitting there as a member of the same college course nearly two years before them.

'About a year ago the world was electrified by the escape of HMS *Amartyst* from its virtual imprisonment by the Chinese army. There has been time, since it happened, to ponder on the manner and result of that event. Today, the man who presided over the escape is here to tell us about it and to help us to learn some of the lessons from it.'

Tim was given a warm welcome.

He had been allocated three-quarters of an hour for his talk, followed by questions. After a coffee break he had another slot of the same time, followed again by questions. In the afternoon the time was devoted wholly to workshop activities based on the morning's work.

He had planned the day very carefully. For his first talk he concentrated on the physical, overt aspects of the battle and escape. For the second he focussed on the psychological, unseen backdrop for the entire confrontation with the Chinese communists.

In the workshop he divided the members into groups of four and set the following same three topics to each group. Their findings, opinions, and judgements were reported by each group at a plenary session at the end of the working day:

Review the intelligence and protocols prior to the despatch of the ship.

Consider the wider implications and type of responses to the entrapment.

Relate the level of casualties and damage to the mission's objectives.

It was a long day for Tim at the college. 'How did it all go, darling?' was Vanessa's second question to him when they met at home late in the evening. The first was always, 'Darling, are you really here? It's good to see you. So many times, I have had to imagine you. I dream that you will be here waiting for me to let you in, but oh, you are never here in reality. After the rush of people at the theatre, and all the noise and hubbub of the show, I long to reach home and find you here. It used to be easy for me to cope with it, but it is getting harder. I must be getting old.'

'Nonsense,' Tim reassured her. 'You are not getting old. At twenty-eight you are not yet in your prime. What you say is so true of me, too. I try to picture you sitting, lying, eating, drinking, and singing. I am finding it hard to live with it any more. We should be married. You did ask me if I will marry you.'

'Marriage won't cure the curse of absence if you are absent. But that can wait. Fortunately, I have a stay-at-home job. At least, for the moment,' she said.

Tim outlined the events of his visit to the college.

'It sounds as if you provided a stimulating day for the course. Did they come up with any provocative suggestions, comments, or criticisms?' she asked.

'Well, yes. In the workshop time I divided the members into fours. And they hammered out their ideas. It was quite invigorating to hear the way they saw the whole event objectively and uncovered new aspects and possibilities, which they presented to the whole group as the finale to the day. It was quite an inspiration. The exercise must have stimulated their imagination and came out in the strong competition between the four groups. Of course, I had been through the same process myself and knew the benefit of the exercise.'

'What do you mean by that?' Vanessa asked.

'It's a means to activate the brains of budding commanders. It calls for dredging their knowledge for ideas and seeing things from many points of view,' Tim said.

'I hope you reminded them of the psychology of the situation as well,' Vanessa reminded him.

'As a matter of fact, I did. It was the focus of the second talk in the morning. So, it played an explicit, central part,' Tim responded. 'The shock of the unexpected interference to the passage of the ship, damage, deaths, injuries and the overpowering noise of the artillery barrage created a need for mental space to think and decide objectively. Later on, the pressures the communists subsequently put on us required a build-up of resolve without remission. The entrapment prevented both going forwards and backwards. It created a real problem, in as much as there was no longer a visible solution. Maintaining the morale of the crew in virtual imprisonment was a subject in itself.'

'I hope you didn't raise the question of whether a sailor should be married or not.' Vanessa tried to modify the solemnity of the conversation with what she expected to be a little levity.

'Now why would I do that?' Tim asked, responding to her change of mood. 'They were all eager young officers, and not interested in the preoccupations of the *Amartyst*'s captain.'

'But they might have decided you would have done a better job if you had been married,' Vanessa said, pulling his leg.

'The job I did was calculated to get me home to you, darling,' Tim said, and meant it. 'We have talked it all out before and the time is approaching when we should make a decision about our marriage.'

'That's what I think, too,' Vanessa added. 'I suppose it depends on what posting they will send you to next. Where or to what will it be, do you think?' she asked, but not expecting an answer.

'At least for a while it might be to a training job,' Tim volunteered. 'That means a home posting, to one of the initial officer training establishments in England or Scotland. It's the sort of thing they do with an officer who has been recently involved in something unusual. Perhaps word will get around after my trip to the Greenwich College. Of course, it would likely be only a temporary appointment. And it would depend on the absence of hostilities everywhere.'

At the conclusion of Tim's leave, he duly received his posting. It was to a training job, as he had anticipated.

He was to be the officer in charge of a new cohort of officer cadets, recruited for basic training at the Royal Naval College, Dartmouth.

'I'm so glad you will not be going away,' said Vanessa. 'Are you pleased with it?' she asked. 'Let's hope the scene remains stable for a nice long time.'

'Yes,' he replied. 'It takes me out of the limelight a bit. If I do a good job there I will expect some promotion for my next posting, but that remains to be seen.'

35

For a few weeks, Vanessa was prepossessed by the outstanding success of *King's Rhapsody,* which had all the hallmarks of a long-running hit on the London stage. Since its first staging on the fifteenth of September, nearly a year before, it had amassed a fine reputation, with the promise of persisting into the following year and perhaps even to the year after that.

Tim was similarly stretched to measure up to his new job at Devonport. His performance as a guest lecturer at the Greenwich College had evidently opened-up the new job for him.

Vanessa and Tim were once again glad to wrench themselves away from their jobs to meet each other. They were free to choose, meeting sometimes at their home in London, sometimes in Tim's newly acquired flat in Plymouth.

They were both so engrossed in their jobs, weeks seemed to pass quickly. But late in June, their established life together was rudely shaken.

Tim was unexpectedly and suddenly posted as captain, with a one-step promotion to the rank of commander, to the light cruiser HMS *Kanyard.* The ship had served in the Atlantic and Mediterranean during the war, before being assigned to the Far East fleet. It was paid off into the reserve fleet three years after the war at Chatham, but with the growing concern for an uneasy situation in the Far East, it was subjected to an extensive refit and update, followed by being commissioned again to the Far East fleet. As it happened, many of HMS Amartyst's crew were posted to the *Kanyard,* when the decision to scrap their long-suffering destroyer was taken at about the same time.

After briefly working-up, the *Kanyard* was ready to sail at the end of October. The time scale set only left Tim with a few days' leave before taking up his new job.

Vanessa was full of questions when he received his official notification. Her disappointment was as great as Tim's excitement over the advancement it meant for him.

'It's a bit sudden to interrupt your posting to Dartmouth, isn't it? Does it mean you have proved unsatisfactory or is there something else in the wind, which you haven't told me about?'

'Oh, no, there is nothing sinister about it, darling,' he replied. 'Managing a cohort of new officer recruits is a changing routine. They like to keep the blood flowing at Dartmouth. It would not do to have people ensconced there too long. In my case the time was unusually short but only because a set of circumstances has arisen which justifies it.'

'What has come up, then?' she countered. 'There is a newly fitted ship which requires an able young captain?' she said, laughing.

'Well, that could be said to be true,' Tim admitted. 'But the fact is that the belligerence of the North Koreans has rattled the cage of the Admiralty in London, as a member of the United Nations.'

He explained that North Korea's invasion of the south of the country had invoked the involvement of the United Nations to defend South Korea. As a prominent member, this had repercussions for Britain and so for the Royal Navy. That august body was spawned by the Second World War in the hope that it could deter, and perhaps prevent, hostilities between nations, which had shattered the world in war.

'Are you telling me that you are likely to be involved in it?' Vanessa, becoming serious, put the pointed question. 'Is there no end to it all? All those long years in the recent war and then the fracas with the Chinese communists, and now this.'

Tim could see that Vanessa was reaching the end of her patience and long-suffering with his exposure to injury and death.

'I have been thinking that I shall regard this commission as my last potential combat job in the navy,' Tim volunteered. 'If I stay in the navy I shall opt for a desk job, possibly at home, if they will accept me. With the training element now on my record I should stand a good chance landing something like that. Would you like to get married before I go?'

'Now you are switching from the terrifying to the sublime. How can you mix the two up so blandly?' she reprimanded him.

'As a matter of fact, I have good reason. If we married before I go – and if, by chance, I was killed – you would get a widow's pension. If not married, you would get nothing.'

'No, and no again, darling. You will come back to me. Then we will get married. In any case I would forego the pension. I don't want to earn it by your death. You must come back to me without a pension. I shall live for the day when I shall be Vanessa Denton as well as Vanessa Coles. Or shall we copy the Spanish and be Mr and Mrs Denton-Coles or Coles-Denton?'

Her last remarks were meant to be a challenge with a touch of humour that took the sting out of their mutual concerns.

Tim felt put in his place. Her resolve was so clinical and final.

36

HMS *Kanyard* moved away from Portsmouth naval harbour at the end of October. It was a light cruiser by classification, of ten and a half thousand tons displacement, with a crew of seven hundred and thirty, plus a company of Royal Marines. It was not an old ship, having been launched in August in Glasgow, just before the Second World War began.

It sailed to Malta in the Mediterranean to join the 5th Cruiser Squadron for a while, before sailing on to Suez, where it picked up a British representative for a commonwealth conference being held at Colombo, Ceylon. While crossing the Arabian Sea it came across a disabled ship, which it rescued by towing it into Colombo.

On its way to war, the ship was employed to carry out an act of peace. The British government had arranged the repatriation of religious relics to be transported by the *Kanyard* from Colombo to Rangoon. The ship diverted north-east to Rangoon in Burma to deliver them before sailing south to Singapore, where it rendezvoused with HMNZS *Tutira* and HMNZS *Pukaki*, two frigates of the Royal New Zealand Navy, to escort them to the Korean War, sailing to Hong Kong.

From Hong Kong the three ships joined the commonwealth base at Sasebo in Japan, from which the

Kanyard conducted operations against the Korean peninsula. At first, it took part in the blockade against North Korea, trying to stem the flow of enemy warships, supply ships, and troop transports southwards.

For two months, the war was regarded as a localised struggle, which might end in a stalemate. But in reality, it gave way to a series of victories by the North Koreans. The *Kanyard* took part in the evacuation of South Korean troops from the Chinnampo Peninsula, where they had been cut off by attacks from the north.

With two other warships, a second British and one American, the *Kanyard* was patrolling off the east coast of North Korea, when it met four enemy torpedo boats, arriving with a convoy of ammunition ships they were escorting to their destination. Rather than retreat, the enemy ships immediately went into action against the three United Nation vessels, hoping to torpedo them in close combat.

The gunners on the *Kanyard* were already at action stations. They combined their firepower with that of the other two ships, to destroy three of the attackers before they were able to position themselves to aim their torpedoes. The sinking of their three escorts, and flight of the fourth, left the unarmed ammunition ships exposed to the same firepower that had deprived them of their escorts, ending eventually in their own destruction.

Soon the world was alerted to a major development in the course of the war. The forces of the south were on the point of being finally defeated, signalled when the North Koreans occupied Inchon, a coastal location west of Seoul, the capital city. The capture of Inchon by the enemy gave them potential control of the city. Only a swift and decisive counter-attack by the southern forces could save the day.

An overwhelming response was put into action. During September the United Nations, led by the United States, assisted by twenty-one other countries, including Britain, made a sea landing at Inchon, cutting off a large part of the north's troops, forcing those who were not isolated and captured, back northwards onto the border with China, or into the mountains inland.

As well as bombarding the landing area before the assault, the *Kenyard* landed her contingent of Royal Marine commandos alongside the other forces to achieve a strategic victory, reversing the course of the war.

But it proved all too soon to be a victory, which China was unable to tolerate. The sleeping giant had been finally alerted. China entered the war, driving the United Nations forces southwards, a retreat that lasted until the middle of the following year.

The *Kenyard* became one of the ships that had the task of covering the withdrawal of the United Nation forces from Inchon, previously so beneficially won.

Following other bombardments on the west coast of Korea and on Wonsan on the east coast, the ship left the war zone, sailing first to Hong Kong on its way to being withdrawn to Singapore for a refit and subsequent transfer to the East Indies station. The main naval base was at Trincomalee, in Ceylon, but with lesser bases at Aden, Bombay, and Basra for covering British interests respectively in the Red Sea, Indian Ocean, and Persian Gulf. It was time to rest the crew and refurbish their ship while at Singapore.

In those few months of action in Korea, the *Kenyard* had fired over five thousand six-inch and four-inch shells in bombardments, and three times that number of shells of smaller weapons against surface ships and in anti-aircraft defence. The wear and tear of such extensive usage, as well as the accumulating need for servicing the damage and imperfections from continuous ocean sailing, pressed for urgent remedial attention in a fighting ship.

The break in action enabled Tim Denton to re-establish his contact with Vanessa. For so many months he had been incommunicado in warfare and totally preoccupied with directing the safety and performance of the *Kenyard*. He found the job of being captain of a light cruiser was essentially similar to that of his captaincy of the *Amartyst,* but there was just so much more of it to manage. The crew was over three times as large. In addition, he had a company of Royal Marines, who doubled up for jobs in the ship on a long voyage. He had more guns to think about and one novel feature. The *Kenyard* was equipped to carry two seaplanes, used for reconnaissance, but more importantly, to identify any land-based targets for directing the ship's firepower as accurately as possible.

Vanessa had grown accustomed to the silence of her absent captain. But when she heard that he had completed his contribution to the war and was in refit at Singapore, her joy knew no bounds.

She and Tim evoked the use of a long telephone call.

'Do I take it that sometime you will be heading back to Portsmouth?' she asked.

'Sometime is the operative word, darling,' he replied. 'You once sang to me that a slow boat to China would take a long time. I think it will also take a long time to return from the voyage. But I can tell you, I am pointing myself in the right direction.'

'Am I pleased to hear it, darling,' Vanessa responded.

'How is the show going?' he queried.

'Still as strong as ever. We think it has steam up to go into one more year,' she informed Tim. 'So, you see, I shall have plenty to occupy my time in the interval before we meet up again. What are you finding to do in Singapore, waiting for your ship to be serviced?'

'Resting, sightseeing, and socialising with the navy men who are also in port,' he replied. 'But of course, I have ongoing duties every day either on the ship or in the offices. There are always a score of matters about repairs, supplies, crew members, and so on, to be handled every day.'

During its service in the Indian Ocean, the *Kenyard* visited Calcutta, Mombasa, and Madras. Tim never had much time to spare from his captain's duties. But those leisurely, goodwill visits to show the flag were opportunities to take a few hours off away from the ship.

In Calcutta he travelled across the vast sprawling city to pay a call at RAF Comilla, where around three years previously he had arrived by air to wait overnight before taking the last sector of his flight to Nanking, on his way to becoming the assistant naval attaché at the British embassy. Most of the members of the officers' mess had moved on, but Jeffrey Purbeck, the pilot of the Dakota aircraft in which he had first flown to China, had become the commander of the base.

'Welcome again, Tim,' he said, shaking hands. 'I see you have come from a different direction this time.'

'Yes, I thought it better to stick to the sea after the parachute drop I was subjected to on my second visit to Nanking,' Tim responded, filling him in with what had happened.

'I see we have both been promoted out of our field of competence.'

They both had a good laugh at Tim's well-known reference to the dictum of self-effacement.

'Come on over to the mess and have a drink.' Jeffery's welcome invitation paved the way for a long yarn about service conditions and the fading power of Britain in the east.

'It's a different world now for Britain in these parts,' Jeffrey said. 'It made sense to promote me to command a base that has ended its great days and will close soon. But I gather the same could be said of the navy. Since the fiasco at Singapore during the war, the great days of the navy have waned in the east.'

'Yes, they certainly have,' Tim replied. 'I have been one of four British ships taking part in the operations against the North Koreans and Chinese communists. It's all American staffed and directed now. Their ships vastly outnumber the rest of the twenty-one countries contributing to the United Nations in the war.'

'So, what have you been doing, then?' asked Jeffrey.

'Mostly bombarding land targets. In a big way. We have sailed over sixty thousand miles in one year, firing over three thousand six-inch, over two thousand four-inch, and over fourteen thousand forty-millimetre shells. We were able to sink some ammunition ships, kill hundreds of enemy troops, and know we destroyed arms dumps, munition factories, vehicles, barracks, shore batteries, and strong points. Then we were taken off to Singapore for a refit and rest. I have just about recovered from the fray. I'm looking to going back to England in about a year.'

It was well into the next year when Tim Denton received sailing orders to join the Mediterranean Fleet. He realised the westward posting was one step more to returning home. It was also near enough to Britain for Vanessa to fly out to meet him at one place or another.

HMS *Kenyard* was directed to join the 5th Cruiser Squadron again, at Malta, the main base in the Mediterranean Sea. The navy still commanded the other important base at Gibraltar at the western end of the sea, although Port Alexandria in Egypt, at its eastern end, as a long-standing naval base, had been vacated a year after the end of the Second World War. Nevertheless, a chain of guarantees still existed that British sea routes to the Far East would remain protected.

The *Kenyard* arrived at Malta and slowly entered Valetta Grand Harbour, surrounded by its historic and beautiful skyline of forts, strong points, honey-coloured buildings, and the cranes, dry docks, and harbours for shipping.

The ship had been allocated a berth for its initial arrival. It would later be assigned to a sea site out in the harbour on anchorages strong enough to moor a battleship.

To the surprise of the crew, a small group of people was standing on the quayside, evidently waiting for the ship to secure its moorings. They included a privileged few relatives of some of the crew, who lived in or who came from Malta and had discovered the ship's arrival date and time, plus navy officials, and some sightseers. They were keen to give the ship a welcome, having learned about its recent exploits in the East.

Tim Denton was too busy to bother about such niceties. He had not told Vanessa of his whereabouts. Nothing could distract him from his job. At the moment, he was concerned about berthing the ship and the sequence of events that would follow from his arrival – such matters as crew sickness, engineering faults requiring onshore attention, completion of documentation, and the whole process of food, water, ammunition, and medical replenishments. He worked in conjunction with his senior officers, who were in charge of the various departments of those responsibilities on the ship.

It was later in the day, when he had established contact with the senior commander of the 5th Cruiser Squadron, that the captain and his officers were informed of a cocktail party to be held in their honour. It would take place in the officers' mess on the next evening, followed by dinner.

Crew members in rotation were given thirty-six hours' shore leave from noon of the day of their arrival. During the next week or so, while the ship was in harbour, crewmen could get short leave passes for off-duty time. Many of them were able to make direct contact by telephone or reliable post with their wives or girlfriends in Britain.

Being summertime, the island was already trying to attract tourists. It welcomed the sailors on their short leaves. In some cases, wives or partners, who had been informed of the ship's arrival at Malta, had secured accommodation to spend off-duty time with their men. Hotel prices were cheap against the British pound.

Next day, Tim duly turned up at the naval officers' mess, glad to have firm ground under his feet again. He was greeted by the Commander-in-Chief, Mediterranean, Admiral Sir John Edstone, who then took his leave for a prior engagement.

The commander of 5th Cruiser Squadron, Rear Admiral Colin Hawkins, took the opportunity to give a toast to the new arrivals.

'Welcome to Malta, Commander Denton. We are glad to have you with us after your long trip in the Far East. I have a little surprise for you.' He raised his glass. 'To Commander Denton and crew of the *Kenyard.'*

As if it were a signal, a corridor was formed among the officers and out from an ante-room walked Vanessa.

Tim internally gasped with surprise. He felt his blood pressure rise enough to burst through his skin. Fortunately, no one had cause to be looking at him at that instant.

He tried to be as welcoming as the rest of the officers.

But there could be no histrionics in that relaxed but formal gathering.

He could do nothing except watch her walk towards him, offering her hand. 'Welcome home, captain,' she whispered. 'This is certainly an unusual place to meet.'

Tim hoped nothing in his demeanour gave him away. He thought it was a cruel but exquisite trick to play. But who had played it? At dinner, sitting together, Tim was keen to find out.

'How on earth did you know about my arrival at Malta?'

'It was quite easy,' Vanessa explained. 'I simply rang up Captain Bruce Fowler and he did the rest for me. I told him you had been away for a long time and wanted to give you a surprise, if you were putting into port in easy reach. I suppose he has plenty of contacts in the Admiralty, from his position at Greenwich. He just got back to me and said you were joining the fleet at Malta and gave me the day when you would arrive. But a few women, related to crew members, also found out the same information. I got through to the navy at Malta and arranged it, offering to contribute thirty minutes of *King's Rhapsody* for this very dinner, if they would have me. They were in fact enthusiastic about it.'

'How long can you be in Malta?' was Tim's anxious question. He knew he could not excuse himself from duty except for short periods and not for at least two days.

'I have been released from five performances. So, with the Sunday and Monday at each end of them I have more than a full week's holiday. I have booked a room at the Imperial Hotel in Rudolph Street, in Sliema, in the hope that you will be able to take off a day or two as well as the off-duty hours each day.'

'That should all be possible,' Tim responded. 'How thoughtful of you to take such an initiative. We ought to be able to make a decent week of it.'

After the dinner, the commander of 5th Cruiser Squadron introduced Vanessa. 'This evening we have a special guest for the occasion. She is a star from the London stage and will sing songs from her current long-running show. It is an unusual event for a mess dinner but the visitor happens to be in Malta and wanted to welcome the officers of the *Kenyard,* who have been away from home for so long.'

Vanessa then ran through her cycle of excerpts from the show, accompanied at the piano by an officer with the reputation of being the foremost pianist in the navy. As the sound of her voice echoed throughout the premises, other officers and local staff drifted into the back of the mess to listen spellbound to her singing.

When she had finished her recital, the polite clapping between the songs gave way to prolonged applause. The audience actually stood up to reinforce their delight.

Eventually, Vanessa was able to speak.

'I thank you all for your kind appreciation. It has been a joy for me to meet you and to sing to you. But I have to tell you that your captain, Commander Tim Denton did not inform me of the arrival of your ship at Malta. It was a surprise for him to see me here. He and I are due to be married soon after he returns to England.'

With that announcement, the protocol of the mess was laid aside. A loud cheer went up and clapping resumed, while Vanessa kissed and embraced her embarrassed intended.

Their time together proved to be a homecoming festival. Tim was restricted for three of the days, but he managed to stay overnight with Vanessa and meet her on the other days for most of the time.

'This is my first visit to Malta,' Vanessa said.

'It's one of the places taking an early initiative to get its tourist trade going,' Tim stated. 'They are trying very hard to entice people from Britain to take a holiday here. The island was awarded the George Cross in the Second World War.'

'I thought that was only given to individuals?' Vanessa queried.

'It is the only example of a collective award,' Tim answered. 'Malta was subjected to constant attacks during the earlier years the war. Well over three thousand air raids by

German and Italian aircraft were recorded on the island. It is so close to Italy and even France after Germany occupied it. They desperately wanted to wipe it out if they could not invade it. It played such a strategic part in the war in North Africa for the British to preserve its usefulness.'

'So many air raids must have done a lot of damage, even so,' Vanessa observed.

'Well over ten thousand buildings were destroyed or badly damaged and over fifteen hundred civilians were killed,' Tim told her. 'But the main loss of life was among the British Navy, Army, and Air Force, suffering seven and a half thousand casualties. At first, the RAF was ill-equipped to meet the attacks. Ships were sunk on their way bringing supplies of food, munitions, oil, and other necessities. Epic stories abound about exploits in the air and on the sea, but once the Germans were repelled from North Africa, the navy and air force were able to save the island.'

Vanessa and Tim did some travelling around the island by bus, starting out from the bus station at the entrance to Valletta. But their great achievement was completing the five scheduled and sign-posted walks around the island, each ranging from five to nine miles in length. They seldom saw anyone else. Apparently, they were the only people who could tear themselves away from the sea, sand, and attractions of the towns to explore the out of the way countryside.

They were astounded by the extent of the ownership of seemingly savage guard dogs on every property situated away from the towns. Alsatian and Doberman dogs – thankfully secured on long chains – were constantly barking for most of their touring on foot. But the walks enabled them to view the sea from precipitous cliffs and see the off-shore installation for removing salt from the sea for the island's human consumption. The one feature that disgusted them was the ubiquitous traps for migrating birds, set to lure them tired from their long travels to and from their annual retreats. It had been a traditional source of food for the poorer population of Malta and still practised in an age of conservation.

They discovered ancient tombs, untouched by the centuries. Their finds made them realise how many civilisations had had a hand in occupying the island. Each had transferred and developed its own culture there, from the Phoenicians and Carthaginians through Greeks and Romans to Spanish, French and British.

All too soon, their time together vanished. Tim and Vanessa had to face up to going their separate ways.

HMS *Kenyard*'s first commission was a patrol at the eastern end of the Mediterranean Sea. British interests had been compromised with the foundation of the Israeli state after three years of hostile, increasingly anti-British activity, and the continuing enmity between Israelis and Palestinians.

On its patrol, the ship rescued the crew of the *Champollion,* which had run aground south of Beirut. It later rescued another ship, the *Burica,* whose engines had broken down, towing it to Port Said.

The rest of the year was taken up with more patrols and exercises with other ships. It was the stuff of activity of a navy in peaceful times.

For Tim, it had been a comparatively restful westwards withdrawal from the war in Korea, first in the Indian Ocean, then in the Mediterranean Sea. The next leg was expected to be home. It came sooner in his expectations, rather than later. The ship sailed away to England in February of the following year, having played a part in the Korean War, which was still raging and would not end until the armistice was declared in July of the same year.

37

A few months had passed since Vanessa turned up in Malta. Such long gaps in their physical contact only raised their mutual passion to be together again. Vanessa and Tim longed to be permanently living side by side, fearing no distractions and disappointments caused by the familiarity of co-habitation, knowing that new skills and additional relationships would have the chance to appear between them and aid their growth into previously unknown joy, comfort, and understanding.

'How about the promise you made to those sailors in Malta?' was one of the early, if not the first question, that Tim levelled at Vanessa when he finally arrived home at their London flat.

'You know me, my darling. I meant it and we should set about organising it as soon as possible,' Vanessa replied.

By chance, Tim was invited to pay a visit again to the Royal Naval College at Greenwich, to speak to the current members of the course about his service in Korea. In talking with Bruce Fowler, he happened to mention their intention to marry.

'Where will the marriage take place? Where does she come from?' he asked.

'She comes from Swindon. Her father is a well-known doctor in the town,' Tim told him. 'It is also my own home town, the place where I was born and brought up.'

'How about getting married here instead?' Bruce questioned.

'Where do you mean?' Tim asked.

'I mean here, at the college,' Bruce answered. 'There is a chapel and reception hall as you know. We do have weddings here but they are not ten a penny. We usually reserve the privilege for the higher ranks of officers only.'

'Are you inviting me to apply for it?' Tim asked, wanting to make sure of his ground.

'I certainly am. You have served the navy with distinction for the last two ships you have commanded. With the rank of commander, you come within the usual practice followed by the college.'

'Thank you for the suggestion. I will talk with Vanessa about it and let you know as soon as possible.' Tim shook his hand and turned away.

'Give her our love,' Bruce called to him. 'We look forward to seeing her again.'

Tim felt the excitement rising in him. The idea had been far out of his ken, for the simple reason he had not known of its possibility. Perhaps it was the kind of venue a pair of lovers, who intend to marry, dream about, but believed it could never be within the realms of reality for them. He could not wait for Vanessa to return from the theatre that night, to tell her about the opportunity.

'Darling, Bruce Fowler bowled me over today at the college. He asked me where we would be getting married. I had assumed at Swindon and told him so. But he wondered if we would be interested in applying to marry in the college. It would be in the chapel there followed by a reception in the great hall, where we went to the cocktail party. I wasn't aware of couples getting married in Greenwich College but, apparently, they are few and far between, according to Bruce.'

'Then the real question for us will be whether to have a quiet wedding or a large affair. In Swindon it will be easy to have a private event but the college in London will almost certainly require a larger celebration. You may wish to invite your officers from the ship. I will have to consider the cast of *King's Rhapsody*,' Vanessa declared.

'I have always expected a quiet wedding, discreet and no frills. If we have it in the college all the media will hear about it,' Tim added.

'In that case we ought to give them something to shout about,' Vanessa said jokingly.

'As a matter of fact, I have been thinking that if we came around to having it as a large affair in the college, an idea is running around my head that would nicely take care of it,' Tim suddenly said, becoming thoughtful.

'What is that, then?' Vanessa demanded.

'Oh, I wasn't planning to tell you,' Tim defended his reticence.

'What!' Vanessa exploded in anger. 'I happen to be in this, too.'

Tim invisibly cringed. Vanessa's temperament could change so dramatically. It brought back to him the very first day they ever met.

'Yes, of course, of course,' Tim hurried to explain himself. 'It is so unusual I was going to look into it to see how feasible it would be before I told you.'

'You tell me right here and now,' Vanessa said. 'If I like it I will support it. If not, you will not have the trouble of exploring it. Now isn't that considerate of me.'

It was not a question. She meant it as a statement of fact.

'Instead of the usual cars, we could employ boats, using the river for your arrival. Would you fancy getting on a bridal boat at Westminster Pier and making your way down the River Thames to the Royal Navy College and stepping out onto a red carpet to go into the chapel?' Tim elaborated, putting it as a question to her.

There were a few seconds of silence. Vanessa was visibly astonished. Unusually, she was lost for words.

'I am shocked at the suggestion,' Vanessa cried out.

Tim's face at first reflected her outburst in dismay. And then he saw her shock was of the ecstatic kind.

'Darling, I never thought you had it in you to dream up such a solution, which is worthy enough to grace a play in the West End.'

'I must have caught the habit from you,' Tim replied. 'I must have been affected by all the tricks and surprises you have played on me over the years that have made my life so cheerful and interesting. I admit it's a long way from the engine room of a ship at sea to make such a suggestion, but you are so wonderful I thought only a wonderful solution would be good enough for you at your wedding. You are from the stage and from it you will come to the wedding. It is an idea that persuades me to go for the larger affair. We shall have to invite the parties you mentioned to justify the venue and make it all worthwhile.'

'Well, we have been lucky so far – six times in fact,' Vanessa pondered. 'It has all depended on your safe returns and wanting to come home to me. It was your initiative that made our first meeting. It told us that happiness could be ours. Staying alive until the end of the war, coming back the first time from New Zealand, surviving the wreck at sea, coming back the second time from New Zealand, eluding the Chinese, and then returning from Korea, all reminded us of the same fact. Each time we escaped from our separate isolation and suffering, entering paradise together. But each time it could only be briefly, before it was torn asunder from our grasp by the demands of life.'

'If we go ahead with our marriage at the college, with your arrival for our wedding, courtesy of the River Thames, it will be a special gesture from you. For the first time you will be coming home to me and from the water. I think that ought to count as a lucky step. It will take us from the end of the long road of comings and goings to be finally together and sealing our love for good,' Tim pronounced.

'It will be the seventh time,' Vanessa reflected softly. 'Our rum affair will be over. Always to be together. No more nervous partings. Let normal life begin.'

'Bringing our ecstasy forever,' Tim breathed.

'Agreed.' It was Vanessa's last word before they embraced.